W9-BUW-348

Kincaid

OTHER WORKS BY HENRY DENKER

NOVELS

I'll Be Right Home, Ma
My Son, The Lawyer
Salome: Princess of Galilee
The First Easter
The Director
The Kingmaker
A Place for the Mighty
The Physicians
The Experiment
The Starmaker
The Scofield Diagnosis
The Actress
Error of Judgment
Horowitz and Mrs. Washington
The Warfield Syndrome
Outrage
The Healers

PLAYS

Time Limit!
A Far Country
A Case of Libel
What Did We Do Wrong
Venus at Large
Second Time Around
Horowitz and Mrs. Washington
The Headhunters
Outrage!

Kincaid

BY

HENRY DENKER

William Morrow and Company, Inc.
New York 1984

The author expresses his deep appreciation for the technical instruction and advice on the medical aspects of *Kincaid* to Doctor Herbert Buchsbaum, Professor of Obstetrics and Gynecology, Southwestern Medical School, University of Texas at Dallas.

Library of Congress Catalog Card Number: 84-60199

ISBN: 0-688-02365-7

Printed in the United States of America

First Edition

1 2 3 4 5 6 7 8 9 10

BOOK DESIGN BY BARBARA SINGER

To my wife,
Edith Denker, R.N.

CHAPTER 1

"Nurse! Miss Kincaid!" patient Rose Bellino cried from her bed in the far corner of the Maternity Ward. "It's beginning again!" With a slight moan of pain she called more fearfully, "Miss Kincaid? Please!"

From the bedside of Mrs. Thorpe, Kate Kincaid glanced toward Mrs. Bellino. "One moment, dear!" But she continued to listen very carefully to the heartbeat in Mrs. Thorpe's belly. Urgent as Mrs. Bellino's cry was, it was important for harried Kate Kincaid to monitor Mrs. Thorpe's condition accurately.

Kate was having an even more difficult day than usual. Instead of the one or two usual complicated cases in Maternity, today there were three. And Kate sensed that the third, Mrs. Bellino, might be the most dangerous of all.

"Nurse!" Mrs. Bellino was calling again. "Miss Kincaid!"

"Coming!" Kate rushed toward her.

Mrs. Rose Bellino, a chubby, dark-haired woman who had previously successfully delivered four children, was experiencing difficulty with this, her fifth. A few years ago she had begun to suffer hypertension, which now predisposed her to complications when it came to delivering a healthy baby.

Damn Dr. Morse, Kate thought. Every Thursday morning he liked to "clear the book," as some doctors say—get all the pregnant women delivered and recovering by Friday so he could have his weekend off undisturbed. Therefore, he prescribed large doses of the drug Pitocin to hasten delivery. Never mind the risks to which the drug subjected patients, just clear the book!

Twice before, Kate had had occasion to complain about him to the Medical Board of the hospital. But they had taken no action.

Harried, concerned, Kate brushed back the strand of long blond hair that kept falling down when she was under pressure. For the sake of her patient she tried to appear far more placid than she actually felt as she placed the metal sensor of her stethoscope on poor Mrs. Bellino's bulging abdomen to monitor the heartbeat of the fetus.

She was checking to see how the decelerations of the infant's heart coincided with Mrs. Bellino's contractions. Kate listened carefully. She did not like what she heard. The infant's heart reacted and slowed, not with but after each of its mother's contractions. Late decelerations were an indication of trouble for both mother and infant. They were a sign to be feared when the mother was hypertensive. They could warn of abruption, that disastrous event in which the placenta was slowly torn away from the uterine wall, depriving the unborn infant of its only source of oxygen.

Kate raced to the phone to have Dr. Alfred Morse paged. She wanted him at Mrs. Bellino's bedside as soon as possible. Having put in the call, she again checked Mrs. Thorpe, a young woman with a history of two previous stillborn deliveries, but who seemed to be bearing up well. Nevertheless, Kate was angry with Morse for putting the young woman on Pitocin to stimulate her contractions and hasten her delivery. But "clear the book," damn him!

There was also Mrs. Theresa Nolan, comparatively young, but a good Catholic who had given birth seven times before. In medical terms she was not only a multipara but a grand multipara, the designation for a woman who had borne five or more children. But that label should also have been a warning to Dr. Morse. Grand multiparas were especially prone to complications from Pitocin. Despite this, he had clearly inscribed it on her chart, and, as the nurse on duty, Kate Kincaid had no choice but to follow doctor's orders.

She palpated Mrs. Nolan's belly lightly to detect any reaction of pain, which might signal the worst danger to be feared in such a case: rupture of the uterus and expulsion of its contents, which could be fatal to both infant and mother. Kate also monitored the fetal heartbeat. If it had slowed, that was a sign the infant was suffering a reaction to the Pitocin and might be damaged or die. The infant's heartbeat did seem a bit below normal. But the mother evidenced no pain on palpation. Kate would wait and see about this one. But where the hell was Morse?

By the time the arrogant young resident arrived, Kate made no attempt to hide her anger. "Dr. Morse, have a look at Mrs. Bellino!"

"Bellino?" Morse replied, as if the name were unfamiliar.

"The hypertensive in the bed nearest the window," Kate reminded him pointedly. Doctors were rushed, always rushed, but that was no excuse for patients to become mere objects. They had names and identities aside from their medical difficulties.

She preceded Morse to Mrs. Bellino's bedside.

"What seems to be her trouble?" Morse asked.

"Late decelerations in the infant's heartbeat," Kate warned him. "That could be dangerous."

Resentful of advice from a nurse or anyone ranking below him in the hospital hierarchy, Morse said, "No need to become hysterical, Nurse."

He drew out his stethoscope, applied the cold, round, metal sensor to Mrs. Bellino's belly.

"Having a little pain, are we?"

Sweaty and fearful, for she knew the dangers involved in her effort to deliver, Mrs. Bellino replied, "I don't know about you, Doctor, but, yes, *I* am having pain."

"Well, you've been through this enough times before to know there's always some pain."

Morse located the infant's heartbeat, listened for a moment, smiled mechanically and said, "Fine, everything's fine. A few hours from now you'll be a mother once more, with a healthy baby."

He turned away from the bed to be confronted by the pretty but challenging face of Kate Kincaid. Reading her disapproval, he said curtly, "Come with me, Nurse!"

Ever since the day Kate had refused his invitation to go off on a weekend with him, he had not used her name, addressing her only as "Nurse."

Aware it was better for the patient to have this discussion outside her hearing, Kate followed. At the door of the labor room, Morse turned on her so abruptly that they collided.

"Sorry," she said.

"What seems to be the trouble, 'Nurse'?" Morse demanded, using the title as an expletive.

"Didn't you detect it?"

"Detect what?" Morse asked angrily.

"Late decelerations," Kate said.

"There wasn't a one while I was listening," Morse said.

"Of course not. You didn't take the time," Kate said accusingly.

"I'll be the judge of how much time it takes to detect decelerations," Morse replied, furious. "I do not need instructions from any nurse."

Though younger than the overbearing doctor, she was able to say, "I remember when Miss Curzon had to show you how to insert an I.V. You didn't do it right then, either."

"Just what does that word 'either' mean? Are you suggesting that my actions just now were incorrect?" Morse demanded.

"I am suggesting that the patient might be better off if you went on your weekend today instead of waiting till tomorrow afternoon!" Kate said, glaring up at the tall young man.

Only five feet four, and looking even younger than her twenty-seven years, Kate Kincaid nevertheless presented an imposing figure in her white nylon uniform, required dress for floor nurses at University Hospital.

She had a youthful, well-knit body, with ample rounded breasts rising above a narrow waist. And even in flat-heeled hospital shoes her legs were shapely and enticing enough to make a man notice, once he took his eyes off her pretty face.

She was not vain about her looks. Two years ago when she had been first assigned to Maternity, a television director came scouting for a young, attractive nurse to use in a commercial. Kate turned him down flatly. Huckstering personal female products was not in keeping with her professional standards.

If Kate Kincaid appeared imposing at first glance, she could be far more so when angered, as she was now.

Morse did not reply but strode swiftly down the hall. At the nurses' station he picked up the phone and had the Chief Nursing Supervisor paged.

"Miss Curzon, I have just been rudely insulted by one of your nurses, Kincaid. I demand she apologize. Or I will bring her up on charges before the Disciplinary Board of this hospital!"

Used to dealing with young staff doctors, whose vanity seemed to be in direct proportion to their inexperience, Miss Curzon said only, "I will look into the matter at once."

"You'd better!" Morse said, then hung up. He glanced at the wall clock. Four-fifteen. Two more hours on duty, then he could be off to the mountains and his favorite sport. For he was being accompanied by a young nurse who had just received her B.S.N. at University and was starting to gain her practical experience at the hospital.

With other, more urgent duties to attend to, Miss Curzon did not go immediately to the labor floor. If she had, she would have found Kate Kincaid standing alongside Dr. Walter Irving at the bedside of Mrs. Bellino. Irving carefully palpated the woman's belly, then delicately probed for the infant's heartbeat.

Dr. Irving was a white-haired man, short, thin with age, but with a benign wrinkled face and a kindly attitude that invited patients to unburden themselves to him. He was especially sensitive to the cares and concerns of young pregnant women. To him they were not patients but daughters. The failure of his wife to give birth to a healthy child was responsible for his solicitude, which had grown even more marked since her death three years ago after a long battle with cancer.

Kate had come to know him well when she took care of his wife during her last illness. Thereafter, whenever Kate needed another opinion for her own peace of mind, she called on him, and he never failed to respond.

Now, the small man turned from the patient and said softly, "No doubt. Late decelerations. We must do a cesarean section at once. I'll arrange surgery. You prep the patient."

As he turned away, Kate pursued him with one further request. "Doctor, the patient in the bed on the other side, Mrs. Nolan. . . ?"

"Oh? What?"

"Grand multipara. On Pitocin."

"Who the hell . . . ?" Walter Irving exploded, but immediately regained his composure and said quietly, "I'll have a look."

In short, swift steps that belied his age, the white-haired doctor reached the bedside of Catherine Nolan. Then, as if he had all the time in the world, he examined her very carefully, palpated her belly, found the infant's heart and monitored it for some minutes.

"Any pain?" he asked Kate.

"Only contractions."

"Good." Irving sounded relieved. "Discontinue the Pitocin." But as he spoke he noticed that the needle, while taped to the patient's arm, was no longer inserted. He glanced toward Kate questioningly.

"I discontinued it on my own," she replied.

"Good girl!" Irving said. "I'll go arrange for surgery. You stay with Mrs. Bellino until it's time to go up."

Before he left he could not resist saying, "Katie, I will never forget how kind you were with Dorine. I remember how she held on to your hand that last day." Irving's eyes misted over. He patted Kate's cheek. "I can never decide if you're prettier than you are nice, or nicer than you are pretty." And he was on his way in short, quick steps.

Strange, Kate thought, the little man was always in a hurry, except when he was at a patient's bedside. She wished more doctors were like him. So that patients would not fear to ask those questions which really troubled them, instead of feeling that doctors were above being intruded upon by mere patients.

Now she had to prep Mrs. Bellino for that cesarean.

While Kate was escorting Mrs. Bellino up to the Operating Room and being spelled in the labor room by a young trainee, Dr. Morse came by for what he hoped would be his final rounds for the afternoon. He approached the bed in which Mrs. Nolan lay, experiencing contractions which were neither so severe nor so frequent as to indicate immediate delivery. As he started to examine her, he noticed that her Pitocin I.V. was no longer inserted. He called out angrily, "Nurse!"

The young replacement came rushing to Mrs. Nolan's bedside.

"Who did this?" Morse demanded.

"Sorry, Doctor, I don't know! It was out when I took over."

"Damn that Kincaid! This is not the first time! When she returns tell her that I want to see her at once!" Morse said. He realized that he would be gone by then so he amended his order. "Tell her the first thing Monday morning I want her to explain this action taken against my orders!"

"Yes, Doctor," the young nurse responded.

"Now replace that I.V. And keep it going!" Morse ordered.

"Yes, Doctor."

"Damn nurses!" he growled. "A little experience goes to their heads. They start making decisions on their own."

He left the room without completing his rounds, still growling about nurses and their lack of discipline.

Up in the O.R., Dr. Walter Irving and his hastily assembled team were performing what fortunately turned out to be a routine cesarean section. He lifted out the infant, examined it closely. From all outward appearances he judged it to be normal. He handed it to Kate to perform the initial Apgar test.

"The Apgar's okay," Kate said. But she and Irving exchanged a look that said the placenta had not been as completely adhered to the uterine wall as it should have been. This baby might not have received all the oxygen it needed.

"Let's hope it stays okay," Irving said.

In infants who suffered late decelerations sometimes the neurological damage did not show up for months.

The short, slight, white-haired obstetrical surgeon, his shoulders hunched with age and personal cares, trudged out of the O.R., muttering to himself, "Damned young doctors, no time, only arrogance. In my day we may have learned less but we used it a lot better."

Kate Kincaid was due to go off duty at four. The wall clock in the O.R. said four-seventeen. One more look into the labor room and she would be free from what had been a taxing day in a long series of such days. She would have time to go home, take a leisurely bath, perhaps even a nap, and still dress in time to have dinner with Howard, then see that play which was on its nationwide tour and which would be in the city only for the week. With the original Broadway cast, it should prove one of the highlights of the season. Kate looked forward to it, if only as a respite from her hectic day. And she did enjoy Howard. An attorney in his early thirties, Howard Brewster still had all the enthusiasm of a young man fresh out of law school. He loved the practice of law. To him each new case was an adventure. It was already apparent that in a few years he would be a partner in the firm.

All this made him a highly eligible husband, which he took every opportunity to remind Kate. In his opinion there was no acceptable reason why she should remain in her demanding profession when soon he could afford to marry her, move her to a fine home in the suburbs, and provide her with a life of comfort and, eventually, of luxury. Despite her frequent evasions, Howard was sure that one day, very soon, she would say yes.

Today had been one of those difficult days when Howard's persistence made great sense to Kate. By the time she had her bath and her nap she might feel differently. But right now, on her way back to the labor room for one last look, she would have said yes to Howard, and quickly.

Her first glance from the doorway told her that Mrs. Van Cleave and Miss Benthal had both been removed to the delivery room. Perhaps had even delivered by this time. There was a new patient in the bed at the far end of the room. But Mrs. Nolan was not only still there, she appeared to be writhing in pain, quite distinguishable from that caused by the usual contractions. Kate raced to the side of her bed. The first thing she saw was that the Pitocin I.V. had been replaced in Mrs. Nolan's arm. She pulled it out, immediately monitored the infant's heartbeat and found it erratic. She asked Mrs. Nolan to describe her pain. Once she did, Kate knew she was confronted by an impending rupture of the uterus, which could cause the mother to hemorrhage and the infant to die!

She raced to the phone to have Dr. Irving paged. Fortunately, the operator caught him on his way to the parking lot. Within minutes Irving was hurrying down the hall in short, quick strides. His swift, expert examination of Mrs. Nolan forced him to the same conclusion as Kate's. Immediate surgery was necessary to prevent fatal damage to the uterus. Hemorrhaging might have already begun.

"Damn it!" he exclaimed. "Who restarted her on Pitocin?"

The young trainee, tense and trembling, said, "Dr. Morse gave the order. He was furious."

"He won't know what fury is until the next time I see him. Get her on a gurney and up to the O.R.!"

Brushing aside all thoughts of a warm bath, a nap, a pleasant evening with Howard, Kate accompanied Mrs. Nolan up to the O.R. There, she watched as Dr. Irving's nimble if aged fingers worked skillfully and swiftly to circumvent the threat to Mrs. Nolan and her baby. He was able to find the source of the hemorrhage and tie it off.

Unfortunately, her infant was too far gone to be saved.

Almost two hours later Dr. Irving turned from the table and asked one of the younger men to close for him. He went to the stainless-steel stool in the corner of the O.R. and sank down. He exhaled in a deep sigh, a mixture of exhaustion and utter defeat. For in all respects that had been a healthy baby boy. Only the last-minute deprivation of oxygen had proved fatal.

Irving beckoned to Kate with a single motion of his forefinger. When she was close enough so he could whisper, he said, "I am going to personally appear before the M. and M. conference next week and burn that young bastard's hide. I am sick to death of these upstarts who think that Medicine was invented for their convenience and profit. Do you hear, Katie? Together we are going to put a stop to this kind of practice!"

"Yes, Dr. Irving, of course." She mopped his sweaty brow with a gauze pad. "Don't you think you ought to go home and get some rest?"

"Home?" Irving asked. "What for? Dorine won't be there. Nobody will be there. But, sure, I'll go home. Where else have I to go?"

Weary to the point of exhaustion, Walter Irving started out of the O.R.

It was the last time Kate Kincaid saw Dr. Walter Irving alive. That night he died in his sleep, at age sixty-nine.

CHAPTER 2

When the matter of the death of the Nolan baby came before the Morbidity and Mortality staff conference the next week there was no one to dispute Dr. Morse's version of what had happened.

Kate Kincaid sought to volunteer information, but the presiding physician dismissed her as a disgruntled nurse seeking to satisfy a grudge against a young resident who was admittedly abrasive in his manner. But that could hardly be called malpractice. When Kate persisted, Miss Curzon cautioned, "It won't do any good. As you know from past experience, they'll never believe a nurse over a doctor."

That night, after Morse had been completely exonerated of even a hint of guilt, Kate had dinner with Howard. In the middle of the meal she suddenly brought her cocktail glass down hard on the restaurant table and declared, "To hell with the whole damn profession! I'm no longer going to serve as a doormat for doctors whose main aim in life is to protect one another. If Dr. Irving were alive he wouldn't let them get away with it!"

"Katie, darling, I know exactly how you feel. In the law we face this quite often. We know our cause is right but we haven't got the witnesses to prove it, so we lose." Howard reached across the table for her hand to comfort her. "We've learned the best thing is to forget the ones you can't win and go on to the ones you can."

"A perfect baby!" Kate protested. "He had every right to live!"

"I know, I know," Howard tried to console her.

"Take me home, darling!"

"But we haven't even started our dinner. . . ."

"Take me home!" she insisted, and he knew her well enough to comply.

They were in Howard's car, headed for her apartment, when he was suddenly aware that she was weeping, silently, but weeping.

"Darling?" he asked.

She did not reply except to continue weeping. Then she wiped her eyes with the palms of her hands and said softly, "Sorry, darling, to spoil your evening. I couldn't help it. I keep seeing that tiny, perfectly formed infant lying in my hands. So still, when it should have been crying aloud and kicking its legs and arms with life—new life. Well, he's not going to get away with it!"

"Kate?" Howard asked, pulling the car to a stop.

"Tomorrow I am going straight to Dr. Minter."

"The Medical Chief?"

"Yes! I am going to tell him the last thing Walter Irving said. He'll be forced to do something about Morse!"

"Katie, darling, sweet, if you love me at all, if you believe me at all, don't!" When she did not reply, he continued, "Think of it this way. This would be a good time to quit. We'll get married. In a month, in a week, tomorrow, if you'd say yes. You could spend your time looking for a house, making plans to furnish it, instead of brooding over what can't possibly be changed."

Kate did not respond.

"Even if Minter believes you and convenes a meeting of the Medical Board, can that bring back the Nolan baby?"

"No," she was forced to concede.

"So what have you accomplished?"

"Somewhere out there are other unsuspecting Mrs. Nolans who, simply because Morse is called Doctor, will put their lives in his hands. There'll be other Nolan babies. Born dead."

"You can't stop that," Howard warned.

"It's my duty to try!" she declared.

Howard knew well that determined anger which always possessed her after she had witnessed some medical injustice. So he embraced her, kissed her tenderly and said, "One thing I love about you, Katie. You only get angry about the right things. And when you do, your blue eyes get bluer, and your pretty face gets more determined. Do what you have to. I'm with you, all the way.''

Bradley Minter, Chief of Internal Medicine, had a habit of sitting forward in his swivel chair, leaning intently in the direction of his patients, peering at them through his thick bifocals. While he took their histories and inquired about their symptoms, his ruddy face radiated a warmth and friendliness that reassured patients and encouraged them to talk freely.

He also adopted that stance and attitude when dealing with hospital personnel. Now he was leaning in Kate's direction as she finished relating what had occurred in the labor room on the night Mrs. Nolan's baby was stillborn.

''I feel sure, Dr. Minter, that if Morse had not restarted that Pitocin I.V., Mrs. Nolan wouldn't have ruptured and that baby wouldn't have died. It was not only negligent, it was stupid. Sorry, but I have to say it, stupid and arrogant!''

Minter nodded gravely, his florid face and blue eyes emphasizing the seriousness with which he viewed the entire matter.

''Kincaid, let me investigate further. On my own. In a discreet manner. We don't want to create a scandal if it can be avoided.''

''Just so long as you don't try to cover it up,'' Kate warned him.

Minter readjusted his bifocals and stared at her, resentment obvious in his eyes.

''I apologize. I know you better than that. I'll wait to hear from you,'' said Kate.

''And be ready to testify, if needed,'' Minter reminded her.

Two days later, when she was coming on duty, Kate heard herself paged. She went to the phone, expecting it to be Howard reporting on another house he heard about that was up for sale. It was Dr. Minter. He ordered her to come to his office at once.

''Kincaid, I've done some investigating. I even talked with Dr. Ahmanson, Chief of Obstetrics. He assures me that while Pitocin is a bit more risky for grand multipara than for most other women, it is neither unprecedented nor considered bad practice. He did say caution is advised. But that's about all. That clearly rules out any question of malpractice.''

''Dr. Minter, for the sake of this hospital, something should be done about Morse before even a worse disaster occurs!" Kate insisted.

"If his own Chief says it's not negligent practice . . . I mean, without proof . . . there's nothing I can do."

"Proof?" Kate countered. "Take a look at the Ob-Gyn charts of all cases under Morse's care. See the frequency with which he prescribes Pitocin late Thursday or early Friday. That should be proof enough."

Minter appeared quite distressed as he admitted, "I've done that, *unfortunately*."

" 'Unfortunately'?" Kate repeated, puzzled.

"Once, I sent for those charts. Morse got wind of it. He came to see me to find out why. I didn't tell him, but he could guess. I'm afraid a pretty nasty situation may develop."

"What do you mean?"

"When Morse left my office, *he* was making threats about bringing *you* up on charges," Minter admitted.

"Bringing *me* up on charges? Because I tried to stop him from killing the Nolan baby?" Kate asked. "I'd welcome it!"

"I wouldn't. I wish this whole thing would stop right here. It can't do anyone any good. Not this hospital. Not Morse. And most especially, not *you*."

"I have nothing to fear," Kate protested.

"If this leads to a hearing, it'll be before a panel of doctors, not nurses. This isn't the first brush you've had with a resident and lost," Minter said. He leaned forward and patted Kate's hand. "Kincaid, Kate, I have a daughter, older than you. So I can speak to you as a father. Take my advice and put this whole distressing thing behind you. We've no time to fight old battles when we should be concentrating on today's patients and tomorrow's. We all make mistakes, doctors, nurses. We're only human. Take my advice, let this rest."

Near the end of the day Miss Curzon, who knew her staff well, finally cornered Kate in the nurses' lounge.

"You spoke to Minter, didn't you? I hope you accept his advice."

"But it's wrong, wrong!" Kate responded heatedly.

"No one knows that better than I," Curzon agreed. "I've spent almost thirty years watching young interns and residents come along. We have to teach them how to do procedures that we are not permitted to do. Sometimes we have to do them secretly because those young inexperienced boys and girls can't. Then we watch them become full-fledged doctors and lord it over us. Many's the time I've wanted to say to some staff doctor, 'Look, sonny, I remember when you couldn't find a vein to save your life, or your *patient*'s life.' So I know how you feel about Morse. But Minter's right. You'll only create trouble for yourself."

With a determined resentment that had been building since her talk with Dr. Minter, Kate replied, "Miss Curzon, precisely because of what you've just said, for the sake of all the nurses in this hospital now, and those to come, I have to make an issue of this. A nurse is entitled to dignity and respect. Her years of study in college and afterward can't remain forever secondary to young doctors, or old ones, who go on making mistakes that should be avoided!"

Curzon shook her head sadly. "You know, Kate, in my day, when we didn't get nursing degrees from colleges, we had to take all this guff from doctors. I guess I never got out of the habit. But if you want to have a go at it, I'll help you. I can't promise you'll win, but I'll do my best. It's the least I can do for my daughters." She smiled as she confessed, "That's how I think of my girls. White, black, no matter where they're from, they're all my daughters. And you're right, you deserve better than my generation received. So go to it!"

"Katie, honey, I beg you, don't go through with this," Howard pleaded as they sat across from each other in their favorite small French restaurant.

Howard was well over six feet, with dark brown hair which tended to become unruly when he was under stress, as he was now. He always blamed this on the undue number of showers he used to take when he played basketball in high school and college, claiming he had washed all the natural oil out of his hair and it never returned. Medically Kate dismissed that explanation, with no effect on him, however.

His solid frame, his muscular arms and legs were a testament to his early athletic career, and though he now spent long nights over legal papers and casebooks, he had not allowed himself to go soft. He jogged to the office, then ran up the fourteen flights to his floor.

The memory of his high school coach, who dropped dead at the age of forty-four, still haunted him. He was determined not to fall prey to the fate reserved for athletes who quit cold.

His lean face was strong. Kate teased him about the cleft in his chin, calling him Kirk Douglas. The comparison irritated him, since he fancied he was more like Cary Grant. In truth, he resembled neither, being a nice-looking young man but not quite handsome. He still resisted wearing glasses all the time, though he was forced to admit he needed them for reading. With his glasses on, he looked extremely studious, which was a more truthful representation of the man.

"Someone has to stand up in that hospital and speak the truth about Morse!" Kate insisted.

"Kate, any lawyer will tell you that the most self-destructive thing in this world is a righteous, angry, emotionally involved person fighting for what he or she thinks is a just cause!"

"Medically I'm right! They must admit that!"

"Medically, yes. But professionally you'll be a threat to every doctor in that room. Each one will be sitting back, thinking, 'If I agree with this young upstart nurse now, tomorrow some other nurse may be hauling *me* up before some committee to answer for *my* errors of judgment.' They don't dare side with you."

When Dr. Minter reached his office after making his early morning rounds, he found the note Katherine Kincaid had slipped under his door. Courteous in tone, it was quite definite in its demand for a hearing before the Medical Board on the matter of Dr. Morse and the death of the Nolan baby.

Damn, Minter thought, *why does a very pretty, extremely capable young woman with her whole career ahead of her keep looking for trouble?* After a second thought he had to admit perhaps it was because she *is* so capable and so principled.

He told his secretary to photocopy Kate's note and send one to each man and both women on the medical staff who were qualified to sit on such a hearing, asking if they would be willing to serve.

Before the day was out, he received four replies, none in writing, but by phone and in a confidential tone that begged not to be quoted.

"Brad, do you realize what would happen if we held such a hearing and word got out? Not only would the Nolans sue this hospital for malpractice, every woman who's ever given birth to a stillborn here would be suing us. We can't encourage this sort of thing. Absolutely not! I won't serve!"

By the end of the day Minter knew what he must do, but he had to devise the proper phraseology in which to do it. That evening he dictated a letter. The next morning he revised it. By late the next afternoon he reread his new version and signed it.

My dear Ms. Kincaid: After intensive discussions with my colleagues on the Medical Board we find that the statements in your letter do not constitute sufficient grounds to convene a hearing.

Sincerely,
Bradley Minter, M.D.

Kate found the hand-delivered letter waiting for her when she went to the nurses' station to check out for the day. She read it and crumpled it, furious. She called Howard from the pay phone on the floor. He listened indulgently, and when she was done, he said, "I guess there's nothing more you can do, is there?"

He was enormously relieved. She had got it off her chest and would now settle down. Maybe she would be disillusioned enough to consider marriage more seriously than she had heretofore.

"If only . . ." she started to say.

"Katie," he interrupted firmly. "There are no 'if onlys.' The Medical Board is the final authority on such things. They said no."

"What about the Board of Trustees?" she persisted.

"Trustees do not become involved in purely medical decisions," he answered.

After a long moment of silence, he heard her concede grudgingly, "Okay, if you say so."

"I say so," he declared with finality. "Now, go on home, get into a nice hot tub, soak out all your hostilities. So when I come pick you up you'll be relaxed, happy, sweet-smelling and generally delicious. Because I have ideas for us tonight. Terrific ideas."

He had no need to be more specific than that. He was a very tender, considerate, satisfying lover.

Kate hung up the receiver slowly, pulled open the door of the phone booth. Across the corridor, glaring, obviously furious, stood

Dr. Alfred Morse. Kate ignored him, starting toward the elevators. He moved swiftly to cut her off. When she tried to avoid him, he seized her by the arms.

"Let go of me!" she said angrily but keeping her voice down to a level that would not attract attention.

"What the hell do you think you're up to?" Morse demanded.

"Let go of me," she said with a precision that accompanied her attempt to free herself from his painful grip.

He ignored her protest. "I know about your note to Minter. What are you trying to do? Get me fired from the staff? Ruin my career?"

She made one final determined effort to break free. She succeeded.

"Kincaid," the young doctor warned her, "you haven't heard the last of this!"

She ignored his threat and raced to catch the elevator, whose red beacon light indicated it was going down.

Two days later Kate Kincaid received a notice from the hospital's Disciplinary Board. She was being brought up on charges of insubordination for deliberately disobeying specific medical orders.

Normally she would have been concerned about such a grave charge. Now she looked forward to it. What she could not accomplish before the Medical Board she would be able to do in the disciplinary hearing. Morse was asking for it. Well, she would let him have it!

"Kate, I am not going to let you go into that hearing alone," Howard insisted as soon as she told him.

"Miss Curzon will be there."

"Darling, you don't realize how serious this is. As a lawyer, I tell you this hearing may only be the beginning. Because if the Board finds for Morse, he might sue you for slander. For damaging his professional reputation. So I don't care what you say, *I* am going to be there. *I* am going to defend you!"

"Howard, this is a medical dispute to be settled among people in the profession."

"Kate, hearings, charges, countercharges are legal matters, even when they concern medical disputes What kind of man do you think I'd be if I let you go into that jungle alone?"

"Howard, I am a big girl now. Well able to take care of my own problems. I want to face that arrogant bastard by myself!"

"Then promise me one thing," Howard insisted. "If it gets rough, worse than you anticipate, you'll ask for a recess and call me. I don't care what I'm into, I'll leave and rush right up to the hospital. Promise?"

Because it was the only way she could avoid his appearance at the hearing, she finally agreed. "All right. I promise."

Dr. Lewis Crane, who presided over the hearing, was a man of mature years, graying at the temples and with hints of white in his trim moustache. Tall and distinguished, he created confidence and hope in patients merely by coming down the corridor in his crisp military stride. When he entered a ward or a patient's room, there was an immediate sense of relief and gratitude. Crane was here. The great Dr. Crane.

Among his colleagues he was more highly regarded for his bedside manner than for his diagnostic abilities, and more envied for his outlandish fees than for his cure rate.

From the first statement Crane made, Kate had the uneasy feeling that he had been very well briefed by Alfred Morse, who sat across the table from her, a faint smile of smug confidence on his face.

"Miss Kincaid, I want you to know that there is nothing personal in this proceeding. We are only here to determine the facts involved in this complaint. And since Dr. Morse is the complainant, I think it is proper for him to state the nature of his grievance."

In a manner far more benign than his attitude of the other day, Morse related his version of the facts, appearing as innocent and conscientious as he could. He had made a very careful examination of Mrs. Nolan, had monitored her infant and its heartbeat, was fully aware that she was a grand multipara, was also aware of the possible risks involved in giving her Pitocin, and so had prescribed a small dose in a sufficiently large infusion of water so that it could be stopped without danger to the patient or the baby if signs of danger presented. But to his dismay, when he went back to observe the patient, he discovered that the Pitocin drip had been discontinued by Nurse Kincaid. He ordered Pitocin resumed in full expectation of a normal, uneventful delivery. He made a mental note to report Miss Kincaid's outrageous act of insubordination, but on reflection he decided not to be harsh with her and to forget the entire episode. Except, of course, when the Nolan baby died, he decided he must bring this whole sad affair before the Disciplinary Board.

Even Miss Curzon could not resist glancing in Kate's direction at such a flagrantly dishonest recounting of the events.

Dr. Crane turned to Kate. In his most benign and indulgent manner he said, "And now, Miss Kincaid, I think you should have every opportunity to defend your actions. After all, Dr. Morse has made some very serious charges."

Kate felt her hands begin to tremble, so she kept them below the conference table to conceal her tension and her anger. She glanced in the direction of Alfred Morse before she began.

"Dr. Crane, you said there was nothing personal in this. But there are certain personal characteristics which are part of this problem."

"This wouldn't be the first time that 'personal' frictions between a doctor and a nurse have created problems," Crane said, smiling in a way that indicated he suspected an intimate and unhappy relationship between Kate and Dr. Morse.

Her face flushed in suppressed anger. "*I* was referring to Dr. Morse's determination to 'clear the book' every Friday."

"I resent that remark," Morse interrupted.

"You'll resent even more some of the things I have to say before I'm through," Kate shot back. She turned her attention to Dr. Crane, who, while he made no attempt to silence her, plainly revealed that he did not welcome her further testimony. "Neverthe less," she went on, "I don't expect any doctor to feel that he owes his patients twenty-four hours of every day. But I do expect that while he is on duty he will devote himself completely to his patients' comfort, security and health."

She turned on Morse as she continued. "To compromise their health by using Pitocin to hasten delivery because it fits his own personal convenience is not only self-indulgent, it is unforgivable."

Morse replied angrily, "It was *my* decision to give Mrs. Nolan Pitocin. It was *your* job to monitor her to see that she did not get into difficulty. And if she did, to call *me*! Not discontinue the I.V., but to *call me*!"

Kate waited out the doctor's arrogant tirade before replying softly but quite firmly, "Dr. Irving agreed with me. In fact, he was very upset to discover the patient was on that medication to begin with. And if he were alive, he'd be here today to say that on his own."

A smirk spread across Morse's face. "Dr. Crane, how long are you going to permit her to continue? She can make up any lie and say, 'Dr. Irving said that.' He is dead. How can I disprove it?"

Kate leaped up from her chair to lean across the table toward Morse. "I am not lying! Dr. Irving *was* furious! In fact, when he found that I had discontinued the I.V. he complimented me. Said it was the right thing, the safe thing to do. And the way things turned out, he was right. And *I* was right. Only I should have acted sooner."

She sank back into her chair, saying quietly, "That baby might be alive today if I had."

Dr. Crane tugged at his trim moustache before he spoke. "Miss Kincaid, did I understand you to say that the course of events was as follows? Dr. Morse prescribed Pitocin by I.V. You monitored the patient. Then decided on your own to discontinue it. And it was only *after* that Dr. Irving became involved?"

"I sent for Dr. Irving to look at the Bellino case. Since I had detected late decelerations . . ."

"Never mind the Bellino case," Crane interrupted. "The Nolan case! *You* discontinued the prescribed drug on your own. And only after that Dr. Irving expressed his agreement. Is that correct?"

"Yes," Kate admitted.

"Well," Crane exclaimed in his most condemnatory manner, "that puts an entirely different light on things."

Miss Curzon felt compelled to intervene. "Dr. Crane, there is nothing in the rules preventing a nurse from seeking the opinion of a senior physician in case of doubt. That is perfectly professional and highly desirable conduct. It reflects her concern for the patient's welfare."

Crane listened witn an intolerant attitude that indicated he was not moved by anything she might say. "Miss Curzon, you have addressed yourself to the wrong issue. No one, I am sure, not even Dr. Morse, disputes the right of a nurse to seek another opinion when she feels it is in the interest of her patient. However . . ."

He paused to accent the word once more. "*However*, that is not what Miss Kincaid did. First she discontinued the I.V. And only *then* did she summon Dr. Irving. In other words, on her own she went contra to specific medical orders. That Dr. Irving agreed later, or that she tells us that he agreed . . ."

"He did agree," Kate insisted.

"Please, Miss Kincaid, let me do this my way," Crane said with the kind of mock deference one accords inferiors in rank and intelligence. "The issue here is Dr. Morse's complaint. A nurse, against orders, discontinued a prescribed treatment, placing her medical opinion above that of the physician on the case. That presents this board with a very grave situation."

"While your board is considering that," Kate said, "let them also consider that because a doctor in a rush to clear the book used Pitocin, an infant, who had a right to be born alive and healthy, is dead. And a woman is suffering from the emotional trauma of that tragedy. Consider Mrs. Nolan!"

With that, Kate Kincaid shoved back her chair and left the room. Miss Curzon raced out and caught her in the corridor.

"Kate, don't run out now."

"What good would it do to fight? Crane's already made up his mind. And what he says the rest of them are going to say. You know that."

She brushed aside Curzon's restraining hand and started toward the elevator to go back up to Maternity and resume her duties, for however long they would let her.

Miss Curzon reentered the hearing room in time to hear Dr. Morse explain, "So you see, by stopping the Pitocin as she did, and then my having to start it again, my carefully planned course of treatment was interrupted and the result was most unfortunate. We wouldn't be here today if Kincaid hadn't gone against orders."

Crane nodded, indicating his agreement with Morse's version of the affair.

"Dr. Crane, gentlemen," Miss Curzon protested, "before you come to any conclusion I would like to be heard. I don't have to tell you the difficulty we have staffing a hospital these days with capable nurses. Half my time is spent recruiting young women with the proper degrees and training. But the day when a nurse was an automaton is gone. If she is to take pride in her profession her opinion has to count."

"Miss Curzon, how would you describe Miss Kincaid's actions, other than as a flagrant violation of doctor's orders?" Crane challenged her.

Her pale skin flushing in contrast with her graying hair, Curzon replied, "Gentlemen, from my point of view the question here is quite clear. Because of a mere technicality in the rules you are going to deprive this hospital of a valued nurse, a young woman I have been planning to make my assistant, to take over for me one day when I retire. Yes, she did what she did against doctor's orders. But *she* was right. It was the doctor who was wrong!''

She turned her accusatory glare on Morse. ''As he was wrong about Mrs. Bellino. He didn't detect late decelerations, but Kincaid did. Dr. Irving did. . . .''

''We've heard enough about Dr. Irving,'' Crane interrupted. ''I regret he is not here to testify for himself, but he isn't.''

Not abashed in the least, Curzon replied very firmly, ''Dr. Crane, there is a hospital record. It shows that Dr. Irving also detected late decelerations. When he did, and before the baby could suffer damage, he rushed Mrs. Bellino up to the O.R. and did a cesarean. Proving that Kincaid, not Dr. Morse, was right about the baby's heartbeat. If she hadn't summoned Dr. Irving that baby might have died or been born brain damaged.''

Curzon rose to her feet. ''If you take steps against this intelligent, devoted, capable nurse for doing what was in the best interests of her patients, then you will be doing this hospital and medicine in general a great injustice.''

Crane was obviously distressed and perplexed. He tugged at his moustache, frowned and turned to his colleagues. ''Gentlemen?''

Wesley Rossiter, also an Ob-Gyn specialist and younger than Crane, spoke up first. ''I trained under Irving. Was his assistant for five years before I went out on my own. I knew that man as well as anyone. What Kincaid describes Irving said and did strikes me as exactly what he would have said and done. If he were here today he would make a strong and eloquent defense of her.

''Unfortunately, he isn't. Yet we have to come to some conclusion. So I will state how far I am willing to go. For the record, I would give Miss Kincaid the very mildest reprimand we can phrase so that we have paid our respects to the technicalities. Then, I think each of us should personally apologize to her for having to do that. She is one hell of a capable nurse. I would entrust any of my patients to her and feel very secure. If this board votes for any stronger measure than that, I will object and make public my objection. Is that clear?''

The longer Rossiter spoke, the more flushed and resentful Crane's face grew.

"Well," he conceded finally, "if there's one thing this hospital does not need it is a public scandal. I think Dr. Rossiter may have given us the way out of this sticky situation. Unless Dr. Morse wishes to be heard again."

Morse looked across at Miss Curzon whose glare challenged him. "Just so long as the principle that a nurse cannot overrule a doctor's express orders is upheld I have no more to say."

CHAPTER 3

Two mornings later, as Miss Curzon was checking her schedule of nurse assignments, there was a knock on her door.

"Yes?" she called out.

"Miss Curzon?" she heard Kate Kincaid respond.

"Come in, Kate, come in."

Kate entered, held out an official-appearing letter. Miss Curzon read it, looked up at her.

"It says some very complimentary things about you, about your work." Curzon was trying to put the best face on this note of which she strenuously disapproved.

"What about the part that says, 'We are sure your act of insubordination was hastily considered, and will not be repeated in the future'?" Kate demanded. "No matter how you interpret it, it says that my education, my training, my professional opinion, gained from continuous observation of the patient, are inferior to those of the doctor who comes rushing in, takes one look, gives one listen on his stethoscope and prescribes. I refuse to accept that."

"They had to do something, for the record." Curzon tried to console her.

"I don't give a damn what they had to do for the record!" Kate exploded. "Somewhere there must be a place where a nurse's value is recognized and her intelligence respected."

"Kate?"

"I don't think I can stay on here," Kate declared simply but with unmistakable determination.

"You've just received this letter. You're hurt. I don't blame you. But don't do anything hasty. You might regret it for the rest of your life."

Those final words made Kate look into Miss Curzon's eyes.

"Kate, University is the finest hospital in this city. If you want to find another place, a better place, you'll have to go elsewhere. That means giving up your seniority here, your chance to succeed me. *And* . . . it means giving up the other side of your life."

She took Kate's hands in hers in a way that reminded Kate of her mother. "I've seen Howard when you brought him to the Staff Christmas Party and the annual Interns and Nurses' Show. He's a handsome young man, and extremely nice. He loves you very deeply. I've seen it in his eyes when he looks at you, at times when you don't even notice. But you can't expect him to abandon his law career here and go wherever you decide to go. That wouldn't be fair."

"No, no, it wouldn't," Kate said thoughtfully. "I'll . . . I'll think about it."

Kate was rinsing her long blond hair after having washed it in a fragrant shampoo that had created huge billows of suds. She raised her clean, wet face, leaned over the washbasin and wrung out her hair until it stopped dripping. Then she twisted it into a knot atop her head and wrapped it, turban style, in an aquamarine towel that contrasted with her fair skin and her hair. Her regular features stood out sharply. Howard always thought she was at her most beautiful that way. She stared into the mirror of the medicine chest, appraising herself as women do at such times. Her face was fresh, youthful, scrubbed clean and, she admitted a bit vainly, pretty. She studied her blue eyes and was about to break off the contact until she realized to do so would avoid answering the question Miss Curzon had asked her.

Was it only hurt feelings, mere vanity that had driven her to the determination to resign? What would resigning do to her and Howard? Would it threaten their relationship? Even end it? Or was that reprimand all the incentive she needed to quit and get married? Why not? There was a whole other life waiting for her. Being a good wife, being a good mother. Her own mother had made a very satisfying career of being a wife, and she'd been wonderful at it, right up until the day her father died. On the other hand, there was Kate's aunt Sybil. Syb had studied nursing, devoted her life to it and was successful at that. Two sisters out of the same family, choosing two entirely different careers, and both were very good in the lives they chose.

There were two elements in Kate's early life that had inspired her to choose nursing as a career. Aunt Syb was one.

Even as a child, Kate had not only loved Syb but admired her as well, especially the way she bore the sacrifices her profession exacted. Kate could remember times when it was Christmas or Thanksgiving and the whole family was assembled, except for Syb, who was on a tough case and wouldn't take time off. But she could always manage to call from the hospital and insist on talking to every member of the family, most especially to Kate, who was the youngest. Then Syb would say, "Now, darling, I have to say goodbye. My patient needs me."

Never any resentment, never any regret, only a desire to serve those in need, which, even as a child, Kate had come to admire. God, would there ever be nurses like Syb again? Not if one were to judge from the complaints of patients these days. Well, there are, Kate insisted to the Kate in the mirror. *I* will be one! Her house phone rang. She raced to the bedroom to answer it.

"Darling?" It was Howard down at the front door wanting to be buzzed in.

"You're a little early but come on up."

She dialed the number that would open the front door for him, but she was determined not to mention her thoughts of resigning until she had decided where to go, when to go . . . and *if* to go.

She had already added the milk to her mixture of butter, flour and seasoning and was about to add the well-beaten egg yolks when she became aware of Howard, drink in hand, standing in the doorway to the kitchen, staring at her.

"Darling, what's wrong?" she asked.

"I was going to ask you that," he said, rotating the ice in his Scotch and soda. "I'm here. But you're still off somewhere."

"I'm cooking," she said a bit impatiently, "and I'm at the most important point in making a cheese soufflé. All the ingredients have to come together just right."

"No, it's more than that. I'm here, but you're still off somewhere battling that monster Morse. I say, forget the whole thing. Medicine. Nursing. Sacrifice. Devotion. You've only got one life. Live it for yourself . . . and for me."

She didn't respond because she was concentrating on folding the blended ingredients into the stiffly beaten egg whites. She poured the whole mixture into the fluted white casserole, checked the oven temperature to make sure it was 475 degrees.

Having done that, she set the timer for ten minutes and turned to him.

"Hawk . . ." she said, addressing him by the nickname he had acquired during his basketball days at college when he was known as a ball hawk. "Hawk, I've given that a lot of thought the past few days."

"About time," he said, encouraged.

"I have devoted the last seven years of my life to studying, preparing and practicing a profession I chose very carefully. Now, I have to ask myself, have I made a mistake?"

"Good question," he said. "There's no thanks, no glory in it. Forget it. Let's get married. You can start a whole new way of life. It'll be you and me, babe, as the song says. And after a while, little Hawk, and maybe a little blond-haired girl or two. That's life, Katie. That's what it's all about. And darling, we will have a great life. If only you didn't have this unreasonable compulsion to go on with a career that's already betrayed you."

Before she could protest, he insisted, "Yes, betrayed! You study, work hard, give yourself physically, emotionally and totally to it, and what's your reward? They have told you, politely of course, that you are a second-class citizen. A hired hand. You just take orders. Hell, that note they sent you, that ever-so-diplomatic reprimand, was an insult to your intelligence. You want to know the truth? I was more outraged by that note than you were. They said, 'We'll put the medicine on a cube of sugar and it'll go down easily. And then our unselfish, devoted Miss Kincaid will go right back to knocking herself out on behalf of this hospital! The doctors! The whole profession!' "

"If only Dr. Irving . . ." she started to say.

"A perfect case in point!" Howard interrupted. "When you needed him, he wasn't there. Because he'd given up his life to doing what you are now doing. Sacrificing. If he had retired ten years ago he'd still be alive today."

"There are a lot of people alive today who wouldn't be if it weren't for Walter Irving," Kate pointed out.

"If it hadn't been him it would have been some other doctor. Just as in your case. If you quit there'll be someone else. Why does it have to be you?"

"I don't know," Kate confessed. "It's something I feel and can't explain. You can't watch the suffering, the fear, and walk away untouched. At least I can't. Call it a compulsion, a drive, a need to serve."

"Or call it a Syb complex?" Howard said accusingly.

"If you want to," Kate responded, equally contentious.

"You know, of all the people you talk about from your childhood, you speak most lovingly of her. Of course you loved your mother and father. But when you talk about Syb there's something more. Hero worship, I suppose. It reminds me of my senior year at college. The local papers back home ran stories about the possibility of my making All-American, which I never had a chance at, believe me. But when I came home on holidays, kids would actually gather outside my house and wait to get a look at Hawk Brewster. And if I showed up at the local schoolyard and practiced my turnaround jump shot, kids came running from all over the neighborhood to watch. Then they would try to imitate me. It was flattering in those days. But by the time I graduated from law school no kids hung around outside my door. They'd forgotten about me. They had new heroes, new interests. And that's as it should be."

"Hawk, what are you trying to say?" Kate asked.

"It is immature to carry into one's adult life the dreams, ambitions and heroes of one's childhood."

"Meaning?" she asked.

"Meaning that the little girl who so admired her aunt is now her superior in every way. Your aunt Syb didn't have half the training and education you do. Wasn't half the woman you are. If I may venture a guess, wasn't as beautiful as you are. Or as loving and passionate a woman. Instead of trying to emulate your aunt, you've surpassed her by far and don't even realize it. It's time to give up your childhood fantasies and do what's best for Kate Kincaid. And, of course, for Howard Brewster, too.''

When she did not reply, he prodded. ''Katie? Honey?''

''So that's what you secretly think about me. Immature. With little-girl fantasies.''

''You can't deny how you feel about your Aunt Syb!'' he insisted.

''Howard Brewster, if I didn't know you so well, I'd say you sound like a male chauvinist!'' she countered.

He was about to reply when the timer interrupted and Kate had to reset the thermostat at four hundred degrees.

She did not have to ask how he liked her cheese soufflé. He had already helped himself to a third heaping dish of the light, fluffy, golden mixture. She admired the gusto with which he ate. It was a compliment to the success of her latest venture into the art of *haute cuisine*.

She leaned back from the table, studied his strong face, and asked, ''Did they call you Hawk, too?''

He looked up, fork poised in midair, and responded, ''Who?''

''The kids who gathered at your front door.''

''Oh, sure. I wonder what they'd say if they could see me now. With reading glasses. And stoop-shouldered from delving into law books.''

''You are not stoop-shouldered,'' she corrected.

''Maybe not, but I feel that way after hours in the library.''

''Don't they have assistants, junior lawyers, to do that kind of thing for you?''

''I like to find my own cases. Suppose some young kid fresh out of law school reads a case and doesn't give it the proper relevance and importance to my case? I may be deprived of a crucial weapon during trial. So I insist on researching them myself.''

''Those nights when I'm off duty and you're busy, I had fantasies of you being out with some devastatingly beautiful woman,'' Kate joked. ''When all the while you were right where you said you were, the law library. What devotion. To the law, I mean.''

''And what about those nights when you have to fill in because there's a shortage of nurses at the hospital and I'm left waiting around?'' he countered.

"Which you wouldn't have to do if we were married and I quit nursing. Right?"

"Exactly!"

"Then, of course, *I'd* be home waiting. In some nice but dull house in the suburbs. While you are having a wildly exciting time in the law library. It hardly seems fair," she teased.

"Kate, darling, this is nothing to joke about. The law is my profession. If a man wants to practice it diligently, it's very demanding. But it'll provide us with a very enjoyable and gracious way of life. So don't begrudge the sacrifice."

"Meaning it's perfectly all right to make sacrifices for your profession, but not for mine," she said in rebuke.

"When there's a clash between a husband's profession and a wife's, yes!" he replied.

"Well, I don't know if I want to spend my life waiting in the suburbs while you're working late hours. During my seven years of college and nursing experience I didn't study waiting. I don't know if I'd be any good at it. I studied nursing. I know I can do that. And damn well! To just sit around waiting now would be like being all dressed up with no place to go. Ready to play basketball and no one blows the whistle to start the game.

"Well, Counselor, for the same reason you like to track down those cases yourself, I like to take care of patients and not leave it to the others." Before he could protest, Kate anticipated him. "And don't tell me about little-girl fantasies! People in pain are not a fantasy. Women in labor are not little-girl dreams. Life in the balance because of some doctor's mistake is not just something my aunt Syb told me about. I have seen it. I have lived through it. I've been there when a baby is born dead and didn't have to be. When a woman has bled to death because no doctor was on the floor. I have had my hands covered with her blood. That, my dear Hawk, is not fantasy!"

She pushed back from the dinette table and rose to her feet. She seemed about to say something but did not. Instead, she strode into the bedroom, slamming the door behind her.

He did not pursue her, much as he wanted to make love to her on this night. But he knew her well enough to know that, though it took a great deal to anger her, once angered it was best to allow her to calm down on her own. He also realized that their lives had reached a critical stage.

Until now he had proceeded with complete assurance that when the time came, be it because of some professional frustration, or some emotional crisis, he would be able to convince her to forgo nursing for marriage. Tonight for the first time, he was forced to admit that his confidence might have exceeded the realities.

She heard the door close as he left. Turning off the bedside lamp, she lay there quietly. She reached out to the other pillow which, on those nights he stayed over, was his pillow.

She felt a strong sense of guilt. Unless she could come to terms with her own life it was unfair to him to continue their relationship. For he was a man with normal desires and needs. He wanted a home, a wife in that home, and children. He wanted children very much. In fairness to him, she would have to decide soon. To give up nursing would not be easy. Can a woman simply make believe her career never happened, and settle down to keeping house and producing babies? Many women did and found it rewarding, enriching. What was this devil in her that prevented her doing it? Why this need to persevere in a profession so fraught with frustrations?

When she had applied for the nursing course at college, one of the questions on the application was: *Why do you wish to choose nursing as a career?*

In the brief space allowed on the form she couldn't very well explain in detail. So she wrote simply: *Because it will give me a chance to serve the sick and comfort the fearful.*

How could she tell them about that terrifying night long ago?

Even now she could never see the rotating red and white lights of an ambulance or a police car without being reminded of that time. That was especially true on any night when an ambulance pulled into the emergency dock at the hospital, or if when driving home after the late shift she sighted a police car in her rearview mirror.

Because it had happened at night.

In those days before smoke alarms, the smell of smoke would rouse a household. Or the barking of the family dog. In the Kincaid house it was Rusty. Not exactly an inspired name for a shaggy, brown-haired golden retriever who had been part of the family since before six-year-old Kate was born.

Rusty's barking had saved their lives. Dad being away on one of his too-frequent business trips, only Mom, Kate and little Scott were home. Mom had rushed into Kate's room, snatched her out of her warm bed, and raced to Scott's room, above the kitchen, where the smoke and the heat were most intense. She seized her son in her other arm, carried both children down the stairs, stopping only long enough to call the fire department before escaping into the night.

Shortly after they had reached the safety of the front lawn, Kate could hear the distant sirens. First to arrive was a police car, red and white lights cutting through the night. It had pulled up with a screech, the officer at the wheel calling out, "Anyone still in there?"

"No," her mother had called back, then tried to reassure Scott, who kept crying bitterly. "Nothing to be afraid of, lovey. We're going to be all right." But Kate realized that her brother continued crying.

From down the street came the big red hook-and-ladder fire truck, horn blaring rhythmically. By that time neighbors in nightclothes had come pouring out of their homes. In the window of the Kincaid kitchen, where the fire had started, flames leapt into view. Internal heat had caused some windowpanes to explode, and smoke began to pour out.

Terrified at seeing the only home she had ever known in flames, little Kate joined her brother in weeping as she pleaded, "Scotty, don't cry, don't cry. Please?" She clung to him while he held his right hand with his left in such a way that caused their mother to kneel down to examine it.

After one close look, she discovered the reason for his intense and prolonged crying. The angry red blotch on the side of his little hand was a serious burn.

Terrified, Mother had cried out, "Someone! Help my son! Please!"

A woman, a stranger, dressed in white uniform and sweater, rushed to their side.

Kate recalled that all Mother said was "My son!"

The woman dropped down beside her mother to examine Scott's hand. Then without a word, she went off, to return in moments with a large red and white metal first-aid kit. As she selected the proper medication and bandages, she continued to comfort little Scott in a soft, reassuring voice. "We'll have you better in no time. The pain'll be gone and you'll be fine again. And you won't cry. Like the strong little man I know you are."

She handed him a lollipop to divert him while she made a more careful diagnosis of his condition. It was evidently more serious than her previous opinion, for Kate observed that the woman discarded her medication of first choice for a different one. Carefully she applied an anesthetic spray to Scott's burn, then with a wooden tongue depressor, she gently applied a layer of antiseptic unguent. She covered the area with a moist, treated layer of gauze, finally bandaging it lightly so as not to create any undue pressure on the painful area.

When she was finished, she held Scott in her arms, asking, "Now, isn't that better?"

Gradually Scott gave up crying for sniffling, then he nodded. She peeled off the cellophane from his lollipop. Once he began licking the candy, he was quite content to remain in her embrace.

When the fire chief needed Kate's mother for information about the layout of the house, the lady in white said, "I'll take care of the little girl, too."

Her mother passed Kate over into the arms of the woman, who took her gently, held her close and comforted her softly. "Come, dear. Now we'll get you both some hot cocoa and cookies. You'd like that, wouldn't you?"

Kate nodded through her tears. The woman carried them to the small van at the curb. It was white except for the big neat cross painted on it in red.

"Anne," the woman said to her colleague in the van, "we'll need some hot cocoa for this young man and this little lady. And one of our special sugar cookies for each. Maybe even two. How would you like two?"

Kate clung to her and nodded. But once offered a cup of hot cocoa, Kate realized she would rather cling to the friendly woman than have cocoa or even sugar cookies. It was comforting to feel the woman's soft white sweater against her cheek, to hear her reassuring voice whisper, "You'll be fine! Your brother'll be fine. And they'll save your house. I've seen them do it many times. So you can stop worrying. You can even fall asleep if you like."

The sound of Rusty's frantic barking, the men calling to each other, for assistance, for equipment, the chief giving orders on the bullhorn, the strange-sounding voices of cross talk from the police car radio, the revolving lights on all the cars and fire trucks were too much to allow a terrified little girl to fall asleep. She only nestled closer to the kind, white-clad woman, feeling warm and safe.

When her mother was free to come searching for them, the

woman in the van gave her hot coffee, wrapped a blanket around her in place of the robe that, in her panic, she had forgotten to take with her. They stood side by side, her mother holding Scott and the nice lady holding little Kate tightly, giving her comfort and reassurance.

It was almost dawn by the time the firemen were sure the fire was completely out. The lady in white offered to find a place for Scott, Kate and her mother to stay. But though the smell of smoke was heavy and bitter, her mother insisted they would remain in their own home.

When it came time for the nice lady to hand Kate back to her mother, she was reluctant to go. Before she finally did, she hugged the woman and kissed her on the cheek.

Little Kate Kincaid had thought about that woman often after that night. She wanted to send her a letter of thanks, as Mother had taught her to do after she received a gift or had been to another child's party. But Kate never knew the woman's name. She was just a kind lady in white who had come out of the night to tend a slightly burned little boy, and comfort his frightened sister. To offer warmth and shelter to them, then to bandage the wound of a fireman cut by shattering glass, to soothe the burned hands of two others, and to keep supplying hot coffee to big, brawny men with smoke-smudged faces, in their wet black raincoats with the wide yellow stripes across the backs.

Later, her mother explained that the nice lady was a nurse, a Red Cross nurse, whose work it was to assist at emergencies like fires, at disasters like floods and earthquakes.

"Like Aunt Syb?" Kate asked.

"Aunt Syb works in a hospital. Red Cross nurses go wherever people need help, all kinds of help."

"Could I do that when I grow up?"

"Yes," her mother answered, assuming that like most dreams of the young, it would be forgotten as soon as Kate was captivated by some other ambition.

But the memory of that night stayed with her, renewed each time she saw revolving red and white lights. She would smell the smoke again, hear the sirens, the shattering glass. She would recall Scott's painful crying and her own fears, and then remember the kind nurse who took away his pain. As much as Aunt Syb, that woman had influenced Kate's choice of a career. To Kate Kincaid, nursing

would always mean more than administering medication and alcohol rubs, and assisting doctors. It would mean comfort and support and reassurance. And she would be especially sensitive to the fears and feelings of children.

Now, after four years of training, three years of experience, after not only Dr. Morse but a dozen other arrogant young interns and residents, she still felt the same devotion. Nursing was an opportunity to serve the sick and the needy. At strange hours. In the face of all kinds of difficulties. Despite the opposition of doctors. Kate looked beyond doctors, beyond the hospital bureaucracy, to the patients. Their lives, their welfare, their security, their assurance were the purpose of her work and her sacrifice. It was difficult to contemplate giving those up.

It was difficult, too, to contemplate the alternative. Many times Howard had urged, "If you insist, you can go on working after we're married." But would he be content with a part-time wife? Those early mornings when she was due on duty at seven she would have to leave their warm bed at five-thirty, dress, grab a cup of coffee and drive into the city, leaving Howard not only alone but forced to make his own breakfast, wash his own dishes. And he would. He was one of those meticulous men who couldn't stand the sight of an unclean dish. Plus who would have time to make sure his shirts were properly ironed, his suits pressed so he would look well when he stood before a judge to argue a motion, or before a jury to plead his client's case? Also there would be nights when it was his duty to entertain a client, or a partner, or anyone else who could aid his career, and she would be forced to say, "Sorry, darling, but I have to be up at five-thirty."

Just before falling asleep, Kate decided she wasn't being fair to Howard. She awoke thinking, *most unfair is not making a decision.* Either marry him or set him free. She promised that she would decide very soon. When she did, she would tell him forthrightly and with finality. Yes or no. Marriage or freedom. She was full of earnest resolutions this morning.

By midmorning, after Kate had confronted two emergencies that demanded surgical intervention, had assisted in the delivery of four babies and allowed three phone calls from Miss Curzon to go unanswered, she was all out of resolutions. She was running hard just to keep up with the pressures of the day. Her lunchtime relief was late arriving, so by the time she was able to go off the floor, she had time only for a muffin and a cup of coffee. She was finishing when Curzon sat down at her table.

"Sorry, Miss Curzon. I planned to call back soon as things eased up. But it's been one of those mornings," Kate apologized.

Curzon smiled and nodded. She had spent the first twenty-three years of her career living on the basis of what she would do when her hectic duty in the wards eased up. It never had. She said nothing, but drew a folded pamphlet out of her sweater pocket. She slid it across the table.

"Not now, but when you have a chance, this evening maybe, read this."

"What is it?" Kate asked.

"Just read it," Curzon urged her, thinking, *it might be just what you need to learn that even in nursing there is a time when humility and compromise must take precedence over determination and unyielding idealism.*

As soon as Kate arrived home, she washed her hair to get rid of the medicinal smells of Surgery. She had been up in the O.R. for two stretches today. Not really part of her regular duty, but it reassured her patients. She fixed herself a light supper and settled down to read the pamphlet Curzon had given her.

It was simply written and contained photographs of a modest institution called Mountain Hospital in a small town named Adelphi in the Appalachian Mountains. To judge from the photographs, the entire hospital was not even as large as the Maternity Wing of University Hospital. How big could it be, Kate wondered, forty beds? Probably less. And if less, what kind of equipment would they have? CAT scan? Definitely not. Surgical staff? In a hospital so small? Not likely.

The pamphlet also described what it called Outposts, small local clinics away from the hospital that served patients in isolated mountainous areas. This was primitive, backwoods medicine.

Had Curzon given her this as a subtle warning that if she left University Hospital, she might be reduced to this? Of course not. A capable, experienced nurse could find employment in any large hospital in these times.

Then why?

Kate ignored her supper to read on. She discovered that this remote institution was not only a hospital, it was a training school. But its standards were extremely high. It accepted only those who were already experienced registered nurses. The school gave two courses: one in Family Nurse Practice, one in Midwifery. Kate resented the idea of going back to school. By training and experience she considered herself above that. Yet she read on.

The essence of Family Nurse Practice was the right—and the responsibility—to treat entire families, take their histories, observe their signs, listen to their symptoms, diagnose, prescribe and follow their progress. Except in cases where illnesses or conditions were grave enough to demand the intervention of a surgeon or a physician, the health of the entire family was in the hands of the Family Nurse Practitioner.

This was what Kate had been searching for. The opportunity to *do* on her own, *treat* on her own, *be responsible for* the health of whole families, *on her own.*

She read on. Midwifery. From the various medical and nursing papers she had read she knew Midwifery was having a resurgence in America. An old tradition which had accompanied immigrants from European lands and been so crucial in our own frontier days, it had virtually disappeared during the twentieth century. Obstetricians had taken over. Large hospitals had taken over. Birthing had become institutionalized, and the midwife had been relegated to history. But within recent years the skill had begun to stage a comeback. At this little mountain hospital it was the accepted way of caring for the pregnant and aiding in the birth process.

Imagine, Kate realized eagerly as she read on, the patient would be in her complete charge, from the time she became pregnant until she gave birth.

What if she had been in charge of Mrs. Bellino from the time of conception? There would never have been any need for a cesarean. And Mrs. Nolan. Her baby would have been born alive if someone who had followed her case for nine months had been in charge of her.

As soon as Kate finished reading the slim pamphlet, she reread it. She studied the photographs of the hospital. Much as they were intended to impress the reader with simple architecture and interior decor, it was still only a small hospital, in an obviously tiny mountain town.

Finally she put the pamphlet aside and went to bed. In the morning she tried to ignore it. She ended up shoving it into her bag when she took off for the hospital. By noontime she could not resist calling Curzon. She asked if she could meet her in her office instead of having lunch.

"I thought it would excite you," Curzon said. "But I wonder how you would do in a small out-of-the-way place like that."

"That's what puzzles me," Kate admitted. "This place, so small, so off the beaten path of advanced medicine, yet experienced women go there to train. Why?"

Curzon pulled a sheet out of her desk drawer, slid it across to Kate.

After one glance, Kate looked up at Curzon. "Are these figures accurate?"

"I reacted the same way you did. So I had them checked out. Yes, they are accurate."

"You mean that in over forty years, after more than seventeen thousand maternity cases, they've lost only twelve mothers in childbirth?" Kate asked.

"Yes."

"Our rate in this hospital isn't that good," Kate said.

"Nor in any big hospital."

"Amazing," Kate said softly. "That's the only word for it, amazing."

Through that day and night, and until the moment she drifted into sleep, one thought persisted in Kate's mind. The next morning she woke with the same thought.

Freedom! Freedom and responsibility! To treat her patients as she saw fit, using all her skills, experience and intuition. No medical hierarchy to determine her choices. No young interns or residents, who by virtue of a degree outranked her, to overrule her experience and knowledge.

She must write to this unusual place and find out more.

CHAPTER 4

Kate was anxious to go off duty for lunch to read the new information which had arrived yesterday from Mountain Hospital in answer to her letter of a week ago. She had had no chance to read it last night because Howard had insisted she accompany him to the annual Bar Association dinner at which he was announced as a new member of the Ethics Committee, an honor unusual for a man who was only a junior member of a large law firm.

She was very proud when he stood up to acknowledge the applause of the guests. With some amusement she whispered, "Go get 'em, Hawk!"

The gray-haired wife of Howard's senior partner, sitting beside Kate, smiled and asked, "When will it be?"

"Be? What?"

"Arthur and I always make it a point to go to the weddings of all the junior men. And women," she added, realizing that in Kate she was addressing the new generation. "Arthur says it gives a sense of familial continuity to the firm."

"That's very . . . very thoughtful and touching," Kate said.

After seemingly endless speeches, which consisted of lawyers lauding the law and its practitioners, she and Howard arrived back at her apartment. Howard insisted on staying over, and, frankly, she wanted him to. So, once again, early in the morning, she had to slip out of their warm bed, leaving him still sleeping, dress by the dim light from the living room, and go off while it was still dark out. At the hospital a quick glass of orange juice and a cup of coffee, and she was on duty once more. Still no opportunity to read that bulky letter from Mountain Hospital in the town called Adelphi.

The morning started badly and grew worse. A young pregnant diabetic woman who had been admitted during the night was already in difficulty. A resident had been summoned, but since there was a change of shifts, none had appeared as yet. There was also a primagravida (first pregnancy), only fifteen years old and with unusual contractions. A young nurse-trainee who was supposed to assist Kate had not come on duty when she was scheduled. It was one of those mornings when Kate could easily have been convinced to give up nursing altogether. Especially when she kept thinking of Howard, warm, asleep and snoring just slightly. How nice it would feel to be cuddled up to him and drifting back to sleep for that last delicious hour.

By lunchtime she had sufficient relief to take her full fifty minutes. Finding a quiet corner of the cafeteria, she settled down to read that bulky envelope.

The forwarding letter had been written by Christine Abbott, Director of Mountain Hospital. Abbott answered all of Kate's questions very directly and made no effort to influence her judgment. The director's attitude was "this is what we offer, but you have to qualify and be prepared for hard work and sacrifice if you want to be part of our training in family nursing and midwifery." Kate was surprised. She had expected they would be begging for trained and experienced women like herself. Her sense of self-importance was diminished considerably when she consulted the accompanying booklet to discover that Christine Abbott had four college degrees, including a doctorate in philosophy. No mountain hillbilly, this director, Kate concluded.

The final paper in the envelope was a form that asked for her *curriculum vitae*, the record of her education and her experience in nursing. To fill it out and send it meant in essence applying for admission.

Did she dare fill it out? Should she tell Howard before she did? Or should she tell him only after she had sent back the form so he would have one less opportunity to talk her out of applying. She folded the sheet, slipped it back into the envelope and glanced up at the wall clock. She had to hurry back to Maternity.

* * *

Kate shopped for their dinner, arrived home, had her bath and hoped to take a short nap before Howard arrived from the office. Instead she decided to glance at that *curriculum vitae* form. It asked the usual questions: *Name. Date of Birth. Place of Birth. Education*, from primary school to the present. *Nursing Degree. Nursing License. Area of Specialty. Work Experience.*

The very last question was: *Marital Status.* What she and Howard had was a deep and loving relationship which was an important part of her life. One word from her, and it would change to a formal marital status. She would then be able to fill in the space calling for *Spouse.* They had even provided a space for *Children.*

The form suddenly presented her not only with a complete review of her past life, but challenged her to decide what her future life was going to be. One thing was very clear. She would have to speak to Howard before she filled it out.

All through dinner he told her about his day in court. The evidence he had planned to introduce, the manner in which his opposing counsel sought to prevent him, the Memorandum of Law which he presented to the judge that enabled him to proceed with his case as he had planned. It was a crucial decision. For without that evidence, his case might have been thrown out. When he returned to the office they were ecstatic.

"And Mr. Kilbourn, the senior partner, you remember his wife, the woman you sat next to at the Bar Association dinner, he said it was brilliant. Something about the way he said it indicated a partnership might not be far off."

Kate shared his excitement, smiling, nodding, yet all the while worrying, shall I tell him while he's on such a high? Is it fair?

As she cleared the table he was still ebullient about his triumph in court. He trapped her in the kitchen, embraced her, held her close in a way that on another night might have led to making love. But on this night she felt that it would be dishonest to make love with him while withholding the truth. When she sought to slip out of his embrace, he was taken aback.

"Darling?"

"I have something to tell you."

"You're pregnant! Great! Now we *have* to get married!" he joked.

"Darling, come into the living room. And just talk. Not embrace, not hold hands, not even touch. In fact, you'd better sit there and I'll sit here."

"Okay, sure," he said soberly, puzzled.

She sat on the edge of the couch, stiffly straight and determined. "Howard . . ." she began.

"When you call me Howard that way it means trouble. So let's have it. No preambles. No buildups. What is it, darling?"

"There is a place in West Virginia . . ."

"West Virginia?" Howard repeated. Surprised but unconcerned, he settled back in the armchair, prepared to listen.

She related to him everything she had discovered about Mountain Hospital and the Family Nurse-Midwifery School. Finally she concluded, "Today in the mail I received a form calling for my *curriculum vitae*. You know what that means."

And because he did, Howard was leaning forward, now not only concerned but deeply troubled. He reached out to take her hand.

"Kate . . . darling . . . everything I am about to say you can dismiss as self-serving. You can think, he's only saying that because he wants me to marry him. But I think between two people like us, two mature people, who not only love each other but who respect each other, there comes a time for plain, honest talk.

"Do I want you to stay here? Of course I do. I love you. I want you. I want to marry you. But even if I didn't, it pains me to see a woman as intelligent and conscientious as you succumb to an emotional impulse at such a crucial time in her life.

"Examine coldly what really happened. The Hospital Board that should have condemned Morse and defended you, did the reverse. Surprise? No. Doctors sitting in judgment are always going to favor doctors. Yet now, instead of facing that fact squarely and unemotionally, you respond like a hurt child. You want to run off to some Godforsaken place in the Appalachian Mountains. What do you expect? That University Hospital will come after you, begging you to return? Accept this for what it is, an injustice at the hands of an unjust system, and go on. Be the nurse you can be. Become an administrator, if you want. God knows, you're capable enough. But don't run off and pout."

"What if the episode at the hospital only brought to the surface a problem I've been wrestling with ever since I got out of college?"

"Kate?" he responded, puzzled, for this was the first time she had ever made such an admission.

"I sat all through dinner hearing about your victory in court today. I loved the look on your face when you told me about it. The look of achievement that said, 'Today my education, my training, paid off. I proved to the court and to all my senior partners that I could do it damn well.' I shared that excitement with you.

"Well, I want that same sense of excitement, that same appreciation, admiration and praise. I would like you to share my feeling with me as I shared yours with you."

"How? By being a thousand miles apart?"

"Now you *are* being selfish," she pointed out.

"You know there are times when I think . . ." But he stopped precipitously.

"Times when you think *what?*" Kate demanded.

He hesitated before admitting, "Times when I think, instead of becoming such an overdetermined nurse, a woman with your brain, your desire for learning, could have become a doctor. Or gone to law school and have become a very good lawyer."

"And then given that up to move to the suburbs to be a wife and mother," Kate said, challenging him.

"If you were a lawyer that wouldn't be necessary. We have two women in the firm who are damned capable lawyers and still raise families. It's not easy on them, but they manage."

"So it isn't my having a profession that bothers you, but that by your standards nursing is one of the lesser professions," Kate pointed out. "Well, outside of getting some murderer off free, when was the last time a lawyer saved someone's life? Or when did some lawyer ease someone's pain? Or hand a newborn to its mother and see that wonderful look on the mother's face? Nursing may not have the social status of the law, but given a choice, I'd rather do what I do than what you do!"

There was a moment of painful silence between them before she said softly, "Sorry, darling. I didn't mean to say that. All I do mean is it's important to me, very important, to find out if my sacrifice was worth it. This may be the way to find out."

Howard did not answer at once. Then he asked, "How long would it take?"

"The course is divided into four trimesters."

"Four trimesters? A whole year," he said slowly. "You'll be twenty-eight. I'll be thirty-two." He paused before he said soberly,

"Kate, darling, if you decide to do this, it could mean the end for us."

She felt the tears well up in her eyes, but was determined to keep from crying. "There must be school breaks when we can see each other. I'll come back here. You can come down there."

"And what if, in between, there's another woman? I don't mean just a passing affair, another woman I fall in love with?"

"You're free, if that's what you want," she managed to say, though it was painful. "I'll understand. I won't like it, but I'll understand."

"You're willing to take that risk?"

She hesitated, then said, "Yes. . . ."

He embraced her. And they did make love. After that, his cheek pressed against hers, he said softly, "I'll wait. At least I'll try to wait. But a whole year . . ."

"Only one year," she whispered. "And not a minute longer, darling. I promise."

CHAPTER 5

The plane had flown over miles of the rugged forests and towering mountains of the Appalachian range before it banked to the left. Its silver wing seemed to fall away, allowing Kate Kincaid to see the blooming, green, cultivated country below. They were passing over towns and farms. Off in the distance she could see the small city which must be the plane's destination. She could just make out the airport and the two runways when the wing leveled off and obscured her view.

She sat back, checked to make sure her seatbelt was fastened for landing and exhaled, trying to relieve her tension. She was beginning an adventure about which, no matter how strong her determination, she still harbored some grave doubts.

She was taking a great risk leaving Howard for a whole year. But her strongest doubts were about herself. Not about her professional competence. But being city born, city bred, educated at a large university, and for four years a highly capable nurse at one of the largest and best-equipped hospitals in the Midwest, she questioned how she would fare in this isolated hospital, in a place like Adelphi, which, to judge from the photographs in the folder, could barely qualify as a small town.

The plane wheels made abrupt abrasive contact with the concrete runway. Doubts or not, she was here. It was too late to turn back.

* * *

While she waited for her luggage, she looked about the small baggage area. Abbott had written that someone would drive up from Adelphi to meet her. Did she mean in the baggage area or outside at the taxi stand, where only a single cab waited? Would the person carry a sign with Kate's name on it? Or the hospital's name? Why were people so careless about important details that could lead to embarrassment?

She sensed someone staring at her. She turned from the baggage rack to find a tall, rawboned young man, no more than thirty, in well-kneed jeans and a worn, scuffed brown leather jacket, studying the handful of arriving passengers. He glanced at Kate from time to time. She made an obvious point of ignoring him, in the way of women who wish to discourage strangers.

The baggage handler was getting out the luggage. Kate found both her pieces. She was about to heft the larger one when a strong, tanned, muscular hand intervened.

"Katherine Kincaid?"

She was looking up at the young man who had been staring at her. She had no need to answer. Her luggage tag did that for her.

"I'll be taking that," he said.

"So you're the one," she said.

"For whatever that means, yes, I'm the one," he said, unsmiling. He seized both pieces of heavy luggage and lifted them with very slight effort. Without a word he started away so quickly that Kate had to snatch her carry-on bag and race to keep up with him.

They had been on the road for more than an hour before the Jeep turned onto a broad interstate highway. Little had been said between them. Kate had had all she could do to hold fast while the battered old Jeep, which seemed to have no springs at all, bounced her about in what she considered a very aggressive manner. She had begun to resent this rugged young man who drove as if determined to win the Indianapolis 500. Once the old Jeep settled into a steady seventy miles an hour on the smooth interstate, Kate felt she could relax her death grip and asked, "Do we have much farther to go?"

"Hour and a half, maybe a little more considering the slow time we're making." He was not smiling.

When the flat highway started to cut between towering mountains, she could enjoy the fragrance of the April air, perfumed by rich green pine and blue spruce. She felt sufficiently adjusted to the rhythmic jounce of the Jeep to ask, "You live in Adelphi?"

"Not exactly *in*. Up a holler a little way out," he said.

How quaint, Kate thought, *up a holler.* "Lived there all your life?" she queried.

"Nope," he responded, but gave her no further clue.

"Born there?"

"Yep," he answered.

"Where did you spend the rest of your time?" Kate asked.

"Places," he said.

Curiosity and frustration made her ask, "What sort of places?"

"Well, ma'am," he said, still without turning to glance at her, "first four years I was at the University of West Virginia. Then I took my master's in mining engineering at Texas A. and M., College Station, Texas."

After a slight, embarrassed pause, Kate said, "Sorry. Very sorry."

"Why, ma'am?"

"You can drop the ma'am now," she said. "Okay, I misjudged you. Now if I admit I made a mistake, can we be civil to each other?"

For the first time he took his eyes off the road to glance at her. "You did. And you didn't. Where you're going you will find exactly the kind of mountain people you expected. Uneducated. Simple, reclusive. But good people. Honest people. You will also find men and women who've been away from mountain country, lived in your cities, been educated in your universities. It's a strange bag we have here. Maybe it was better when there was only one kind of mountain people. Too late to speculate about that now. We are all here in one mix. Trying to make a go of things while one part catches up with the other and all of us catch up with the rest of the world. Though, you being here would seem to indicate we have something of value to offer."

She felt justifiably rebuked and at a loss for an answer. Until he asked, "You?"

"B.S. in nursing at the University of Chicago. Master's in nursing administration after that. I've been working at University Hospital since."

"Not for long, I reckon."

"What does that mean?" she asked, offended.

"So young, couldn't have been working very long," he said.

"Almost five years." Which was stretching the truth a little.

He did not respond but continued driving, eyes focused on the road. She stared up at the mountains on either side.

"The country around the hospital, is it as primitive as these hills?"

"More. More beautiful, too. Rivers and streams, and in fall and spring, colors that'll set your heart to quivering, if you've an eye for beauty," he said. "That's why I came back. When I lived here as a boy I just took it all for granted. But once I left and started living in cities, I realized I was homesick for these mountains and hollers every day I lived away. 'Specially on early spring days like this 'un."

After a brief silence she asked, "What do you do here?"

"Mining engineer, superintendent actually," he said modestly. "Since the energy crunch, coal became the oil of these mountains. It's our job to supply it."

"You didn't tell me your name," she reminded.

He smiled for the first time. "Jessup. Harlan Jessup."

"Harlan?" Kate asked. "Isn't there a Harlan County in Kentucky? Bloody Harlan County?"

"My grandpaw was one of the miners killed in a strike there. My paw never wanted me to forget. So he named me Harlan."

"Your family always been mining men?" she asked.

"Runs in the blood, I guess. Though if my grandpaw, who I never saw, were alive now, he'd take a shotgun to me for what I do."

They had turned off the interstate onto a narrow road that curved gracefully downhill, the mountains looming taller and greener above them. At the bottom, Jessup turned the vehicle onto a rutted blacktop road that betrayed all the effects of the freezes and thaws of tough winters and the floods of many springs. Each rut had been carved in that road by years of great changes in climate and temperature. Ahead was a narrow street which appeared to run only two of the city blocks to which Kate was accustomed, then it turned sharply left and out of her sight. On one side of the short street was a two-story building, new and official-looking. She would discover that was the public library. On the other side an older and more stately building was both county courthouse and county seat. The rest were shabby one-story frame buildings, a grocery, a hardware store and one gas station. The place looked as weathered, gray and bleak as a Grant Wood etching.

"That's it, Adelphi," Harlan Jessup said, his blue eyes stealing a look to see her reaction. She noted that he pronounced the name Adel*phee*, not Adel*phy*, as she had done.

"All of it," he said. "Library, newspaper office, courthouse, general store. Can't see the old school, that's around that bend."

He turned the Jeep to the right and onto a broad short incline that led up to the one building that Kate recognized: the modest two-story Mountain Hospital. Her original estimate was confirmed. It would not serve even as the Maternity Wing of University Hospital.

Jessup sensed her disappointment. "Not big, but good Emergency Room. More than once I've had to bring in one of my men. They always get good treatment. Good nurses, damn well trained. That's what you're here for, isn't it?"

"Yes," she admitted. "And I was damn well trained before I got here."

Jessup smiled. "Didn't mean to infer otherwise. Just doing a little bragging on my own, that's all."

He pulled up the Jeep at the front door, jumped down and swung the two heavy bags out of the backseat, carried them into the waiting room and set them down. As he turned to leave, Kate said, "I want to thank you for making the trip all the way up to meet me."

"I had to pick up some things for Big Betsy. Abbott asked me to fetch you on the same trip," he said. "Though if I'da known how pretty you are, I'da made the trip just for you."

She couldn't help blushing. She glanced up at him, realizing how tall he was, reminding herself he was even taller than Howard. "Who's Big Betsy?"

He smiled and said, "You'll see, someday."

"Well, I guess I'd better meet Miss Abbott," she said.

"I hope you like it here."

With no further word, he left. She watched him ease his lanky frame into the Jeep, which now seemed too small for him. The battered old car started down the broad road that led back to the town street.

* * *

Kate addressed the young girl at the reception desk. "I am here to see Miss Abbott, please."

"Abbott's not in her office at the moment," the girl replied, "but if you have a seat I'll try to reach her. Your name?"

"Kincaid. Katherine Kincaid."

She took one of the few empty seats near the reception desk and looked around the waiting room, which was large, bright and had chairs ranged along the walls. Obviously the area also served as the waiting room for outpatients, since most of the chairs were occupied by elderly people and by young mothers with restless children. One mother clutched a child too feeble in body or mind to be restless. Other older children sprawled on the cream-colored terrazzo floor, playing games of make-believe. Most of the play involved warfare of one kind or another, since the children pointed finger guns or toy guns at each other, and made the appropriate explosive noises with each fancied shot.

Many of the adults had begun to stare at Kate, for by dress alone, she was obviously an outlander. They not only made her feel self-conscious, but they themselves suddenly seemed embarrassed by their plain, worn attire. As casually as she could, without staring, Kate studied their faces. Most of the young women seemed to be in their late twenties or early thirties. Young enough to be mothers of children of eight or nine or ten. But their faces betrayed the physical and emotional wear Kate was used to seeing in women much older.

The young woman closest to Kate stole furtive glimpses at her out of the corner of her eye. Her discomfort expressed itself in the way she sharply reprimanded her young son for playing on the floor. After he refused to come sit beside her, she remarked apologetically to Kate, "Don't know what's got into him today. Usual he's such a good child."

With that, she lurched forward to yank him up from the floor. In that precipitous move her worn leather purse slid from her lap, struck the terrazzo floor, causing a loud explosion and creating a terrifying echo. Startled, Kate pulled back sharply. As she did, she noticed that across the narrow waiting room an elderly man had seized his chest and was toppling forward.

Fearing the explosion had precipitated a coronary episode, Kate raced across the floor, dropped beside the man and turned him on his back to take his vital signs. But she discovered that her right hand was stained with bright, warm, fresh blood.

"A gurney! Someone get a gurney!" she ordered with the same authority and efficiency she had used in the Emergency Room back at University Hospital.

The young receptionist quickly rolled up a stretcher. Together, Kate and the girl lifted the old man onto it.

"Which way to Emergency?" Kate demanded. The girl preceded her around the corner of the waiting room and toward the Emergency Room. "Call a doctor!" Kate told the young trainee on duty in Emergency.

"Doctor isn't in the hospital right now."

Kate ripped open the old man's shirt to reach his injury. It was a small entry wound, just below his rib cage. From its point of entry and the direction it had taken, Kate feared it might have invaded his liver. As she took his vital signs, she ordered, "Get a doctor! I don't care how or where. But get one!"

The old man was recovering consciousness. His pulse was irregular and weak, but there seemed no immediate danger of his slipping into shock, which could be fatal. She refrained from giving him medication, for she wanted him as alert as possible.

He reached out desperately to grasp her hand and held it tightly. Behind her, she sensed that someone was breaking through the crowd of curious observers. Kate turned, "Doctor?"

Instead, she was facing a woman in ordinary street dress who said, "No."

"Miss Abbott?"

"Yes. Kincaid," Abbott assumed.

A robust woman with graying hair and eyes that keenly reflected a high degree of perception and efficiency, Abbott said, "You seem to have things under control here." But Kate noted that Abbott also made her own appraisal of the old man's vital signs. As she did, she said, "I phoned for Dr. Boyd. He's at one of our Outposts. He'll be here in about an hour."

"You mean there's no doctor in Emergency at all times?"

"Sometimes, like now, there's not a doctor in the entire hospital," Abbott replied. "We're not exactly overwhelmed with medical talent down here. This isn't University Hospital, Kincaid."

"Of course," Kate agreed, rebuked. "I'll just watch him till the doctor arrives. Monitor him for vital signs."

"Good," Abbott said. "When Dr. Boyd takes over, come see me in my office. Second floor."

As Kate turned to watch Abbott leave, she was confronted by the curious mothers and children who were gathered at the Emergency Room door. She was startled to notice that they exhibited no shock, surprise or fear, only curiosity. Nor were there any sounds of police sirens converging on the hospital in response to what would, in her own hospital back home, be considered an event demanding police intervention. She reminded herself that she must stop referring to University Hospital as her own hospital. This was her hospital now and would be for the next twelve long months. She must inquire again about that Dr. Boyd. Was he on his way?

Dr. Raymond Boyd burst into Emergency on the run. From his sweaty face, Kate knew that he had driven at a reckless rate of speed to get there. Tall, with a close-cropped brown beard and alert dark eyes set in a tanned face, wearing an old corduroy jacket and an open-throated flannel shirt, he looked more a woodsman than a physician.

"Let's have a look!" Boyd said, brushing by Kate. He approached the patient and began to take his vital signs. There was an efficiency about him that convinced Kate that he was a highly capable physician.

Before examining the entry wound, he observed, "Vital signs pretty good. No danger of shock. When they said a chest wound I was worried. Well, let's get him up to the O.R."

"I don't even know where the O.R. is," Kate replied.

For the first time he took note of her. "Oh. You're new here."

"Kate Kincaid," she introduced herself.

"Ray Boyd." Then he asked, "One of the new trainees?"

"Yes."

He smiled. "Good!" He looked at the patient, then back at Kate. "What a welcome to Adelphi."

Kate noticed that he, too, pronounced it Adelphee, the way Harlan Jessup had, like a native. Boyd turned to the young nurse in charge of Emergency.

"Get him up to the O.R. Prep him. I'll be scrubbing." He turned back to Kate. "I hope this didn't discourage you."

He started toward the elevators, stopped, turned back to take another look at Kate. "Yep. Welcome to Adelphee."

Abbott was on the phone when Kate was shown into her office. The administrator was just as crisp and blunt on the phone as she had been in the Emergency Room. She finished her conversation with a direct "then do it!" and hung up to confront Kate. "Yes?" she asked in her usual brisk fashion. Then her face relaxed into a slight smile. "Sorry. I forgot. You're new here, just one hour new. And what a greeting. I hope you won't think too badly of us."

"Back home, people are brought into the hospital with gunshot wounds. They don't get them there."

"We get our share of gunshot wounds brought in, too," Abbott said, "especially on Saturday nights. You could say it's part of the local culture." She changed the subject abruptly. "How was your trip down?"

"A little rugged," Kate said. "But an interesting drive. Beautiful country."

"Beautiful," Abbott agreed, "and, like many of the people, rugged, primitive and, at times, forbidding."

Kate could not resist remarking, "I noticed that after that man was shot, no one made any attempt to apprehend the woman or take away her gun."

"Why would they?" Abbott asked simply. "It wasn't an intentional shooting."

"For a young woman with a small child to carry a loaded pistol in her purse as if it were her compact, is that usual around here?"

"Handguns, shotguns, rifles are a hangover from pioneer days. Civil War days. Times when a man was forced to leave his wife and kids for days to hunt for food for his family. But there were marauders, deserters from the army, and just plain outlaws who lived on anything they could take, food, drink, women. A man couldn't leave his home unprotected. Every household had a shotgun or a rifle. And every woman and child over eight knew how to use it. And they still do. It's a long tradition here in the mountains."

"But this is 1984," Kate protested. "The age of cars, radios, television, telephones. And no army deserters roaming the forests."

Abbott took off her spectacles and started to polish them. "Kincaid, we live here on the cusp, so to speak, between two civilizations. One goes back two hundred years in speech, habits and customs. The other civilization is as up-to-date as tonight's television news. Sometimes you find both in the same household. Harlan's a good example. Between him and his widowed mother there must be a gap of several generations at least. In some families the gap is even greater. This place is a mixture of ignorance, superstition and a primitive way of life combined with the sudden prosperity of the 1980's brought on by the energy crisis. Our coal became very valuable again, so we have a booming economy for some, while others struggle for survival. You'll find poverty and affluence side by side here.

"It's important for you to remember that. Because you will come in contact with both kinds. Will have to treat both kinds. More of the depressed than the other kind. But remember one thing. In this hospital we believe every individual, regardless of economic status, is entitled to dignity. We consider that a God-given right. The educated and the ignorant are treated the same in our hospital. We do not judge these people. We treat them. And I hope you will do the same. For so long as you are here."

The way Abbott searched Kate's eyes while she enunciated "For so long as you are here" made Kate suspect that the woman doubted her ability to survive the course.

Abbott gave her a little time to speculate.

"Your indoctrination class is about to start. Classroom A. Main floor."

CHAPTER 6

Kate looked about the small room and discovered that except for its size it was no different from many of the other classrooms in which she had spent most of her life. A plain table served as the instructor's desk. The simple blackboard was bare of any writing. There were only six student chairs, attesting to the select classes that were trained at Mountain Hospital.

Today only three of those chairs were occupied. Correspondingly, on the table were three high stacks of looseleaf manuals, which aroused Kate's curiosity.

The instructor, Adele Sawyer, a short, plump woman in her early forties, Registered Nurse, Family Nurse Practitioner, Registered Nurse-Midwife, studied her new students very critically before she launched into her orientation lecture.

"It would be very helpful if you were to forget where you came from and what you did there," Sawyer began.

"We do not want to hear what you did back in some big city in the East, or on the Pacific Coast, or in some large hospital in the Midwest or in one of those overendowed health centers in Texas. Here we serve under quite different conditions. Our facilities, while adequate to most of the demands of our patients, are not always able to afford complete medical and surgical care. From time to time we are faced with situations that demand diagnostic and surgical facilities beyond our means.

"When that happens, your immediate tendency will be to complain, 'This is medicine as practiced in the Dark Ages. Where are those magnificent facilities in that big, rich hospital I left?'

"At such times I urge you to ask yourselves, if those hospitals had been so satisfying, why did you leave?

"This is my way of saying we don't want to hear what you miss from back home, unless you're also willing to tell us what it was you *didn't* like that brought you here. So we will start with that."

Sawyer called on the young woman at the end of the short row. "You!"

Kate leaned forward slightly to take her first good look at the thin-faced, mild-appearing, plainly dressed dark-haired girl whose black eyes reflected surprising conviction and determination.

"Mahoney. Ellen Mahoney," the young woman introduced herself. "My name in my order is Sister Bernard."

From Mahoney's slacks and plain blue shirt, Kate had not suspected that Mahoney was a nun, and from an order in which nuns were free to choose masculine names on taking their final vows.

"However," Mahoney continued, "from now on I would prefer being called either Mahoney or just Ellen. Because it is quite obvious to me since I arrived yesterday that Catholics are very rare in these parts. I do not wish to spend the next twelve months explaining how I happen to be Sister Bernard.

"Now, as to why I am here, that is due to a conflict with my bishop," she announced.

Kate could not resist leaning even farther forward to watch Mahoney's thin, delicate face, which seemed to grow stronger before her eyes.

"As you know, birth control as generally practiced today is not in conformity with Church dogma. But having seen the price of poverty, of large families that are not equipped to give their children a decent childhood or a fair start in life, I decided early in my nursing practice that family planning is essential. Therefore, I chose to give instruction in all forms of birth control to the poor. I was ordered to stop, even threatened with expulsion from my order if I did not. So I decided to leave, come here, learn more than I now know, learn to tend whole families, to help them regulate their rate of childbirth so each child can be born as nearly perfect as possible, with as good a chance in life as possible."

Kate noticed that Mahoney's eyes filled with tears as she announced, "In that way I feel that I will be fulfilling my duty to God to serve His poor. After I have finished here I will seek out the poorest section of this great country and go there to serve. I believe that is what Christ wants me to do."

There was a long, respectful silence before Sawyer called on the next candidate.

The young woman stirred slightly in her chair, as if undecided whether to rise. She remained seated finally, but turned to her right and then her left as she spoke, seeking acceptance from her two fellow students. Even seated, she was obviously a tall, robustly built young woman. Brown-haired, with classic features, she wore her short hair in a simple swept-back style.

"Emily McClendon," she began. Her soft speech revealed that she was from the South. "What I will say might be misinterpreted, so I want to make clear right at the start that I am not a racist. My purpose here is to learn enough to minister to the poor whites whom I have seen come and go down home. By come and go I mean like the seasons. They are the migrant workers who twice each year come through down home, pick their fruit, live like animals, and then are gone until next season.

"Some people look down on them, thinking no one lives that way who doesn't want to. Or that they are too lazy to work themselves up in this world. But I have never seen people work harder. Or receive less for it. Since childhood that troubled me. Then I went away to school and no longer saw them twice every year. When I received my nursing diploma and went to work in the city hospital back home I was relieved not to have to watch them.

"Except those times when they would bring one of them in. Perhaps a father with a coronary from overwork in the orchards. Or a child with some disease no child should have. I would watch their faces. Faces of the mother and her children as they waited, terrified, to learn if husband and father would survive. The face of a sick child, pinched, hungry, with eyes that stared at you, begging to be part of your world. But you knew, and that child knew, it was a vain hope. Then they would be gone. Either died or kept moving. I had many restless, miserable nights thinking about those faces. Once I wanted to organize a unit at the hospital to serve those poor people, but the orchard owners refused. So the hospital refused. 'We've enough of our own to care for,' the trustees said. We did. Yet who could refuse those poor kids? But the thing . . ."

McClendon stopped suddenly, debating whether to go on. Finally, she continued:

"The thing that made up my mind happened during the last peach harvest. They had come like locusts, in a swarm. Except they came in battered, noisy old trucks, in cars that seemed on their last journey. They had picked the fruit, and moved on. When the farm help were cleaning out those miserable shacks, one of them came upon a dark green plastic garbage bag. A sound came from it. There was movement inside. The farmhand thought a rat had got into it somehow. So, before he dared touch it, he beat it with his broom handle until it stopped moving. When he was sure it was dead, he opened the bag."

McClendon dared not look either to her left toward Kate or her right toward Sister Bernard. She stared past Sawyer, who stood before her.

"It was a baby. Not more than a month old, we discovered when they brought the body to our hospital. A healthy baby. Born without any defects. Yet some mother had disposed of it, thinking, 'Better it die here than live as we have lived. Better it die than become another hungry mouth we can't feed.'

"I don't blame that mother. God knows, she didn't want to do that. How much better it would have been for her and for that unfortunate child if it had never been conceived. Or if conceived, that it had been born under such circumstances that if she didn't feel able to cope with it, it could have passed into eager, loving hands that would have given it love and a good upbringing.

"That's when I decided to come here, train, then go back and serve those people. I don't know if I will move with them or if I will wait for the seasons, but I am determined that no such cruel death will happen again if I can prevent it."

Sawyer now looked directly at Kate.

"Katherine Kincaid," she introduced herself. She proceeded to relate what had determined her to leave University Hospital and enlist for training as a family nurse and midwife.

When she had finished relating those events, Kate said softly, "If my reasons seem less idealistic, I can assure you that I will not be less devoted to my studies or my work. I have not decided where I will go when I leave here. But I promise that I will put this training to good use for the benefit of those who need my help."

Sawyer had listened patiently, then she eyed them before she said, "I know your records. You are all professionally qualified. And I've heard your good intentions. What we don't know, what you don't know, because you have never been tested, is how much guts you have. How well you can face a true emergency when human life is on the line, and, different from the hospital you came from, that life will depend solely on you. There will be no doctor to summon with a buzzer or a phone call. You may be facing a sudden cardiac arrest and no Code Blue to bail you out, because you are in one of our Outposts or in the simple bare cabin of the patient. If you can't face emergencies like that and function well, then you don't belong here. So, if at any time we feel you don't measure up, we will terminate you."

Kate glanced furtively to one side, then the other, to see if her new classmates were as sobered by their instructor's words as she had been. They were.

Sawyer turned to the three piles of folders on the table. Each pile contained nine manuals, creating a stack more than a foot high.

"Everything you will have to learn is in these manuals. Your first trimester will be devoted to physical assessment skills. In a word, diagnosis.

"Your second trimester will concern the management and treatment of common health problems, colds, stomach ailments, hypertension and the like. You will report your findings to the physician and together you will decide on the management of the patient.

"Your third trimester will involve considerable classroom instruction in midwifery. Including the normal mechanism of delivery, plus prenatal, postpartum and neonatal care. Throughout those three months you will alternate one day in class, one day in clinic.

"Your fourth and final trimester you will devote to actual deliveries. You will be required to complete fifteen successful deliveries on your own before we consider you qualified.

"Now, the material for the four trimesters is contained in these manuals. But that's not all. Because in these manuals you will find references to hundreds of medical textbooks and papers that you would do well to become familiar with in order to broaden your knowledge. Each of you will come up now and take your stack."

When Kate lifted hers she estimated it weighed at least ten or twelve pounds. Once they had returned to their seats, Sawyer said, "Don't make the mistake of trying to learn everything at once. You will only confuse yourselves. It will be tough enough to study those manuals that correspond to the particular trimester and to put the material into practice in your clinical work. We give them all to you so you can form a long-range attitude to sustain you through the next year."

Sawyer dismissed them with a curt "first class in Family Health Assessment tomorrow morning promptly at eight. Get settled in your new housing. But don't delay. You are expected back here at four today to go on night floor duty."

She handed each of the three students a slip of paper with the name of a family and an address written on it.

Kate's slip read: *Mrs. Elvira Russell, 33 Ridge Street.*

CHAPTER 7

Kate struggled through the front door of Mountain Hospital with her two suitcases and her heavy load of manuals. She put down the suitcases, but the manuals slithered out of her arm and fell haphazardly to the ground. A field nurse who was warming up her Jeep in the parking lot noticed and called out, "Need some help?"

"I sure do," Kate said.

The nurse hopped out of the Jeep, came to scoop up the manuals. "Put your suitcases in the back and I'll drop you."

"Thanks," Kate said. "I had no idea how I'd make it with all this stuff."

"Where to?" the nurse asked as she climbed in behind the wheel.

"Mrs. Russell's."

"Oh, yes," the nurse said, smiling as if she had some special knowledge.

"Kincaid, Kate Kincaid," she introduced herself.

"Braden, Emma Braden," the driver replied. She shoved the Jeep into gear, turned sharply, swiftly heading for the main road. "Nervous?"

"I'm a pretty fast driver myself," Kate said.

"I meant about your first day."

"Oh, that," Kate equivocated.

"You can admit it," Braden said. "I was nervous as hell. Sawyer really knows how to put the fear of God into a new class."

"Yes, yes, she does," Kate said, relieved to find some company for her own concerns.

"Only thing is," Braden continued, no longer smiling, "she was really being easy with you. You'll be tougher on yourself. All those mistakes you used to blame on doctors will now be your mistakes. And that doesn't make for quiet, peaceful sleep, I can tell you."

Mrs. Russell's modest white frame house was down the two-block main street and just around the bend, actually within walking distance of the hospital. As Kate started to get out of the Jeep, she remarked, "But you're still here."

"They need me," was all Braden said. "Want a hand?" she asked, indicating Kate's luggage.

"I'll manage," Kate answered, lifting down the two heavy pieces of luggage. She gathered up her manuals. "Tell me . . ." she started to say, but Braden had already put the Jeep in gear again and was off, the thick-treaded tires making a rasping sound on the rutted old blacktop road.

Kate turned to look at the small white house set behind a neat, well-tended flower garden. She started toward the front porch, which could have benefited from an overdue coat of fresh white paint. As she mounted the two steps, she noticed behind the lace curtain in the window the face of an elderly woman whose hair appeared whiter than fresh paint and whose wrinkles were so deep they seemed to have been carved by a sculptor.

The door opened. Kate asked, "Mrs. Russell?"

"Yes, child," the elderly woman responded.

"I'm Kate Kincaid."

Mrs. Russell's stone-blue eyes appraised Kate and for a moment it seemed she might not accept her. But then there was the hint of a smile in them as she said, "I shall call ye Katherine."

"It's what my mother called me."

"I thought so," Mrs. Russell said. "Come in, come in, Katherine."

She stepped aside to welcome Kate into her home. Beyond the foyer was a parlor only as large as such a small house permitted. The furniture was old, but neat and very clean. Ancient hand-crocheted antimacassars were pinned atop every chair. And the black bombazine upholstery shone with age and quality. The carpet had served so long that at certain places the backing showed through the pattern.

There was a hand-crank phonograph in one corner and no sign of a television set. Beyond the archway that separated the parlor from the dining room Kate could see a large, dark wood table with a heavy carved armchair at its head. Kate could imagine what the rest of the house looked like.

"Well, ye'll be wanting to see yere own room," Mrs. Russell said, turning to lead the way. Instead of heading for the stairs she led Kate to the end of the carpeted hallway toward the rear of the house. She opened the door.

"This is it."

Kate found herself staring into a room that was decorated in a soft, light blue with accents of red, a combination quite colorful and startling compared to the rest of the somber house.

Her surprise was obvious, for Mrs. Russell said, "It was Louise's. Done for when she was to come back. Only she never did."

"I'm sorry," Kate whispered, for want of something more appropriate to say.

"The girls prefer being down here 'stead of upstairs. So when they come off night duty or are up late studying, they won't be disturbing me. But I hear them. Any hour, any time of night, I hear them. Not that I listen for them. I wouldn't eavesdrop. It's Louise I keep listening for."

"I'll do my best not to disturb you," Kate promised.

"Don't worry over it," Mrs. Russell said. "It's always a comfort to know there's a body in the house. That's why I like the girls to come and stay. 'Cept for the year of the big snow, was always someone in Louise's room."

"How long ago . . . ?" Kate started to ask but changed her mind in midsentence.

But Mrs. Russell understood and replied, "Last year of the war. Same's when President Roosevelt died."

Thirty-nine years, Kate thought, *thirty-nine years this woman has lived with the memory*. She was tempted to ask how Louise had died but refrained from doing so.

"Well, ye'll be wanting to unpack," Mrs. Russell said. "And when ye're done, please come have a cup of tea with me?"

"Yes, of course, I'd love to."

Mrs. Russell closed the door softly. Kate was free to look around the room, which was larger than she had expected. From the rug of light blue, red and white with tiny flowers, to the spread which repeated those same colors, to the starched white curtains on the two windows, the room was bright and cheerful. The large dresser offered a wide, high mirror to dress by. A heavy oak door opened to a closet roomy enough to walk into. It smelled of cedar, pungent and fresh. She hung away the few simple dresses and slacks she had brought. When she opened the dresser drawers she found them lined with clean white paper and smelling of violet sachet.

When Kate returned to the parlor, it was empty. She passed through the dining room and into the kitchen, which was warm from the heat of the coal stove. The table was covered with an embroidered cloth that had obviously been set out especially for company.

"Do ye like yere tea strong, my dear?"

"Strong," Kate said, "with only a little sugar."

"Sugar to taste, I always say," Mrs. Russell agreed.

Once they were both seated and Kate was stirring her tea, Mrs. Russell pushed a plate of homemade cookies across to her. "Make 'em myself, but they're good."

Kate tried one, and good it was. As she savored it, the woman asked, "And what brought *ye*, child?"

Kate explained her reasons for coming to this remote place while Mrs. Russell kept nodding. She understood and agreed. Yet when Kate finished, the woman said sadly, "And your man, who was sparking ye . . ." When Kate reacted to the strange word, Mrs. Russell explained. "I was born up a holler pretty far from here. Lived there till I was fourteen. That's when Mr. Russell come through looking to string the first telephone lines. Young he was. And very handsome. And he must of thought well of me, for he kep' coming back. Till one day, I was scarce sixteen, when he asked for me to marry. I was frightened of his world and his ways. But I said yes. And my maw said yes, since she was wasting and had little time and didn't want to leave me up there in the holler for the rest of my days.

"So I married. And we moved down here to the town. I promised myself I wouldn't shame him by talking mountain talk. So I studied hard to overcome it. Even went to school after I was sixteen, married and in a family way. Sitting amongst girls of nine and ten, seeing them smile and snicker at me. But I learned to speak proper.

'Cept every once in a while a word or two creeps in from the old days."

Mrs. Russell leaned close to Kate and said very seriously, "You must have studied about such things. These days I notice more and more words from the past creeping in. Is that a sign of old age? To go back to the language in which one was raised up?"

Kate smiled. "I don't see any signs of aging."

"Ye're being polite and thoughtful. The way Louise used to be."

Kate could not resist asking, "Louise? How did she . . . ?"

"She'd been trained a nurse. Right here at Mountain. So when the war come along, and when her man was signed up to go, she went. He come back. She never did. Killed in an air raid in England. One of those flying bombs. Never even found her body. Just sent back her things. Some clothes. And letters. All the letters I wrote her. And those that Mr. Russell wrote her. He was ailing then but still able to write. And of course there was the letters from George. About plans for their wedding soon as the war was over."

A glistening from unshed tears welled up in the woman's eyes. But her wrinkled face showed her determination not to weep. The lines in her face appeared to deepen and the muscles of her jaw stood out more prominently.

"I don't mean to weigh you down," she apologized. "I was only intending to tell you how come I speak like I do sometimes. So's ye'll get used to it. Because up there in the mountains they talk like that all the time, and half the time ye won't know what they're intending. Those as come here, like ye, have to get used to their ways, for they won't be quick to get used to yours."

She leaned closer, as if to impart a secret which might cause her to be accused of disloyalty. "They're not warm and friendly at the start. Fact is, some young ladies like yourself has been scared off and refused to finish. Felt people was cold and ornery. Wasn't. Just they treasure friendship and trust so high they don't give it easy. You'll get used to it. I hope."

"I'll try," Kate promised. "I give you my word, I'll try."

"They don't take easy to foreigners," Mrs. Russell felt it necessary to warn again.

"I understand."

Mrs. Russell nodded, then interrupted herself suddenly to stare at

Kate. "Girl so purty and not married. Will ye be going back to him?"

"I don't have to answer that for a whole year," Kate said.

She had bathed in the large white old-fashioned tub that rested on giant claw feet. She had done her long blond hair in the efficient manner she had always used in University Hospital and was slipping into her clothes, the serviceable ones the instructions had specified as acceptable in the hospital. Sturdy, flat-heeled shoes, navy slacks, plain shirt, over which she would be required to wear a white lab coat when on duty. She appraised herself in the mirror, decided she looked proper and was ready to return to the hospital.

Before she could reach the front door, she heard Mrs. Russell call to her from the kitchen: "Child!"

Kate stopped at the kitchen door. "Yes, Mrs. Russell?"

"Didn't mean to scare ye afore. 'Bout the folks hereabout. But if ye'd like, some nights when ye've the time, I can teach ye the language."

"I'd appreciate that," Kate said.

Mrs. Russell nodded and drew out of her apron pocket a small object which she held out to Kate. It was an old-fashioned cast-iron key.

"For the back door," the woman explained. "Late at night no need to come in the front door. The back door'll do. Especially if ye don't come home alone."

For an instant Kate was puzzled. But she saw the frank, unashamed look in the woman's light blue eyes. "I was young once. And I never forgot what it was like. A young woman, a purty young 'un at that, won't be alone for long. I don't think God nor nature meant for it to be so."

Without a word, Kate took the key which felt warm in her hand, as if it had been fondled for a long time before it was handed to her.

CHAPTER 8

The long morning session had been devoted to the proper procedure for taking first histories of new patients. Dr. Boyd, the general practitioner and surgeon attached to Mountain Hospital, stressed the importance of learning as much about the family as about the patient, for as he pointed out, "The thing that will eventually kill your patient, if a gun or an automobile doesn't, is what he inherits from his family. If you would lengthen his life, discover the family weaknesses and set up a regimen for your patient to follow to enhance life. Good medicine is nine-tenths prevention. Because the one tenth that is cure is not nearly as dependable as not getting sick in the first place.

"The demands on the family nurse sometimes seem too much to cope with," Dr. Boyd continued. "And yet, through training and hard-gained experience, most of you will learn to manage. The vast amount of medical knowledge that may now seem such a jumble to you will somehow, almost by magic, fall into place when you are faced with the need to use it. You are suffering now the same pangs and doubts that interns feel when they first begin the clinical application of their knowledge."

Kate studied the young physician, thinking to herself, *he's not so far removed from internship that he has trouble remembering*. She estimated Boyd to be no more than thirty-two or three. He had obviously grown that beard to give himself an appearance of greater maturity than he actually possessed. She was debating whether to judge him handsome when she heard her name called.

"Kincaid!" Dr. Boyd addressed her directly. Kate sat erect, and as her face flushed, she realized she had become so involved in her thoughts about him that she had ignored what he was saying. "What would be your response to such a question?" he asked.

Question? What question? Kate was forced to ask herself. She was aware of the deepening flush in her cheeks as she found herself unable to answer.

"There was such a faraway look in your eyes I figured you'd left us. Now, if you are with us again, we will continue," Boyd said.

Much as she resented his reprimand, she found herself unable to respond with more than a soft "I'm sorry, Doctor."

"The subject I was about to introduce was this: 'Nurse, can you give me something for my headaches?' You will hear that many times in your work as a family nurse. It will almost always come from the woman of the house. You will look about her simple home, at the sparse furniture, the plain wood floors, scrubbed down to the grain of the wood. Just outside the window the long clothesline hung with the family 'warsh.' On the floor the young 'un playing near the coal stove on which, side by side, are boiling the evening's stew and the baby's diapers, and inside it, the whole week's bread baking. And you will say to yourself, small wonder this woman suffers headaches. Of course she needs something to help her.

"And precisely when you are feeling such sympathy is the time to stop and say to yourself, no! Because if you are discerning enough, you will find that this woman is suffering from an ailment common to the city housewife and the suburban housewife. What I call the drugstore philosophy of life. The false confidence with which we have been raised that all our problems can be solved by some bottle or box that can be found in every drugstore. It is the kind of thinking that leads to drug addiction of various kinds."

Kate was not the only one who sat up a bit more tensely at this. Drug abuse, yes, she had run into cases of it, more than enough cases, back at University Hospital, among women facing the burdens and cares of city life. But here, among these simple, almost primitive people?

"Alcoholism, drug abuse, wife abuse and child abuse exist here to the same degree as in the places from which you came. You must be alert and on guard against these dangers. If you see any of the signs of those troubles, you will note them. And, if you form a distinct suspicion, you must report it on the proper forms you will be given. Above all, never feel 'If I inform on them it will destroy my relationship with them, their trust in me.'

"For while you are thinking that, some unfortunate child may be going untended by a drug-laden mother. Some other child may be suffering physical abuse or emotional deprivation because her mother is an alcoholic. In family nursing you are responsible not for only one patient but for generations of patients. The child who is abused today becomes tomorrow's abuser. The child who is deprived of love and care today becomes tomorrow's depriving parent. Whole generations will be in your hands.

"So do not condescend. Do not pity. Do not 'make allowances' for their culture or their way of life. Exercise firmness with a loving heart, but exercise firmness. We are no different from you. Remember that."

His last statement made Kate aware that Boyd himself had come out of these mountains. It was a surprise, for he sounded no different from most other young doctors with whom she had come in contact.

"We will break for lunch," Boyd announced abruptly.

Though she took her breakfast at the house because Mrs. Russell insisted, Kate made it a point to have her lunch at the hospital cafeteria. It saved time, of which there never seemed to be enough. It also gave her a chance to review her copious morning notes before what she had learned could be crowded out by hectic afternoons in the busy clinic.

With her sandwich in one hand and her notes in the other, she was engrossed when she heard a man's voice. "Kincaid?"

She looked up into Boyd's face, and in that moment decided he was indeed handsome.

"May I?" he asked as he set down his tray alongside hers.

"Of course," she said tensely, prepared for an additional rebuke. Before he even sat down across from her, she said, "I'm sorry about my mind wandering in class. It won't happen again."

"No," he said, smiling. "*I'm* sorry. And I'm afraid it *will* happen again.'' She stared at him, puzzled. ''The entire episode was my fault. I did it to hide my own embarrassment.''

''You . . .'' Kate began to ask, but did not finish.

''I found myself staring at you more and more. Until I felt I must put some distance between us. I also noticed that your mind had begun to wander from my lecture. So I decided, I will compel her to concentrate on my lecture again, and in her embarrassment she will resent me. That will maintain the proper professional relationship of teacher and student. That's why I pretended I had asked a question that you were not prepared to answer. Forgive me?''

Kate smiled and asked, ''Did you really come out of mountain people?''

''Does that strike you so strange that it couldn't possibly be true?''

''You have none of the characteristics, none of the speech patterns. . . .''

''It wasn't easy,'' he admitted. ''But it would take hours to tell you about it.''

''Sometime, when there are hours enough, I would like to know.''

When Boyd's face flushed, Kate realized that he had misinterpreted curiosity about local life and traditions for a more personal interest. She decided to correct him at once.

''Dr. Boyd, let's get one thing straight right now. Yes, you are an attractive man. But I am here for twelve months of intense study and practice to further my education. And that's all I'm here for.''

''Of course,'' Boyd said coolly. ''Class resumes in exactly eight minutes.'' He left the table and his untouched lunch as well.

For the next two hours Boyd lectured his three students on the proper examination of eyes, ears, nose and throat. He pointed out the differences they should be aware of when examining a young patient as distinguished from a geriatric patient. He dwelled on the nuances involved in examining the iris, which presented more revealing signs than merely the state of the patient's sight.

It was an intense session. Just before he excused them, he read from the slip that had been delivered to him.

''Sister Ellen, you will go to Pediatric Clinic. McClendon to Surgery. You, Kincaid, will come with me.''

Puzzled and embarrassed, Kate nodded, while trying to avoid glancing at her fellow students to discern their reaction to this unusual invitation.

The others had gone. Boyd and Kate alone.

"Back to the cafeteria," Boyd ordered. Though she resented his order, she followed. They reached the cafeteria to find that the kitchen crew had shoved back all tables and chairs to clear a large area in the middle of the room. There stood two tall ladders that reached to the ceiling.

On one of the tables was a huge carton. Boyd ripped open the sealed top and began to unload large rolls of decorative paper.

"Don't just stand there, Kincaid," he ordered. "Make yourself useful!"

Instead of obeying, Kate said, "Dr. Boyd, if this is your way of humiliating me because of what I said at lunch, I don't enjoy it. I am a qualified nurse. And I wish, no, I demand to be given duties consonant with my training and experience."

"Well, well, well," Boyd said, dropping a roll of red, white and blue streamers as he turned to her. "It seems that in college, indignation was the course you studied hardest."

"I would prefer an assignment like Sister Ellen's or McClendon's," Kate said as coolly and professionally as she could.

"If I didn't think this was a way of educating you to your responsibilities as a family nurse I wouldn't have asked you to participate."

"I'm sure whatever it is you're intending to celebrate can be done without me," Kate replied.

"If you insist, relieve Sister Ellen in Pediatrics and send her here to work with me," Boyd said sharply.

"You call this 'work'? . . ." Kate began to ask.

Boyd interrupted. "Send Sister Ellen here. And you relieve her. But change your attitude. You'll be working with little children who are not aware of your previous excellent training and experience," he added sarcastically.

She was about to respond in kind but refrained. Instead, she turned briskly and left. Boyd watched her go, then resumed unloading rolls of colored paper, string, lanterns and other party decorations.

* * *

Pediatric Clinic was crowded with mothers and their children, ranging in age from six months to twelve years. There seemed an unending stream of them. Kate did not have a moment to stop or think between seeking out their records, asking some basic questions as indicated in those records, and passing them on to Nurse Ledyard, who did the actual examination, evaluation and treatment.

Kate also barely had time to admire the dispatch yet the warmth and attention with which Ledyard handled each little patient. She particularly noted the amount of time Ledyard took in explaining to each mother the child's condition, the child's expected recovery and any danger signs that demanded immediate return to the hospital.

From time to time Ledyard would whisper to Kate, "Hold that file out for me."

By the end of clinic, which ran well past the scheduled five o'clock, six patients' files had been held aside. Though exhausted from her intensive work, Ledyard studied each file again before she concluded, "Anemia. Two cases. One from malnutrition. The other from some deep-seated cause that demands more testing. This one needs surgery. Deviated septum. These two need chest X ray. Disturbing rales."

Ledyard held the sixth file for a long time before she said, "This one needs a complete blood workup. And a scan."

"Scan?" Kate asked, alert to the dangerous implications.

"Possible sarcoma."

"Is this a typical day in Pediatrics?" Kate asked.

"Oh, no," Ledyard said, "today was very light. Usually they come out of the mountains in much larger numbers. I think many of them are waiting until tomorrow and the circus."

"Circus?" Kate asked.

"You'll see" was all the older nurse said. Because Ledyard seemed so involved in her depressing suspicions about that sixth child, Kate did not question her further.

On her way out of the hospital, Kate could not resist stopping to discover what Boyd and Sister Ellen had accomplished during the afternoon. But the glass panels in the cafeteria doors were covered by red, white and blue paper that obscured any view. On the wall alongside the doors was pasted a small, neatly typed notice: *All personnel will be appropriately dressed in circus costumes tomorrow morning. Let ingenuity be your material and imagination your designer. Abbott, Director.*

Still smarting under the doctor's earlier rebuke, Kate thought, *Not me! I'm not here for amateur theatricals. No matter what Boyd thinks!*

After such a long day and evening, after poring over her instruction manual on patient assessment until past midnight, it was not difficult for Kate to sleep uninterrupted until almost six the next morning.

The sound that woke her was a heavy, unaccustomed, rhythmic vibration directly over the house. It was so loud and persistent that she leaped out of bed, raised the window shade just in time to see a huge helicopter pass by low and in the direction of the hospital. It was khaki-colored and bore Marine Corps insignia.

Kate's first reaction was it must be a life-threatening military emergency! Somewhere very close by, a Marine unit engaged in a training maneuver must have suffered an accident which endangered some young lives. Else why come to Mountain Hospital when only sixty miles away there was a city hospital, larger and better equipped? *They'll need me* was her next thought.

She dressed hurriedly and ran all the way to the hospital. There she stopped, for she had encountered a phenomenon she had not seen in her brief time in Adelphi.

In a single long line stretched a caravan of motor vehicles of every type and vintage: battered, rusting half-ton trucks, old jalopies from twenty-five years ago, some cars newer, but none less than seven or eight years old. And in every vehicle not merely a driver but a whole family. Father, mother, and as many as three, four, five, even six children of varying ages. Kate raced past the line of cars toward the parking area where the reason for the waiting cars became apparent. The huge Marine helicopter occupied the entire center of the parking lot.

But instead of Marines in uniform, men in civilian clothes were busy unloading boxes and cartons from the copter. They were all strangers to her. Until she saw Dr. Boyd. Like the others, he, too, was helping unload supplies and equipment. Boyd spied her while he was lifting a large brown cardboard carton.

"Kincaid! Lend a hand. We need all the help we can get. They're already here. And we're not ready!"

She hurried to the open copter, took a carton held out to her by one of the unloaders. As she struggled with it, making her way to the Emergency Room entrance, she saw a large black word inscribed on top in marking ink. Instead of medical supplies it said TOYS.

As she looked for a place to set down her carton, Boyd came to her rescue.

"I'll take that," he said, sliding his hands under the carton.

Before he could turn away she asked, "What's this all about? Toys? That lineup of cars? A Marine helicopter?"

Instead of answering, Boyd asked, "Where's your costume? Didn't you see the notice?"

"Costume?" Kate responded, puzzled, but only for a moment. "Oh, you mean about the circus?"

"Of course, about the circus! You're part of it. Get into costume."

"I didn't plan anything," she admitted.

"Well, then, come as you are!" Boyd said. He studied her for a moment, smiled and said sarcastically, "We'll say you're the fairy princess from the big city." With that, he started in the direction of the cafeteria.

Though Kate resented his remark, she followed him. Before she could reach the cafeteria she passed the Ear, Nose and Throat Clinic. Inside, more men were busy than the place could comfortably accommodate. One man was laying out surgical equipment that Kate knew was required for intricate throat and nose examinations. What made her remain to stare was that the other men were dabbing makeup on their faces. Red, green, blue, large white circles under their mouths. They were making up to be clowns, laughing, joking, admiring or criticizing each other's efforts, until one of them said, "You make a better clown than a surgeon."

Doctors in makeup! Kate wondered silently. Where else but in a rustic backwoods town would such a thing be possible! It would never have happened in staid, regimented University Hospital! The chairman of the Surgical Department would forbid it. The Board of Trustees would be outraged.

One doctor, short, powerfully muscled and older than the others by some dozen years, put the finishing touches on his makeup, then said, "Okay! Give the word. Get that copter up and away and let the people in!"

Kate watched from one of the windows as the huge copter blades started in motion, faster and faster until they generated enough lift to take it up and out of the parking area, safely over the tops of the lined-up motor vehicles. The cars, trucks and jeeps started to move in orderly fashion. As each vehicle parked, a family piled out. From children in arms to thirteen- and fourteen-year-olds, they piled out. Their attitude was joyous, the children were laughing, shouting, calling out to friends from other cars. Hundreds of them, all happily converged on the front entrance to Mountain Hospital.

Abbott was directing the human traffic toward the cafeteria when she spied Kate.

"Kincaid! Get with it! We need every hand in there!"

Kate went along with the torrent of happy families. She reached the cafeteria to discover that her two classmates, dressed as clowns, were already serving milk and doughnuts to the children. Farther down the line, adults were being offered coffee and tea and sweet biscuits. Kate took a place in the serving line, doling out milk and doughnuts to fill eager, grasping young hands.

All the families had been admitted and fed. They were seated on every available chair, with at least half a hundred ensconced on the floor for lack of seats. Now the man Kate had identified as the senior surgeon of the group appeared in the doorway. He was dressed in a clown costume which she recognized was an ingenious adaptation of surgical greens. He made his entrance with a loud, vocal improvisation of a circus flourish.

"*Dadah!*" he exclaimed, to the delight of the youngsters. "And now, one and all, welcome to Dr. Abrams's traveling circus!"

To the accompaniment of circus music on the loudspeaker, the other doctors, all in makeup and costume, burst into the room, racing around it to the wide-eyed awe of the children until surprise turned into delight and laughter.

Dr. Abrams proceeded to do a number of mystifying magic tricks, all of which involved common surgical instruments, clamps, scissors and other equipment that could be handled with impunity and without risk. The children applauded each trick, including even those that failed. It soon became apparent to Kate that Abrams was deliberately failing at some of them because he obviously possessed the manual dexterity to perform them all.

He was followed by two other surgeons, Bethard and Wilson, who pretended to be a ventriloquist and dummy. Since Wilson was the taller of the two by at least a foot, he pretended to be the dummy, sitting on the smaller Bethard's lap. The incongruity caused the children to roar with laughter.

Songs followed the ventriloquism. Then one of the younger doctors brought out his violin and played mountain music as only an experienced and talented native could play it. It was the highlight of the show for both adults and children. It ended with cheers, shouts, laughter, applause and calls for more.

Kate noticed that when Abrams subtly signaled to his contingent, one by one they slipped out of the room during the encore. Kate followed. Down the corridor they went in the direction of the E.N.T. Clinic. But first each man made a stop at the small dressing room. When he emerged, all the makeup was gone from his face and he was wearing fresh, sterilized greens. They entered the clinic, stopping to scrub at the three shiny metal sinks. In a matter of minutes, men who had been merry, comical, ridiculous clowns had been transformed into an efficient team of surgeons.

Assuming Kate had been assigned to him, Abrams ordered crisply, "Okay, girlie! Into a lab coat and start bringing in the little ones!"

She had found a lab coat in the supply closet and was on her way back to the clinic when she almost collided with Boyd, who was holding a two-year-old in his arms. He seemed about to make some comment about her, but instead he smiled and with a gesture of his head beckoned her to follow him to the entrance of the clinic.

Abrams was already examining the first young patient. Two other men were also making intensive ear, nose and throat examinations. Without orders, Kate assumed the duty of keeping the children in line and amused until their turns came. Soon she was dividing her time between supervising the young and observing the doctors. She had seen many E.N.T. examinations during her service at University Hospital, but she had never seen them done with such care yet with lighthearted banter so that if any serious defect was discovered, no child was aware of it. But among the doctors there was a level of silent communication that indicated "I've found a bad one here." Or the look that said to Abrams: "Surgery, extensive surgery is going to be required here." Abrams would glance at that child, as if to fix him in his memory for later in the day.

Abbott came by to make sure that things were running smoothly. She saw Kate and asked, "Who assigned you here?"

But Abrams called out, "I drafted her, Christine. You know I always draft the prettiest ones."

That seemed to resolve the crisis, for Abbott said nothing, only nodded, giving her reluctant consent.

As more complicated cases came into Abrams's hands, he ordered Kate to assist him. When he needed to study a nasal polyp, he asked her to bend the light in his direction so the mirror he wore on his forehead would reflect it more strongly. When the next case revealed a peritonsillar abscess deep enough to demand surgery, he ordered Kate to hand him a probe. Before long, most of her time was spent passing instruments to Abrams or replenishing the supply of fresh sterile ones.

After more than four hours of such intensive examinations and when the entire team was exhausted, Abrams called for a lunch break. The others went off to the cafeteria. Fatigued, Abrams sank down onto a shiny steel stool.

"Doctor, may I get you some lunch?" Kate asked.

"Not me, but get some for yourself," Abrams said.

"Then coffee?" Kate insisted.

He smiled. "It won't make me feel better but it will at least give you some satisfaction. Coffee."

The cafeteria was full to overflowing. Children everywhere, parents hovering over them to make sure they were fed properly. Kate saw both Sister Ellen and Emily McClendon moving among the children, refilling their glasses with milk while offering coffee to their parents.

Kate prepared a tray for Abrams and herself. Despite his refusal, she brought two sandwiches, two coffees, even two pieces of circus-decorated cake the hospital baker had prepared for this special day.

Abrams toyed with the sandwich, but it was obvious he was only being polite. It was the coffee he needed. But he dawdled over it, luxuriating in the respite it afforded him.

"You're a very good nurse," he said, "very efficient."

"Thank you."

"I noticed you right from the start. Even before we started to do our examination. You were the one who didn't wear a costume or get into makeup."

The comment was a rebuke and called for a reply.

"I didn't realize what this was all about."

"Seemed foolish to you," Abrams assumed.

She hesitated before admitting, "Yes, it did."

Abrams swirled the remaining coffee in his plastic cup as he said, "The basis of good medicine is not necessarily to bring the patient to the therapy but to bring the therapy to the patient. These people live a different kind of life than we do. They love their mountains, their rivers, their hollers. They love their isolation, their way of life. We might not choose it for ourselves. But that is no reason to deny it to them.

"And yet they need medical attention and help. So twice a year, the boys and I . . . I call them my 'boys,' but there isn't one of them who couldn't head up my department . . . the boys and I fly down from the city and hold this great mass clinic. The Marines are kind enough to lend us a helicopter for the occasion so we can save time. The people here put themselves out for us. And all of us together try to make it a show, a circus. It makes Medicine fun. The doctor is a clown, a magician, a ventriloquist, a dummy, a fiddler to be laughed at, not a man to be feared."

Abrams took another sip of coffee. It was tepid now and not so refreshing, so he put the cup aside.

"I can see you are a young woman who takes nursing seriously. Just by the efficient way you pass instruments I know that you were well trained in some excellent medical facility. Yet you are here. Why you are here is no business of mine. But as long as you are here, relax. Unbend. Blend in with these people. Be part of the community. Be part of the human race."

Kate felt a surge of anger at the implied accusation that she was not.

"Wear a clown suit. Dab your face with idiotic colors. Make fun of yourself. As we do. You'll get to like it. And the kids will love it. As my father used to say, in such situations, be a *mensh*. A human being among human beings."

He reached out to touch Kate's firm, dimpled chin. "I would like to see laughter in those eyes. I want you to feel that if Abrams can become a clown for the occasion, then so can . . . what is your name?''

''Katherine Kincaid.''

''Then Kate can be a clown.'' Having said that, he handed her a cup of cold coffee. ''Get me a refill. And then I want you to be my scrub nurse for the rest of the afternoon.''

The afternoon extended far into the evening. Abrams occupied one Surgery, and his chief assistant, Ron Wilson, occupied the other. The clinic was used by two other doctors for the minor procedures.

Kate had seen many surgeons operate during her service in University Hospital, but none seemed to work so swiftly or so expertly as Abrams. With his young patients under anesthetic, there was no need now for him to be the smiling, affable surgeon. He was all business. He reached out for instruments and expected they would be there. He made neat, small incisions, and handled human tissue with care and reverence. But when it was required, as in two of the cases that involved malignancies, he did not hesitate to use both skill and strength. Of one of the cases he said finally, ''This one has to come to City Hospital. We'll fly her back with us.''

By nine o'clock that night all the tonsillectomies and adenomectomies had been completed. The more serious cases had been done. Only one case required transmission to the city. That would wait till morning when the copter would fly in again to take the team out.

The cafeteria had been kept open and was ready with fresh hot suppers for the surgical team. Abrams invited Kate to join them. She tried to beg off, saying, ''I have an early class tomorrow.''

Abrams laughed. ''Young lady, when I was an intern and your age I would go forty-eight hours without sleep. So you can afford to get by with a few hours tonight.''

After their late supper of stew, grits and home-grown greens, the doctors compared their findings. The usual run of inflamed tonsils, large adenoids, minor ear infections. But there were those two tumors. And just a hint of another one from which Wilson had excised a sufficient amount of tissue to turn over to the pathologist.

Wilson turned to Kate. ''I'll send you my report in three days.'' Then he thought to ask, ''Your name?''

But Abrams interceded. ''Kate. Kate Kincaid. But I think you'd better send the findings to'Abbott. Am I right?'' he asked, smiling.

''Yes, I think so,'' Kate agreed.

It was almost midnight when Kate left the hospital. She could not forgo making one last round of the wards. They were filled with young patients, some of whom were sleeping, others whimpering in afterpain from earlier surgery. But at each bedside was a mother or father ready to comfort the child.

Out in the corridor, beds were lined up, and in each bed was a patient being solaced by his or her parents. Families were being treated here, whole families, not merely patients. It was the first time that Kate Kincaid truly appreciated what family nursing was. You did not isolate the patient from the family, you brought the family into the treatment.

By the time she stepped out into the cool late night Kate Kincaid had a deeper realization of purpose than she had when she first chose this isolated place. She walked back to the house feeling not tired but exhilarated.

She woke just before dawn. After dressing hurriedly, she ran all the way to the hospital, for she could already see the rotors of the huge Marine copter in the parking area. Dr. Abrams's team would be leaving now.

She arrived just as Abrams was supervising loading his young patient aboard. When he spied Kate approaching, he called to her, ''Kincaid! Come say good-bye!''

He greeted her with a paternal kiss on the cheek. ''If you decide to leave here, get in touch with me.''

''I'm not leaving here until I finish,'' Kate said firmly.

''Good!'' Abrams replied.

He swung aboard the craft. The huge rotors began to spin, slowly at first, then whipping the air and causing Kate to pull back out of the blade wash. Soon the helicopter lifted off.

She waved until it disappeared beyond the first green mountaintop.

Bring the Medicine to the people, the man had said. It could serve as a motto for the rest of her career. This had been the most rewarding twenty-four hours during her brief time in Adelphi.

CHAPTER 9

Days of instruction and clinic duty turned into weeks, then months. It was already June. The course in Assessment and Diagnosis of Common Health Problems was nearly completed. Three months of daily classroom and clinic work and long nights of studying additional material had become such a habit for Kate it was difficult for her to remember when it had not been so.

Many nights she fell asleep in the Russell kitchen over textbooks and medical monographs which enlarged on the subject matter in the thick manuals. Some nights Mrs. Russell woke her for a cup of hot tea before insisting she go off to her room and get the relaxing sleep she so desperately needed.

Some of those nights, while enjoying a cup of hot, spicy tea, the two women talked of themselves and of the past. After one particularly arduous week, Kate confessed to her elderly confidante that there were difficult days when she began to question the wisdom of her choice.

There were nights, when, alone in bed, her thoughts of Howard were especially disturbing and arousing. His letters, their conversations on the phone, too often interrupted by the frequent breakdowns in the local phone service, were not only not enough, they only served to remind her how much she missed his lovemaking. How much she missed his maleness, missed his light snoring, even missed having to leave him sleeping while she went off to the hospital. Most of all, she missed what she had not fully appreciated when it was available to her, the stability and comfort he offered her by insisting they marry.

There were times when Kate thought, *I might as well be Sister Ellen. I've given up all earthly pleasures, all self-indulgent comforts. I've chosen a life of celibacy, without the religious conviction that motivates Ellen.*

The only way she could dispel such moments of regret was to force herself to be even more determined not to fail here. She would not only meet Mountain Hospital's stringent standards, she would exceed them. It had become a battle between her and Abbott, whose every glance seemed a critical appraisal of Kate's work.

On the night before their end-of-trimester exams, a night which Kate had planned to devote to intensive study, she received a call from Abbott. Nurse Ebert, scheduled to take over the Emergency Room, had suddenly come down with the flu. Abbott assigned Kate to cover for her.

"I'm afraid you can't figure on studying too much. You know how Saturday nights are in Emergency," Abbott warned her, then added, with what Kate took to be a tinge of sarcasm, "but then, by now you're probably well prepared for your exams."

Though Kate resented the unexpected duty, she looked upon it as a challenge, a chance to prove to Abbott that she could do both—cover Emergency *and* do her studying. Armed with manuals, medical periodicals and two textbooks, she went on duty.

For the first few hours she was able to study undisturbed. The night watchman interrupted once, and then only to bring her some fresh coffee.

It was past one o'clock in the morning when she began to bone up on Brower's *Evaluating Growth and Posture in School Age Children* that she was startled by the loud screech of tires outside the E.R. entrance. A heavy vehicle had come to an abrupt halt. She heard the excited voices of angry men. In her haste to get to the door, her book dropped to the floor. As she bent to reach it, the door burst open. She was confronted by two roughly dressed, bearded men who were carrying a third. The third man was bleeding profusely from his left shoulder. His two comrades pushed past Kate and carried their unconscious friend to the treatment table. The older of them ordered gruffly, "Git the doctor!"

"There's no doctor on duty," Kate informed them.

"Then find one!" the bearded man commanded.

Kate pushed the belligerent man aside to take charge of the patient. She seized a surgical scissors, cut away his old shirt and discovered a large bleeding wound in his shoulder. She had spent enough time in the city Emergency Room to recognize a gunshot wound. Though this one was larger than any she had seen before. The condition of the surrounding tissue indicated that the bleeding wound was probably where the bullet had exited. It must have entered from his back. That was of no importance now. To stop the flow of blood was Kate's first obligation. She pressed a large gauze pad against the open wound. She had to discard pad after pad as they became soaked with blood.

Meanwhile, the patient's two companions stood across the table, scrutinizing her every move, obviously doubting her ability.

"Damn it, git us a doctor!" the leader ordered.

"Damn it, shut up!" Kate replied, as she drew on a pair of sterile plastic gloves. She reached into the open wound, feeling around until she found the artery that was the source of the hemorrhage. She tried to tie off the damaged artery with a surgical clamp. Slippery from blood, the vessel kept eluding her. On her fourth try she seemed to have snared it, for the flow of blood ebbed, finally oozing only from the smaller vessels in the area of the wound.

"Better," she said softly.

"Which way was it?" the leader asked.

The question being of no consequence to Kate, she ignored it to attend to more urgent problems. Seizing another large sterile pad, she placed it against the wound to hold the clamp in place. She ordered the older man, "Hold this right here. Don't move it."

Before he obeyed, the man repeated, "That there bullet, front or back?"

Kate ignored him to reach for the telephone and summon Dr. Boyd. The man seized her by the shoulders. He spun her around so that she was forced to face him. His breath proved that he had done considerable drinking and might be dangerous. She struggled to free herself from his big strong hands, hands that had dug coal, tilled land, built roads and done other physical labor. She was unable to break free.

"The bullet? Front or back?" he demanded.

Because she sensed her answer was of great consequence to this angry drunken man, she knew she had better not reveal it.

"I'm a nurse. That question can only be answered by a doctor. I'm trying to get one now. And if I can't, I don't know how long your friend has to live."

"Not my friend, my boy," the older man admitted, releasing his fierce grip on her so she could telephone for the doctor.

Within moments after she called him, Dr. Boyd's Jeep pulled up outside the Emergency Room entrance. With enormous relief, Kate heard his car door slam shut. In a moment, the door of the E.R. flew open and Boyd was demanding, "Okay, let's have a look at him!"

Kate stood aside to reveal the young wounded man who was still unconscious. Boyd asked for a pair of surgical gloves. Kate slipped them on his outstretched hands. He began his examination. He was silent while he worked, only nodding his head occasionally as he determined the full extent of the injury. Very tenderly he examined the area and the manner in which the clamp had been applied to the torn artery.

"Good work, Kincaid. This could have been bad. Very bad. Blood pressure?"

"Didn't take it."

"Then take it!" Boyd said, annoyed with what he considered a serious oversight.

"Didn't have time," she explained.

"Don't explain. Take it!" Boyd ordered impatiently.

While she put the cuff on the patient's other arm, Boyd continued his examination, wiping away the oozing blood while probing gently. "Well?" he asked.

"Eighty over fifty-five," Kate informed him.

"He'll stabilize. No need for a transfusion, thanks to this clamp. Main thing, no signs of shock yet."

That assurance freed the father from his gravest concern, so he asked. "Doctor? Which way, front or back?"

"Look, we've got other things to worry about right now," Boyd said.

But as he had with Kate before, the father seized Boyd and pulled him away from the patient.

"This one here," he said, referring to Kate, "she's a furriner, she don't know no better. But ye're one of us. So ye got to tell us. It's yere bounden duty."

"Until I find the bullet . . ." Boyd started to say.

The irate father interrupted. "Ye ain't goin' to find no bullet! It's sticking in the wall of the bar where this here happened. So we got to know. Or do I have to guess?"

Kate did not know the consequences of "guessing," but she knew it constituted a threat. Boyd turned back to the patient. Kate could tell he was only pretending to make another examination so as to avoid answering. Then he turned to the irate father. "If you don't let me get on with my work, you may get your answer from the county coroner."

"Ye said yereself he ain't in no shock."

"But he may be soon if you two don't clear out and let us do our work," Boyd threatened.

"Ye do what ye have to do. We'll do our'n," the father said. He beckoned to the younger man who had helped carry his son into the E.R. They left. Kate heard their old truck start up noisily, make a sharp squealing turn and roar away into the night.

"Damn, damn, damn!" Boyd said as he began making the surgical repairs and applying the preventive procedures needed to keep his young patient alive and free from infection. After Kate inserted an I.V. to prevent the patient from going into shock, she had a chance to study him for the first time. Shiny black hair accented his thin pale face. A handsome face now, one day it would be like his father's, old, gnarled, and exhibiting just such hostility as his father had displayed.

Several times, at frequent intervals, Boyd had Kate check his blood pressure. Each time it improved. Then it was up to 100 over 60. Finally they lifted him onto a gurney and moved him into the small ward, where he was entrusted to the care of the night nurse on duty.

Kate was surprised when in taking over, the nurse asked only one question of Dr. Boyd.

"Front or back?"

Boyd shook his head and admitted, "Back."

"Too bad," the nurse replied.

From her own experience Kate knew enough about gunshot wounds to know that from the front or the back, the medical consequences of such a wound were the same. Why the nurse's comment?

* * *

When they returned to the E.R., Kate said, "Sorry to have bothered you, Doctor. But under the circumstances . . ."

"You did the right thing. Though from what I found, you could have handled it yourself."

"Couldn't have handled *him*," she said, referring to the angry father.

"Mountain people" was all Boyd would say before asking, "Coffee?"

"Of course. I should have offered," Kate said.

They were both relieved to get hot cups of coffee into their hands. Between sips they were able to converse for the first time in weeks.

"How's it been going?" Boyd asked. "Tough grind?"

"I've had tougher," she said.

"Why this need to avoid admitting how tough it really is? What is it about you, Kincaid?"

"I hadn't noticed anything 'about me' that's so different," she protested.

"Your two colleagues don't hesitate to admit to me how difficult it is. But not you," he pointed out. "What are you avoiding?"

"I am not avoiding anything," she insisted.

Boyd smiled. His smile, attractive and friendly, only irritated her.

"Something I said amuse you?" she asked angrily.

"I was thinking, if I were the visiting psychiatrist instead of the staff doctor, I would label your attitude aggressive, overdetermined, hence overtly and suspiciously defensive."

"Well, *you* are not the visiting psychiatrist and *I* am not any of the things you labeled me," Kate replied. "Now, sorry I disturbed your night."

"Are you dismissing me?" Boyd asked, laughing.

"There is no further need for your presence here tonight."

"That's what *you* think. I'll wait. If you don't mind."

"Why? To practice amateur psychiatry on me? I don't need it. And frankly, I resent it."

"Kincaid, you know what your trouble is?" Boyd replied. "You're down here to work off a grudge. To prove something to those people who offended you back where you came from. That's not good enough. Here, you have to get to understand these people, to love them, to become part of their way of life for as long as you're here. *If* . . ." Boyd paused before he repeated, "*If* they will accept you."

Before she could protest, he continued. "Yes, if *they* will accept *you*, not the other way around. Now, you don't have to stay here. You're not a prisoner. No one here is. We're here because we love what we do. The only thing *we* want to prove is that ministering to these people is one of the finest things we can do. Until you believe that, you won't be happy here. So maybe you *should* quit."

"I've never quit on anything in my whole life," Kate shot back.

"Of course not," Boyd agreed, too quickly for her comfort. "Another sign of your overdetermination."

"You're using that word again," Kate warned him.

"Right, lady. The difference between us is that I only use it, you live it. You're an overachiever. Always have been. Why? To prove you have brains as well as beauty?"

She glared at him, resenting his assumption. But he was quick to respond.

"From the first time, I was curious about you. So I looked up your *curriculum vitae* in Abbott's files. You are an extremely bright woman. Have been ever since grade school. I'll bet where you came from you were considered the best maternity nurse around. Right?"

She refused to give him the satisfaction of admitting it.

"Well, here we take it for granted you are one of the best. Else you wouldn't have been admitted. But we want more. Much more. We want love. Want respect. Get to know us. Let yourself go. Be human. Do ridiculous things like painting up your face on Circus Day. Do whatever it takes to minister to the whole patient."

"You and Dr. Abrams . . ." she started to say.

"Good!" He intruded on her angry response. "That's a place to start. Abrams. He could serve as a model for you. When he first came down here, he was considered an outcast. Because he is a Jew. Some of these people never actually get to see a Jew in their entire lives. Now Abrams could have said, 'To hell with them, I don't need them and their prejudice.' But he decided to prove something to them. That he and they were human beings together in this beleaguered world.

"Today there are folks in this valley who wouldn't entrust their children to any surgeon but Abrams. I have seen a mother refuse to allow an orthopedic surgeon operate on her little girl's leg until Ear,

Nose and Throat Surgeon Abrams gave his approval. That is respect and confidence and love. You don't study that in books. You learn it from people. Until you do, Kincaid, you are not going to make it here."

"If you've said all you want to, I would like to be alone," Kate replied.

"I can't leave," Boyd said.

"There's nothing to detain you," Kate replied.

"Oh, yes, there is," he insisted.

"What? More psychiatric diagnosis?" she asked sarcastically.

"You'll see," he answered, provoking her even more. "Meantime I'll go have another look at the patient."

She watched him leave. Her anger succeeded only in partially obscuring the realization that, despite his manner, she found him interesting, provocative. Finally, she realized, he reminded her of Howard, who often spoke to her so directly and critically.

Both men had used the same word to describe her devotion to nursing—overdetermined. Would that word plague her forever? It was used by those who did not understand, could not understand unless they knew. And how could they know, since she could never bring herself to tell anyone.

It went back to the time when her father had made a special effort to return home from one of his business trips for her graduation from grade school. Since she had always scored so high in English, he was sure she would win the gold medal for excellence. So, without telling Kate or her mother, he had bought a special gift, a small frame and easel, which he would keep on the desk in his office next to her photograph. Her gold medal would fit in there and enable him to brag to all his business associates about his daughter Kate, who was not only the prettiest but the brightest girl in her entire school.

But on graduation night when the prizes were announced, the English medal was awarded to Priscilla Waybright. And though the principal announced that Katherine Kincaid was only three tenths of a point behind, it did nothing to soften Kate's disappointment and pain.

She would never have known about the frame and easel except that later that night, unable to sleep because she was so unhappy, she slipped out of her bed and came down the stairs in time to overhear her mother.

"Fred, you can't tell her about the frame, it would be too cruel. Find some other present."

"What'll I do with the frame?" her father asked.

"Give it away. Throw it away."

"It was very expensive," he protested. "I had it specially made."

"Then keep it. She'll win something else one day. She always does."

"I even wrote to the principal to ask the exact size of the medal," he confessed. "I feel so foolish now."

"You had your heart set on it, I know," her mother said.

As quietly as she had come down, little Kate went back up to her room, closed her door and wept the rest of the night. In the morning she was determined never again to disappoint her father. Losing was bad enough, disappointing others was even worse. She would never do that again.

Her sophomore year in high school, she won the Latin medal. It fit the frame almost precisely, and she had to pretend the gift was a surprise. But nothing would ever wipe out the failure about which her father had felt so deeply.

If wanting to do your best, be your best was being overdetermined, then she was. And at this moment, she felt stubbornly proud of the fact.

Her thoughts were interrupted by what seemed a rerun of what had happened earlier that night. The same startling sound, a screech of deep cleated tires on the driveway outside Emergency. Angry voices. The slam of truck doors. The door to the E.R. burst open and three men appeared, two of them carrying the third man, whose shirt was bloody from an uneven, wide bright-red stain that warned of considerable bleeding from a critical artery. Without a word they placed the man on the examining table. Kate called to the night watchman, "Get Dr. Boyd!" She immediately ripped away the bloody shirt to find the wound. She knew from its location that the wound, from whatever cause, had damaged the aorta. She knew, too, what thc probabilities were. Kate was desperately trying to find a pulse when Boyd came racing into the room. He edged her aside, began to make a cursory examination. Then he stopped and looked at Kate. His eyes confirmed her own diagnosis. The young man, no more than nineteen or twenty, was dead. D.O.A. was the note Kate eventually would inscribe in the E.R. log before this night was over.

"How did it happen?" Boyd asked the man who was apparently the leader of the group.

"Pete Crispin," the man replied. "Is Lafe here?" When Boyd did not answer, the man repeated, "Ye holdin' Lafe here?"

"He's here," Boyd finally admitted but added, "If you try to get him, I'll have to witness against you."

The leader looked to his companion. Kate realized Boyd's warning had consequences beyond any she understood. The younger of the two men shrugged and seemed resigned. But the leader went out abruptly, only to reappear some moments later with an old double-barreled shotgun. He broke the shotgun and deliberately inserted two shells. He snapped the barrels into firing position and started for the door that led to the hospital corridor.

"I'm warning you," Boyd shouted after the man, "I'll not only witness against you, I'll have to say Lafe was unconscious. So it couldn't be self-defense."

Those words caused the man to stop, turn back to glare at Boyd. For a moment Kate feared he might raise his gun and aim it at Boyd. But the other man, younger but no less angry, was forced to concede. "He means it, Ez, he means it." The man called Ez lowered his shotgun, paused, silent for a moment, before he said huskily, "There'll be another time, another way." He stomped out of the E.R. and his companion followed.

Once they heard the old truck start off, Kate asked, "Is this why you insisted on waiting?" Boyd nodded. "And is that why Crispin was so insistent on finding out if his son was shot from front or back?"

"It's the code of the mountain people. That man there, lying dead? He knew that if you shoot a man in the back you are begging for retribution."

"And now what?" Kate demanded. "Will there be more retribution?"

"If his folks think that his killing was unjustified, yes, there will be."

"And what does the law have to say about this?" Kate asked.

"You've just seen the law operate," Boyd said simply.

"But that's savagery, not law. No trial, no jury, just grab a shotgun and be your own law! This is 1984, not pioneer days!"

The outraged look on her face prompted Boyd to take her hand and hold her dimpled chin so firmly that she had to look into his face.

"Before you condemn them, try to understand them."

"All I know, there was a killing, a cold, deliberate killing, and you, a physician, are trying to justify it!" But in that moment she realized, as did he, that she had turned her anger at the mountain people against him. Suddenly it was important to her what he thought and said and felt. She tried to turn away. He couldn't let her.

"What I think matters to you, doesn't it?" he asked.

She tried to deny it with a shake of her head, his strong hand wouldn't permit it. He kissed her, a fierce kiss, which seemed to contain a mixture of love and anger. She resisted kissing him back. But it was plain to both of them that next time she might not be able to resist. He allowed her to slip free.

For a moment they were silent at their discovery of each other's feelings. To evade further intimacy, Boyd began to explain.

"You have to understand how these people came to be this way. When they first came here they chose this place because most of them were from the highlands of Scotland. They chose these mountains, these hollows, these valleys and rivers because it reminded them of the grandeur of their homeland. And like all immigrants in this new nation, they wanted to live among their own kind, for safety, for reassurance.

"Listen to them talk, and you can still hear accents of Elizabethan England, the burr of old Scotland. Their language may sound quaint to you but not to the English ear. Isolation from the outside world has deprived them of taking the usual course of other immigrants, who, in a generation or two, assimilate with the rest of the population.

"Their seclusion hasn't all been of their own choosing. When the first railroads were laid out, these rugged mountains were considered unconquerable. When state roads were built, it was deemed too costly to build through here. So history bypassed these people as well as the abundant natural resources buried here.

"Funny," he said, beginning to chuckle. Kate admired the way his eyes lit up and his tan cheeks wrinkled when he laughed. Even his close-cropped beard could not hide that. "History plays odd tricks. Thousands of miles from here the Arabs and the Israelis get into a war. The Arabs declare an oil embargo and the echoes are heard up here in our mountains. Suddenly Big Betsy is brought up. The trucks start to roll. There is prosperity in the land."

Big Betsy, Kate recalled hearing that name before. The first day. Harlan Jessup had mentioned it.

"Of course," Boyd said, no longer amused, "now that the Arabs don't have their greedy hands on the throats of the western nations, who knows what will happen here?"

"Who is Big Betsy?"

Boyd chuckled again. "You don't know? You've never seen her? Well, one day when you can tear yourself away from your studies I'll drive you up to have a look. Quite a sight. Now, if you're off duty, I'll walk you home."

The early summer sun was rising in the east. It cast its red-gold light on the mountaintop. To the west the silver crescent of a moon was still in sight but beginning to set behind the tallest range. The single main street of Adelphi was quiet. The huge coal trucks had not yet begun to rumble by. There was silence except for the far-off baying of a hound, companion to an early-morning hunter.

As they walked along, Kate looked up at the grandeur of the surrounding mountains. This was far far different from the early walks along city streets that she was used to.

"Take a good look," Boyd said regretfully. "Who knows how long these mountains and valleys will remain green and sweet-smelling."

"You love this place," Kate said.

"Love it, yes. But I hate some things about it. The poverty. What it does to people."

"They aren't all poor," Kate reminded. For she had seen some fine homes on the edges of the small town.

"My people are," Boyd said.

"You've come out of it," Kate said.

"True. But there are children back in those hills with far greater abilities than mine who will never get the chance. Whose eyes are never turned to the outside world, who are never given the incentive . . ." His voice trailed off.

They had reached the Russell house.

"Some coffee?" she asked. "Mrs. Russell bakes delicious cake.

She's taken to spoiling me, I'm afraid. Thinks I'm getting too thin, that I work too hard. Nights she'll get up and bring me some tea and cake while I'm studying."

"Some coffee would go down nicely right about now," he agreed.

So as not to disturb Mrs. Russell, she led him around the house to the back door. Soon she had the coffee bubbling in the percolator and the kitchen table set. Through all the preparations he watched her, admiring the graceful way she performed even the most ordinary household task. Until he realized it was her face and her shining blond hair he really admired.

"Will you be staying on here?" he asked.

"I have to, for nine more months," Kate explained.

"I mean after."

"I only planned on the year."

"And then?" Boyd asked.

"Some place where my training and skill will be appreciated."

"They'd be appreciated right here," Boyd pointed out.

Kate felt herself blush. For his invitation sounded more personal than professional. "My plans don't call for it," she said.

"Your plans . . . there's a man in them, isn't there?"

"Yes," she admitted, feeling a little self-conscious.

"If I'm being too inquisitive, say so."

"I've nothing to hide," Kate said.

"Are you sparkin', courtin' or already talkin' to?" he asked, and smiled at her puzzlement. "That's mountain language."

Now she smiled, too. "Then you'd better explain."

"Well," he began, "sparkin' in your language would be dating."

"Courtin' I can guess would mean something like going steady?" When he nodded she asked, "And talkin' to?"

"That's mighty serious. Talkin' to means courting with a view to getting married."

"Ah, I see."

"But you haven't answered *my* question," he pointed out. "Which is it with you, sparkin', courtin', or talkin' to?"

She hesitated, then a shy smile stole into her face. Her eyes sparkled as she teased. "Is there a mountain word for when one party is in the 'talkin' to' stage but the other isn't?"

Boyd smiled, too, as he responded, "The right word for that is 'encouraging.' "

"I don't get the connection," she said, puzzled.

"Well, ma'am, if'n one party isn't in the 'talkin' to' stage, then *I* am very very encouraged. And that isn't mountain talk."

Now he was no longer smiling but frankly declaring his feelings.

"Look," Kate began, protesting. "I don't want you to think . . ."

"You can't stop me from thinking," he said. "Or hoping."

"I told you why I'm here. And when I'm going to leave. I wouldn't want you to feel that I misled you in any way."

"And I wouldn't want to mislead you, Kate. So I'll tell you my feelings straight out. I think I'm falling in love with you. No, I think I have already fallen in love with you," he declared simply.

"You don't even know me," she said.

"I know enough."

"Schoolboys talk that way, not mature men," she said, trying to discourage him.

"Love is an emotion, it's not supposed to be mature."

"I told you, there's another man," she protested.

"You also told me you aren't sure."

"Look, Doctor . . ."

He interrupted. "Don't call me Doctor. Right now I'm not being professional. I am a man with a given name. Say it. Raymond. Ray. Try it. It can't hurt."

"Okay," she said reluctantly, "Look, *Raymond*, I told you there was another man. And if I haven't made up my mind, that doesn't mean I intend to encourage any other man until I do. So please, don't let's get involved and find out it's been a mistake. That would be painful for both of us."

Boyd shook his head. "I don't think you're afraid of being hurt. I think you're afraid of having your careful plans upset. Nine months to serve and you're free. You're not here to serve but to be served!" he accused.

"Look, it's late and I've got an early morning test."

"Of course. Sorry." He started for the kitchen door. She rose to see him out, but he said, "Don't bother. But thanks for the coffee. And tell Mrs. Russell she bakes good as ever."

"You've had her cake before?" Kate asked.

"When I was just a mountain kid I used to gather wood for her, build up her fires on winter mornings, so when she came back from the hospital the place'd be nice and warm for her."

"The hospital? She never told me . . ." Kate said.

"She was one of the first of the family nurses. And one of the best of the midwives. She's a legend up in the mountains. They still talk about Aunt Elvira," Boyd explained. "She was the one inspired me to go to the university. And later to med school."

"She's never said a word about anything like that."

"She is a great lady, and therefore not much for talking about her own accomplishments," Boyd said. He stared at her for a long, meaningful moment, then said softly, "Kate Kincaid, I'm 'afeared' it's too late. I'm already too much in love to be discouraged."

CHAPTER 10

The onset of summer, the warm, clear, inviting days of late June to which the three students had looked forward, only served to increase their hospital duties. Twice they had planned to ask Abbott for a day off together to go climbing up into the mountains for a picnic. Twice their plans were frustrated by sudden assignments. For in the mountains, summer meant an influx of tourists. And with tourists, especially those unused to driving the narrow, twisting mountain roads, came the inevitable increase in automobile accidents, as well as snakebite victims and an occasional patient in shock from an anaphylactic reaction to a bee or hornet sting.

As if intentionally, Abbott always managed to assign one of them to Emergency at all hours of day or night. Once, immediately after they had completed their first trimester exams, Kate, Ellen and Emily did manage to steal off together. But then only for a few hours, hardly enough time to scale any mountains. They spent the hot afternoon at the school's outdoor swimming pool, which was opened to the public once the academic year was over.

Even on that afternoon, Abbott had dispatched a messenger to find them and summon Kate back. Emergency was overloaded and a radio message from State Patrol put them on alert for an accident victim being helicoptered in after a mountain fall. Kate was to receive the victim.

The same afternoon she had to call in Ray Boyd from the Critchfield Outpost where he was holding clinic hours. But for this particular emergency he arrived too late. A four-year-old girl, unprotected by a seatbelt or a safety seat, had crashed head first against the windshield of the family camper when her father lost control of the vehicle and it went off the road. By the time Ray was able to get there, the child had expired in Kate's arms.

For the first time since she arrived at Mountain Hospital, Kate Kincaid broke down and cried. Ray tried to comfort her, embracing her, pressing her wet face against his chest.

"Wasn't anything you could do, Kate. Nothing anybody could do to save that little girl." He tried to console her. "In fact, with that kind of brain damage, maybe this was the best way."

"The best way would have been if she hadn't been injured in the first place!" Kate protested. "Murder, that's what it was. And because of her father's carelessness." She burst into a fresh flood of tears.

"Kate, Kate, you've been going at it too hard. For too long. Three months without a letup. You need to get away from classrooms, medical books, clinics and emergencies. You need a break. Let's go get some fresh air."

"I can't leave. They need me," she insisted.

"If we had to answer every time they 'need' us we'd have no lives of our own," Ray said. "Let's go."

"But Abbott . . ." she started to protest.

"I'll tell her that you deserve a break, especially since you passed your first trimester exams with flying colors."

"I did?" Kate asked.

"Yes."

She was delighted and relieved, because for the past week she had been reliving that long, difficult exam and regretting some answers she would have improved upon if Abbott had given them a second chance.

"How did you know?" she asked.

"Simple. I asked," Ray explained. "I am interested in everything you do. I look upon you as a terminal addiction."

"Ray, please."

"Okay. Sorry. But that doesn't change the fact that you need a break. Let's go! If there's any problem later I'll explain to Abbott."

She hesitated only a moment before agreeing.

* * *

Ray Boyd's Jeep climbed the rough road that had been bulldozed out of dense forest. Wide enough to be a superhighway, it was unpaved and packed down by the huge, deep-treaded tires of giant trucks, some of which passed them on the way down.

Kate leaned back, staring up at stately pines that almost crowded out the sky. The warmth of the day enhanced the fragrance of the pines, like warming up brandy enriches its pungency.

"Do we ever get to the top?" Kate asked.

"Soon," Ray said.

Coal trucks so large it seemed each could engulf half a dozen Jeeps descended in a steady flow. The drivers, recognizing their doctor, waved to him. Ray waved back.

Soon his Jeep catapulted up over the last rim of a hill. Kate was startled. She sat up stiffly and peered straight ahead.

There, in the center of a vast clearing, stood a huge, intricate machine taller than a fifteen-story building. Its structure of bare metal girders resembled the skeletons of prehistoric dinosaurs Kate had seen when as a college student she had visited the Museum of Natural History in New York. But this monstrous mechanism stood taller than those, far, far taller. Perched at the top was a cab housing one man who seemed to control the beast.

Extending from its body was a long steel arm, at the end of which an enormous bucket was digging into a vein of exposed coal in the raw earth. In one groaning, grinding move the scoop lifted a load so great that the single bucketful filled to overflowing the first of a line of huge trucks that stood waiting.

One loaded truck drove off and the next in line pulled up. Another deep sweep of the monster's arm and its bucket dug into the coal with an angry crunch that echoed from the mountaintops. It dropped its cargo of coal into the second truck and sent it on its way.

As she stared at the spectacle of man tearing nature's bounty out of her belly in such giant bites, Ray said, "You asked about Big Betsy. That's her. That's why the need to cut that wide road through the trees. She had to be brought up here on her own, like a ponderous, slow-footed monster laboring across the face of the earth."

"You resent her?" Kate asked.

"She put three thousand miners out of work. She can dig more coal in a day than they could in a week," he said. "So now all that's left for them is to drive trucks or go on relief. Which all of them hate to do."

He took her hand. As they started for the monster, a man at its base came toward them. When he drew closer, Kate recognized Harlan Jessup. He recognized her, too, waved and broke into a trot to reach them sooner. Or, Kate wondered, to keep them from coming too close? Because there was something defensive in his attitude when he reached her.

"Come to see my girl, have you?" he asked. "Well, there she is." With a wide sweep of his hand he invited Kate to take a closer look.

She started toward Big Betsy, Ray on one side of her, Jessup on the other, ready to catch her if she stumbled on the broken earth. She made it to the foot of the monster without incident.

"It's a great view from up top," Harlan said.

He held out his hand, she gave him hers. The three of them started to climb. All the while the monster strained and clanked while it gouged bucketfuls of coal out of the earth and dropped them into the trucks with an explosive crash. The sound of the scoop ripping into the coal was awesome. It reflected a grinding struggle, as if the earth were fighting to retain what belonged to it.

"Look around," Harlan Jessup said.

From up in the cab, hundreds of feet above the mountaintop, Kate had the most imposing view of the Appalachian Mountains she would ever have. Viewed from a plane, the forests were too remote. From this height they were real. She could look out and see tall pine and spruce that stretched to infinity. And here and there a patch of blue where a lake inhabited a crater left by some Ice Age formation. She could see silver rivers threading their way through green forests to get lost and then reappear when the trees thinned out and afforded a view once more. Around her the air was fragrant with the smell of pine and wildflowers, but it was also tainted by the smell of fresh-turned earth, which caused her to lower her eyes from the distant horizon and stare down at the devastation the monster, Big Betsy, had created on this single mountain.

Below there was no green. Every tree had been cut down and hauled away. All that remained was rough earth and, where the monster had not yet attacked, underbrush. Where the monster had invaded, there were gaping holes in the brown-black soil. It was a scene of devastation that rivaled World War II films Kate had seen.

"Good God!" she said softly, in shock.

"Yeah," Harlan Jessup said. "Looks pretty bad now. But it won't stay that way. You see, the company has a whole plan laid out. When we're done, another crew moves in. They level this place, seed it, grade it to make the most of the rains that will come. And someday—it'll take time, but someday this whole flattened area will be . . ." He broke off suddenly. To cover his embarrassment he shouted an order to the operator who, until that moment, had run the monster very efficiently.

"Look," Jessup said, "if you two have seen enough, we can go. I have work to do."

Kate looked at Boyd, who nodded and said, "Sure. We've seen enough."

Jessup climbed down with them. At the foot of the monster he said, "I'm glad you came. Hope you enjoyed it." His words could not quite conceal his discomfort.

"It's incredible," Kate said. "I never would have believed it."

"Was a time I wouldn't either," Jessup said. "My grandpaw sure wouldn't."

Mention of his grandfather made him look around at the mountains.

"He loved these mountains. There's a magic in them. People born and brought up here never forget them. No matter how far away they go, or high up they get in this life. There was something fine and clean and righteous here, even about the poverty."

He glanced back at the monster before saying, "Sometimes I feel I'm being disloyal to my heritage. Tearing down the trees, digging out the mountains."

"It's brought prosperity to some of these people, Jess." Boyd tried to console him. "Long overdue for most of them."

"I reassure myself from time to time by saying we're going to replace the tops of useless mountains with great flat plains that will turn into golden fields of grain, orchards bearing all kinds of rich fruit. But"—he paused before confessing—"at night, especially when it's raining hard, I lie awake, thinking, we're tampering with nature. What if one of these rainy nights these flattened mountaintops, with no trees to bind them, just slide down into the valley, choke off the rivers, sweep the cabins before them and devastate everything?''

Kate had to respect the tender sensibilities of this big, brawny young man, expert in his profession but with grave doubts about its ultimate purpose and value.

''That's progress, Harlan,'' Kate said consolingly. ''Every advance in civilization exacts its price.''

''Price?'' Harlan questioned. ''Do you realize it'll take hundreds of years to return this mountaintop to what it was? Our civilization may be gone before that. You have to wonder, is it worth it?''

He took a long look at the monster as it scooped up tons of the coal in one angry lurch. ''One thing to the good. We're actually cutting down now. With the oil glut, we're digging less, using fewer trucks. Maybe soon it'll stop altogether. Maybe.''

On the drive down the wide rugged road, passing empty coal trucks which were on their way up, neither Kate nor Ray Boyd spoke.

Near the foot of the mountain road Kate said, ''It's an inevitable struggle. Nature against progress.''

''Now I'm going to take you up into *my* mountains,'' Ray said.

He was heading his Jeep up a narrow dirt road that only a four-wheel-drive vehicle could conquer. With the top down and the light early summer breeze on their faces, the air was refreshing, relaxing. Kate breathed it in as if drinking new spring wine. This was the first time since she had arrived here that she felt completely at ease and free. There was no class awaiting her, no assignment in the Clinic, no demonstration she had to attend, no manual to grapple with, no stack of medical monographs to read. Free. To lean back in her seat and stare up at the blue sky. To have the luxury of watching a cloud go by shepherded by the summer wind.

Boyd glanced at her from the corner of his eye, observing the change in her. She was no longer the tense, overpurposeful young woman whose beauty was ofttimes marred by furrows of worry in her brow. She no longer appeared to be on trial or angry with the world. He wondered, is there such a thing as being too dedicated?

She was staring at the mountain peaks ranged one beyond the other to infinity when she felt the Jeep come to a stop.

''This is it,'' he said.

"What?"

"The place we used to climb to when we were kids," he explained. "We'd come up here, lugging our rifles all the way, thinking if we came across something, a rabbit, a wild hog, a deer or even a bear, we'd bring home some fresh meat. But we knew that mainly we had come up to see the world. Our world. Like off there." He pointed to the distant mountains. "Places we only studied about. Names like Kentucky, Virginia, Ohio. They were schoolbook names to us. We never thought we'd ever see those places, not really. This was our home, our hollers, our mountains, our rivers, and they were enough."

"It is beautiful," Kate said.

"Which your cities are not," Boyd said soberly.

"That why you came back?"

"Yep," he said, as if he were a barefoot mountain boy again. "It was uncommon good, our hill country. Not just tolerable, but uncommon good."

"Is that the only reason?" she asked.

"Nope," he admitted. "I felt I owed them. They're my kin, and those who aren't kin are related to me by a tie almost as strong. They're mountain people. Part of me, and me part of them."

"I've seen doctors from the best medical schools and in one of the best hospitals. You're as good as any of them. You could do very well out there," Kate said.

"I'm content here."

"You don't know, you didn't give yourself a chance."

He smiled. "Now who's the doctor, who's prescribing?"

"*Are* you running away?" she asked frankly.

"No!" he protested at once. Then he relented and after a silent moment he said, "Yes, but not from what you think."

"Then what?"

"It don't bear talking about," he said, sounding like a mountain boy again.

"Well, if it ever does . . ." Kate said. "I'd be willing to listen."

He climbed out of the Jeep and walked to the edge of the precipice, below which was a sheer wall of exposed rock that seemed to plunge a thousand feet into the tops of an endless forest of green pines. He looked out over the valley and toward the mountains beyond. Kate came to stand alongside him.

Never once taking his eyes from the vista that stretched before them for hundreds of miles, he started talking.

"What it was, was a girl," he admitted softly. "Am I allowed to use the word 'girl' to a liberated woman like you? She was dark-haired and just about shoulder high to me. Pretty. With sparkling black eyes that spoke to you. I mean you could read every thought, every feeling in those eyes. And she was bright, bright as anyone in our class."

"Med school?" Kate asked.

"Uh-huh. She had ideas, big ideas. Bigger than any I ever had. In our last year we studied together." He hesitated, and admitted, "'Course, that wasn't all we did together. She had her own place. We were alone a good part of the time. It was natural, what happened. And wonderful. We talked about getting married. Talked a lot about it. She had me to her home, to meet her folks. Nice people. Nice as they could be to me. Her father mainly. I got the feeling her mother'd rather she had picked some other man, more her own kind of man. But not her father. First time I met him he told me how he had started as a door-to-door commission salesman of household things, then worked his way up to banking and investing.

"Came graduation, we both got appointments to the same hospital. Her father arranged that. He had influence in all kinds of places.

"End of our first year of internship, just living together didn't seem enough. Not to me, anyhow. So I went, like a man is supposed to, to call on her father and announce my intention. He seemed amused about how seriously I took the matter of marrying. I said where I came from that was the most serious thing a man ever did. He laughed and said, 'In our circle, marrying is serious, too, but divorce settlements are more serious.'

"Then he got around to talking about my prospects. When I told him what I wanted to do, he seemed highly disturbed. He didn't see the value in our just practicing medicine. When I protested that's why we spent years studying, he got up from his chair and started pacing the length of that long long library of his. Bigger than our whole public library in Adelphi, I can tell you.

"'Son,' he said, 'I didn't send my daughter to medical school so she could come out and practice in some little town, romantic as that might sound. Nor did I educate her so she could open an office on Park Avenue in New York, or in Dallas, Beverly Hills or those other places where doctors are supposed to make fortunes. Which they in turn pay to the damned government. Practicing medicine is okay, I guess. But in this day and age a doctor has to be a businessman, too. And a tax expert. There is a way to make money in medicine and keep it. That's the secret, son, not earning money, keeping it! That's the bottom line!'

"I sat there and listened while that man unfolded an idea he'd had from the beginning. His bank would lend us enough money to buy a CAT scanner. Almost a million dollars. And we would set up an office just to do scans. The interest on the loan would be deductible, the rent and the staff would be deductible. So we'd pay practically no taxes. When that was under way, we'd open another office with another CAT scanner and another staff. And then another. The trick was never to pay taxes and to keep using the bank's money. After seven or eight years, when we'd opened maybe a dozen of those places and paid them off, we'd sell it all for millions, make one big capital gain and be set for life.

"All without practicing medicine. When he was done he looked at me as if he expected me to applaud. I didn't say anything. Not till I could talk to Sandy. She wouldn't agree with her father.

"But she did. And she'd always assumed I'd be delighted to go along because the money would mean so much that Medicine wouldn't matter. Once she found out I didn't feel that way, things changed between us.

"First we stopped talking about marriage. Then we just stopped talking. Then we stopped seeing each other. It was over. Quietly. No big quarrels. But it was as over as anything between two people could be.

"So I came back here."

"Where you can practice medicine among people who appreciate it," Kate concluded.

"Funny thing," Ray said. "Folks all thought I came home because I had no choice. They always think that a doctor only comes here when he's a failure."

They stared at the awesome expanse of land before them. After a time, she asked, "Do you still think about her?"

"Times," he said, "but not lately."

"It's wearing off," she said.

"No," he said. "Now there's someone else I think about."

Immediately the atmosphere between them changed.

"We ought to go back," Kate said. "We've been away almost all afternoon."

She started to go. He reached out and caught her hand. She resisted. But when he drew her to him, she went easily. They embraced. They kissed, a long kiss, deeply felt. She broke free.

"We're both doing this to forget someone else," she said.

"That part of me is long gone. Buried. In the past. Like it never happened. You?"

She didn't answer. Because she didn't know the answer. He kissed her again. When he started to unbutton her blouse, she did not resist. When he kissed her breasts, she pressed his head against her body.

When it was over, they lay on their backs staring up at the blue sky and each wondered what would be the end of it.

CHAPTER 11

Kate was putting on the one dressy dress she had brought with her, a pink and white print, which was a welcome relief from dark slacks and plain blue shirts or the white pants and jackets she sometimes wore in the clinic. This was the first time she had worn it since she arrived. The occasion was the night of Adelphi's Fourth of July celebration. The parking lot in front of the hospital had been cleared of cars. Lights had been strung over the area, the wires wrapped around with red, white and blue bunting. A small, temporary bandstand had been erected. From her room at Mrs. Russell's, Kate could already hear the native fiddlers and banjo players beating out rhythmic square-dance music that sounded brighter and more genuine than the imitations heard at sophisticated country-club square dances, which were only city people playing at rustic dancing.

She stood before the mirror, appraising herself. Her dress hung a trifle more loosely than it once had. The arduous past three months had taken a bit of weight off her. But she was satisfied that she looked good. She felt defiantly satisfied. For Howard's letter, which she had received only yesterday, was a proposal of marriage and practically an ultimatum, which had both touched and angered her.

If only Howard had not written, "By this time you must have got hillbilly medicine out of your system, so admit it's a mistake and come home."

But she had resented even more the sentence that followed.

"When a man becomes a partner in the firm, his wife is expected to entertain clients and other partners."

She resisted being cast in the role of a business appendage. Getting married seemed more important to Howard than getting married to *her*. So it was with special and almost vengeful care that she dressed and made up for this evening. She took one final look at herself in the brightly colored dress, touched up her makeup for the last time, wrapped her white knit shawl around her shoulders, pulled it down in front to see how she would look with a little cleavage showing, and was defiantly ready for the evening as she murmured, "How do you like that, Hawk?"

Once she stepped out onto the porch, the music sounded louder and brighter. Mrs. Russell was leaning against the porch pillar, her head bobbing in time with the music, as she said, "Nothing to the ear like a real mountain violin."

"Aren't you coming?" Kate asked.

"Who'd dance with an old lady?"

"Please come," Kate insisted, "if only to watch."

The old woman considered it a moment. Then, with a saucy smile, she replied, "By God, there must be an old man or two there."

They reached the dance area and found it crowded. Hospital staff, townspeople, families from out of the mountains, all mingled together. The little band—a guitar, two banjos, and two violins—was vigorously playing a stomping kind of music that compelled one to dance. Kate seized Mrs. Russell's hand. They moved into one group, which broke formation to make room for them. The caller interpolated his personal welcome to them into his rhythmic chant.

Kate was surprised and delighted to see Sister Ellen dancing as lustily as the rest of them. When Kate smiled at her, Ellen smiled back, as if to say, yes, nuns are human, too, they know joy and love to show it.

The music and the dancing continued without a break. From time to time dancers dropped out to refresh themselves from the two large galvanized iron tubs of lemonade and punch afloat with chunks of ice. Kate was ladling herself a cup of punch when a familiar voice said, "Let me." She turned to confront Ray Boyd. She allowed him to pour for her. They stood side by side watching the dancers in the glow from the varicolored lights.

"I haven't seen you the last few days," he said, "except to pass you in the corridors."

Trying to evade the real intent of his rebuke, she said, "I've been busy. Studying for exams, clinic, you know how it is."

"No, I really don't know how it is," he said.

"Ray, what happened between us was . . . was an accident."

"What happened between us happened because both people wanted it to happen."

"Please, I'd rather not talk about it."

"Why? Howard?"

"The one thing you may be sure of, it's not Howard," she said, her early anger rekindled by the mention of his name.

"Then what?" Ray persisted.

"There can only be frustration and great pain for both of us. Nine months from now, I'll be leaving here."

"You'd never consider staying on?"

"Not a day longer than it takes to finish. The world I'm looking for is bigger than this."

"I've been there," he said. "It may be bigger but it's hardly more satisfying."

"Please, Ray, I'd rather dance," she said, starting toward the dancers, but he seized her hand suddenly. She stared into his eyes, then down at his strong hand.

He released her at once. "Yes; let's dance."

They joined one of the groups. For the rest of the long dance, though the order of the call kept them apart, Ray kept his eyes on her, and she was conscious of him every moment. The more aware she was of his glances, the more she was reminded of that afternoon on that secluded mountain. If it was not love, she could not deny that it was passion. She had been a woman alone too long.

She deliberately avoided him by fixing on the other dancers. She was surprised and delighted to see that Mrs. Russell had found a friendly, smiling, ruddy-faced white-haired man; they seemed to be dancing animatedly and enjoying each other.

The music had ended. Everyone faced the mountain that towered behind the hospital and waited expectantly. Soon an explosion of red and gold light burst above them from the mountaintop. The long-awaited fireworks display had begun. The explosive sounds of giant firecrackers echoed from mountain peak to mountain peak, reinforcing the flashes of colorful light that burst, then seemed to float in space and slowly disappeared until the sky was dark again. With every fresh burst of light, Ray Boyd watched Kate's face, her graceful profile accented by the brightness until it faded away into the night.

Eventually the sight and sound of the fireworks were over. The warm July air was still again and smelled of gunpowder. The sky was dark. The little band did not start up again. The dancing was over. The tubs of lemonade and punch had been drained down to melting ice. Most people had begun to depart for their homes. Kate looked around for Mrs. Russell, but discovered she had gone. The night air was cooler now. Kate pulled her shawl about her and started for the house. Ray caught up with her.

"May I walk you home?"

"Yes. Please," she said, for the celebration, the dancing, participating in such a happy event with strangers had made her aware of how lonely she had become in the busy months she had been here. She was glad to have a man by her side. She was even willing to reconsider Howard's note a proposal, not an ultimatum.

Realizing how vulnerable she was, when they reached the front gate of the house she tried to bid Ray Boyd good night. Somehow she could not, without first justifying herself.

"Don't misunderstand, Ray. I didn't come here to use this place and then desert it. I came to learn, to qualify if I can, so I can go out and practice what they taught me for the benefit of many other people."

"No matter your reason for being here, as we mountain people say, it shore pleasures me a heap ter have ye around," he said.

She looked up at him and could not resist smiling. He smiled back.

" 'Course we also say, don't go hurryin' away none."

"Please, Ray . . ."

"And when someone gets ready to go, we say, honey, take keer o' yereself 'n' git nice and fat. Though with a terrific figure like yours, don't do anything as foolish as that."

"I really have to go in. We have our first class in Family Practice tomorrow at eight."

She started up the path to the porch. He took her hand, gently this time, and drew her close. He kissed her. She made a pretense at resisting, but knew she did not want to. She kissed him back. It felt good to be in a man's arms again and to feel him wanting her.

In the seclusion of her own room they made love. And after, in the hush that followed, he whispered, "Kate Kincaid, I love you. No matter where you go, no matter what you do, that's a burden you'll have to carry with you. Making me fall in love with you was your doin'."

"I never intended . . ."

He smothered her protest with a kiss.

Some time later when they lay spent and quiet, she asked, "Coffee?"

"Would go right fine 'bout now," he agreed.

She wrapped her robe about her and went out to the kitchen. The kettle was on the stove, steaming. There was a fresh-baked cake waiting. And the table had been set for two.

Mrs. Russell, of course. Had she anticipated what Kate herself had not even suspected?

Early the next morning Kate dressed hastily to be in time for class. When she came out into the kitchen, Mrs. Russell was waiting with coffee and fresh biscuits. There was no hint of reproach or even acknowledgment. The old woman poured the coffee for her and asked, "Would you like some peach preserve with your biscuits, dear?"

"I really have no time . . ." Kate said.

"It's my own homemade . . ."

"All right, a little," Kate said, to please the old woman.

CHAPTER 12

The three months of the course in Family Practice had gone by quickly, almost too quickly for Kate. She would have wanted to learn more, to be better prepared before having to face the difficult written and oral exams that would qualify her to become a practicing family nurse.

But here they were, Kate Kincaid, Sister Ellen and Emily McClendon, listening to their last lecture from Mrs. Sturges, a review really, in preparation for their exams.

Successfully completing this second trimester was a milestone for them. It marked not only the completion of their first half year, but would qualify them to go out and practice in many states. Some students settled for family nursing and left after the first six months. But not Kate, not Ellen, not Emily. They were here for the duration, but the duration depended on successfully concluding this course. Failing now would prevent them from going on to their main objective, Midwifery.

Sturges was stressing the detection and treatment of a pulmonary embolus, citing the signs and symptoms to be alert for in making the diagnosis.

"Sudden breathlessness is the most usual presenting sign. Sometimes followed by hemoptysis. This spitting up of blood is often accompanied by pleuritic pain. In some patients this may be preceded by recent thrombophlebitis . . ."

She reacted with great annoyance when the door opened suddenly. It was a messenger delivering a note. Sturges glanced at it hastily, prepared to ignore it, but then read it a second time.

"Kincaid, Abbott would like to see you."

"Yes, ma'am. Soon as class is over," Kate replied, embarrassed to be the subject of the interruption.

"Her note says 'at once,'" Sturges informed her.

"At once?" Kate was puzzled by such an unaccustomed interruption in their class routine. "Yes, of course."

She left her books and accompanied the messenger.

Abbott was most formal. "Kincaid, I've been looking at your record."

"I thought I've done well during my second trimester," Kate started to protest.

"Sit down, sit down," Abbott urged impatiently. "I have a problem. An emergency."

"If there's anything I can do . . ." Kate started to volunteer.

"Samuels, one of the two nurses in our Wildwood Outpost, has to go into City Hospital. An ovarian difficulty. May need a biopsy."

"Oh, I'm sorry," Kate said.

"That leaves us one nurse short in an area where there should be at least two nurses on duty at all times. I want you to fill in until Samuels returns. It may be a day or two, but possibly longer. However, I cannot make allowances as regards your exams. That's a state requirement. So if you have any doubts about making up any missed study and all the reading that goes with it, say so now."

"I'll do my best," Kate said.

"The question is, will your best be good enough?"

"It always has been before," Kate said.

"Dr. Boyd said you are always quite sure of yourself," Abbott remarked.

At the mention of his name, Kate felt a flush rise into her cheeks. She studied Abbott's eyes to see if the older woman detected what their relationship had become. Abbott gave no indication.

She said only, "There's a Jeep out in the parking lot. Take one of the saddlebags, make sure it is filled with all the medication and supplies required for house calls, and get going. I have sketched out this little map to show you how to get to Wildwood."

As Abbott held out the map, Kate asked, "Why me?"

"What?"

"I'm curious. Sister Ellen and McClendon have both done very well this trimester. Why did you choose me?"

"Because nursing isn't all cramming, filling in in clinic or even getting good grades. We knew you could do that before we accepted you," Abbott said. "So don't consider this a reward."

"You mean, I'm still on trial?" Kate asked, trying to conceal her resentment.

"Until the day you three finally qualify, you are all on trial," Abbott said firmly.

"Mostly me?" Kate asked.

"Kincaid, if you'd rather not replace Samuels for a few days . . ." Abbott started to say.

This time Kate interrupted, "Now, I insist on replacing her!"

Abbott studied her for a long moment, then held out the map once more. Kate proceeded to the supply room and the pharmacy to collect all the equipment and medications she would need. When she slipped into the driver's seat of the Jeep, she did so aggressively.

Still on trial, was she? She'd show Abbott! She'd show them all!

The drive along the remote two-lane blacktop road convinced her of one thing. Potholes were not an affliction limited to city streets. Twice she had to wrestle the Jeep back on the road after it almost catapulted off when it struck a deep, jagged hole. She persevered, wondering all the while what would happen if she were traveling the same road with a sick patient who needed emergency hospitalization. Or suppose she were confronted by one of those huge coal trucks while fighting to control the Jeep.

She passed through two little towns, which consisted of no more than a gas station and a general store displaying weatherbeaten old signs advertising bourbon and chewing tobacco. Beyond the second town she found the turnoff road Abbott had designated on her rough map. She started up the hill. At the crest of it she came on a small, brown-stained wood-frame building with a modest handpainted sign: *Wildwood Outpost.* She pulled up alongside the squat one-story building.

When she entered the waiting room, she found all four chairs occupied and several mothers and their small children standing. Kate announced herself to the young dark-haired girl at the reception desk.

"Thank God" was all the girl said. She immediately directed Kate toward an inner room, where she found another nurse examining a young woman who, to judge from her size, was at least in her seventh month.

Without looking up from her patient the nurse asked, "Kincaid?"

"Yes," Kate replied. "Just tell me what to do and I'll take some of that case load off your hands," indicating the waiting room outside.

"I'll handle those," the nurse said. "But there are folks up in the hollers that need looking after." She had completed her examination and said to the young mother, "You're coming along fine, Annie. No problems. But come back in two weeks, hear?"

"Yes, Leona," the young woman said and began to get dressed.

"Now then," the nurse turned to Kate. "Owens is my name. Leona Owens."

"Kate," she informed the nurse.

"Okay, Kate. Eva out at the desk will give you a list of families to visit. And instructions on how to get to them. She will also give you their charts. After that, you're on your own. Try to get back before dark, else you'll get lost and we'll have a devil of a time trying to rescue you."

As they reached the doorway to the crowded waiting room, Kate asked, "Is it always this way here?"

"This is nothing. But you have to take the time to talk to each of them. If they ever get the feeling you're rushing them, you lose their confidence."

Owens turned Kate over to Eva, the young secretary, who gave her the list and all pertinent medical data about each member of each family. She also gave Kate a brief description of the hollows, roads, streams and rivers she would have to overcome to reach her patients. After studying the instructions, Kate set out, aware for the first time of the burden of responsibility that rests on a family nurse.

Her first stop was a wooden shack hardly perceptible from the paved road. It was perched atop a hillside like some stray boulder that had been deposited there by an Ice Age glacier. The Jeep would never make it, so Kate seized her saddlebags and started to climb, rehearsing in her mind the medical history of the occupant. Rufus Bates, age seventy-two, widower, no family. Health good for a man his age, despite a tendency to certain nutritional deficiencies due to existing on his own crops and cookery. His greatest need was for vitamins by injection, especially vitamins A and E. On his chart were the underlined words: *Refuses to take vitamins by mouth, resents them as newfangled inventions*.

The sight that greeted Kate as she climbed was one that would become quite familiar during her stay in Adelphi. Though no two homes in these hollers were exactly the same, they all had certain characteristics in common.

The houses themselves were of weathered wood, gray from age, many rains and much snow. Each had a roof that slanted down in the direction of her approach. To one side of the house was a small patch of land, tilled and planted and, depending on the time of year, either low with sprouting stalks or tall with a crop of corn or beans, or green and yellow with ground-level growths of squash, pumpkin or watermelon. Bushes of wild berries abounded everywhere, blueberries, raspberries, strawberries.

And always, either in front of the house or to the side, there was some ancient possession, such as an old bedspring or the empty shell of an automobile forty or fifty years old, ofttimes covered with wire to serve as a coop for the chickens all mountain families kept and relied on for eggs and poultry. Their hard life had taught these people to discard nothing.

Now Kate observed another phenomenon to which she would become accustomed. Beyond the Bates house, farther up the holler, she could make out the simple headstones of a family burial plot. Mountain people buried their own, and close to home.

As Kate approached the Bates cabin, she was halted by the sound of a dog's angry growl. In a moment, from out of the door came tall, extremely thin Rufus Bates. He glared down at her suspiciously.

"Who are ye?" he called.

"Nurse Katherine Kincaid, from Wildwood," she replied.

"Ye don't look a nurse. Ye're too small. And too fair. Mostly they's sturdier in size and more plain to the look." He eyed her suspiciously until he relented. "Ye can come closer."

She climbed farther up the hill toward the bare wood porch,

which even from this distance showed the wear of so much scrubbing that the grain stood out clearly. Whatever else the man was, he was clean and neat. She felt somewhat encouraged.

"Show me," he said suddenly.

Puzzled, Kate did not know how to respond.

"If ye're what ye say, ye should have the stuff in that there bag. Eunice always did."

"Eunice?" Kate asked.

"If'n ye're the one ye say, ye'd know who Eunice is," he said accusingly. "Since ye say ye come to take her place."

"Oh. Yes," Kate said. "Miss Samuels. She's ill."

"Drinlin', is she? Too bad. Nice woman. Leastways, friendly." This last he said as if comparing the two nurses to Kate's detriment.

The word "drinlin'" was new to Kate but she assumed it meant sick, ill. She was sure of that when Bates asked, "Is she drinlin' bad or will she be comin' this way again?"

"She'll be back soon. In time for your next visit. Now, can we have a look at you, Mr. Bates?"

He shook his head sadly. "Mr. Bates, is it? Ye're from off, that's for sure. Mr. Bates," he repeated disapprovingly. "Come ye." He beckoned with his head, granting her permission to ascend to the porch.

Kate stood face to face with Bates and only then realized how tall the man was. He towered over her by two heads at least. She stared at his scrawny neck, where his weathered skin hung in loose wattles. His face was almost skeletonlike in its bony leanness, but tanned from exposure to the sun. She noted two discolorations on his left cheek that might be due to age, but were also cause to suspect skin cancer. She would note that on his chart.

"Says here," she began as she started to take out the equipment for his injection, "you're due for one of these shots today." She began to fill a hypodermic with the colorless solution. "Take off your shirt, please."

Bates balked at complying. "Eunice always give me that in my arm. Left arm, seein's how I'm right-handed."

"I'd like to give it to you in your side," Kate said, with other purposes in mind. "Either take off your shirt or just pull it out of your pants so I can reach the flesh just above your hip."

"Damn," the man said. "Seems like we just get a nurse broke in when they send a new one. And each one more bossy and from off than the one before. Four years . . . took four years to make a decent nurse out of Eunice and now ye show up."

"Your shirt, please, Mr. Bates?" Kate insisted softly.

He started to unbutton his shirt, glancing at her hostilely from time to time. When it was off, Kate saw what she had suspected. Obvious signs of malnutrition. To carry out her pretext, she squeezed a thin fold of skin just above his hip, inserted the needle as gently as she could and completed the injection. She swabbed the area with an alcohol pad and said, "That wasn't so bad, was it?"

"I've felt worse."

Kate started to make a note on his chart, recording the date and contents of the injection, but also used the diversion to conceal her primary objective. "Been eating well, Mr. Bates?"

"Ye don't lak me, do ye?" he asked suddenly.

Taken aback, Kate did not know how to respond. It was a serious reflection on her professional conduct if she had indeed given the patient cause to think she harbored any hostility. Confidence and a sense of caring were two indispensable attributes for a nurse.

"Have I done anything to indicate I don't like you, Mr. Bates?"

"Ye jes' did it again!" he accused.

"What?" she asked, now both puzzled and resentful.

"Ye come into my house. Ye say ye come to help me. Yet ye keep calling me Mr. Bates. Didn't nobody teach ye manners, girl? If'n ye want to be friendly with a body ye call him by his name, his real name, which for me is Rufus."

"Oh, I see." Kate, relieved, understood now.

"One's dumber than the next," Bates muttered, as if complaining to some other presence. "Used to, we didn't change nurses every few years and have to train a new one. Ye'll never do, never." Then he asked warmly, "Now, ye'll have a cup of tea?"

Ray Boyd had told her once, "If ever a patient invites you to have a cup of coffee or a meal, you must, by mountain etiquette, accept."

"Yes, a cup of tea would be fine," Kate said, adding a bit tentatively, "Rufus."

He glanced at her out of the corner of his eye to make sure she meant it, then he put a chipped old white enamel teakettle on the wood stove to boil up some water. Kate used the time to suggest, "Rufus, long as you have your shirt off, mind if I examine you?"

"Ye know I cain't stand ye," he said, but he turned to present himself as a patient.

She performed an examination which included his chest, heart, back, eyes, blood pressure and throat. Most especially she concentrated on those two discolorations on his left cheek. He grew self-conscious.

"Anybody'd know they's liver spots."

"Have they ever been tested?" Kate asked, though she meant biopsied.

"Nope. No need. 'Sides, wouldn't allow it."

If it were not outside her prescribed duties, Kate would have taken a specimen then and there. But she decided on other means. "Dr. Boyd said he'd like to see you down at the hospital. Thinks maybe you need a change in your injections. Will you be coming down to the town?"

"Might," he replied.

"Do that. And soon. Better still, if you tell me when, I'll make sure Dr. Boyd is there to see you."

"Don't know," Bates said evasively, then asked, "What ye see there, girl?"

"I don't like these spots," Kate admitted. "How long have they been there?"

"Recent" was all Bates would say. "Look, the water's boilin'. I'll make us our tea."

The two cups matched neither each other nor the saucers. Obviously remnants of old sets now long gone, they seemed to have a history of their own, bespeaking a lengthy marriage to a woman who had had simple good taste in the possessions she gathered around her.

"Have you been a widower a long time?"

"Years. Lots of years," Bates answered sadly.

"Children?"

"Seven. Buried five," he said with quiet resignation. "Two from the wars. Folks from off, they always say mountain people are quick to use a gun to settle disputes. But I notice, come a war, which we ain't got no part of, and they take our sons to fight it. Two boys, Lester and George . . ." He rose and went to a corner of the cabin and brought out a small box. He lifted out two ribbons, at the ends of which hung silver medals. He held out one. "That's George. And this un's Lester. Fine boys, both."

The tall, gangly man moved to the window at the far end of the cabin and looked out as he said, "Dug their graves myself once they bodies was returned. Had the preacher come say a few words. Nice words. The boys would have been proud."

"What about your other two children, Rufus? Those still alive?" Kate asked.

"Helen. And Clara. Married. Moved off. Husbands went to the city looking for jobs. Found them. Sent for Helen and her children. For Clara. They went."

"Do you ever see them?" Kate asked.

"Nope. But they write. Often. Sometimes three, four times a year. And they send me money. But I always send it back. A father's place is to do for his young, not make them do for him."

Kate realized she had to overcome the man's stiff pride to discover what she wanted to know. "You keep the place so neat and clean. Do it all by yourself?"

"Ain't nobody else," he said.

"Do all your own raisin' of food, cookin'?" Kate asked, adopting as nearly as possible the short, clipped speech of her patient.

"I told ye, ain't nobody else."

"Do you cook often?"

"Often enough," he responded, but by now her questions had obviously made him uneasy.

"What?" Kate persisted.

"Corn, pertaters, snap beans, lak that."

"Meat?"

"Sometimes I go a-huntin'. Used to, I went a-fishin'," he admitted, "but it's too troublesome these here days."

"I can understand that," Kate said. She made a mental note to have him down to the hospital for a thorough examination before his malnutrition became life-threatening.

He must have suspected, for he volunteered, "These days, seems my aim's not so good as it used to be. I ain't brought down a buck nor a rabbit for weeks." Then he admitted, "Months." And as if reluctant to talk any further, he suggested, "But ye got to get along to others."

"Yes, yes, I do," Kate said.

He saw her out to the porch, carrying her saddlebags for her. When he handed them to her at the top of the steps, he said, "Next time, if ye want to be real friendly, ye'll call me Rufe."

She smiled. But her smile was short-lived, for he added, "And ye won't go nosying into things lak how I eat and what I eat. I'm alive, ain't I? And feelin' tolerable. Which is more'n some can say."

"You'll come down to see Dr. Boyd anyhow, won't you?"

"I'll think on it" was all Bates would concede. "I'll think on it."

Kate was at the bottom of the steep climb up to the cabin of her next patient, Mrs. Hildy Persons. She had to determine if it was safer to climb the hill on foot or try to drive up. She decided that sturdy as the Jeep was, and even with its four-wheel drive, it might overturn. She would try it on foot. It was a difficult ascent up a rough, stony path that had been gullied by the year's rains and snows. The house ahead and its surroundings differed little from the Bates place.

She was halfway up when a woman's voice challenged her.

"Who be ye?"

Before Kate could answer, a rifle shot rang out. The bullet lodged in a tree high above her head, so she knew it was only a warning. She dropped to the ground, called, "Nurse Kincaid from the Outpost."

"Don't know no Kincaid," the woman shouted back. "Where's Eunice?"

"She's ill. Sick," Kate said, then remembered. "She's drinlin'."

The woman came to the edge of the porch to look down in Kate's direction. "Drinlin', is she?" she asked, the familiar word having diminished her suspicions. "And did ye say what your name wuz?"

"Kincaid," Kate said, adding, "Kate."

"Kate . . ." The woman seemed to consider, then spat a stream of brown tobacco juice. "Wal, Kate, ye can come closer."

Kate rose from the rough earth, brushed the twigs and dust from her slacks and jacket, seized her saddlebags, and started up slowly, not wanting to advance too fast or too far lest she anger the woman again. When she was within fifteen feet of the porch, she looked up and saw a woman of about sixty, heavy-set, dressed in a well-washed cotton housedress and holding in her right hand a rifle the barrel of which rested across her left arm. The woman's suspicious look made Kate stop to await a further invitation. The woman looked her over.

"Kate, is it? And ye say ye're a nurse?" Mrs. Persons considered her. "Ye don't look like much. For size I mean. Pretty enough. But pretty ain't no measure of no nurse. Now ye take Eunice, there's a nurse. Homely as sin. Can't get no man's the reason she's up in these here mountains. But what's yere reason?"

"Because I want to help people," Kate explained.

"Sure, charity work," the woman said contemptuously. "Well, we ain't charity!"

"I didn't say you were," Kate replied. Then, remembering the instructions she had received from Rufus Bates, she added, "I'm just here to help in any way I can, Hildy."

Mrs. Persons finally lowered her rifle. It was a signal that Kate would be permitted into the house. From Hildy Persons' chart Kate knew that she had to test her for sugar level. The woman was diabetic and had been since her last birthing at age thirty-eight. She was now sixty, somewhat overweight and, based on her last examination, had been spilling sugar. Her insulin dose had been increased and today's visit would determine if the increased dosage plus a more modified diet had remedied the condition.

Mrs. Persons' modest home consisted of one large room which was kitchen, dining room and parlor all in one. There were two doors in the wall on the right side which Kate assumed to be small bedrooms. The large, worn, gray, once-black cast-iron stove in the corner served not only for cooking but as the only source of heat. Kate noticed that in each corner of the room was a brightly polished brass vessel, the purpose of which she discovered when Mrs. Persons aimed a stream of tobacco juice at one of them and hit it with the unerring accuracy of an expert marksman.

"So Eunice is bad took and ye're here in her place. Reckon ye're going to be the same nuisance she wuz, 'cept worse. Seeing as ye don't know nothin' 'bout nursin', 'cause ye're too young and too pretty. Girl like ye, 'fore ye know it she's married off and never see her again. Don't know why they send ones like ye. Waste of time. Suppose ye want one of them there specimens?"

"If you don't mind," Kate said.

"And if'n I do? I cain't stand ye nurses. No matter what ye ask, I got to do it. Wal, just wait."

While the woman was out of the room Kate pondered the phrase which both Rufus and Mrs. Persons had used, "cain't stand ye nurses." Yet they had done exactly as she requested. Perhaps the words had another meaning. Could "cain't stand" actually mean "can't withstand"? Can't resist, can't refuse? Why else would they say the words but then comply so readily? She must find out.

Hildy Persons was back with a specimen of urine. Kate tested it only to make a disheartening discovery. Despite the increased insulin dosage and changed diet, her sugar level was up so high it did not require a blood test to confirm it. There could be only one of two reasons. Either Mrs. Persons was not taking her insulin or else she was cheating on her new diet.

To confirm her suspicions without arousing the patient's anxiety or resistance, Kate proceeded under the guise of doing a routine examination.

"Please remove your shoes and stockings," Kate started to ask, until she observed the woman wore plain, worn flat-heeled shoes but no stockings. "Please slip off your shoes."

Mrs. Persons looked at her with hostile condescension. "Ain't nothin' wrong with my feet."

"Please," Kate insisted.

"Reckon ye got to practice on somebody, so go ahead," she replied, slipping off her shoes.

While Kate examined her feet, looking for signs of lesions or other breakdowns in the skin likely in advanced diabetics, she asked, "Been eating regular?"

"Yep."

"Plenty of greens, and milk and cheese?"

"Greens, milk and cheese," the woman repeated impatiently.

"Bread?" Kate asked.

"Some."

"How much?"

"I said some," the woman reiterated, "which means not too much, like ye're thinkin'."

"Cakes? Pies?"

"None!" the woman responded firmly.

To add emphasis to her denial she spat a stream of tobacco juice in the direction of the nearest brass bucket.

Her answers did not fit with the medical facts Kate had discovered. Yet she knew that patient relations made it unwise to challenge the woman directly. Kate had satisfied herself on one point: The woman had been carrying out prescribed hygienic practices; her feet were clean, in good condition and showed no disturbing signs. In an advanced diabetic, infection of the feet was a constant danger.

After consulting the diabetic flowchart which contained all the vital facts of Mrs. Persons' case, Kate asked, "Do you do your daily walk?"

"When I can."

"It is important to do it even when you feel you can't. Force yourself to do it. You can't give in to laziness."

"When I say, 'When I can,' I mean if'n it's raining cats and dogs or snowing a blizzard out there I ain't like no fool going to go prancing around and have my neighbors stare at me like I am tetched in the head," the woman explained.

Kate could find no adequate response to that bit of basic logic. She decided to do a fasting blood sugar test to determine if perhaps the root of Mrs. Persons' trouble lay in the fact that her insulin dose was still too low.

"Have you eaten yet?" she asked.

"Yep," Mrs. Persons said, then added in rebuke, "as ye say on them there instructions. Breakfast every morning. One egg, one slice a bread, some butter and coffee, with a bit of sweet milk to tone it down."

Since she had already eaten, there was no possibility of doing a fasting blood sugar test. Kate decided on more direct means of detection.

"Mrs. Persons, we have a problem."

"Ye, who is obvious one of them fools with a college education, may have a problem. But not *me*. And not *we*!"

There was no other way but to say it straight out. "For some reason your blood sugar level is up beyond the level of tolerance."

"'Tain't my fault. I done what Eunice tol' me. So if'n that ain't workin', 'tain't my fault," the woman said. Kate could see her resistance building.

"Have you been taking your insulin as prescribed?"

"Have," the woman insisted.

"Eating what you've been told?"

"Yep!" She spat again at the brass cuspidor, hitting it.

"No more than you've been told?" Kate persisted.

"No more!"

"Not just a little sugar with your coffee?"

"Nope!"

"Some honey?" Kate asked, since the sugar content of honey was as dangerous to a diabetic as refined sugar.

"No honey, no sugar, no nothin' as could harm my diet!" the woman insisted.

Almost half-aloud, Kate thought, "Something wrong, somewhere there is something wrong."

"I think, Miss whatever yere name is, ye better be going from here," Mrs. Persons said, drawing on her shoes. "Ain't nobody going to come into my own house and 'cuse me of lyin'!"

"I'm only trying to discover the cause of something that is obviously wrong with the management of your condition," Kate tried to explain.

"Don' know about management and such, but ye much as called me a liar. Used to, we had nurses come visiting was nice decent ladies. Didn't go round suspicionin' or accusin'. Now ye go down there and tell 'em that less'n Eunice comes back I don't want to see no more nurses up here!"

She went to the door, yanked it open and stood aside to make it quite plain that Kate was being evicted. Kate tried to explain. "I'm sorry. I'm new at this. And I may not be as good as Eunice was. Maybe I never will be. But all I'm trying to do is find out what's caused the change in your condition."

"If ye couldn't do that without accusin', ye hadn't ought to do it at all," the woman said with finality. With that, she spat out the door and beyond the porch as if the distance was meant to emphasize her vehemence.

"Mrs. Persons, Hildy—" Kate made one last appeal.

But the woman interrupted, "Sure. Go ahead. Do like they tol' ye. Call me by my first name so's ye'll seem friendly and one of us. Cain't fool me. Just git!"

"I would like to come back tomorrow. I would also like you not to eat breakfast, so I can do a fasting blood sugar," Kate explained.

"Ye can come back if ye want, but I ain't promisin' nothin'!" the woman said, spitting again. This time the brown juice exceeded the mark set by her previous effort.

Kate started down the path, with the baying of a distant hunting hound a mournful accompaniment. When she reached the Jeep she settled in, but instead of starting on her way to the next patient, she studied Hildy Persons' file again. It revealed nothing unusual for the history of an adult diabetic. No extreme diminished vision, no marked kidney disease, not even a note as to ischemic heart disease. In all respects a controllable case of diabetes. And yet that sudden rise in sugar level indicated that it was not being controlled. And if the woman was truthful, she was doing everything she had been instructed to do. Diet, exercise, insulin.

The only proper thing to do was to bring her in to the hospital for further examination. All the facilities for further testing were there, and she might be more forthcoming with a local doctor like Ray Boyd than with an outsider, someone "from off" like Kate Kincaid. She would discuss it with Leona Owens when she returned to Wildwood at the end of the day.

She started up the motor of the Jeep and was about to put it in gear when she recalled one phrase the obstinate woman had used.

She had said she added "sweet" milk to her coffee. What was in that milk? Sugar? Honey? Molasses? What made it sweet? Kate turned off the motor and, determined not to be put off, she started up the steep path again. Before she drew close, Mrs. Persons was on the porch. She must have been watching Kate, for she gripped her rifle, muzzle pointing down at the ground. But she seemed quite ready to raise it if she felt inclined to.

"Aye?" she challenged her, as if asking, what is it this time?

"Hildy, how do you make your sweet milk?"

The woman studied Kate before she let go a stream of brown tobacco juice. She smiled condescendingly. "Trouble with educated folks, they got so much education they ain't got no room in their haids for plain simple sense. They go foolish from too much larnin'. Body don't 'make' sweet milk. Sweet milk just is."

The answer sounded evasive to Kate. She decided to risk antagonizing the woman even more. "I'm sorry, Hildy, but to sweeten milk you must add something to it."

Hildy Persons shook her head intolerantly. "Ye're even dumber than I thought. Less ye're doin' this to give me some more sass."

"Believe me," Kate said, "I'm only trying to learn."

"Larn, is it?" the woman considered. "Wal, sit ye down." She indicated the top step. Hildy Persons leaned her rifle against the porch post and sat down beside her. "Cain't hold yere ignorance against ye. Not if ye're willin' to larn. They is only two kinds of milk. They is sour milk, which is what is left after ye churn yere butter. And they is sweet milk, which is what comes from the cow."

"Nothing added? No sugar, no molasses?" Kate asked.

"Just like it comes from the cow, sweet and creamy."

Kate was glad to have this new knowledge of mountain talk. But it only created further mystery about the case of Hildy Persons. If not sweet milk, what was it that caused the woman's high blood sugar level?

"Think about what I said," Kate reiterated.

"'Bout comin' down to the hospital in town?"

"Yes. It's important," Kate tried to impress on her.

"I'll study on it," the woman answered, but remained stubbornly noncommittal.

CHAPTER 13

The last call on the day's list was the Torrence house. Following the directions, Kate approached it to discover a stream that separated her from the house. She studied the clear meandering water, judged it to be fordable and set her Jeep in motion. She was halfway across when one of the front wheels started to settle into the soft bed. For a precarious moment she feared the vehicle would capsize. She gave it a surge of gas, and with the water up to her hubcaps, she made it to the other side. The Jeep climbed out of the stream like a prehistoric monster waddling up from a swamp.

Profiting from her experience with Mrs. Persons, Kate parked a distance from the house, seized her saddlebags and cautiously made her way toward the path that led to the house. The Torrence house appeared in good repair. In addition to the vegetable patch, the path was bordered by early spring flowers which had been planted and tended with obvious care. The porch had been swept clean. There were no sagging boards. In the two windows Kate could see simple colorful cotton curtains.

There was no one in sight, but as Kate reached the bottom step of the porch stairs, she caught a glimpse of a child's face peeping out of one window. As soon as she noticed, the face disappeared.

Kate climbed to the porch and hearing nothing, she called out, "Mrs. Torrence?" Still no sound or sign. She called again, "Anyone home?" There was a rustle inside the house. The front door eased open a bit. A woman peered out guardedly.

"Mrs. Torrence?"

"Yes" was the cautious reply. "Who are ye?"

"Kate Kincaid, from the nursing service."

"I don't know ye," the woman said, refusing to open the door any wider.

"Eunice is sick. I've been sent in her place. She'll be coming back," Kate explained. "But you'll have to make do with me in the meantime."

Matilda Torrence opened the door. Kate saw that she clutched a rifle in her hand. The woman put the weapon aside, apologizing. "Cain't be too keerful. Not these days."

Kate judged her to be younger than she had first appeared, no more than thirty, possibly even less. She wore a well-washed, faded cotton housedress. Her face was thin, pale, betraying more wear than a woman her age should. As she stood aside, she afforded Kate a view of the inside of the house. It was meticulously clean. The floors were bare and showed signs of much scrubbing.

"Come in, come in," Matilda Torrence invited her. "We been waitin' for Eunice. Ben and me, that is."

"Your husband?" Kate asked. "Is he ill?"

"Ben's my boy," the woman said. "Don't ye know about Ben?"

Among the myriad details about all the new patients whom she would meet today, Kate recalled that the Torrences had two children, one a boy of seven, Benjamin. And, she remembered now, he was retarded.

Kate found the boy sitting at table, fixed in a high chair that had been constructed especially for him. Before him was a bowl of steaming soup. Obviously, Kate had interrupted his mother while feeding him.

"Benjy gets hongry 'tweentimes," his mother apologized.

"Please," Kate said. "I can wait."

"Would you care to have a cup of coffee?" Matilda Torrence invited. "Or maybe a bowl of soup?"

As she had been instructed, Kate agreed. "A cup of coffee is exactly what I need."

The old enamel pot was steaming on the back of the wood stove. The woman poured, asking, "Anythin' in it?"

Kate was pleased to respond in the vernacular. "Some sweet milk if you have it."

"That we do."

Once Kate was settled with her coffee, she observed the woman complete feeding her son. Except for the deformity of his jutting jaw, the boy was almost handsome. He giggled often, enjoying the attention his mother lavished on him. But at age seven he was unable to hold a spoon correctly, even when his mother assisted him. From time to time, Mrs. Torrence glanced at Kate, to apologize for her unfortunate son. Finally the feeding was over.

As Kate turned from the table to open her saddlebags, she noticed once again a small wraithlike face stealing a glance at her from behind the door of an inner room. But the door closed at once.

"I would like to examine Ben, if you don't mind," Kate began.

"Ye may," Mrs. Torrence said, turning to the boy. "Benjy, this nice lady is going to examine ye. But she won't hurt ye. So don't be afeared."

She lifted the boy out of the chair and placed him on the bare wooden table, hovering over him in case he attempted to wriggle off.

Kate made her examination in accord with the routine detailed in the manual. In all respects the boy's condition conformed to the report Eunice had made three months ago. Children born with his mental deficits also suffered certain physical difficulties. He was slowly deteriorating. Kate had no way of determining if the cause of his condition was genetic and inherited or was due to some trauma during gestation or birth. Whatever the reason it mattered little now.

These were the cases that most tormented Kate, when she ran up against the limits of what medical science could accomplish. The days, months and years of love and anguish that devoted parents lavished on such children were both inspiring and depressing. As Kate studied the Torrence family chart she discovered a note there.

"Eunice says here your husband had a bad cough last time."

"Seems 'twas the same as Benjy's cold. Heavy in the chest. He was bad took for a spell. But it's better now."

"Can I examine him?" Kate asked.

"He's out back. Don' know if'n I can find him."

The woman went to the kitchen window that faced out of the back of the house. She stared a moment, searching, then opened the window and called, "Homer! There's a new lady from Wildwood come to visit. She'd like fer to see ye."

She turned back to Kate. "He'll be comin' soon now. He's layin' in wood fer winter s'long as he's not workin'," she explained. "With the price of oil droppin', they's digging less coal these days."

"Your husband a coal miner?"

"Big Betsy does all the digging now. The men only do the drivin'. 'Cept now ain't nearly so many trucks needed. Them's as is drivin' is makin' good money. The rest is mostly on the draw. Homer was one of the first to get the sack. So all's there to do is raise some vegetables, the hog, some diddlers and cut enough wood to keep us through the next season or two. After, maybe we have to go on the draw again. Hate to do it," the woman said very sadly. "Not good for the little 'uns, to see their father that way."

Realizing Kate did not understand, she explained, "When we's on the draw that means welfare. Man should be able to care for his own without no government needin' to help. He's a pride-proud man, my Homer. Sometimes makes him ornery. Person got to be keerful 'round him," thus alerting Kate to how her husband should be treated.

Kate nodded. The women understood each other. Waiting for Torrence to appear, Kate had a chance to observe the room. She was impressed that within limited means the woman had made every effort to improve her modest home. The cupboard shelves had been bordered in neat, colorful, hand-sewn strips of flowered material. On closer examination, Kate realized that they were of a fabric that came from a worn-out cotton housedress. The dishes and other crockery were simple but clean and neatly arranged. On the wall above the stove hung a meager array of pots and pans, no two of which matched. Some were cast iron. One aluminum. Some old white enamel. But all had been polished till they appeared surgically clean.

The striving of this poor woman to set an example for her family of what a home should be was evident in every detail.

The slight squeak of the worn old floor made Kate turn in the direction of the bedroom door. But the door was shut instantly. The second Torrence child was evidently too shy and sensitive to reveal herself to strangers. Before Kate could speculate further, she heard heavy footsteps at the back door.

Homer Torrence flung open the door in a manner that betrayed his resentment of strangers. He eyed Kate before he finally entered the room.

"Ye're from Wildwood, are ye?"

"Eunice is drinlin' and I've been sent to take her place for a short time."

"But she'll be back?" Torrence asked.

"She'll be back," Kate promised.

The man seemed to doubt Kate, for he asked guardedly, "And what do ye want of me?"

"According to your chart, you had a bad cold."

"Did," Torrence conceded cautiously.

"Also, last time, Eunice said you needed surgery for a hernia."

The man glanced at his wife to inquire if there had been any discussion between the two women about a subject obviously sensitive to him.

"I'd like to examine you," Kate said. "Would you remove your shirt, please?"

After some hesitation, Homer unbuttoned his faded cotton-flannel plaid shirt. Kate stethoscoped his chest and back, listening carefully for any vestigial rales from his cold. She heard none. His heart was strong and regular. From all signs he had recovered from that illness.

Now she must address herself to the more intimate part of the examination.

"Would you lower your trousers?"

The man glared at her.

"I have to examine your hernia," Kate explained. Matilda Torrence was tense. She wanted to intercede but dared not. "Homer?" Kate persisted.

"I ain't 'lowing any stranger to take such liberties with me," Torrence said.

"Homer, it's important. If your hernia's gotten worse it might strangulate. That could be dangerous. Might even kill you if it becomes gangrenous." Still the man did not relent. "If you've no concern for your own life, think of your family. Would you want Matilda and Benjy and your daughter to have to make do without you?"

"Ain't much help to them as it is," Homer Torrence said grimly.

"Things'll get better," Kate said, trying to reassure him. "Now, please, I have to examine you."

"Wouldn't do no good," Homer said. "All's ye can tell is I need the opyration. And we cain't afford it."

"Let's find out first. Now, please?" She indicated that he let down his worn, patched denim pants.

He still resisted sullenly until his wife interceded. "Homer? She's asked very proper. She don't mean but the best."

"Wal, not this way," he said, his attitude now somewhat more conciliatory. "What if'n I laid down on the bed and ye . . . ye did what ye had to?"

"Of course," Kate agreed.

He led the way into the other bedroom. The bed frame had been handmade, hewed out of native trees. The mattress, which had been new many years ago, sagged and showed clearly the outline of two bodies. He lay down, loosened his trousers but did not pull them down. Very gingerly Kate began her examination. She felt the protrusion. Her own estimate, compared with the one Eunice had made several months ago, indicated it was now several centimeters larger. It should be treated surgically.

"Wal?" Torrence asked.

"It's somewhat worse," Kate said.

"Thought so," he confessed. "Been feelin' kind quicky there. More'n a body laks to feel."

"We'll have to do something about it."

"Reckon," Torrence said, accepting that surgery was inevitable. "Wuz layin' in the wood and tryin' to get in some meat afore I went. To see 'em through whilst I wuz gone."

So that was it, Kate realized. He had accepted all along what needed doing but was willing to risk his health, possibly even his life, to provide for his little family. She had to admire the man. They stared at each other in the dimly lit room. His eyes begged for her cooperation, and hers assented.

"We won't tell them until you've done all your chores," she agreed.

"Last year and afore wuz different. I wuz workin' steady and we had things. This year is bad. And I don't want to go back on the draw."

"I understand," Kate said softly.

"People always sayin' mountain folk got too much pride for what they are. I don't call it too much pride for a man to want to take care of his own. Do ye?"

"No, Homer, I do not," Kate agreed.

* * *

She had completed her examination of Matilda Torrence and had found her to be in fair health for a woman of twenty-nine who had borne three children under hard circumstances, one of whom had not survived. It was time now to ask about the shy child who peered furtively out of windows and from behind partly opened doors.

"The little girl," Kate asked. "Can I see her now?"

"She's terrible shy of strangers," Matilda Torrence said.

"Still, I have to examine her," Kate said.

"I'll fetch her."

Matilda Torrence was gone for some minutes before the door opened. Haltingly, out came a timid girl of ten, slight, with golden hair so fine and wispy that she seemed a character from a fairy tale. Her blue eyes were wide with curiosity. She was tense and fearful, yet she was obviously not mentally deficient like her brother.

"Eloise," Mrs. Torrence urged her toward Kate.

To establish some communication between them, Kate said, "Eloise is a very lovely name."

"Was a name I read oncet in a book about a fairy princess," her mother explained.

"Eloise?" Kate said invitingly.

She came a bit closer. Kate held out her hand. The child pulled back shyly. When Kate looked into her pale blue eyes, she turned away. But not before Kate was able to appreciate what a pretty child she was.

"Now, Eloise, I have to examine you."

The child drew back. Her mother intervened. "She won't be hurtin' ye. She's right nice, one of the bestest nurses we ever had up here in the holler."

Eloise finally relented. Kate reached out to run her fingertips lightly across the child's smooth pale cheek. *Soft, soft as only a child's skin can be,* Kate thought. Then she gently slipped the straps of the simple homemade dress off the child's shoulder. She allowed her dress to be removed. Kate was careful to fold it neatly before placing it on the bare wood table. Since the child wore no undergarments, she stood naked. While her mother and father watched, Kate performed a complete examination, eyes, ears, nose, throat, chest, arms, legs, percussing both her chest and stomach, listening for any revealing sounds. She performed the stethoscopic part of the examination with good results. The neurological tests proved the child's reactions to be excellent. Kate measured her height and estimated her weight. When compared with her chart of several months ago, in all respects Eloise was developing normally for her age.

"You may dress again, Eloise," Kate said, wondering at the genetic perversity of nature, that in one family there should be two children so dissimilar.

She was putting her instruments back in the saddlebags when the child moved close to stroke Kate's cheek as Kate had done to her.

"Pretty lady," the child said, the only words she had spoken during the entire procedure.

"Thank you, Eloise."

"What do they call ye?" the child asked in her native lilt.

"Katherine. But since I hope that we are now good friends and always will be, you may call me Kate."

"Kate," the girl repeated. "Maw, we had a Kate oncet."

"Yes, child. We had a Kate," the mother confirmed sadly. When Kate looked to her for an explanation, Matilda Torrence glanced at her husband, requesting permission. He finally yielded with a single curt nod. "Was our firstborn. Like little Benjy she was. We messed over her more'n a little. But didn't help airy a bit. She turned quare and just passed on. Hardly more'n eight. Eloise was seven at the time. But she ain't never forgot."

With a sad sigh in memory of her departed child, Mrs. Torrence brightened as she said, "We wuz just settin' to have supper. Would ye eat with us?"

Not wishing to impose on people who could ill afford to feed another mouth, Kate said, "I would love to, but it's getting close to dark and I'm still strange here, so I would like to start back."

"Please?" little Eloise begged. The eager look in her eyes made Kate relent.

"Of course, I'll be delighted to stay."

"I'll be settin' table, won't be but nary a minute," Mrs. Torrence said.

Eloise took Kate's hand and pulled her in the direction of the room where she had hid. It was a tiny bedroom with two homemade beds and just enough room in the corner for an ancient cradle which must have sheltered all Torrence babies for generations. Eloise closed the door carefully before she said, "Used to I had mah aunt Bessie to show to. But she's passed on."

Baffled, Kate nodded nevertheless, smiled and pretended to understand.

The wraithlike child looked up at her, "Aunt Bessie wuz mah onliest friend. Till you, ain't nobody sayed they was a friend of mine. But I got to be sartain."

She held out her delicate hand, the little finger bent and extending from the others. As a child herself, Kate had used that same gesture to solemnize bets with other children. So she extended her hand, and they locked little fingers in firm commitment.

This appeared to assure the sensitive child, for she dropped to her knees and crept under the bed. When she slid back out, she was clutching close to her breast a worn old shoe box from which she extracted some wrinkled sheets of lined writing paper.

"I ain't nary showed these to anyone. Sartain not Paw. Don't pay fer to make Paw mad."

Puzzled yet intrigued by this child who, once shy, now seemed so relieved to talk, Kate said, "No, we wouldn't want to make Paw mad. What are those, Eloise?"

The child held out her treasured papers to Kate. In the fading light of an early fall evening, Kate began to read:

> *We was all sad when Kate was took with the fever. Paw was gettin the old truck ready to take her to the hospital fer treatment when Maw called out of a sudden. And I knew that Kate was arrived at her death. Maw cried, and I was frightened near to death myself. But Paw was like in a franzy, sayin as how Kate was quare like all his family. And 'ceptin for that she would a never died. Pore Paw, to be sad and blamin' hisself all at the same time.*
>
> *Preacher Hoskins said some nice things over Kate's little wood pine coffin. Lak what a sweet chile she was, and as how she was now better off for where she was. And I say to myself, whut kind of world is it if'n one is better off out of it than in it? But I dit'n dare ask, special with Maw cryin and Paw so self-blamin' he coutn't hardly look a body in the eye.*

That brief description of a death in the family clarified several things for Kate. Why Matilda Torrence was so reluctant to speak of young Kate's condition in the presence of her husband. There was a genetic strain in the Torrence side of the family that, for whatever reason, spawned children like Benjy and the unfortunate girl who had died at an early age.

But for a child who had been only seven at the time to understand it all and attempt to put it in writing revealed a surprising perception. In this family, shy, pretty Eloise was a genetic anomaly. Kate read on. The child had written down her observations and feelings in the language she knew best, her mountain vernacular. Words she had never seen or learned to spell she simulated from their sounds. But every so often a word or two crept in that indicated that schooling had had some beneficial effect on her limited vocabulary.

Near the end of one of her papers she had written a comment that Kate found both amusing and pathetic.

Words we larn in school is spelled funny, since they no how is spelled lak they sound.

But it was the final page that touched Kate more than any other.

Benjy is the lucky one. He got Maw and Paw fussin and doin over him all the time. But Eloise is allus alone. Hearin folks talk lak they do when they's shore no young uns is listenin, they say Benjy's quare. But seems lak Eloise is the quare one, seen's how she is not lak anyone else in this here world.

When I die, will some preacher be sayin over me, she is better off there than when she was here?

She looked down at the young child who was tremulously awaiting her response.

"This is very nice, Eloise. Have you ever shown these writings to anyone else?"

"Aunt Bessie was all," the child said.

"I want you to know that I'm very flattered that you showed them to me," Kate said.

"I seen you wuz common like the rest of us," the child said.

Only later, when Kate asked Ray Boyd, would she discover that Eloise had bestowed on her the supreme compliment a mountain child could offer to an outsider. For the moment, it was enough that little Eloise obviously found her worthy of her confidence.

"Eloise, you've never shown these to your teachers?"

"Wouldn't be proper seein's how Paw would think I was sassin'."

"Of course you wouldn't want to upset your paw," Kate agreed, wondering how long the family would try to keep secret this weakness in the Torrence line, which was no secret at all.

"Supper is on," Mrs. Torrence called from the kitchen.

The table was set with an odd mixture of dishes, knives, forks and spoons, obviously a collection of family heirlooms for a hundred years or more. If the pieces did not match, they all shone brightly.

Mrs. Torrence lifted a large cast-iron pot off the stove and hefted it onto the table. She trussed up Benjy in his oversized high chair. Homer Torrence took his place at the head of the small table. There was a moment of bowed heads and silence. Though no one spoke a word, grace seemed to have been said. Mrs. Torrence ladled out the stew, which was fragrant with an aroma which was foreign to Kate but not forbidding. When she tasted her first mouthful, she realized it was a form of meat she had never eaten before.

Matilda said, "Homer shot him just this afternoon, skinned him and hung him just in time for supper."

"Excellent," Kate said, forcing herself to eat and wondering all the while what sort of animal Homer had shot. When she had eaten what she considered a polite amount of stew and fresh-baked bread, she sought to excuse herself. "It's quite dark and I'll have to find my way back."

"Shore," Matilda agreed. "Homer'll show you down to your Jeep."

As Kate gathered up her things, she did so near the single electric light that hung from the ceiling. She managed a look at the family file. She was relieved to see that Eunice Samuels had placed Matilda Torrence on a regimen of birth-control pills. There would be no more Benjys or Kates unless bad luck or some accident intervened. She also noted that Eunice had suggested a vasectomy for Homer. But he had rejected that.

Oil lamp in hand, Homer waited on the porch to see Kate down the path. Matilda took advantage of the moment to corner Kate for a brief confidential opinion.

"About Benjy?" she asked softly. "Will it be same as with little Kate?"

"I'm afraid so," Kate had to admit.

"Too bad," his mother said. "Drinlin' all his life, but such a sweet child, such an uncommon sweet child. Ye won't tell his father? He takes on so."

"No, I won't tell him," Kate agreed.

Because it was dark and the road was unfamiliar, the ride back to Wildwood seemed longer. Or did it seem so because of her disturbing thoughts about the Torrences?

Poor Benjy, born to suffer and die at an early age. His mother, Matilda, struggling to keep her family clean and decently fed despite their deprivations and at the same time trying to sustain her husband's spirit throughout his present unemployment and his corrosive sense of guilt. Torrence, a proud man, fervently striving to provide for his own, in a world that conspired to prevent it, a man tormented as well by the knowledge that the reason for poor Benjy lay in his blood, though he surely had never heard the word *genetics*. Yet how tenderly he picked Benjy up and caressed him. Kate had never seen any father evidence more love for a child.

Finally, there was little Eloise, named for a fairy princess in a book. Her light, wispy golden hair, her pale face with such delicate features made her appear more the creation of an artist who had a great love for children than a real child. And whose pale blue eyes were piercing with an intelligence trying to fight its way out, make itself known through her touching efforts at writing. Couched in the speech of her mountain people, they revealed a sensitivity that exceeded her limited language.

It would be a waste of a human life to allow her to grow up in the image of her mother. Yet, unless she was given the opportunity, that was exactly what would happen to her.

By the time Kate reached Wildwood she had decided someone should do something about that little girl.

CHAPTER 14

At breakfast the next morning Kate reviewed with Leona Owens the long list of patients she would have to cover today. Owens gave her helpful bits of personal background to aid in her approach to these families. But when Kate mentioned the patient Will Spencer, she noticed that Owens was about to pass some remark, but then for some reason deliberately refrained from doing so. Kate decided to be on the alert for him.

She drove along the narrow blacktop road rehearsing her family nurse's catechism: Call out from afar before you approach any house. Use first names, not last names. Never appear to pry. Never seem surprised or disapproving. Never suggest by word or deed that you do not accept totally what they say. The widow Persons had made an indelible impression when Kate even hinted she was being less than totally honest about her diet.

Her catechism ended when she arrived at the Redmond house. That visit went well. Grandma, mother, three grandchildren, two boys, one girl, all submitted to her examination without protest. Their health checked out well when compared with Eunice Samuels's family chart. Kate could not examine the father, who was off seeking employment at coal mines in another county.

After the Redmonds, she visited the Clintons, then the Martins, where she was invited to have dinner, meaning the midday meal.

She tasted bear meat for the first time in her life. It was different but not as unpleasant as she had feared. Fresh biscuits hot from the oven, coffee with sweet milk, and a pie Mrs. Martin had baked from dried peaches made a very satisfying meal. Kate thanked them profusely and set off to the next stop on her itinerary.

Will Spencer.

The Spencer place was farther off the blacktop road than any of the others. After Kate left her Jeep at the end of the unpaved road, she had to climb several hundred feet into what seemed a tangle of woods, beyond which she could barely make out a rustic cabin.

"Spencer? Will Spencer?" she called, standing off some fifty feet from the front porch. When he did not appear, she called out again, "Will Spencer? I'm Nurse Kate Kincaid from Wildwood!"

She was about to abandon seeing Spencer when the door opened. A man came to the edge of the porch. The first thing she noticed was the great shock of white hair that crowned his florid face. He wore small framed glasses which sat far down on his nose. He peered over them in a way that told Kate they were reading glasses. Kate recognized him now. He was the man Mrs. Russell had danced with on the Fourth of July. Spencer carried something in his hand. She thought at first it was a baton of some kind. As he motioned her to come closer, she realized that it was a simple flutelike instrument made of wood.

"Nurse Kate Kincaid, is it?" he asked. "And where is my good friend Eunice?"

"I'm afraid she's ill," Kate said.

Spencer appeared very concerned. "Not bad, I hope?"

"They don't know yet."

"Oh, one of those," Spencer remarked sadly.

One thing Kate had already determined, he was not mountain people. He spoke with the diction and enunciation of a well-educated man, which only increased her curiosity. What was he doing up here in mountain country? And in this remote cabin?

He beckoned her into the kitchen of his small cottage. She laid out her basic instruments on the table. She glanced at his chart. The only note of significance was that Eunice suspected a slight cardiac defect in Spencer's mitral valve. The condition was not serious, but it predisposed him to occasional momentary blackouts, sometimes accompanied by falling, which could be dangerous. The defect was not detectable by stethoscope, so Kate decided to study his head, chest, arms and legs for bruises or discolorations.

Once she finished studying his file, he asked, "Know me like a book now, do you?"

"Know you like a chart," Kate corrected him, smiling. "Now, then, any recent fainting, blacking out?"

"You mean episodes of syncope?" Spencer asked.

He took her by surprise. *Syncope* was a medical term she had not expected even from a layman who was well educated.

"Yes," she agreed. "Any episodes of syncope?"

"No, none," Spencer replied.

He watched her, amused, as she carried out her examination, asking every so often, "Well?"

"So far, so good" was all Kate would say, intending to be as provocative with him as he had been with her.

"Aren't you going to remark on the fading black-and-blue mark on my left side?" he asked.

"You said you had no episodes of syncope."

"Still, I might have been concealing one and this would be the evidence," he pointed out. "However, it would also be misleading. I got this when I accidentally collided with the door while carrying in a load of logs for my fire."

She performed her stethoscopic examination. No rales in his chest. Heartbeat free of any adverse signs. She examined his eyes carefully to see if the fundi revealed any complications from his high blood pressure. They did not. But when she took his pressure it was indeed high, even for a man of his age.

"Been taking your potassium pills?" she asked.

"Yes," Spencer informed her. "And my Inderal. In fact, I take so many pills now I often wonder how I stayed alive all these years without them."

Kate could no longer control her curiosity. "Mr. Spencer," she demanded, "you will have to tell me why you're here, since you obviously don't belong here."

"Let's strike a bargain," Spencer said, smiling. "I'll tell you why I'm here, if you tell me why you're here."

"I'm here to render good nursing care. So my personal life should be of no interest to you."

"Yet mine should be to you?" Spencer countered.

"You are the patient," Kate said. "Everything about you, including your background, is part of your medical history."

Spencer laughed. "All right. But let's have a cup of coffee first."

Over coffee, he apologized. "I'm sorry, my dear, it was unfair of me. But life here is quite dull. I like these people. I enjoy listening to their speech, their songs, their folklore. While that is professionally satisfying, it doesn't make for much company. So I am a lonely man. Have been ever since Claire died. And that's been quite a spell now, as mountain folk say. So whenever Eunice came up here to see me it would be a pleasant break in the monotony, and we would talk about all sorts of things.

"Then today you show up. Frankly, I was disappointed. I said to myself, I'm to be deprived of my usual pleasant visit with Eunice. I wonder what this one will be like. You were so businesslike, so efficient, I thought I'd have some fun with you. But you didn't join in. You were *too* efficient. *Too* professional. More coffee?"

He poured from a blue enamel coffee pot too shiny to give evidence of much wear. Like the man himself, it did not seem to belong among these ageless mountains. A few more sips of coffee and Kate asked, "And now, about yourself?"

"You first," he insisted, smiling.

Kate told him briefly of her background and what had brought her to the mountains.

When she was done he said, "My story is simple enough. For a man who has been a professor of English and American dialects for almost thirty-seven years and whose wife dies suddenly, leaving him alone, this seemed one of the more desirable things to do."

"No children?" Kate asked.

"Children. And grandchildren," Spencer admitted. "But these days when the airplane has led to the dispersion of us Americans there are no real families anymore. When I was a boy we had a family. I had a grandfather and a grandmother. They lived right around the corner from us back in Ohio. And when my granddaddy died, my grandmother just naturally moved in with us. In these days of small families and small houses there's no room for grandmas." He added sadly, "Or grandpas. Mind, girl, it was not a case of being dependent. With my lifetime savings and investments, with my pension from the college, I've more than enough to keep me through several lifetimes. It was just that there was no convenient room. And I didn't want to live in Southern California anyhow. I'm an

Ohio boy, born and raised. I like my winters cold, my falls brisk. I like my springs green. And my summers hot. I wouldn't have been happy with them, even if there was room.

"So I said to myself, and to Claire, even though she's gone I still talk things over with her." He chuckled. "You might want to put that down on my chart. Say that my high blood pressure has led to softening of the brain. But we talked it over, Claire and I, and she suggested, 'Will, you've been teaching local dialects, accents and music so long, why not go and do some fresh research right there while those things are still alive and taking place?' That's how I come to be here these last eighteen months. Since the best medical care around these parts is at Wildwood, I've put myself in their merciful hands. And since I can pay for it, or the government has kindly agreed to pay for it because of my age, I enjoy these visits up here. Sometimes I go down to Adelphi and present myself for perusal and study at Mountain Hospital. I feel I'm offering my body to science."

They both laughed.

"Now, if you've done studying me, I'll have to be getting along," he said. "Promised I'd be at church early this evening. Special service today. More snakes than ever, I was told."

Kate looked up sharply from the saddlebag into which she had begun to stow her instruments.

"More . . . snakes?"

"Haven't you heard?" Spencer asked.

"I've been warned to look out for rattlers before I start up any path."

"You mean no one's told you? And you've not even seen one of them down at the hospital?"

Kate had witnessed the bloodiest surgery without becoming squeamish, but the thought of rattlesnakes still frightened her. "You mean they show up even in populated places like Adelphi?"

"Of course not," Spencer said, "but some religious sects here handle rattlers as part of their worship."

"They couldn't," Kate protested at once. "In ancient history back in college I read about the Egyptians and some Greeks worshiping the snake as a holy object. That's why it's on the medical caduceus. But in this country, in these modern times? You're pulling my leg."

"Oh, but I'm not," Spencer disagreed. "We have two churches

where the men handle live rattlers to prove their faith."

"That's insane," Kate declared.

"To you and me, maybe. But not to the local Pentecostalists."

"Have you ever witnessed such a service?"

"Once," Spencer admitted. "Frightening, yet fascinating. The absolute faith with which those men handle those wriggling deadly beasts! All the while proclaiming they're protected by their faith in God. Would you like to see it for yourself?"

If she had not been quite so frightened of the idea, Kate would have begged off. But, overdetermined as usual, she impulsively accepted the challenge. "Of course. Why not?"

On the drive to the church, Kate could not resist asking, "Don't any of them ever get bitten?"

"Happens," Spencer said.

"And if he dies?"

"Like all religious fanatics, they have an explanation. They simply say, 'His faith wasn't strong enough.'"

They were silent again until Spencer said, "There it is, up ahead on the right. And try to be as inconspicuous as possible. They won't normally allow a woman into their church if she's wearing slacks."

The Redeemer's Pentecostal Church was a small wood-frame building. Though more than a century old, it was freshly painted white, neatly kept and in good repair. Its modest steeple was just tall enough to accommodate the little church bell and low enough so the bell could be rung using a short, thick, knotted rope that hung down onto the church porch. It was being rung now to announce the early evening service as Kate and Spencer drove up in the Jeep.

More than thirty cars were parked in orderly fashion in the open area before the church. People were streaming in, so that by the time Kate had parked and she and Spencer reached the door of the church, there were no more seats and they had to stand against the back wall. The service had not yet begun, but the congregation remained silent and patient. As Kate studied the backs of their heads, she was surprised at the number of children in attendance. She was also surprised at the number of women who wore bonnets as in the days of the frontier.

Suddenly there was a rustle of activity just outside the front door. Heavy footsteps clomped onto the porch. The door was flung open. As Kate turned to look, she was almost face to face with three bearded, grizzled men, one dressed in clerical black and with the burning eyes of a prophet of old. The man in the center had slung over his back a large, bulging gunnysack. As he brushed by Kate, she could hear the hissing and rattling sound of the contents. She had just been touched by a burlap sack of live, squirming, vicious rattlesnakes. Instinctively she pulled back. Spencer realized this and seized her hand for moral support.

The three men paraded down the short, narrow aisle. When they reached the altar, which was no more than a slightly raised platform with a small lectern, the man unloaded his burden by swinging the sack off his shoulders and setting it down with a loud thump. The sack became alive and active with the writhing, twisting mass within it.

One of the three men, the minister of the little congregation, took his place before the lectern. He began to sing "Rock of Ages," and the others joined in. Kate started to sing along until she thought, *I am not like these people. They are not Christians as I know Christians.* And she fell silent, waiting for what might follow.

The hymn concluded, the preacher held out his arms, palms down, and, with his eyes closed, pronounced a benediction over his flock.

"Lord God of Hosts, these, Yere veriest own most true believers, is gathered for another sign of Yere blessing. Reward those which has faith, as Ye did reward Yere servant Daniel, which'un Ye saved from the jaws of death whilst he prayed in the lions' den. Take kindly to yere servant Josiah Bledsoe, which is about to witness his faith to Ye."

The preacher opened his eyes, glanced down at the man who had carried the sack of snakes into the church. The man Bledsoe pulled open the top of the sack, plunged in his hand, and when he drew it out, he clutched a rattlesnake that appeared to Kate to be at least three or four feet long. The rattler wriggled and fought, straining to bite its tormentor. But Bledsoe had a tight grip on it close to its head, and another almost at its rattle. He brandished the fierce reptile high over his head, shouting, "Glory to God and to His Holy Son. In the name of Jesus Christ, I defy all evil. My faith alone protects me!"

His fellow congregants answered with shouts and cries of "Amen. Glory to God!"

The angry snake twisted and writhed in Bledsoe's strong grip but could not break free. Meanwhile, the sack at his feet became more active and alive as other reptiles intended for further use at this service tried to escape.

Kate watched, regretting the impulse that had brought her here to witness this display. She pressed back against the wall, not in fear for her own safety but in revulsion. Until Spencer said in a whisper, "Would you like to leave?"

Though she was tempted to go, and feared she might vomit if she did not, she shook her head, determined to see it through. At the moment she made that decision, the head of one of the other snakes burst suddenly from the sack. The rattler started to emerge, and a gasp of alarm swept through the congregation. Being closest to the escaping reptile, Bledsoe's attention was diverted just long enough so that he relaxed his grip on the snake he held above his head. Taking advantage of that lapse to strike at him, the rattlesnake sank its fangs into his bicep, where it clung fast, despite Bledsoe's desperate efforts to shake it off.

It was the preacher who finally tore the reptile from Bledsoe's arm. The third man captured the escaping snake. But the congregation was thrown into turmoil and tried to escape through the small door which was the only means of exit. Kate and Spencer remained pinned against the back wall until the church emptied out. Then Kate called out, "Put him into my Jeep! We'll take him down to Wildwood!"

Instead of acting at once, the preacher came halfway down the short aisle to demand, "Who are ye, wuhman? We ain't never seed ye afore."

"I'm Kate Kincaid, replacing Eunice Samuels, who is drinlin'. Better bring him! We've no time to lose!"

"We don't know ye," the man insisted.

"Even if you don't know me, you know Leona Owens. She'll take care of him. But it has to be soon. Time counts!"

"Leona, eh? We know her," the preacher admitted. He gestured to his friend, and together they carried Bledsoe out to a car and followed Kate and Spencer down to Wildwood.

She pulled the Jeep up so fast that the gravel exploded from under her wheels like gunshot. She leaped out of the car, took the three steps onto the porch of Wildwood in one bound, calling, "Owens! A snakebite case! Owens!"

When there was no response, she rushed into the building, found that no one was there. Not Owens, not Eva, the secretary. The place was empty. She raced to Owens's tiny office. There, on the small cork bulletin board, she found a note tacked.

Took patient in difficult labor down to hospital.
Will try to be back before nightfall. Owens.

By that the time the preacher and his comrade were carrying Bledsoe into the treatment room. Bledsoe gripped his right bicep so fiercely that the knuckles of his right hand were white. His face was deadly pale. He was dripping sweat. His cheek bore a stain that indicated he had vomited on the long drive.

Kate recalled from an early lecture during first trimester: symptoms and signs of snakebite—pain, nausea, vomiting, diaphoresis, or heavy sweating. Bledsoe had almost all the signs. There was no time to lose, minutes counted now.

"Put him down." They laid Bledsoe on the examining table. She ripped his right sleeve from cuff to shoulder, forced aside his left hand to reveal the place he had been clutching. There they were, fang marks. She put a blood pressure cuff on him, pumped it up quickly, released it slowly. Hypotension, low blood pressure. Now Bledsoe had all the classic signs.

He trembled under her hand, asking in short breathy words, "Doctor? Be there a doctor?"

"I'm afraid not," Kate said.

"Ye said Leona. We got to have Leona," the man insisted, the sweat pouring down his face.

"Leona is down at the hospital with another case," Kate told him. "So even if you don't know me, you'll have to trust me. Lie back. Be still. And don't be afraid. I won't let you die!" she repeated firmly, since panic was as much a danger now as snake venom.

Since the bite had been inflicted half an hour ago, Kate decided that an incision and an attempt to suction out the venom would be futile. She immediately started the patient on a saline intravenous. Then she examined the bite area for edema. If by any stroke of luck there was no swelling and more than thirty minutes had elapsed since he was bitten, there might be no immediate danger. But she did find pronounced swelling around the area of the fang marks.

The danger and the urgency were clear to her. Snake venom kills by causing a breakdown in the blood. If not treated in time, hemolytic blood, in which the hemoglobin has separated from the red cells, can no longer reveal blood type. Without knowledge of the patient's blood type it would not be possible to give him a lifesaving transfusion.

It was too late to transport him to the hospital. Hemolysis would have set in.

She had to start treatment at once.

She unlocked the drug cabinet, searched hurriedly among the various preparations until she found the antivenin kit. Breaking the kit open, she hastily studied the directions for administering the vaccine.

All the while her patient kept whispering, "Fust time . . . fust time it ever happen."

Kate was tempted to answer him sharply but refrained. It was not her function to serve as a religious missionary.

She performed the prescribed skin test to determine if Bledsoe would be allergic to the injection. He was not. She proceeded to administer the antivenin.

She put Bledsoe to bed, mopped his brow, which was not nearly as wet as it had been. His first signs of panic were evidently subsiding. His blood pressure, which was no longer falling, was still nowhere near normal. She would have to spend the night watching over him.

She dismissed Bledsoe's friends. But they were unwilling to entrust him to the care of a woman they considered a foreigner. Only when Will Spencer reassured them would they leave.

As they drove away, Kate exploded. "Insane! They let him handle poisonous rattlesnakes and then refuse to leave him in my care because I'm 'from off.' That's the phrase, isn't it? 'From off'?"

"Yes, yes, it is," Spencer said. "But you mustn't judge them too harshly. After all, they haven't invaded your world, you've invaded theirs."

Kate finally relented. "I guess . . ."

"Their culture is different from ours. You and I, the nurse and the professor, can mingle with them, yet never be part of them. And always remember they are proud people, possibly the proudest you will ever meet."

Kate asked pointedly, "How proud? So proud they'd lie to cover up their indulgences?"

"It's not their way to lie. What makes you ask?"

Kate told him about her encounter with Mrs. Persons. "My test proved conclusively that her sugar level had risen markedly. Yet she kept insisting she was following her diet exactly."

"If she said she was, then take my word for it, she was."

"Then what accounts for her increased sugar levels?"

"I can't answer that. But this much I know. If they're not going to follow your orders they'll tell you to your face. They won't lie about it," Spencer insisted.

Through the night Bledsoe slept restlessly but evidenced no adverse reaction to the antivenin. He had ceased sweating and his pressure was rising slowly but encouragingly. Kate continued to keep watch over him, while pondering the mystery of Mrs. Persons' unexplained sugar count.

By dawn, she determined that as soon as Leona Owens returned, she would do something about it.

With an equal degree of determination, she drove into Adelphi to the hospital and cornered Ray Boyd in his office before his hours in Pediatric Clinic began. She stated Mrs. Persons' problem and sought his advice.

Before he answered he smiled in a way that caused Kate to ask, "Ray, is there something funny about her case? Something that escapes me?"

"No," Boyd replied, "but it's nice to know that you feel the need for a consultation every once in a while."

"Meaning?" Kate asked, blushing in resentment.

"Meaning, Sister Ellen asks for help, Emily McClendon asks for help. Only you feel you have to do it all by yourself. Relax, Kate, relax. Admit you can be less than perfect sometimes," he cautioned gently. "We all are."

"About Mrs. Persons . . ." Kate brought the discussion back to her problem.

"About Mrs. Persons . . ." Ray considered. "Spencer is right. These people are honest. Bluntly so, at times. They will insult you to your face when it's called for. So if she's not lying, what *is* causing her rise in blood sugar? It must be something that she may not even be aware of. Therefore, this is one of those times when the family nurse has to become the family detective. Something in her life-style is different. Find it and you'll have your answer."

It was a cool morning. The early sun glistened on the dewy branches of the pine trees. Kate drove along the dirt road, her Jeep bouncing over the ruts and rocks on its hard springs.

"Family detective, family detective," she kept thinking.

She reached the foot of Persons' hill, got out, slung her saddlebags over her shoulder, climbed to the foot of the path and called out, "Hildy! It's me. Nurse Kate from Wildwood."

Hildy Persons came out onto the porch, planted herself in a firm, forbidding stance and spat a challenging stream of dark tobacco juice toward the path.

"What is it ye come for today? To make more accusin's?"

"I just want to talk to you, Hildy."

"Seein's how ye tol' me to my face I wuz lyin' ye can leave off callin' me Hildy. Mrs. Persons will do."

"All right then, Mrs. Persons," Kate said. "May I come up?"

The woman considered her request dourly, then said, "'Low as ye might, s'long as ye're here already."

Kate started up the path while the woman's eyes followed her every step of the way, unrelenting.

"I would like to go over your diet, the things you eat . . ." Kate began.

The woman interrupted, "We already done that."

"I would like to do it again, just in case I missed something," Kate replied.

"Ain't nothin' missed," the woman insisted, adamant.

"May I come in and look around?"

"Suit yereself," Mrs. Persons said, spitting tobacco juice once again before leading the way back into the cabin. "Well, go wan, look!"

She set herself to eyeing Kate disapprovingly as the latter made an inspection of the pots on the wood stove, then of the old handcrafted wall cabinet in which Mrs. Persons kept her foodstuffs, lastly the old, round-topped electric refrigerator. She found nothing that was prohibited by Mrs. Persons' prescribed diet. Perhaps the trouble lay in quantity. But the woman was not so heavy as to substantiate that possibility. Then her insulin? She had insisted she was using her newly prescribed dose and both Spencer and Ray Boyd said these people would not lie.

Why, then?, Kate kept asking herself, *why this unhealthy rise in her sugar level?*

"Mrs. Persons, is there anything you do differently now than you did two months ago?"

"No!" the woman replied. "Now, if ye're done . . ." It was a pointed suggestion for Kate to leave.

"Yes, yes," Kate agreed, even though she was far from finished with this problem. She started toward the door, the old floorboards creaking under her feet. Mrs. Persons trailed her to make sure she would indeed depart. At the open door she said, "Would be nice if Eunice was back next time. Least she believes a body."

"I'm sorry about . . ." Kate started to say.

But Mrs. Persons put an end to the conversation when she spat tobacco juice beyond the edge of the porch. Kate started down the path. As she was swinging up into the Jeep she stopped in midair. A thought had suddenly crossed her mind. She climbed down again, headed toward the cabin once more, despite Mrs. Persons, who maintained a forbidding stance at the edge of the porch.

"Fergit somethin'? Like mebbe to go accusin' again?"

"Mrs. Persons, how long have you been chewing tobacco?"

"Near all my life."

"The same kind?"

"Terbaccy is terbaccy."

"I mean, where do you get it?"

"Are you askin' do I buy it or do I steal it?" the woman asked, furious.

"No. I mean, do you buy it in the same place all the time?"

"M' grandson Jeff, he buys it. Where, I don't ask. Just so long as 'tis right-tastin' and gives a body a little comfort from the troubles of the day."

"Did Jeff always buy it for you?" Kate asked.

"Nope, 'fore his paw went to work truckin' coal, he uset to buy it fer me."

"But is it the same brand?" Kate asked.

"'Tain't no business o' yeres, but t'answer is no. Why?"

Kate paused to phrase her next question very diplomatically.

"Mrs. Persons, would you consider it an imposition if I asked you to let me see the plug of tobacco you are using now?"

"That's a lot of words fer askin' a simple thang like kin ye see somethin'," Mrs. Persons said suspiciously.

"Then kin I see it?"

Mrs. Persons pondered her request. Finally she dug into her apron pocket and pulled out the small, brown, hard-packed plug of tobacco which bore teeth marks where she had bitten off her last chew.

Top O' The Crop, the little pasted-on label read. It bore a sketch of golden tobacco leaves as background for the printed matter. Kate studied the words. *Ingredients: choicest tobacco leaves, molasses, salt, preservatives.*

Molasses! The word leaped out at her. Very few foods have a higher sugar content than that! *Molasses!*

The woman had been telling the truth. She had adhered to her diet, had taken her insulin, had done everything prescribed for her. The only thing that had changed was her chewing tobacco. Evidently this new brand had a much higher content of molasses than the old.

"Mrs. Persons, I apologize for doubting your word "

"'Bout time," the woman said.

"I now have to prescribe a little differently for you. You must give up this brand of chewing tobacco. In fact, it would be helpful if you gave up chewing tobacco altogether."

"Cain't," the woman said.

"Can't or wont?" Kate asked.

"Don't matter," Mrs. Persons said stolidly.

"Then at least give up this brand," Kate urged.

"I lak it," Mrs. Persons insisted.

"It's not good for you."

"Tastes better," Mrs. Persons said.

"It's raising your sugar level. I strongly advise giving it up and going back to the old brand."

"Nope!" the woman said firmly, ending all discussion.

Kate thought, *Spencer was right. They may not agree with you but they won't lie about it.*

"We'll have to increase your insulin dose and get you regulated all over again," Kate said.

"Ye do that," Mrs. Persons said.

Kate Kincaid had learned another lesson in mountain ways. She added "stubborn" to "proud" and "truthful."

She surrendered to Mrs. Persons' inflexibility only after taking a blood sample, a procedure to which the woman accommodated with dignity. Once Kate had sealed the test tube, Mrs. Persons relented somewhat.

"Ye can call me Hildy again, if it pleasures you."

On the drive back toward Wildwood, Kate pondered the events of the last forty-eight hours. She owed Ray Boyd her thanks for a valuable lesson in family nursing. And there was Mrs. Persons, set in her ways, stubborn, close-minded, a woman who lived much as her ancestors did two hundred years ago. And down at Wildwood the grizzled mountain man, given to proving his primitive faith by handling deadly rattlesnakes, as if his God had ever asked for such a display of faith.

And in the midst of this strange world, a child like Eloise, bright, sensitive, a budding mind that should grow and contribute to the outside world or it might, by example, follow the way of Mrs. Persons or of that misguided man who had come within an hour of dying a painful death that was no more than fanatical religious suicide.

Kate, Ellen and Emily McClendon had been instructed that a family nurse was just that, a nurse responsible for the total health of each member of the family.

With sudden resolve, Kate brought her Jeep to an abrupt, skidding halt, made a sharp U-turn and headed for Adelphi.

Family nurse, family detective, she would now become family education counselor, if need be.

CHAPTER 15

The Adelphi Town School was a drab, sprawling old building that clearly showed where, years ago, additions had been built to accommodate the combined elementary and high-school student bodies when another county school had been closed down.

As she entered the old building, she could hear the swift stampede of scrambling feet on the hardwood gymnasium floor. Curiosity made her go to the door and peer in. Ten husky boys in their early and midteens were practicing basketball. From the games she had attended with Howard she had picked up considerable knowledge of the sport, and was able to appreciate the skill of these youngsters. She smiled and thought, *go get 'em, Hawks!*

After she inquired of the school clerk, Kate found Willa Talmadge in her classroom. The teacher was stacking away the geography charts she had used in her last class of the day. She was in her early fifties, petite, dark-haired. *Birdlike,* Kate thought. A woman of physical delicacy with a sensitive and alert air, she turned to stare at Kate through her steel-rimmed glasses. "May I help you?"

"Miss Talmadge?"

"Yes," the tiny woman replied, continuing to store her rolled-up charts.

"Eloise Torrence's teacher?"

"Yes, indeed," Miss Talmadge said, abandoning her work to give her full attention to Kate.

"I'm Kate Kincaid, from the hospital. I've visited the family, met Eloise. I'd like to talk to you about her."

"Of course," Miss Talmadge said. "I'm afraid we have no chairs for adult visitors," indicating Kate take one of the students' seats.

Kate squeezed into a front seat, noticing the carvings on the old desktop before her. Hearts with arrows and initials in them. Two derogatory words about a teacher which someone had tried to obliterate without quite succeeding. Some initials carved so long ago that age and wear had smoothed them down to the point where they were barely legible. How many years had this old classroom served to educate the children of Adelphi? How many boys and girls had sat in this same seat, among them perhaps some of the adults she had treated?

"Well, now?" Miss Talmadge asked. "About Eloise. A strange child. No, not strange. Unusual. Withdrawn. Sensitive. I ofttimes think, if only we could unlock her inner mind. But she lives in a world of her own."

"Have you ever thought of teaching her differently from the others?" Kate asked.

"Oh, many times," Miss Talmadge said. "But, my dear Miss Kincaid, there are problems."

"What problems?"

"Eloise is only one child among thirty-three in my fifth-grade class. Much as I'd like to, I can't take time away from them to devote to her. It isn't fair. Besides . . ." She hesitated before proceeding. "Well, let us say that education in these mountains is resisted as well as welcomed. Some can see the economic advantage. At the same time, most parents consider it a threat."

"Education a threat?" Kate found it impossible to accept.

"Children who benefit most from education tend to leave here and pursue their lives elsewhere. So education breaks up families, which are the basis of society here. Therefore, they are hostile to it. No one knows that better than I."

"Yet you stay on."

"I do what I can," Miss Talmadge said modestly. "Unfortunately, in a case like little Eloise, it is not nearly enough."

"If you could only give her a little more time . . ."

"How? When?"

"After school in the afternoon," Kate suggested.

Miss Talmadge smiled indulgently. "My dear Miss Kincaid, the children are all bused in and out together. There is no way for a child to come earlier or remain later. Except the few who live in Adelphi."

"Miss Talmadge, if it were possible for Eloise to be here earlier and stay later would you be willing to give her the time? To give her the benefit of your obvious experience?"

With those last words, the women's eyes met. Kate's look showed she was aware of Talmadge's background, which far exceeded mountain life and culture. In Talmadge's eyes was an acknowledgment of Kate's comment and her demand for an explanation.

However, she said only, "I would welcome the chance to work with Eloise and help her advance as swiftly as her agile mind demands. If it could be arranged."

"I'll work on it," Kate said. "As long as I know you're willing to help."

Kate rose to go, but Talmadge smiled and said, "Aren't you going to ask?" Her soft eyes were peering at Kate through her plain, serviceable steel-framed glasses. "Don't you want to know what I'm doing here?"

"You're not mountain folk. But I didn't want to pry."

"Twenty-seven years," Willa Talmadge said, "that's how long I've been here. Times I love it. These mountains. Their wildness, their timelessness. And these people, who change little more than their mountains. Yet, despite the wide, wild space, the majestic mountains, the broad sky, this place can be a prison."

"Then why do you stay?"

"The people here took me in when no one else would. Your generation wouldn't understand. But twenty-seven years ago people were shocked at the mere hint that the woman who taught their children might have a life of her own, a love of her own. Might even do such a daring unconventional thing as become pregnant. . . ."

Kate's eyes were fixed on Talmadge's. There was a sudden communion between the two women.

"Nowadays, if a teacher is pregnant and unmarried it may cause a flurry, but in the end she remains and teaches and eventually the excitement passes. Twenty-seven years ago, public attitudes were not much more enlightened than in the days of *The Scarlet Letter*. A mere hint of scandal, even if untrue, was enough to ban a teacher from her school. And not only from that school. She couldn't get a recommendation that would secure her a job at any other school. And if the scandal were true, if she really was pregnant, and unmarried, her position was completely untenable.

"Except in out-of-the-way places like this. Where, because of need, they would take in a woman with such a reputation. It also had another advantage."

"The hospital, the availability of midwives?" Kate assumed.

Talmadge nodded. "I can vouch for their skill and their kindness. I was delivered of a perfectly healthy little girl. Megan. Six pounds, eight ounces. And pretty. Very very pretty."

"Where is she now?" Kate asked.

Proudly Talmadge said, "She is now an Associate Professor of Philosophy at a fine small New England college. And has made me a grandmother twice over." Talmadge studied Kate for a moment. "She looks quite a bit like you. Small. Blond as her father was blond. And still pretty. Except now, at her age, I suppose one should call her beautiful or handsome. Good features, and strong. Like yours."

"Forgive me for asking . . ." Kate began.

Talmadge anticipated her. "Her father? He never even knew."

"You never told him?" Kate asked, astonished.

Talmadge shook her head ever so slightly before confessing, "I considered it very carefully at the time. I decided, if I tell him he'll want to marry me. And I will be tempted to accept that obvious way out. Then I asked, is he the man I want to spend the rest of my life with? And I realized, a love affair is one thing, but marriage, a lifetime together, oh, no. So I never told him. I found this place. Came here. Taught. Had my child. Went on teaching."

"Surely the problem of educating your daughter here was much the same as teaching a special child like Eloise," Kate suggested.

"I told you, the problem is time. Not mine. The child's time."

"And if that could be arranged?" Kate asked.

"I would be only too glad to teach her in the same way I taught Megan. But if we light the flame in Eloise's mind, we must be prepared to go all the way with her. Can you promise her that?"

CHAPTER 16

Kate pulled the Jeep to a stop alongside the edge of the dirt road at the foot of Torrences' hill. She got out cautiously, keeping her eye on the old cabin at the top. She called out, "Anyone home?" There was no answer. She called again, "Anyone home up there?"

The door opened. Matilda Torrence emerged to stare down toward the foot of the hill. Her unfortunate little son, Benjy, clung to her housedress. There was no sign of Eloise.

"Matilda? I'm Kate. From Wildwood," she called out.

"And what would ye want?" Matilda Torrence called back suspiciously.

"Just to visit and talk. May I come up?"

Mrs. Torrence pondered a moment, then said, "Might's well, since ye're here already."

Kate could not be sure if it was caution or suspicion that made the woman appear unfriendly, especially since during their last contact she had seemed kindly disposed toward her. As Kate approached the porch, she discovered that the woman's face showed grave concern.

"There's something wrong," Mrs. Torrence assumed fearfully.

"I just came to visit. And to bring some presents for the children," Kate said, showing two little gifts she had been able to buy in Adelphi.

"'N' why would ye do that?"

"I thought they might like it," Kate said, still wondering why Eloise had not appeared. She hesitated before asking, "Can I give this to Benjy?"

"Ef'n he don't care to," the woman said.

Knowing that meant he would like to have it, Kate handed the small, brightly wrapped package to the boy, who seized it with both hands. He tried to unwrap it but could not manage. Kate knelt beside him. To give him the sense of accomplishing it, she carefully helped him unwrap it by using his own fingers as the instruments. She had brought him a brightly painted little pull toy, a wooden dog that she demonstrated by pulling it along the porch floor so that its legs moved and it seemed to be walking. Benjy's face lit up with much delight. He dropped to the floor to push the little dog and watched the way its legs moved in exaggerated unison.

"Hound," he said. He repeated the word, "Hound," and laughed.

Mrs. Torrence smiled at her poor little son's joy.

"And I have a gift for Eloise, too," Kate said, seeking the child's whereabouts.

"Ain't here," her mother said.

"What do you mean, ain't here?"

"She run off," Mrs. Torrence said, confessing the cause of her tense concern.

"Why?" Kate asked, greatly worried now.

"She's allus quick to argy with her paw. Child worries me at times. Benjy's quare in his way, but she's quare in hers. Always off in secret whilst she should be chorein'."

"Chorein'?" Kate asked.

"Somebody's got to feed the diddlers, collect their eggs, tend the hog. Failn' them, we kinda like to starve. It's wuhman work to tend 'em. Any young'un wants to be a good wife best larn how to do that early. She wouldn't. And her paw, he don't 'low it no other way. So she run off."

"Does she 'run off' often?" Kate asked.

"More'n enough," Mrs. Torrence said, "but she'll be back. Come edge of dark and it git cold out there, she'll be comin' back. Hongry as can be." Mrs. Torrence then lowered her voice to confess, "I got to feed her in secret, 'cause her paw don't like fer her to be fed if'n she's run off that day."

"If I wait, will I see her?"

"She'll be back, she'll be back," the woman repeated sadly, as if the girl's return would pose new problems. "Come in, set a spell, whilst I'm a-cookin' supper."

Kate entered the small house and found that Mrs. Torrence had been washing the floor when she arrived. The bucket stood in the middle of the half-wet floor. The smell of strong homemade lye soap filled the room.

"'Scuse me," the woman said as she got down on her knees to resume scrubbing. Kate noticed that though her hands were red and raw from the harsh soap, she seemed not to mind, accepting it as an unavoidable part of her life. Matilda Torrence scrubbed in silence, every so often having to brush her son aside as he dragged his new toy across her path.

Suddenly she looked up to ask anxiously, "What makes ye come wantin' Eloise?"

"She's a bright, pleasant child. I like her and wanted her to have this gift."

"What's it?" the woman asked, glancing suspiciously toward the small, flat, brightly wrapped gift Kate held.

"I thought she might enjoy a new book," Kate said.

"School just about started again and she already plumb wore out the books she was gived."

"I thought she might like something different from the ones they give her in school," Kate said.

"'Low as she might, took as she is with readin' all the time." Matilda Torrence put aside the floor cloth, rose to her feet. Kate noticed that at twenty-nine Mrs. Torrence moved like an arthritic woman of sixty. She drew close to Kate to confess.

"Times she hides in that there room. An' she writes. More'n oncet I snuck in there when she wasn't 'round. I don't read good, but I kin read some. It's quare. Very quare. Each time I say I won't never read it no more. But I cain't stand it, cain't. So I do."

"Matilda, have you ever thought that you have a daughter with an unusual mind?" When she realized the woman did not comprehend, she said, "Your little girl is bright, smart, very very smart."

"She does tol'able in that school," Mrs. Torrence admitted.

"She can do a great deal more than 'tol'able' if she gets the chance," Kate pointed out. "She has too good a mind to waste on chores."

"Oh, she got to do her chores. Her paw won't put up with no sass, not from me, not from her."

"Matilda, I want you to help me convince your husband that Eloise should have extra schooling, in town, someday maybe even in the city."

"The city? We ain't never been, not since the time we took little Kate when she was so sick she lak to die. They didn't help her none 'cause later she did die. Since then my man don't hold with goin' to the city for no reason."

"I'll talk to him," Kate said determinedly.

"No! He'll go into one of his franzies," the woman warned. "Mebbe ye better leave without seein' Eloise. Mebbe ye better take that present with ye. And Benjy's, too. I'll kinda lak to pretend ye wuz never here."

"Don't do that to Benjy," Kate said. "And you can't stop me from waiting for Eloise. Even if I have to wait down by the path."

"Just hope he don' see ye," Mrs. Torrence warned.

She left Matilda to her floor washing, went down the path to the Jeep where she found Eloise sitting behind the wheel, pretending to drive. Without revealing her presence, Kate listened as the child improvised, "'Round the curve we go, fast enough to burn the wind. Bumpety-bump over the holes and the cracks. Through the holler. And now we leave the holler and climb up into the mountains. Up to the sky. And we go sailin' through the sky like them airyplanes, leavin' white tails behind, long white tails."

As soon as the child became aware of Kate, she crouched fearfully behind the wheel, pleading, "I din' do nothin'. I never meaned to do nary a thing."

Kate drew closer, the child began to tremble.

"Eloise, no need to be afeared," Kate said, thinking to reassure her in her accustomed language. She held out the brightly wrapped gift. The child stared at her, suspicious, as all mountain people seemed to be of the unfamiliar.

Though the child's delft-blue eyes grew wide with the desire to possess the bright package, she resisted touching it. Slowly Kate opened the brightly colored paper to reveal the book and its illustrated cover. Eloise was torn between temptation and fear. Kate held the book out to her. Finally Eloise found the courage to reach for it. She stared at the cover, then clutched the book to her. It seemed enough merely to possess it. Reading was a luxury beyond her dreams.

Soon the child held the book away from her to stare again at the colorful cover. Only then did she dare open it. The book contained brief poems, each of which was illustrated by a watercolor on the facing page. Eloise rubbed her fingers over the illustrations, trying to determine if they had a texture she could feel.

"Eloise . . . read one of the poems," Kate suggested.

The child stared at the text. She began to read aloud. She read more fluidly than Kate expected, and with a growing sense of enjoyment. Having read the first poem, she turned the page and read the second more hungrily. Then the third. She looked at Kate and smiled. As her sense of enjoyment and accomplishment grew, she read on and on. Finally she was so exhilarated she was laughing aloud.

Suddenly she turned to Kate, kissed her on the cheek and pressed against her. She had no words but needed none to express her appreciation. All that ceased abruptly when from the cabin she heard her father's voice call out angrily.

"Eloise! Damn! Whar is that child?"

Once again she became a cowering, frightened little girl. Huddling behind the wheel, trembling, she hid her new book to keep it from her father.

"Don't be afraid, Eloise," Kate said. "Let's go up to the house and talk to your father."

"He'll get in a franzy," she warned.

"Come," Kate insisted. She took the child's hand. Eloise left the book on the front seat, but Kate said, "Take it with you. It's a present you've a right to have."

They started up the hill. They could already hear Torrence berating his wife.

"Dang child, always contrary, never whar she supposed to be. Whyn't she out back feedin' the hog, else'n we'll be having nary enough meat and fatback for winter. Ye had ought to be strong with her!"

At the sound of their steps on the squeaky porch, Torrence turned his anger in their direction. "Come in here, girl!" The instant he saw Kate he became even more hostile. "You?" was all the greeting he bestowed on her. "I hear Eunice's comin' back tomorrow. What you doin' up in our holler?"

"Mr. Torrence, I came here to see you," Kate said forthrightly. "Can we set and talk a spell?"

"Don' rightly know why, since it's already decided I'm to have my opyration," Torrence said, seeking to avoid conversation with a woman he obviously distrusted.

"We have to talk about Eloise," Kate said.

"She drinlin'?" Torrence asked, concerned now.

"Her physical health is good. It's her mind I want to talk about."

She put her arm around the child, drew her close and felt her quivering. Kate pressed her to her side to reassure her.

"Mr. Torrence, your daughter Eloise has a fine mind. Better than most I've run across in children her age. She is sensitive, bright and creative." Kate realized she was talking a foreign language to this mountain man to whom survival was the challenge. "Mr. Torrence, your child has the possibility of living a life beyond these mountains. Out in the world she might achieve great things. But like your crops, her mind needs to be watered and tended if it's to yield a harvest. Do you understand?"

Torrence looked at the book Eloise clutched in her arms. He reached for it. If she had not surrendered it he would have torn it free. He glared at it, tossed it into a corner of the room. Instinctively Eloise moved to recapture it, but Kate held her close.

"What air ye sayin'? Or is it so bad ye cain't say it straight out?" Torrence demanded.

"What I am saying, Mr. Torrence, is that this child should have special teaching so she can make the most of her excellent mind."

"She already got enough larnin'," Torrence replied. "Every mornin' she gits picked up on that there yeller bus to get carted off to that school whar they only larn them to get above their raisin'. Leads to nothin' but self-conceit."

"Self-worth, Mr. Torrence, which is a far different thing."

"I don' hold with all this book nonsense. Anything worth rememberin' can be tol', like it used to. Best stories ever I larned was tol' when I was a boy. Tol' by those who remembered, or else singed by someone. My old granny was allus doin' sings or ha'nt stories, lak to scare a chile to death with ghosts and all. We din' need no books nor them there magazines I see in town. Nor that tell-yvision. 'Nuff 'Loise goes to town school,'' Torrence declared with finality.

''That may be enough for most children. But not for her. She should learn more about the world outside. She should learn to talk well, to read and write well.''

''Figger she reads and writes too much as 'tis. Allus in that there room writin' her nonsense,'' Torrence said. '''Sides, oncet she larns all that stuff, then what? She goin' to fergit her own ways? Be a stranger to her own kin? No! Till she gits married she stays right here. After that, if'n she wants to marry somebody from off and then go, that'll be her decidin'.''

''Mr. Torrence, I am trying to impress on you that you have a very unusual child. . . .''

Torrence turned from Kate to his wife. ''She's wantin' to do the same to our 'Loise as was done to your cousin Sam. They said he was a bright 'un. Sent him off to school in the city. Din't last but half a year. They poke fun at the way he talk. Want him to use that picky language of theirs. And when he couldn't do it fast enough they dang near drove him out. He come back here and never been the same since. Lak he didn' belong nowhere, not here nor there. I don' aim to have that happen to my little girl. So, I bid ye good day and ask ye to be on yere way.''

Kate was about to reply, but behind Torrence, his wife shook her head to warn her off.

''I'll come back,'' Kate said.

''Be better for all if'n you don't,'' Torrence warned.

''I'll be back,'' Kate insisted.

Angry, because she was making him confess to what he considered his own shame and failure, he shouted, ''Won't do no good, there's scarce enough to eat, let alone afford such foolishness as ye're talkin'.''

''I'll be back,'' Kate reiterated.

She kissed Eloise on the cheek and started for the door. Torrence intervened. ''Ain't ye going to take yere present with ye?''

Kate glanced at the book, which lay in the corner where he had thrown it, then looked down at Eloise whose eyes pleaded to retain the gift. But Torrence said, ''Girl, git it and give it back!'' Eloise hesitated. ''Yo' paw said, give it back!''

Reluctantly, the child crossed the room, picked up the book, cradled it in her arms, then held it out to Kate. Kate could see the tears in Eloise's eyes, but for the child's sake she accepted it. As she did, Eloise seized Kate's hand, pressed it against her cheek, then kissed it.

Kate got in behind the wheel of the Jeep, started up the motor with a furious twist of the key, thinking, *so it is not only prejudice but poverty I have to fight. Okay, then!*

She shoved the stick into gear and took off with a fury that made the rear wheels spin before gripping the earth firmly.

The next morning Kate found a message in her mailbox that Abbott wanted to see her. She was not surprised, expecting to be graded on her performance during her few days at Wildwood. She started up to Abbott's office, reviewing in her mind the families she had visited, the manner in which she had treated them, especially the emergency with the snakebite victim. In all, she felt that she deserved a good rating.

Her first glimpse of Abbott's dour face indicated otherwise. *God,* Kate thought, *is there no way of satisfying this woman? What have I done wrong now?* She was prepared for a detail-by-detail account of her shortcomings.

"Kincaid," Abbott began in the severe tone that always preceded one of her rebukes, "I received a call from Leona Owens this morning. A very disturbing call."

"Something I did?" Kate asked.

"Torrence," Abbott said, as if that one word stated the entire problem.

"He needs surgery. Even Samuels said that in her report."

"I'm talking about the little girl," Abbott said.

"Oh, yes," Kate said, "I'd very much like to discuss that with you."

Abbott interrupted, "Not nearly as much as I'd like to discuss it with you. Torrence made a special trip down to Wildwood to complain about you."

Kate cautioned herself to remain, if not calm, at least in control. She must present her case unemotionally.

"I have come across a child of unusual sensitivity and intelligence. As a family nurse I feel it my professional duty to do what I can to see that her abilities are nurtured. That her horizons are broadened. That her talent be given a chance to develop, to come alive, not remain something that she hides in the dark because she thinks she is strange. All I want to do is give her that chance."

"It never occurred to you that you are meddling in very private family matters?" Abbott demanded. "These people accept and respect us because we respect them, their customs and practices."

"I did ask for Torrence's permission . . ." Kate started to say.

Abbott interrupted, "There is a line, an invisible line, that we do not cross. We do not intrude in the family's private business or the parents' prerogatives. Due to your lack of familiarity with their ways, you crossed over that line. You could have done this hospital and our family nursing program great harm by stirring up considerable resentment. To say nothing of what this can mean to your own career here."

Despite the threat implied in Abbott's words, Kate insisted, "The first thing you taught us is that we are responsible for the entire family."

"The *health* of the entire family," Abbott corrected her.

"Is that limited to making sure they don't have high blood pressure? Or to treating their colds? Or recommending surgery for their hernias? I believe that when a nurse sees something that is damaging to any family member, physically *or* psychologically, it is her duty to do something about it."

"I repeat, you are to confine yourself to the health of the family," Abbott declared.

"We inquire into their diet, their sanitary facilities, their water supply, we assist in their family planning. None of those are diseases. Yet they are vital to producing and maintaining healthy, stable individuals. That's all I'm trying to do for little Eloise."

"'Trying to do'?" Abbott repeated. "I consider this matter closed."

"I would still like . . ."

Abbott interrupted again. "I understand that Mr. Torrence said no. He is the head of that family. His word is final. Since this is not within the scope of the duties of a nurse, you had best forget it."

"Miss Abbott, I would be less than honest with you if I promised to forget it. I can't."

Abbott's eyes narrowed, her lips pursed slightly. "I can see now why your past record indicates an inability to respect the wishes and orders of your superiors. I will only say that any effort on your part to continue with this will endanger your future here."

Kate stifled the urge to respond, turned and started out. But she stopped in the doorway.

"Yes, Kincaid?" Abbott demanded impatiently.

"It just occurred to me. Since by your own statement this is outside the scope of a nurse's duties, there can be no objection to my pursuing this personally on my own time, can there?"

"If you're asking, can I officially forbid you, the answer is no. If you're asking, do I disapprove? Yes. Most emphatically!"

The two women eyed each other for a long moment, neither giving any sign of compromise. But in the end, it was Kate who had to leave off staring and go on to her next assignment, which was in the Family Planning Clinic, in preparation for the start of their first Midwifery trimester.

She passed a long line of patient women waiting for family planning consultation before she reached the clinic itself. When she entered, Sister Ellen interrupted interviewing her patient to say briskly, "Kate. Phone calls. Three of them. All from a certain person."

They had shared enough intimacies for Ellen to know about Howard and their relationship.

"It sounded urgent," Ellen said. "I hope it isn't."

A single glance between them said the rest of what Ellen had to say. For she and Kate had discussed many times the possibility that Howard might grow impatient, might fall in love with some other woman, might even consider marriage to someone else. Insistent calls from him could mean that he had come to some final conclusions about their lives.

Kate went to the phone, hesitated before lifting the receiver, then decided if it was bad news she might as well hear it now. There was also a part of her that, in defiance of Abbott's last warning, compelled her to think, *damn it, I'll give this up now. I'll go back to Howard and admit it was all a mistake. Coming down here was simply exchanging one form of domination for another. I'm through with nursing.*

She picked up the phone aggressively and dialed.

Howard's secretary responded with a cool "Mr. Brewster is in conference, but he asked me to put your call through at once. Please hold on."

She felt a twinge in her stomach when Howard answered in an impersonal way, without any of his usual endearments or even referring to her by name. *Yes,* she thought, *when the end comes, it must come like this.*

Still aloof and impersonal, he said, "I am arguing my first case before the Supreme Court."

Relieved and delighted for him, Kate said, "Terrific!"

Howard continued, "And I thought since Washington is midway between here and Adelphi, if you could find time to fly up, we might meet and have dinner there. Next Friday evening?"

She smiled and realized, poor Howard, undoubtedly sitting in conference, bursting with his news, yet unable to allow it to show or to let his client know that he was asking her to spend their first long weekend together in six months.

"Darling, I'll have to get permission," she said. "We're coming to the end of the second trimester—there are exams. But maybe Abbott will say yes. I'll let you know."

"Do your best," Howard said, in the same even tone he would have used with a colleague or a witness. "And call back as soon as you can. So I can make a reservation for you. Myself, I'll be staying at the Watergate."

Kate couldn't resist laughing. "Hawk, I don't think you're fooling anyone with 'Myself, I'll be staying at the Watergate.' Okay. The Watergate. If I can make it. Meantime, I love you, you great big Supreme Court lawyer. And stop blushing. I can see it over the phone."

She hung up, relieved, elated. It was exactly what she needed after her confrontation with Abbott, a safety valve for her anger and her concern. Until she realized that so soon after one showdown with Abbott, she would have to have another. She decided to face it at the first possible moment.

On her way to the desk where she would conduct her first family planning interview, she passed Ellen. The young nun looked up questioningly; Kate smiled down at her and nodded. She raised her right hand, two fingers extended in a V-for-Victory sign.

"I'm happy for you," Ellen said softly.

In that moment, Kate remembered the only time the two had ever talked about sex as it related to themselves. They had had a brief conversation over coffee after coming off night duty, which had involved taking care of a girl who had tried to abort herself with unfortunate results.

Ellen had said sadly, "If only she hadn't been so ignorant of sex and the consequences, this would never have happened."

Kate had asked, "Have you ever had a man?"

"No," Ellen replied simply.

"Ever think about it?" Kate asked.

"Sometimes."

"Does it trouble you?"

"Sometimes," Ellen said.

"Do you ever think of . . . of resigning, or whatever it is nuns do when they quit?" Kate asked.

"Sometimes."

"Would you?"

"Never," Ellen said.

That was the end of all personal conversation about sex between them. Yet Ellen could fully understand, commiserate and empathize with Kate and her emotional problems. As now, she could be genuinely delighted that Kate's relationship with Howard was obviously flourishing once more.

Their tour of duty in Family Planning Clinic was finished. It had been a long day, with a number of interviews, presenting a multiplicity of problems, physical, emotional, problems involving frigidity, impotence, and even one case that, as the details unfolded, turned out to be a case of wife abuse.

But now it was over for the day. Kate felt tired but free. Until she realized she had one problem yet to face.

"A whole weekend off?" Abbott considered the request with a frown. "Do you realize your second trimester exams will be coming up next week?"

"Yes, but I think I'll be prepared," Kate said.

"Don't be misled by the fact that you did so well on your previous exam. Family treatment is far more difficult than Diagnosis. Ever hear about Stebbins, in the class before yours?"

"Yes, I know," Kate said. "Passed her first trimesters with the highest grade in her class, then flunked out in Treatment."

"Personally, I'd spend every available moment studying. However, it's up to you, Kincaid,'' Abbott said, more in warning than as a concession.

''If I can be excused from clinic duties for the weekend, I would like to go,'' Kate said.

''Suit yourself,'' Abbott said. ''In fact, it might do you some good. It will give you a chance to reconsider your determination to interfere in the Torrence case.''

CHAPTER 17

The plane began its descent. Kate could see the city of Washington below. Familiar buildings came into view: the tall, slender Washington Monument thrusting into the clear sky, the Lincoln Memorial with its imposing white Grecian pillars, the blue fall sky reflected in the long pond leading to it.

Soon with a sudden scrape, the plane touched down on the concrete runway of National Airport. The pilot reversed the engines and the plane began braking to slow down. It turned off the main runway and taxied toward the landing gate.

In her desire to see Howard once more, Kate broke all the rules. She unfastened her seatbelt long before the plane came to a stop. She was the first on her feet, first in the aisle, first to wait impatiently until they swung open the door.

When her bag appeared on the revolving luggage dispenser in the terminal, she did not wait for a porter. Heavy as the bag was, she seized it and made for a cab outside the terminal building.

Even before she was seated she told the driver, "The Watergate, please, and hurry!" She was distressed that he did not pull away immediately but waited until the dispatcher seated another passenger in the cab, a portly middle-aged man who, with a barely audible" 'scuse me," practically shoved her to the seat on the far side.

His destination being closer, Kate had to restrain her impatience until they dropped him at his hotel, then finally went on to the Watergate.

At the registration desk she discovered that, yes, Mr. Brewster left word to expect her. The bellboy was at her side, taking her bag and leading her to the elevator.

She discovered that Howard had been in the room before he left for the Supreme Court. There were flowers, long-stemmed red roses. A note leaned against the vase.

Kate darling: Get to the Court as soon as possible. I'm scheduled early. Can't wait for later. Love, Howard.

She changed quickly from her travel slacks and jacket into the dark blue tweed suit she had brought for attendance at the Court session. She freshened her makeup, took one last reassuring look at herself in the mirror and was off. She instructed the cab driver to hurry to the Supreme Court.

As she stepped out of the cab at the bottom of the wide granite steps, she stared up at the tall, fluted pillars of the Court building. She began to sense the majesty and the importance of the Court. She raced up the steps, determined to be on time to hear Howard argue his first big case.

She arrived at the entrance, stared into the high, vaulted rotunda, but was distressed to discover a long line of visitors waiting patiently outside the tall doors to the august chamber. If she had to wait until all those people were admitted, it might take more than an hour. She would surely miss Howard at the crowning moment of his young career. Not many law firms would give a man his age the opportunity to argue a case before the highest court.

As she surveyed the long line, she saw one group of a dozen spectators come out of the courtroom while the uniformed attendant gestured the next dozen in. Just before they passed into the chamber, he whispered instructions on courtroom etiquette. The high door closed silently. Kate did not take her place at the end of the line but went directly to him.

"Please, I must get in. My . . . my fiancé is arguing his first case before the Court this morning and I must be there."

"Sorry, ma'am," the white-haired black attendant said. "These people have all been waiting for quite some time."

"But this is his first case and I haven't seen him for months and . . ." She stopped because she knew it wouldn't make sense to anyone else. Yet to have prevailed on Abbott to let her come, to have come this far, and to miss this moment in Howard's career. . . . She broke down and started to cry.

"Sorry, ma'am, but we have our rules," the sympathetic attendant repeated.

The short, portly man who was first on line stepped forward. He had long white hair that reached down to the collar of his dark jacket. His cherubic face was accented by gold-framed spectacles, behind which were moistly sympathetic blue eyes.

"Sir, would it be permissible for the young lady to take my place?"

"If you want to give it up after waiting so long," the attendant said.

"I do," the plump little man said.

"You'd have to go back to the end of the line," the attendant warned. "They might adjourn for lunch before your turn comes."

"I'll risk it."

He stepped out and with a gallant bow from another age, he beckoned Kate to his place at the head of the line.

Impulsively and with tears still in her eyes, she kissed him. The spectators behind her applauded. Then, with an impromptu but unanimous decision, they made room for the man right behind Kate.

The tall door opened, a previous group of spectators emerged. The attendant smiled at Kate and permitted the next eleven others to enter with her.

As she stepped into the august chamber, a sense of destiny overcame her. Here, the nation's laws were interpreted. Here, the Constitution of the United States was argued and defended. Here, the future of whole generations of Americans was decided.

Though imposing, the room was not as large as she had expected, yet the Justices seated behind the long bench seemed distant from her. She made her way down the aisle to the second row of benches. There was an empty seat in the right-hand section. She slipped in, trying to be as inconspicuous as possible.

At the lectern reserved for attorneys, a tall, elderly, distinguished man faced the judges, making a point of law that was obscure to her but which he argued with great passion. The nine judges listened intently, giving no hint of their attitude. Two of them made assiduous notes, glancing up from time to time at the advocate, who spoke swiftly to make the most of his limited allotted time.

At one point a Justice interrupted with a question that appeared to dispute the lawyer's line of argument. He answered, but another of the Justices, feeling that he had not done as well as he might by his reply, asked a question that gave him a second opportunity. By their questions these two had indicated their predisposition in the case. But the other seven Justices gave no hint of their attitudes.

The case itself was of no interest to Kate, for it concerned the dispute between two states over the water rights to the same river. Instead of listening, she took time to study the backs of the heads of those attorneys behind the barrier who awaited the opportunity to present their cases.

She spied Howard. Her first reaction was dismay. She knew the back of his head so well she could tell that he had changed barbers. There was a cowlick on the back of Howard's head which stood up rebelliously. She felt a strong impulse to slip down the aisle, spit on her hand and flatten it into place before he rose to argue.

The present argument ended. There were no more questions from the Justices. The clerk of the Court called the next case. An aging lawyer, distinguished looking in his formal frock coat, rose and approached the lectern, put down his papers and began, "Mr. Chief Justice and honored Associate Justices of this Court . . ."

Kate soon realized that this was Howard's case, for in one of his letters he had mentioned working on the brief. It concerned a decision in which a state judge had ruled against both parents in a case involving custody of a nine-year-old girl. He had held that unless the child were represented by counsel on her own behalf, there could be no adequate and fair disposition of the custody question.

The case had now come before the Supreme Court on the constitutional question of whether the civil rights of the child had been abridged, because she was not the beneficiary of due process of law in what could prove to be the most important decision of her life.

Howard's opponent, a mature and skillful lawyer, argued that whether a child should have legal representation in such a case was a choice for the parents, not a right or responsibility of the state. The judge's ruling was therefore an unwarranted interference in the family relationship. Except where health or life was concerned, courts could not impose their judgments on parents, who had the ultimate responsibility for their children. If, he argued, it could be shown that a child was being abused physically, mentally or emotionally, then the state and the courts would have a right to intervene and, if necessary, to appoint counsel to protect that child. But no such proof had been introduced into this case.

When the first warning light signaled that he had only a minute left, the attorney turned his argument into a summation, the substance of which was the protection of the sanctity of the family unit and the home from governmental interference. He gathered up his papers and returned to his seat.

Kate watched tensely as Howard rose. He looked extremely impressive, attired in a proper frock coat and striped trousers. He made his way to the lectern and laid out his papers. Kate could feel her hands go cold. Yet Howard seemed confident and unruffled as he looked up, paid the usual opening respects to the Justices, eight men and one woman. Before he launched into his argument, he explained to the Court his position in the case.

His firm had a policy of devoting a percentage of its attorneys' time to *pro bono* work, on behalf of clients and causes deserving of legal representation but unable to afford it. In this particular case they had volunteered to represent the child at no fee because of the importance of the issue involved. Too often, Howard began to argue, children's emotions and their future are trampled upon during the arguments and cruel disputes of warring adults. Children are made victims in a vicious game where love has turned to hatred, where they can be held hostage by one parent or the other to avenge real or fancied wrongs committed, not by the children, but by the parents themselves.

He urged that the child in this case should not be treated as the object of a marital dispute but should be considered one of three essential parties. Otherwise, her rights, well-being, health and safety were being jeopardized.

"In truth," Howard argued, "to treat a child as a pawn or a weapon of retribution in a marital dispute may be the most unjust and terrible form of child abuse, short of physically maiming her. We make no attempt in this argument to determine which parent is right. That is a matter for the courts to decide, but only after the child has had fair representation and its rights protected. We ask the

Justices of this High Court to uphold the judgment of the state court in this matter."

Howard started to gather up his papers when one of the judges to the right of the Chief Justice asked, "Counselor, is it your contention that a lawyer not selected by the parent or parents is the proper person to represent a child? Would we, as parents, hold still for such a decision if it was not a lawyer but the child's doctor who was involved?"

Kate leaned forward anxiously to hear Howard's response.

"Sir, if I may take your analogy one step further, let us suppose this child *were* ill. That both parents were involved in the same marital warfare as in this case. And, as a result, they could not agree on the proper doctor to treat the child. Let us also suppose that, as a result, the child was not receiving any medical treatment. Would not the courts be justified in stepping in and insisting that an appointed doctor treat that child? We have numerous precedents where the courts have made it mandatory that certain medical procedures be carried out on children for their safety, even against the express objections of the parents. I think we are in that exact situation in this case. While the parents are in a legal and emotional battle, the rights of the child go undefended. I do not think a court of equity can allow that to continue."

The Justice nodded, smiled faintly and made a note on his pad, thereby conceding that Howard's response had impressed him. There were two more questions from other Justices. Howard countered with answers that proved he was well prepared for all eventualities which might arise during his argument.

As he turned away from the lectern, he caught sight of Kate, who, he was relieved to see, was smiling at him encouragingly. He stuffed his papers into his briefcase and started out.

Kate joined him in the rotunda, and to the delight of the spectators who were waiting in line, they fell into an intense embrace, kissing for what seemed an inordinately long time, as if to make up at once for the long months of their separation.

They finally stood apart and stared at each other.

Kate said, "You were terrific. And so sure of yourself. They never rattled you once."

He held out his hand. She touched it. It was icy cold.

"God!" she said.

"If that's being sure of myself, and unrattled, that's what I am," he said. He sighed wearily. "Let's get out into the daylight. I have this terrible feeling that a few of those Justices will think of questions they should have asked and come after me."

They had ordered coffee, but he did not drink any of it. He was too tense. She reached across the table to take his hand. It was still very cold.

"Let's do what you marathoners do, walk it off. Come!" she commanded.

They strode along Constitution Avenue until they reached the Washington Monument with its white granite spire majestically pointing to heaven. The broad plaza surrounding it was bounded on all four sides by a row of American flags, which on this day were being whipped by the stiff fall breeze. They crossed the broad avenue, stood at the base and looked up toward the top. At the same instant they both said, "Let's!"

They climbed to the top. Since the day was clear, with only a few friendly clouds, they could see for miles—the White House, the dome of the Capitol, the many official buildings of white stone and graceful architecture. Over toward the river they could see the imposing Kennedy Center.

"That's where we're going tonight," Howard said. "I've got tickets for a new play."

They stood pressed together, holding hands, as they watched planes take off and land at National Airport. They saw the traffic flowing across the wide, beautifully designed bridges that spanned the Potomac and united the many areas of the nation's capital.

Howard whispered suddenly, "You thinking the same thing I am?" He made no secret of his anticipation.

"Uh-huh," she admitted softly.

"Let's go back to the hotel," he whispered.

Their room had been the beneficiary of the V.I.P. treatment. A large bowl of fresh fruit, one bottle of expensive Scotch whisky, one of vodka, and a platter of cheese.

Howard also discovered a bottle of champagne in the refrigerator A damp and soggy note was attached:

This time, bring her back. She is exactly the kind of partner's wife we'd love to have.

It was signed by the wife of the managing partner of the firm. He passed the note to Kate.

She read it and laughed. "So much for all your secret plans."

Howard did not laugh but asked, "Well?"

She knew what he meant. "Darling, I have to finish what I set out to do. It's only six more months."

To change her mind he embraced her, kissed her. This time there were no spectators, no inhibitions. It led naturally to what had been in both their minds since the moment they touched hands in the rotunda of the Supreme Court.

Later they were lying side by side enjoying the champagne, along with a feeling of sensual exhaustion, when they were interrupted by a phone call from the office. Howard's partner wanted to know "How did it go?"

"Terrific!" Howard reported.

His partner laughed and said, "I mean in court."

Howard laughed. "That was terrific, too. I think we have a chance. An excellent chance."

"Good. Sorry to intrude. Have fun. Bring her back."

It was late afternoon when Howard suggested, "Let's not go out to dinner. It'll mean dressing early and all that. Let's order dinner up here. We can dress in time to get to the theater. It's only across the street."

They ordered dinner, ate little, spending most of their time staring at each other across the table. He admired everything about her: the way she lifted her wineglass, the way she smiled, her lack of shyness.

She stared at him, wondering, *during all those months has he been faithful or, like me, has he had an affair?* Or more than one? She realized that by trying to involve him in other affairs she was really trying to ease her own conscience. No matter the great change in sexual morality in recent years, she would always be governed by the conscience instilled in her during her youth. She had a sudden impulse to confess to Howard what had happened with Ray. She decided not to. Why exorcise her own guilt by making it his problem!

They never arrived at the Kennedy Center to see the play. They decided to enjoy each other. They would have only two more days before she would have to return to Adelphi.

She woke early. Dawn was beginning to break and the sky was rosy in the east. The pink light bathed the white marble of the Kennedy Center across from their window. Slipping on Howard's robe, Kate walked out on the balcony in the cool morning air. She could see the planes coming in to land at National Airport. Her bare feet on the stone made her feel even colder. She pulled his robe tighter about her. Then she felt Howard's arms reach around to comfort her.

"What are you thinking?" he asked.

"I love you . . ." she began.

"That's a good place to start." He tried to turn her around to kiss her. She resisted, intent on having her say.

"*And* I love my work. I love those people. I love what I'm learning. I love the knowledge that I can now do things that I've been told for the past five years I can't do."

"Katie, darling . . ." he tried to interrupt.

"No, Howard! Listen to me. Please? I am not going to make up my mind until I've finished. Until I'm qualified, really qualified," she said.

"You mean what we have . . . what we had yesterday and last night . . . doesn't mean anything to you?" he asked, rejected and angry.

"It means a great deal, darling. But unless we intend to spend the rest of our lives in bed together, it can't mean everything. Married life is not a perpetual honeymoon. Love is part of life. Career is part of life. Having children of our own is part of it. I want all these things. And I mean to have them. But in time."

"Time . . ." he repeated disparagingly.

"Please, Howard, it's almost over. Can't you wait six more months?" she pleaded.

"It seems like a lifetime. I know the exact date. I have it on my calendar, circled in red. All right. Six months."

He kissed her, a long kiss, after which he said softly, "You're wearing my robe."

"I'll take it off."

"Not out here. Have you no shame, woman?" He picked her up in his strong arms, carried her into the room and to their bed.

It was past two o'clock in the morning. The city of Washington was asleep. Outside the Watergate, the streets were deserted. Inside, in room 1609, two people, who had for the moment satisfied their desires for each other, lay side by side, quietly enjoying their naked closeness.

Howard reached out to take Kate's hand. She pressed it against her breast and held it there.

"What are you thinking?" he asked. "Right now?"

"The argument you made in court today. Or was it yesterday? How long have we been here?"

"Is that all you're going to remember of this weekend? My argument in court. Doesn't say much for my lovemaking."

"I admired how you argued for the rights of children. I wish you'd represented me."

"Darling, what are you talking about?"

"Eloise, the Torrences, Abbott."

He rose up to look down at her lovely face in the darkness. "Katie?"

She told him about Eloise and the warning Abbott had given her.

"Hawk, what do *you* think I should do?"

"I know better than to tell you what to do about anything," he said. "Besides, I'm not exactly an unprejudiced witness. I have a deep personal interest in seeing you leave Adelphi, no matter what the reason."

"You really do believe in what you said in court. You were not just a lawyer up there arguing a case, were you?"

"Of course I believe in it. The rights of children are precious, and must be protected, even from their parents."

"Good. Because I think so, too!"

Though the flight back to West Virginia took little more than an hour, it was enough time for Kate to reach several decisions. Howard was the man she truly loved, the man she would go back to when her training was completed. So, in fairness and total honesty, she would have to tell Ray the first time she saw him in the hospital.

But when they met, she discovered there was no need.

He simply asked, "How was it?"

"It was wonderful. I learned a great deal about myself, and about what I want."

"I expected that," Ray said softly. "I wish you the best, Kate, you know that."

There was no need to say any more. The fact that he knew and accepted it gave her an additional twinge of guilt. He was such a fine, sensitive man that she blamed herself for not being able to love him as she loved Howard.

But now that she was back, she must confront the matter of little Eloise.

CHAPTER 18

"You won't be too firm with them, will ye?" Mrs. Russell asked while watching Kate do the final touch-ups on her lips and cheeks.

Kate smiled. "No, I won't be too firm with them. So long as they do what I ask."

"Watch out for Charlie Greer. He's the quiet one. Puffing on that pipe, way he does, you have no idea what he's thinking. But he makes the decisions in the end. Wilbur Thomas'll do the talking. But Charlie's the one," Mrs. Russell coached.

"You say they both went to the State University?" Kate asked.

"Both. Charlie's paw, he owned the mines and the lumber mill. Greers have owned most everything here since anyone can remember. And what they didn't own the Thomases did. The telephone company. And the power and light. I kin say this for them. They didn't go off and stay off. They come back. Which means they got some feeling for mountain people. Not that they give anything away. You don't get to be a Greer or a Thomas by giving anything away."

Kate turned from the mirror to face Mrs. Russell. "How do I look?"

Mrs. Russell studied her face, then said gravely, "The face of an angel, but behind those blue eyes I see a tetch o' the devil." Then she added consolingly, "Ye mustn't feel too bad if they say no. Sayin' no is a mite easier for folks here, 'specially when dealing with foreigners."

"I'll do my part and hope for the best," Kate said. "But if I fail I'll feel quite terrible. I can't help it."

She embraced the old woman and started for her meeting.

Since the town afforded no special meeting place for the Adelphi School Board, Kate's appeal to the members was scheduled to take place in a small conference room in the county courthouse of Adelphi. It was a room of old polished mahogany and parquet floors, with high windows which admitted daylight yet protected the occupants from any intruding sights or sounds. The furniture was heavy and dark, adding the aura of early-century, pre-World War I history to the place. It was the kind of room in the kind of public edifice that architects at the turn of the century were sure they were building for eternity.

As Mrs. Russell had warned, Charles Greer sucked incessantly on his pipe, emitting puffs of smoke like signals of doom. Wilbur Thomas opened the meeting. "Miss Kincaid . . . it is Kincaid, isn't it?"

"Yes," Kate replied.

"Miss Kincaid, I think it is only fair to tell you that after we received Mrs. Russell's request that we meet with you we received a call from Miss Abbott. She made it clear that neither she nor the hospital supported you in your . . . your *crusade*. That was the word she used. *Crusade*."

Kate felt herself experiencing the same mixture of anger and fear as she had on that morning, almost a year ago, when she appeared to defend herself before the Disciplinary Board of University Hospital.

God, she thought, *am I destined to fight authority for the rest of my life?* Was Abbott's rebuke when they discussed Eloise actually a wise and well-intentioned warning? Too late now. She had asked for this meeting and she was in for it.

"I am not here representing the hospital," Kate stated frankly. "I am not here even in my own behalf. But there is a child in your school, a rather special child. I represent her because no one else does."

For the first time, Greer shifted the pipe to the other side of his mouth, appeared about to reply, but permitted Wilbur Thomas to answer for him.

"Miss Kincaid . . ." Thomas said, "as the School Board, we like to think that *we* represent the children of this area. And if you will excuse a bit of pardonable pride, we like to think we do that quite well. Considering the makeup of our population, their background, their economic circumstances, we send a decent number on to higher education."

"Especially the tall and muscular ones," Kate said, referring to the fact that some of the nation's best college basketball and football players had come out of these mountains.

Greer shifted his pipe again, glanced at Will Thomas to indicate he was obviously not pleased.

"You were speaking of a special child, Miss Kincaid," Thomas said.

"Yes, yes, I was," Kate said. She proceeded to tell them about Eloise Torrence and her possible undeveloped talents and intelligence. She concluded by saying, "It is criminal to squander those talents. We cannot permit that child to waste her life as she now seems destined to do. Both she and society will suffer the loss unless we do something about it. And so I did."

This time Greer did remove his pipe and while knocking out the ashes, he asked, "And exactly what did you do?" It was not an innocent inquiry, but hinted that whatever she had done he would disapprove.

"I have arranged with Miss Talmadge that she will give Eloise additional time and special instruction if the child can be made available," Kate said.

"And just how is the child to be made 'available'?" Greer asked.

Now it comes, Kate thought, *they are going to put roadblocks in my way, as trustees and board members always do. Well, damn all board members.*

"Gentlemen, I have arranged with my landlady, Mrs. Russell, that five days a week, every school day, Eloise will be boarded at her house. Mrs. Russell is willing to convert her sewing room into a little bedroom. She will see that the child is well fed, well cared for, clothes washed and pressed, everything. I can testify to how well she cares for those under her roof."

"Uh-huh," Greer grunted. "And I suppose Mrs. Russell had plans to do all this as an act of Christian charity."

"You gentlemen know full well that living on a pension she is not able to afford that," Kate said. "Time, attention, concern, special teaching, all those are freely donated by Mrs. Russell and Miss Talmadge. But food, special books, and other supplies which must be purchased will have to be paid for by someone else."

"Meaning the School Board," Greer said. "Well, young woman, I don't know where you came from, but it is obvious you haven't the faintest notion of how local school boards run in times of economic stress. We can't get a decent budget accepted by the voters in this township. Last year our budget was voted down three times before we could get it passed. And then only after we cut it way below what we consider adequate. Judge Stark, our third member, could tell you. Unfortunately, he is on the judicial circuit this month and could not be here today. But he went out and made a personal appeal to the voters and they even turned him down. So, while it is very easy and sounds quite noble to come to us on behalf of this child, I can tell you now voters who would not approve a decent budget to educate their own children are not going to vote a dime to educate one little girl beyond the level afforded all other children."

Wilbur Thomas nodded his unshakable agreement with Greer's flat rejection.

"It is all well and good," Greer continued, "for you people to come from outside and tell us how to run our affairs. Like the government does. Except they are willing to put up some money at the same time. You are telling us what to do and asking *us* to pay for it. No chance. No chance at all, young woman!"

He turned to Thomas. "I assume this meeting is over, Will?"

Thomas began to nod in approval, but Kate interrupted.

"Not over yet, gentlemen."

Greer, who had been reaching for his pipe, was caught with his hand in midair. "Miss Kincaid . . . it is Kincaid, isn't it? . . . We've been kind enough to grant you this meeting. But we do have businesses of our own to attend. So we have to be getting on."

Kate felt a surge of anger at being shunted aside so lightly. She leaned across the small conference table to look Greer in the eye.

"Mr. Greer, you haven't been 'kind' at all. You were just going through the motions. You two had your minds made up before you ever arrived here. Miss Abbott made your minds up for you."

"Now, just one moment," Wilbur tried to interrupt.

But Kate rode right over him. "Deny it, if you can! I can tell you what she said, that Torrence doesn't approve, that this might endanger the relationship between the hospital and the local folks. Now you're telling me the local people will resent the little added expense in the school budget. And all the while, that child is being deprived, so starved for knowledge and a window to the outside world that she lives in a form of solitary confinement.

"Well, gentlemen, I'll tell you what I am going to do. I am going to set up a little stand just outside this courthouse. And I am going to put out a bucket and ask for public contributions. And in my spare time, of which I don't have much, I am going to be out there collaring every passerby, asking, begging if I have to, for the money to give that child the chance she needs and deserves."

"You don't want to make a public nuisance of yourself," Thomas warned, then added, "Charlie, isn't there a local ordinance against soliciting funds?"

"There's a public ordinance against soliciting, but I don't think it applies to funds," Greer replied. "We'll ask Judge Stark when he gets back next month."

"That'll be too late for me," Kate warned. "I mean to start now. 'Fore the edge of dark today!" she said, resorting to a local expression to make her point.

"On a proper complaint, the town policeman will arrest you," Greer warned.

"Promise?" Kate asked.

Both men exchanged concerned glances. Greer asked, "What does that mean, young woman?"

"Local TV news reporters are always hungry for any kind of human interest story," Kate said. "Well, here is this young nurse out on the town street, begging for funds for a worthy cause, and they cart her off to jail. So this young lawyer comes down here to defend her, since his big law firm up in Chicago does *pro bono* work without charging any fee. That would make quite a story. And when they add to it some pictures of that little girl, that lovely, sensitive little girl . . ."

When Kate realized she had given them cause for great concern, she made one last extravagant threat. "This is just the kind of story that *Sixty Minutes* would pick up on. And Harry Reasoner would be the man. He's from Iowa, the heartland of America. He goes for this kind of thing. Yes, Reasoner is the man!"

"Young woman, if you intend to intimidate us," Greer said, "it won't work."

"Oh, I don't know," Kate said. "The whole School Board against one little girl. It's the kind of story Americans love. David against Goliath. Except this isn't a tale from the Bible. This is real.

This is now. And when I get that little girl to read some of her writings before the TV cameras there won't be a viewer in this country who won't side with her."

Kate turned and started for the door. But Charlie Greer called out, "Wait. Just a moment, young woman."

Kate turned back. "Kincaid . . . it *is* Kincaid."

"All right, Miss Kincaid, come back here. Sit down again."

Once Kate was ensconced in her chair, Greer said, "What we said before is true. We simply cannot get the money from a budget that is already overspent. We didn't even have enough money to buy two extra basketballs the boys need for practice. So, off the record, Will and I donated them. The only way this matter can be worked out is on the same basis."

"Private donations?" Kate asked.

"From the two of us," Greer said. "But there are conditions attached. First, it never gets to be known that we are the ones. We have a reputation to maintain in this locality. We are considered practical businessmen. A dollar paid for a dollar's value. Else we'd be easy marks for anybody with need."

"No one will ever hear it from me," Kate promised.

"Second," Greer emphasized, "none of this can be done without Homer Torrence's consent and approval."

Kate nodded soberly. If getting the promise of funds had been difficult, getting Torrence's consent would be much worse.

"I'll do my best," she promised. "And thank you, gentlemen, for your kindness."

"Just remember, this meeting was never held, and no promises were made by the two of us."

Kate nodded and rose to leave, when Greer asked, "That young lawyer, there really is such a person, isn't there?"

"Oh yes, Howard Brewster. He's even known in the Supreme Court of the United States. Appears there all the time."

She felt justified in taking a little liberty with the facts.

She stood at the foot of the hill looking up toward the Torrence house. Finally she summoned her courage and called, "Hello up there! I'm Kate Kincaid from Wildwood. Anyone home?" She waited for a sign of welcome. She saw the front door open. Eloise came bursting out, hurtled to the edge of the porch, but did not dare come one step closer. Behind her came her father, holding his shotgun, which he had evidently been oiling and polishing.

"What's yere business, seein's how Eunice was here only three, four days ago?" Torrence asked.

"Homer, I would like to talk to you and Matilda."

"Talk? 'Bout what?" Torrence replied, looking through the muzzle end of his shotgun to see if the barrel was clean.

"If I have permission to come up . . ."

"Might's well," Torrence said, starting back into the house without another word. When Eloise did not follow, he ordered her inside with a sharp, impatient gesture of his forefinger.

Kate discovered Matilda Torrence carefully spooning warm grits and milk into little Benjy's mouth, wiping his chin after every swallow. Torrence sat down at the other end of the table, oiling his shotgun, polishing it, staring down the barrel from time to time.

Without looking at Kate, he said gruffly, "Ye said ye wanted to talk."

"Mr. Torrence, Homer," Kate began, "I would like to talk about Eloise."

Torrence gestured the girl out of the room before he felt free to ask, "'Loise drinlin'? Eunice ain't said so."

"I would like to talk about her education," Kate announced with some trepidation.

"That child is right smart book-read," Torrence replied defensively.

"Indeed yes, she is," Kate agreed. "But not nearly as much as she could be."

"Young wuhman," Torrence said, turning to eye her for the first time, "them durn books costs too blame much for a pore man to git for his young'uns. Like that there book ye tried to give her. I knew that was goin' to be the start of trouble. And now, here it be." He turned to glare at his wife. "'Tildy, did I tell ye? Din' I say, watch out fer that furrin wuhman, she goin' to mean trouble?"

Kate persisted. "What I am suggesting won't cost you anything."

"Lakly," Torrence said in skeptical anger. "Ain't nothin' these days don' cost too much."

"Whatever it costs will be paid for by others. I give you my word."

"I ain't land proud, nor money proud, but I ain't no need to take charity neither," Torrence said hostilely.

"This is not charity, Homer," Kate insisted. "It is an investment in the education which this child needs."

"Don' see why. I never did larn to write. I always jes' read. Din' do me no harm."

"We are in the last twenty years of the twentieth century!" Kate exploded. "Children are going to need more than just to read or write in order to get along. It's a big changing world out there. And a child only ten years old now will have to be able to get along in it."

Torrence slammed his shotgun down on the table, turned to face Kate directly, his eyes flinty and fixed.

"Ye come to say somethin' and ye ain't said it. What is it ye want?" he demanded. Behind him, Matilda Torrence put down her spoon and stopped feeding little Benjy. She wiped his chin one last time, breathless, and waited.

"Mr. Torrence, I know that to you I'm a foreigner. I come 'from off.' From another world. But I couldn't be more concerned about Eloise if she were my own child. She is unusual. Special. She has to be educated that way. To do that I have arranged that she can live in town five days a week and receive additional after-hours instruction from Miss Talmadge. Special books, special materials. She will live at Mrs. Russell's. She'll be well fed and cared for. And it won't cost you anything."

Torrence glanced accusingly back at his wife, suspecting she might be part of what he considered a conspiracy against him. But Matilda Torrence shook her head, pleading to explain she knew nothing about it.

"And who'd be takin' care of the diddlers?" Torrence asked.

Matilda Torrence dared to explain. "Diddlers is chickens, Kate."

"And the hound? Man's dog got to be minded real good. 'Specially this 'un. He git the scent of a rabbit or a buck and run so fast he durn near burn the wind. Not many's got so fine a hound. Someun got to feed 'im, care for 'im."

"Homer, I could do that," Matilda Torrence started to say, but he silenced her with a sharp look.

"I seed too many families get broke up with too much larnin' hereabout,'' Torrence said. '' 'Sides, she couldn't be fit for marryin' if she gits so uppity.''

"Before you worry about her getting married, worry about the kind of person she can become. She is pretty and bright. There is no danger of her living to be a spinster lady,'' Kate said.

Torrence eyed her skeptically before remarking, ''You are purty. And bright like. But you ain't married.''

"That's my own choice,'' Kate replied.

"Mebbe a woman kin git so larned she don't know how to make a right choice,'' Torrence said.

The accusation stung. But Kate was determined not to be swayed from her primary purpose.

"Homer, it isn't as if you'd be losing her. She'll spend four nights a week in town. But she can be back here from Friday evening until Monday morning. I'll drive her myself. She'll have time to do all her chores then.''

Matilda Torrence spoke with the tenuous air of a woman taking a great risk. ''Homer, give the young 'un her chance. She's lak Kate sayed, spaycial. She'd be the fust of the family to get that kind of larnin'. Think of it, Homer, a Torrence who might one day go to college, even. Like Doctor Ray. He 'us the fust Boyd ever to go. He become a doctor and din' fergit his people. He come back.''

Torrence considered that, but he did not relax his adamant attitude.

Kate pleaded softly, ''Think of it this way. You have it in your hands to give your child the most precious present in the world, an education. Your own preacher can tell you, it says in your Bible, 'What man, if his child asks for bread, will he give him a stone?' Your child is asking, Mr. Torrence. What will you say to her? Will you give her a stone?''

Torrence turned away from Kate to call out, '' 'Loise! Come here!''

The child came out from behind the partly opened door. She stood obediently before her father.

"Yes, Paw?''

Torrence knelt down until they were eye to eye. ''They sayin' ye'd mebbe stay in town to get more schoolin'. That it'd be spaycial good. Would it pleasure ye to do that?''

Aware of what her answer would mean, the child hesitated, before saying, ''Yes, Paw, would.''

"Ye won't be fergitten yere own or wantin' to stay on there all week, would ye?"

"I'll come home lak Miss Kate said, every Friday. An' do my chores. You'll never even know I'm gone, Paw."

"Oh, yes, I will, child," Torrence said, embracing the child and holding her tenderly. "Yes, I will."

Matilda said softly to Kate, "When ye come for her I'll have her things all fresh and clean."

"Monday," Kate said. "I'll be here first thing Monday morning."

"And thank ye," Matilda Torrence said. "Thank ye more'n a heap."

On Monday morning, early, when Kate Kincaid's Jeep pulled up at the bottom of the hill, she found Eloise Torrence already waiting. The child held two objects: an old, worn suitcase tied round with clothesline, and the shoe box in which she kept her poems and writings. Her face was scrubbed bright and she was smiling. She turned to wave to her father, her mother and Benjy. Her mother waved back. When Benjy did not wave, Mrs. Torrence lifted his hand and waved for him. Homer Torrence did not wave, but stood there, unsmiling, like a man who might break into tears if he gave way to his emotions.

Once Kate had installed Eloise's few worn but clean dresses and underthings in the little back room on the second floor of the Russell house, and after Mrs. Russell had fed her a good, hearty, hot breakfast, Eloise marched off to join her classmates at the school.

As they watched her go, Mrs. Russell said, "It'll be like olden days in this house again. To have a young one to do for."

Abbott said nothing to rebuke Kate about her determination to provide little Eloise with advanced schooling.

The only comment that might be so interpreted was when Abbott said, "Kincaid, perhaps now you'll be able to settle down to studying for your second trimester finals. Some women find them to be the most difficult."

And they were. Several times during the written part of the exam, Kate pored over an exacting question and wondered if Abbott had created it especially to frustrate and defeat her.

When the grades were announced, all three, Ellen, Emily and

Kate, were within five percentage points of each other, and all were well above the passing level.

They were given the rest of the week off and told to report for their first class in Midwifery on Monday morning at eight. The privilege was not so magnanimous as it sounded, since it just meant they had Friday afternoon, Saturday and Sunday to themselves.

Kate decided immediately. *Home, I'll go home, two whole days and nights with Howard, two mornings when I can luxuriate in bed, and not have to wake early to go to class, two whole days I don't have to rush from class to clinic, or clinic to class, or to the Emergency Room.* Two whole nights with Howard. It had been weeks since Washington.

She consulted the airline schedule hungrily, only to discover that the first plane out was in the morning. She wouldn't be home until Saturday afternoon and would have to leave Sunday at noon in order to be back in time for her Monday class. She was forced to content herself with a phone call.

"Howard . . . darling . . . I passed. Only two more trimesters to go now."

He tried to sound enthusiastic, but could not forgo the temptation to say, "You could quit now and be certified as a family nurse. Wouldn't that be enough?"

"I signed up for the whole course. I have to stay. But I'll be home for Easter. Just think, Easter together, darling."

When she hung up, she tried to overcome her guilt by feeling more determined. Half her time was over, there were only six months to go. Six long months, she had to admit. But Easter would be something to look forward to, possibly the best Easter in years for her. Certainly the best since her whole family had been together, Dad and Mother and her brother Scott. They hadn't had an Easter like that since her father died and Scott had been transferred to Hong Kong by the bank for which he worked.

Emily McClendon decided to visit cousins who lived a four-hour drive from Adelphi. Ellen chose as her special postexam reward a trip up to the city for mass on Sunday morning. There being no Catholic church within many miles, she had gone without mass, confession or communion since arriving in Adelphi.

Friday afternoon Kate picked up Eloise at school, drove her home for the weekend. On the way the child bubbled over with newly acquired knowledge gained in her after-school hours with Miss Talmadge. During her excited recital the child recalled, "She said I was even brighter than Megan. Who's Megan?"

Kate glanced down at the puzzled face of the curious, animated child. "Megan is Miss Talmadge's daughter, who was once a little girl just like you."

Knowing how highly Talmadge thought of her own daughter and what she had become, Kate thought if she ever needed justification for what she did, she had it now. She had surely not overestimated this child's abilities.

There was a tinge of regret when they reached the foot of Torrence's hill and the child kissed her good-bye. For a fleeting moment Kate thought, *if Howard and I had been married three years ago as he insisted, a few years from now we would have had a child of our own almost Eloise's age.*

"I'll pick you up at seven Monday morning, dear," Kate said.

"Monday. Seven. Cain't hardly wait. Now, I bestest . . . best hurry. Whole week I ditn't do my chores. . . ." She stopped to correct herself. "For a whole week I haven't done my chores."

She turned, leaped out of the Jeep, scampered up the hill calling, "Maw . . . Paw . . . I'm back!"

Saturday was one of those Indian summer mornings in fall when a heavy mist is low in the mountains, obscuring the peaks and settling in the hollows. By nine o'clock the sun began to break through. With a whole day to themselves, Kate and Ellen decided to go exploring. They packed a lunch and drove up into the mountains. Because Ellen had heard of Big Betsy but had never seen the gigantic piece of earth-devouring machinery, Kate drove up the rough road hacked out of the side of the mountain. It being Saturday, when they arrived at the top they found the powerful giant abandoned, like an object out of ancient history. There was no crew, no trucks or other vehicles around. But the scarred and devastated earth gave convincing if silent testimony to the havoc it had wrought on the landscape.

Ellen stood at the foot of the monster, stared up at its enormous height and girdered sides, whispering in awe, "Incredible. It's like those battering rams we used to read about in history books back when cities were fortresses."

"It's even more incredible when you see what it can gouge out in one bite," Kate said. "It's like remaking the earth."

"Seems almost sacrilegious," Ellen said softly. "And what's to become of all this?" she asked, pointing to the raw earth around them.

"They say they're going to replant, that it'll be rich and blooming, better than before. They say!"

"I pray to God it's so," Ellen said, then added quickly, "Let's get away from here," as if the place were cursed.

They left the Jeep at the foot of a tall mountain that was virgin green with pines. Taking their lunch, they started to climb, determined to reach the top. But halfway up they realized they had miscalculated the height and steepness of the climb and were forced to stop by a broad stream that blocked their way. Breathless, perspiring and feeling delightfully exhausted, they decided to have their lunch.

The noon sun was directly overhead, and it had become very warm for an October day. Impulsively Kate said, "Before lunch let's go skinny-dipping." Then she realized what she had said and added, "Sorry, I didn't mean that."

Ellen laughed. "You'll have to get over your preconceived notions about nuns." She kicked off her shoes, started to unbutton her blouse. In a few moments they had both slipped out of their slacks and underclothes and were wading naked into the rushing stream.

Since the water was too shallow for swimming, they splashed about and it was good to feel the cool water flowing across their warm young bodies. It seemed to wash away all the tensions of preparing for their exams, taking them, then sweating out the results. Free, uninhibited, they lay staring up at the clear blue sky, at the bright hot sun, experiencing the sensuous joy of the refreshing water, their young breasts floating level with the tide.

It was the freest, most enjoyable day either of them had had since arriving in Adelphi six months ago.

Half the year was over. The most difficult half was yet to come. But today they banished all thoughts of that. They were enjoying the world around them.

CHAPTER 19

Kate Kincaid, Sister Ellen and Emily McClendon waited impatiently for Dr. Boyd to arrive for the eight o'clock class, their first in Midwifery. When he arrived, without a word he took his place behind the desk, faced the blackboard and wrote only one word:

Life.

"From now on," he began, "for the next six months, you will be concerned with only one thing. *Life!*

"The reproduction of it, but also the prevention of it. Many of the women who will become your patients will be desperate to have even one child. But many will be desperate never to have another. Others will need to have their minds opened to the fact that it is a crime to bear children without giving them the opportunity to live a useful productive life.

"Since mountain women do not believe in abortion, for them the answer is prevention. Contraception."

Boyd directed his gaze toward Sister Ellen. "You understand that, Sister?"

"That's why I'm here, Doctor," Ellen replied firmly.

"So, though this is termed a course in Midwifery, it is also a course in how to plan births and, if necessary, to prevent them. In short, you women will become advisers, consultants and medical aides to women in all those categories.

"For the next three months you will alternate one day in class, one day in Midwifery Clinic. So theory and practice will go hand in hand.

"Your last three months will be devoted solely to performing actual deliveries. Then human life will be in your hands, figuratively and literally."

He paused to allow that solemn thought to sink in on the three young women before him.

"And now we will begin with how to conduct the first interview and history of a woman who does *not* desire to become pregnant for whatever personal reason. Too many children. Fear of having children. The unhappy state of the marriage. Or, she may be an unmarried teenager with an active sex life who wants to avoid becoming pregnant."

Boyd proceeded with a detailed discussion of the various kinds of contraceptives: intrauterine devices, oral contraceptives, the rhythm method for those whose religion forbade mechanical means, and other methods, not excluding abstinence.

"More recently the Pill has taken over," he continued. "But let me warn you now, when the time comes for you to assume complete management of patients, you must never lightly make the decision to prescribe the Pill for them."

He glanced suddenly at Kate. "Kincaid, using the patient history form you have before you, cite the factors primarily involved in the decision to prescribe the Pill."

Kate had no need to glance at the form as she recited, "Age at which menstrual cycle commenced. Length of cycle. Events involving failure to have regular cycle. Intermenstrual bleeding."

Boyd turned to Sister Ellen. "Medical history?"

The slight, dark-haired young woman responded quietly and precisely, "Presence of diabetes, history of cancer, or embolus, kidney disease, liver disease, epilepsy."

Boyd turned to his third student. "McClendon?"

"It is important to know if the woman has a history of headaches or psychiatric problems, either of which might become important due to the changes induced by regular and longtime use of the Pill."

"Correct," Boyd agreed. "And, in addition, if the woman has recently had a child, it is important to know if she is currently breast-feeding. Also the frequency of her sexual contacts. All those factors, and more, are important.

"I know this sounds overwhelming. But, I can assure you, once you start assisting an experienced midwife in clinic, and observe how it is done, it will eventually become second nature.

"However, never let it become so routine that you forget for an instant that you are dealing with the most sensitive area of your patient's life. At one and the same time you have to be physician, midwife, psychiatrist, family counselor, friend, and, in some instances, strict parent.

"Actually, your contact will be even more intimate than those of the physician. Because our patients all have the same complaint about us physicians. We don't give them sufficient time. We are too rushed. While you, as family nurses and midwives, have the time to chat with them, to answer all their questions, to quell their fears. We are only professional acquaintances to them. You should become intimate friends. But you must earn their friendship."

"God knows they make you work for it," Kate remarked, remembering her own experiences at Wildwood.

"Ah, but what a valuable relationship, once you earn it," Boyd said. "Now, using your manuals as a starting point, prepare yourselves for your first day in the Midwifery Clinic tomorrow."

To Kate, as to Sister Ellen and Emily McClendon, the amount of study material seemed overwhelming. At first, the number of forms, the hundreds of detailed questions seemed impossible to master. To assemble all this information about even a single patient seemed like a career in itself.

Yet their manual described in detail the specific reason for each question and answer before encouraging either pregnancy or its opposite. The phrase "family planning" took on a meaning far beyond any they had ascribed to it even during their nursing practice.

On alternate days, Kate, Ellen and Emily spent endless hours with the women who streamed through the Midwifery Clinic. The experienced midwives knew the procedure so well that very few had to resort to forms and charts. They worked with dispatch and efficiency. Yet Kate noted they never gave any patient the feeling that she was being rushed. Some women were hesitant to ask. Some were forthright, almost aggressive, in their questions and complaints. But all of them looked with admiration and kinship upon their midwives. It was that look of appreciation and respect which, more than any words, told Kate how much a part of their lives their midwives had become.

She wrote on the inside cover of her manual, "Be friend, confidante, and adviser, but always a discerning observer of your patient, of her physical and mental condition."

CHAPTER 20

"This is Gynny," Mrs. Carberry said. The short, plump, efficient instructor in Midwifery held in her strong, broad hands a naked doll made of spongy plastic and weighing about six pounds.

"Gynny is not short for Virginia but for gynecological. To prepare you for your final trimester of obstetrics, she will be your constant companion for these next three months. Just as will this life-size plastic replica of a mother's thighs and reproductive organs. You must practice with Gynny and this model until you become so accustomed to the process and the feel of delivering a live infant that you can do it blindfolded.

"Along with the theoretical knowledge you will gain in my classes you must develop the manual skills necessary for the birthing process. Because much of what you decide to do as a midwife will depend not only on what you can see, but on what you can feel. Your stethoscope and your hands are the two most important instruments you have to aid you in accomplishing a successful delivery. So we will commence now to become familiar with both.

"Kincaid, come up here."

She handed Gynny to Kate.

"Place her in the womb as we would normally expect her to be, in the vertex position."

Kate placed the doll in the womb, head down and not quite resting at the top of the birth canal.

"Now, assuming we have the proper degree of assist from the mother and from nature, easily, gently bring her down and effect the delivery."

Carefully, Kate eased Gynny slowly down into the birth canal and finally out through the vagina.

"Exactly," Mrs. Carberry said. "The simple, normal delivery, as we expect in most cases. You must continue to practice this, and you three will have ample opportunity to do so. For these demonstration models will be available to you at all hours of the day or night.

"But while you are becoming accustomed to these, remember that in about five percent of your cases, birth will not occur in this way. We do our best to avoid accidents and surprises by monitoring the development of the infant from conception to time of delivery. But surprises can develop in the last few weeks or even at delivery. That is where your training and your experience can become vital. We might as well start learning about some of those problems now.

"So, Kincaid, place Gynny back in her resting place, this time not with head presenting but reversed."

"In breech presentation," Kate said.

"Exactly," Carberry said. "Now what do you do?"

"This is a case I would refer to the obstetrician," Kate said. "The breeches I've witnessed have almost all gone to cesarean section."

"And I have seen too many cesareans which were unnecessary," Carberry said.

Recalling Ob-Gyn men like Dr. Morse, who performed cesareans in cases that seemed not difficult but only inconvenient for their schedules, Kate said, "So have I."

"Then let us suppose the mother you are dealing with was not able to come to the hospital, there is no doctor available. What do you do?" Carberry pursued.

The three students began to volunteer information based on their study of the manual and the supporting literature.

"First, determine the exact lie of the fetus," Kate said.

"How?" Carberry addressed all of them.

"Leopold's maneuvers," Sister Ellen volunteered.

"By making the cross marks, real or imaginary, on the mother's abdomen," Emily added, "and listening for the fetal heartbeat."

"If," Kate continued, "it is in either lower quadrant, it is in vertex or head-down position. But if the heartbeat is in the upper quadrant of the cross marks, then the fetus is in breech position."

"Let us say we have determined the presentation is breech. What next?" Carberry asked.

"Determine if it is a complete breech or a frank breech," Kate responded.

"Those are terms, give me facts," Carberry ordered.

Sister Ellen replied, "If a foot or both feet are presenting, then it is a frank breech. But if the buttocks are presenting, then it is a complete breech, and the most difficult."

"What if it is frank?" Carberry asked.

Emily was ready with the answer. "If you can feel one foot or both, and the baby is beginning to emerge that way, place a surgical towel around the presenting limbs so you can hold its wet, slippery legs, and with the mother assisting by pushing, gradually extract the infant."

"Is that all?" Carberry asked.

"Make sure to place your other hand under the infant to assist the head out as gently and efficiently as you can," Kate said, "to avoid any trauma."

"Remember," Carberry cautioned, "when a breech is involved, the infant is *always* in danger. Because a breech draws the umbilicus and the cord into the pelvis. That compresses the cord, possibly cutting off the infant's oxygen supply. So the head must be delivered as quickly as possible. Otherwise hypoxia can result and may be damaging or even fatal. On the other hand, if you force the delivery in order to hasten it, you can inflict danger to the brain, spinal cord, skeleton or abdominal viscera. So a breech is dangerous, be it complete or frank.

"There is an alternative method of delivery called cephalic version," Carberry continued, "but that can only be done under special circumstances and with utmost care. Since it can mean life or death for the infant, and sometimes for the mother as well. But we will get to that later in our course."

During the succeeding days, Kate, Sister Ellen and Emily spent hours working with Gynny. Simulating every possible form of presentation that might occur and trying to effect a safe delivery. But the more they worked, the more they were impressed by the awesome responsibility that would be theirs if they were ever confronted by some of these challenges in an actual case.

On alternate days they spent their hours in the clinic observing experienced midwives who prescribed birth control methods and instructed the patient how to use them, followed births through the various stages, performed regular examinations from week to week, measured the health and weight gains of the mother. They watched closely as midwives tested for the responses of the fetus to determine if it was developing normally. They accompanied midwives on visits to a patient's home, to make sure that the mother's diet and habits were conducive to the welfare of the unborn child, to make sure the child would be born into healthful surroundings, physical and psychological.

No part of the mother's life or home surroundings was exempt from the experienced midwife's scrutiny and concern.

The day finally arrived when Carberry decided to entrust her three students with the responsibility of interviewing new patients on their own. In the small, tidy examining room, Kate Kincaid observed her first patient. Eighteen, Kate judged, surely no more than nineteen.

The young woman's tense posture made Kate consider: Is she nervous on her own, or does she realize that she is the first patient in Midwifery entrusted entirely to me to take her history, make the initial physical examination, and discuss with her all the aspects of becoming pregnant, bearing to term, and delivering what we both hope will be a healthy baby?

No matter how anxious I feel, Kate thought, *I must not let her know.* She rehearsed in her mind the routine for general assessment of the patient and future mother. Blood pressure. Eyes. Throat. Teeth and neck. Breasts. Abdomen. Hands, arms, legs and feet.

Pelvic examination. Speculum exam. Pap smear. Bimanual examination. Family birthing history. Previous form of contraception. Etc., etc., etc. There seemed no end of etceteras. By now Kate had memorized the routine until she knew it better than the pledge of allegiance to the flag.

Smiling to put the obviously tense young woman at ease, Kate began with the first and basic question. ''Name?''

Instead of answering, the frail young woman toyed with the strands of brown hair that hung in disarray close to her damp, shiny cheeks.

Poised to fill in the top line of the form, Kate repeated, "Name?"

The young woman began to weep silently. Kate put down her pen, suspecting that instead of seeking information concerning this birth, this young woman had come here to effect the opposite result.

"How long have you been pregnant?" Kate asked gently.

The young woman shook her head and continued her silent weeping.

"You're not pregnant?" Kate asked.

The young woman suddenly rose from the chair, attempting to leave. Kate reached out to take hold of her arm. "Just relax. Sit here until you're able to pull yourself together. Then tell me what the trouble is."

The woman sank back into the chair. Kate felt her arm gradually grow less tense, though she continued to cry more freely now. Kate handed her a box of tissues. The woman grasped several, held them to her eyes, as much to hide as to wipe away her tears.

When Kate felt it possible to resume, she asked again, "Name?"

"I'd rather not say. Not right off. Till I tell you."

Puzzled and curious, Kate said, "Of course," though she had already drawn some conclusions. Her accent indicated a Southern background, but she was not mountain people. She did not use words in the same way. Her problem appeared psychiatric rather than physical. Kate knew it was best to allow the woman to reveal at her own pace what tormented her. She had obviously been in great turmoil before coming to the clinic.

"Whenever you're ready, tell me," Kate encouraged.

With one hand the young woman played with strands of loose hair, while her other hand brushed back traces of the tears on her cheeks.

"I . . . I want to say right off . . . I'm married," she declared, obviously feeling she was under suspicion. "Which . . . which is the trouble."

"You're pregnant, but not by your husband?"

"Oh, no," the young woman protested. "Not pregnant at all."

"And you would like to do something about that," Kate said. "No reason to be tense. It's more common than you think. Though every young couple in this situation always feels they're the only ones. How long have you been married?''

''Year and a half.''

''And how long have you been trying to conceive?'' Kate asked.

''Year and a half.''

Kate ran through the statistics she had learned. Among couples who are physically normal and have regular sex habits, 65 percent conceive in the first half year. By the end of the first year 80 percent will have conceived. But there will always be 15 or 20 percent who, unless there is some intervention, will never conceive for any of a number of reasons. Since this young couple had already been trying for more than a year, they were obviously in the last group. The first thing to do was put her patient at ease.

''It would help if you told me your name,'' Kate said. The young woman shook her head. ''At least your first name. So we can speak woman-to-woman.''

The patient considered Kate's request and finally said, ''Sally.''

Obviously an alias. But Kate decided that any name was better than the barrier created by no name.

''First, Sally, rid your mind of one fear. This situation may be no fault of yours. To make sure, we have to determine if you are physically able to become pregnant. So I have to do a complete gynecological examination to discover if your organs can accommodate to conception and pregnancy. Then we will have to do several other tests, X ray and a hysterosalpingogram. That's a big word. But all it means is we have to discover if your ovaries produce ova, if your Fallopian tubes function properly, and if your uterus develops implantation sites so that your husband's sperm can be effective. Just remember, even if we discover trouble, it might be corrected surgically.''

Kate started toward the examining table as she said, ''Please, just get up here and let's begin our examination.'' She was pulling on her rubber gloves when she realized the young woman had not moved. ''Sally?'' she invited, beckoning her to the table.

''No need,'' the young woman said.

''What do you mean, 'no need'?''

''The trouble ain't in me.''

Kate studied her for a moment. ''How can you be sure?''

'' 'Cause I never had any trouble before, even when I didn't want to get pregnant,'' Sally admitted.

"You've been pregnant once before?" When Sally did not reply, Kate asked, "More than once?" The girl nodded. "How many times?"

"Twice," she admitted.

"And what did you do about it?" Kate asked.

"First time . . . first . . ." Sally started to weep again.

Kate took the distraught woman's hands in her own. "Sally, you're going to have to tell someone about this. If only to stop tormenting yourself."

"He'll kill me . . ." the young woman protested through her tears.

"This happened while you were married?" The girl shook her head. "Then when? While your husband was courting you?" Again Sally shook her head. "Before you met your husband?" Finally Sally nodded. "So you weren't unfaithful to him."

"No, but . . ."

"But what, Sally?"

"I think it's punishment," she said. "I think because I got rid of one of them I'm being punished now. I mean I'm able to have a child but somehow God, or whoever, won't let me, because now I do want one. We both want one. Bad."

Kate hesitated, unsure of the answer her next question might evoke.

"Sally, when you say you 'got rid of one of them' exactly what did you mean?"

"Had an abortion," the girl admitted.

Kate was somewhat relieved, for back at University Hospital she had seen more than a few cases in which infants, obviously born healthy, had been brought in dead through abandonment or even more violent means.

"And the second one?" Kate asked.

"Which was really the first one," the girl said. "I was determined to have her. But came time to decide I gave her up for adoption. That's why the second time I had the abortion. I didn't think I could go through that again, having her and giving her up. It stays with you. Nights when you can't sleep. Other times. Like when I was at work . . . I worked in a cotton mill down home . . . times, in spite of the noise of the mill and the machines whirring and all . . . I would think, where is she? Who has her now? Are they treating her good? You read all kinds of stories, hear them on TV. About people mistreating kids, abusing them, and so many times, turns out the kids was adopted in the first place. So you ask yourself, if they didn't like kids why did they adopt them? I mean, nights I would cry for wondering did my little girl get into the hands of people like that? So that's why, second time I decided I wouldn't let no little child of mine suffer that way. But that was even worse. 'Cause I felt like I had done murder. So I . . . I swear I didn't let no other man touch me after that. Not till Jeff. And even him not till after we was married. I wanted everything to be proper. I went to a doctor and had him test me for . . . you know, diseases . . . so I could be sure I was clean and right for him. Because I love him and I want everything to be good for us. And it is . . . was . . . till he started saying we ought to have a child.

"You see, he comes from a big family. And all three of his brothers and his four sisters, they all got big families. When we get together on holidays, like last Christmas, and the house is full of kids, and I mean kids—twenty-six kids—and Jeff's mama says, 'And when are you going to start raising a family, Edna?' . . ." The young woman realized her slip and apologized. "Sorry. That's my real name, Edna. And I don't know what to say. 'Cause . . ."

"Because," Kate suggested, "you think you're being punished now for what happened those other two times?"

Edna nodded in short, jerky, nervous movements of her head.

"Edna, if you want to find out, we have to start somewhere," Kate said, now having to consider whether Edna's abortion had dam aged her present ability to conceive. Kate gestured toward the exam ining table. Edna approached the table slowly, climbed up, assumed the dorsal lithotomy position for pelvic examination. Kate draped a sheet across Edna's knees, then commenced her examination.

When she was done, Kate concluded that fortunately the abortion had been done with care and under properly septic conditions, and had left no residual damage. There would have to be additional tests, but based on her physical findings, and the fact that the young woman had conceived twice in the past, there was no apparent reason why this young woman could not conceive, carry to term and deliver a healthy child.

Therefore, Kate had to consider two other possibilities. Previous emotional trauma might have predisposed Edna to psychosomatic infertility. Though, based on her history, the problem probably rested with her husband. The third, and rarer, possibility, that two healthy, fertile people together might prove to be infertile, could not be dismissed. She would attack the more likely possibility first.

"The thing to do," Kate said finally, "is send your husband in. We'll test him for sperm count and motility and see if, by chance, the problem is his."

"Oh, no, don't!" Edna protested, her eyes welling up with tears once more.

"Otherwise we'll never know," Kate pointed out.

"But then he'll know," Edna protested. "I mean, if it isn't my fault but his . . ."

"Edna, in cases of infertility no one is to blame."

"But if you have to say to him, Edna's okay, you're the one who can't have children . . . I mean, that'll just kill him. He's a very proud man."

"There are many proud men who are infertile," Kate said. "But it's important for you, for him, and for your marriage to discover the truth. Else you'll go on for years tormenting yourself for not having children."

Edna hesitated before asking, "Will he ever find out about the other two times?"

"Only if you tell him. He'll never learn it from me," Kate said softly. "Think about it. And next time, come back with him."

"Will I . . . will I get to talk to you again?"

"Yes. You'll be my patient from now on."

"I would like that. I never told anyone else about this before. Not even my own mother. But it felt better to tell you. I trust you."

"Good. Bring your husband with you next time. Soon, if you can."

Edna was dressed and at the door when she stopped and asked, "What's your name?"

"Just ask for Nurse Kincaid, Kate Kincaid."

"Can I call you Kate?"

"I want you to."

"I'll bring him," Edna promised. "I'll bring him the next time."

As Kate watched the door close she thought, half sadly, half amused, this could only happen to me. My first case in Midwifery, and it turns out to be a failure to conceive.

She went to the door to admit her next patient.

* * *

She had handled four cases that day, taken detailed and meticulous histories, done complete physicals, drawn blood, sent the specimens off to the lab. It had become a routine; to Kate, a reassuring routine. Except, of course, for the physicals. She was constantly tense and aware that any failure to observe some significant sign might have future life-or-death consequences for the patient or an unborn infant. So she had always carefully repeated every step in the procedure. At the end of each examination, she was aware of being bathed in sweat. The burden of responsibility was heavier than she had anticipated.

During the second week of Kate's family planning duties, Edna Ferris returned as she had promised, bringing with her her husband, Jeff, a broad-shouldered blond young man who, while he seemed to be listening to Kate, also obviously resented her. Edna sat nervously twisting the strap of her handbag, prepared to intercede and mollify her young husband if he gave vent to his impatience.

"I have examined Edna thoroughly and there is no apparent reason why she can't conceive," Kate said.

"Meanin'?" Jeff Ferris asked belligerently.

"Jeff, honey, please . . ." Edna tried to mollify him. "Just listen?"

"Okay. I'll listen!" he said, but it was plain he could not be moved.

Kate continued, "There are reasons, at least one reason, why you two haven't been able to conceive."

"Such as?" Jeff interrupted angrily.

Kate knew the time had come for frankness. "Such as, Jeff, the trouble may be with you."

"There ain't never been such a thang in my family. Never was a Ferris, man nor wuhman, had that kind of trouble," he insisted.

"So your wife has told me, and I believe her."

"Well, then?" Ferris demanded.

"It may be that you don't live under the same conditions as the Ferrises who came before you. Pollution in the air. In the water you drink. It's happening all over the country."

"You mean there's something . . ." Ferris began, then said, "No, cain't be. Whut about my brothers? They breathin' the same air, drinkin' the same water."

"Jeff, what kind of work do you do?"

"Drive a truck."

"What kind of truck? Anything to do with chemicals?" Kate asked.

"Coal."

"Coal?" Kate considered. Coal in its primary form was not considered a contaminant. Only when certain types of coal were burned and turned into smoke did they become toxic. That would seem to rule out any chemical cause of Ferris's infertility. Yet the lab tests had proved that his sperm lacked motility, which was undoubtedly the cause of this young couple's failure to conceive.

Unfortunately, in this kind of case, to know the cause did not necessarily point the way to a cure. The only happy solution for Edna Ferris might lie in artificial insemination with the sperm of a donor. But Kate was sure that Jeff Ferris who was, as mountain people put it, a pride-proud man, was not likely to consider that alternative. This case called for a consultation.

"I'll have to talk this over with Dr. Boyd," Kate said.

"I thought this wuz 'tween us. Next ye know it'll be all over the county," Ferris said.

"It's your decision, Jeff," Kate said. "If you would rather no one else knew about it . . ."

"I'd ruther," he said, rising to leave.

"Jeff?" his wife begged, hoping he would reconsider.

"I said my piece, Edna, I'd ruther no one elst knew. I come this fur, done what you asked about the specimen. Didn' help. So's far as I'm concerned, that's the end of it."

He started out. Edna looked helplessly at Kate, then had no choice but to follow her husband.

The disappointed look in the young woman's eyes made Kate feel that she had failed. She had mishandled this proud but uneducated man and had destroyed his wife's hopes of ever conceiving their child.

The case troubled Kate through the day. While she concentrated on other cases in clinic, the Ferrises kept intruding. Coal. There must be something about driving a coal truck that made this Ferris different from his brothers and the generations of Ferrises before him.

Instead of going to supper, she went to the library and started researching among medical texts, monographs and journals for any clue that linked coal to infertility. She found not a single reference. She had best look for other causes.

Defeated, she left the hospital and started walking back to the house. The night air was warm for November. The main street of Adelphi was dark except for the single street light in front of the courthouse. Even the old, red, flickering neon lights that framed the fly-specked window of the bar on the corner were now dark. All Adelphi was asleep. Only Kate Kincaid was not.

She reached the house to discover that the pot of coffee Mrs. Russell had left on the stove had simmered down to a thick black residue. Kate washed the pot clean and went off to bed.

Because of the unseasonable weather, or the Ferris case, she slept fitfully, waking several times to find herself perspiring. She opened the window wide. What breeze there was barely stirred the curtains.

The warmth of the night taunted her. In some way she could not fathom, it related to the Ferris case.

She woke early, before six, and with a sense of great urgency. She had to go back to the library and do some further research before their eight o'clock class. She dressed hurriedly, left the house quietly so as not to disturb Mrs. Russell or Eloise.

The night shift was still on duty when she arrived. She went directly to the library. She began to look up the indexes, tracking two words: *Infertility. Warmth.*

During the night, those two words had become interconnected. She found several references to the medical fact that when a man's testes remained in the inguinal canal instead of descending into the scrotum, body warmth resulted in sterility. But this had no application to Jeff Ferris. Kate had determined that from her examination and his previous history. Yet the thought pursued her. Infertility. And warmth.

She went back to the library on her lunch hour. Finally among the more recent articles in the *Journal of Medicine* she found the one which had eluded her all night. She had come across it several months ago and dismissed it as interesting but irrelevant to her geriatric studies at the time.

She read it through, not once but twice. When she finished, she went to the phone and called Edna Ferris.

"Edna, Kate, at the hospital. I'll be in clinic again tomorrow. Tell Jeff I want to see him."

"He won't come," Edna warned. "He won't see no doctor!"

"He won't have to see the doctor. Tell him I may have the answer."

"I'll try," Edna said. "God knows, I'll try."

Jeff Ferris stood in the doorway of the small consultation room, nervously shifting from one foot to the other, trying to appear less anxious than he was about Kate's summons.

"Edna said ye wanted to see me."

"Don't just stand there, Jeff. Come in, and close the door."

He did, then asked, "Whut was it ye wanted?"

"There was something I couldn't quite remember from when I examined you before, and I didn't write it down in my chart."

"I already tole ye everythin' I could. And we went through that damn specimen test," he said, still embarrassed.

"Only one thing more," Kate said. "Lower your jeans."

"Ye done all the examinin' I'm permittin'!" he protested.

"Just lower your jeans!" Kate commanded in a voice so firm it allowed for no dispute.

Slowly, disgruntled, rebellious, Jeff Ferris undid the big brass buckle on his wide rawhide belt, unbuttoned the top button of his worn faded jeans, pulled down the zipper and let the jeans slide to the floor. He stood with his shirttails hanging down, but not quite able completely to conceal his shorts.

Kate took one look and broke into a broad smile.

"'Tain't funny, wuhman!" Ferris said, blushing now.

"No, 'tain't funny," Kate agreed, still smiling. "But it's great, just great!"

"Whut?" the puzzled truck driver demanded, blushing more furiously.

"Jockey shorts," Kate said.

"Wuhman, are you tetched in the head?"

"No," Kate said. "Now, pull up your jeans and listen."

He obeyed like a bashful schoolboy.

"Jeff, you're as good a man as all the other Ferrises. The trouble is with your shorts."

He still did not regard her any less than mad, nor was he any less embarrassed, so she proceeded to explain.

"The reason nature has provided a special sac for your testicles is to keep them outside your body at lower than body temperature. Because warmth can create the condition you now have. Your kind of shorts have been keeping them close against your body, warmer than they should be. That's why your sperm lacks motility and why Edna doesn't conceive. So I am going to prescribe for you. Wear loose-fitting shorts. And we'll see what happens in a few weeks."

"That's all?" Ferris asked skeptically.

"That's all," Kate said.

"'N' I thought you wuz going to do all kinds of medical things to me," he admitted, relaxing for the first time. "Wait'll I tell Edna, just wait'll I tell her!"

Kate followed the progress of the Ferris case with great interest. She was delighted to confirm some weeks later that Edna Ferris had indeed conceived. She gave all indications of carrying to term and delivering a healthy infant.

Edna's radiance each time she reported to clinic was all the reward Kate needed. If her three months of Midwifery study had accomplished nothing else, they would have proved their worth.

She was ready now for her final exams and, if she passed, for entry into the final trimester, the actual delivery of newborns.

CHAPTER 21

The exams Kate and her two classmates were required to pass before they could go on to their fourth and final trimester were both written and oral.

The written test was intended to determine if they had absorbed the enormous amount of detail involved in all aspects of the birth process, including the special problems of high-risk patients.

The oral portion of the test was to evaluate their ability to respond quickly in emergencies.

Abbott had arranged to be in charge of Kate Kincaid's oral testing. She asked questions in staccato fashion, with the inquisitorial attitude of a prosecutor, until Kate thought, *she will never forgive me for going over her head about little Eloise*. But there was no time for Kate to let her thoughts wander, Abbott was pressing her for highly technical and exacting answers.

"Generally accepted measurements that indicate a safe and successful delivery?" Abbott demanded.

Kate answered briskly, "Diagonal conjugate twelve point five centimeters. Pubic angle greater than eighty-five degrees. Pubic arch ninety degrees. Sacrospinous ligament two to three finger breadths. Intertuberous ten centimeters. Posterior sagittal of outlet seven point five centimeters. Height of pubis less than six centimeters. Spines, flat. Sacrum, hollow."

Without indicating approval or disapproval, Abbott made a note on her pad while asking, "Equipment for physical assessment to determine presence or absence of pelvic abnormality?"

"Light. Drape. Disposable glove. Lubricant. Vaginal speculum. Slides for culture for G.C. Applicators. Pap spatulas. Cytology spray."

"Differentiate between causative factors of first, second and third trimester bleeding."

Kate had barely completed her answer when Abbott followed with question after question.

"Identify fears an expectant father may have toward his role of father, toward his wife or sexual partner, his fears toward the baby.

"What are normal psychological reactions and responses of a pregnant woman during the first, second and third trimesters of pregnancy?

"Explain the significant changes in sexual interest and responsiveness during pregnancy and the possible effects of these changes on the marital relationship."

Kate summoned up all the knowledge she had accumulated during the past three months through observing, listening to lectures, asking questions, poring over hundreds of medical and midwifery tracts and journals.

When the examination was finally over, Kate felt drained. She had relived three months of Midwifery instruction and observation in a compact, torturous two hours. Abbott gave no indication as to whether she had passed or failed.

"Thank you, Kincaid" was all she said.

Four days later, on December 22, Kate, Ellen and Emily received the results of their exams in sealed envelopes. When they compared scores, they realized that all three had passed, with excellent grades.

They had only three more months of actual Midwifery practice before they completed the entire course.

But Abbott gave them little opportunity to celebrate. Or even to observe Christmas. The director had increased their clinic hours to permit those nurses who had been in Adelphi for several years to go back home for the holidays.

Before they left, the family nurses made up cartons of gifts, which they had bought out of their own funds, to give to the children in their poorer families so they, too, might have a happy

Christmas. It was an object lesson to the three aspirants; to these older nurses, mountain people were more than patients, they were very much family. Feeling deprived because they did not have families of their own to give presents to, Kate, Ellen and Emily added their gifts to the cartons and wrapped them in bright red and green ribbon.

For Kate this was the most lonely Christmas she had ever had. Even at University Hospital when she had drawn ward duty on Christmas Eve, she had not felt so alone. Because after she came home there was always Howard, and Christmas dinner, and gifts to exchange. And love to make.

This year, though there were no classes on Christmas morning, she was assigned to relieving in Pediatric Clinic. Then she trudged home through falling snow. Mrs. Russell had done her best to provide a festive dinner. Despite the decorations, the turkey, the other delicacies she had prepared, Christmas dinner for two lonely women was not particularly cheerful.

To make some talk at table, Kate said, "At least the weather is on our side. So much snow, and still falling."

"Dunno," Mrs. Russell said. "Been looking up toward Hell's Mountain. Too much snow."

"There can't be too much snow at Christmas," Kate said.

"Mebbe not. But come March or April or the first good thaw and ye could be seein' floods like ye ain't never seen before. I'd feel better if 'twere to stop now."

After dinner they exchanged gifts. Kate opened her gift from Howard, a very costly robe of expensive wool. Obviously he hadn't known what else to send her that might be of use in such an isolated place as Adelphi.

He had called several times before the holiday, eager to come down. But she was forced to discourage that. She would have no time for him, not with her crowded schedule.

"That Abbott must be a tyrant," he said. "Hasn't she ever heard the word 'enough'?"

"Yes," Kate said. "She doesn't think a year is long *enough* for all the training we need."

"You're not training to do brain surgery," Howard said. "It's only primary medicine."

"Never use the word 'only' as far as I'm concerned," Kate responded angrily. "This is tough, very tough. But I'll show her before I'm through!"

Late Christmas night, Kate retired to her room at the back of the Russell house, and for the first time in many months, she broke down and cried. Holiday depression, she diagnosed, not an uncommon phenomenon. Psychiatrists were forced to deal with it every year. Kate tried to reason herself out of it.

She had no reason to feel depressed. Howard had called, not only on Christmas Eve but again on Christmas night. Her brother Scott had called all the way from Hong Kong, and she had spoken to him, to his wife, Pam, and to their two little ones. Yet all that only served to make her feel more alone. She was strongly reminded of her aunt Syb, who celebrated most of her holidays on the phone, calling from a hospital ward or a patient's bedside.

She reached the depth of her unhappiness when her mother called from Florida. Alone since her husband had died, she always attempted to put the best face on things. She tried to convince Kate, and herself as well, that she was quite content and happy with her life as it was now. She had settled in a very active and congenial colony of senior citizens.

"Fine people, Kate. You'd like them. Cheery. I mean, there's always something doing here. Activities. Games. We put on our own play last week. I got to play the ingenue. It was fun, lots of fun."

But then she began to cry suddenly, admitting, "God, my dear, how I miss your father! Every evening I expect him to throw open the door as he used to when he came back from one of his business trips and call out, 'Darlin', I'm home!'"

Kate, too, fell asleep crying that night. But the next morning she woke early and went off to the clinic as usual. Continuity and habit seemed the best antidote for loneliness. The other antidote was the promise that there were only three more months left. Three months during which she would apply everything she had learned in the past nine to the actual process of delivering new human beings into the world.

The day arrived when for the first time Kate Kincaid was confronted with presiding over the actual process of birth. She had been assigned to carry out her first delivery.

Her patient was Mrs. Elizabeth Downey. A primagravida, twenty years old, married only eighteen months, Mrs. Downey was coming into labor.

She was a slight woman, despite her recent weight gain. She was extremely tense, not only because this was her first pregnancy, but because all the old wives' tales she had heard since childhood spoke only about the pain and difficulty of delivering. Kate was equally tense, but knew she must conceal it, lest she add to her patient's fears.

Before Kate entered the delivery room she reviewed Downey's chart one last time to refresh her mind on every detail. Preparation, Miss Carberry had drilled into them, preparation was the best way to be ready for any complications which might arise. Knowing your patient will usually tell you what to expect, what medications to have ready, what equipment.

Kate checked her medical supplies. If Downey, being a primagravida, suffered unusual pain on contractions, have the proper medication ready. Demerol. But do not use it if the baby might be born in less than an hour, or it would be born in a weak or unresponsive state.

She made sure to have at hand a bulb syringe to suction out the baby's nose so it could breathe. Umbilical clamps to tie off the cord. Bandage scissors to cut it with. Tape to seal it off at the baby's umbilicus. And syringe, needle and lidocaine if a pudendal block became necessary to ease Mrs. Downey's pain. She also prepared scalpels and sutures in the event she had to perform an episiotomy to ease an unusually large head out of the mother's body.

She had studied Mrs. Downey's chart for high-risk factors. Her patient was slightly hypertensive but not sufficiently to indicate a serious problem. During pregnancy she had reported the usual complaints, slight backache, episodes of constipation, nausea but no vomiting, and, during the last weeks of pregnancy, sleeplessness.

Under Abbott's discerning eye Kate performed a complete abdominal and vaginal examination of her patient to determine the lie of the infant, its presentation, the degree of cervical dilation and effacement.

She drew some blood and dispatched it to the lab for a complete blood count, typing, RH finding and cross match. She had her patient's urine checked to make sure there were no ketones or protein present and to ensure that the patient's bladder was kept as empty as possible.

Periodically she checked the fetal heartbeat against the contractions to see that it returned to normal after each contraction. *If* it did not, this could indicate the infant was in trouble and might not survive the procedure. The heart of Elizabeth Downey's infant was responding beautifully. It slowed with each contraction, but resumed its normal beat of 140 per minute shortly afterward.

The infant was presenting in classic, uncomplicated vertex position, head down. The mother's contractions were regular but a bit more intense than those Kate had witnessed before. There seemed no reason to intervene with medication.

The rule had been drummed into her head during their three months of theoretical study: Do not intervene if it can be avoided. Intervention only increases the risk of patient reaction and infection. Let nature do as much of the work as possible.

Kate continued to monitor the mother's pulse, respiration, blood pressure and the fetal heart rate. Periodically Abbott checked Kate's observations. Everything normal.

Now the actual process of delivery was beginning to take place. Dilatation was maximum. The patient's pain increased in frequency and intensity. Kate knew it was time to put the mother on a Duke inhaler, add 15 ml of Penthrane, set the inhaler to maximum and permit the woman to administer it in accordance with her contractions. Penthrane was the drug of choice, since it did not affect the patient's contractions or run the risk of being flammable.

Coincident with Mrs. Downey's contractions, Kate urged, "Push! Push!" From the change in the patient's vocal reactions and the stress of her contractions, Kate knew the baby was about to appear. Now the head was crowning. It was emerging nicely, if with considerable strain on the mother. Soon the head was fully out. Since the amniotic fluid had been clear, Kate reached at once for a bulb syringe to aspirate the infant's nose so it could breathe on its own for the first time. If the fluid had been stained with meconium, that dark green material from the intestine of a full-term baby, she would have summoned Dr. Boyd at once. Fortunately, it was clear. She had been spared that emergency in her first delivery.

Kate helped ease out the infant. The mother's body seemed relieved to surrender it. Kate clamped off, then cut the cord. She obtained a cord blood specimen and sent it off to the lab. The placenta was separating and the uterus was contracting.

Kate turned her attention to the infant. She took its vital signs. Performed the Apgar test. Everything normal. She examined its eyes and administered medication to prevent any damage. She wrapped the infant in a fresh blanket and handed him to his mother, who took him gingerly, fearing to damage him in some way. She smiled down at him and then up at Kate. It was a smile of relief and thanks and wonder at the miracle she held in her arms. The pain, the difficulty, the fear, were gone now, hardly to be remembered compared with the sight of this tiny new human being who lay in his mother's embrace, his mouth already contorting in the sucking action of normally born infants.

Within minutes Mrs. Downey had expelled the placenta. The birth had been completed successfully, but Kate's work was far from over. She had to check the vital signs of mother and child every fifteen minutes. Make sure the mother's fundus had contracted normally.

Two hours later Elizabeth Downey had been returned to her bed. The infant boy had been fed and lay in his crib in the nursery along with two other newborn infants.

Kate Kincaid was finally free to relax, and she realized that she had sweated through her uniform. Her hair was still damp and pasted against her temples. She felt she had herself given birth and suffered every pain, action and reaction of both mother and child.

Abbott said only, "Get yourself some coffee. Then we'll talk."

Kate went off to the cafeteria, wondering what Abbott meant. She proceeded to review every step of the delivery, every problem that had come up, every procedure she had effected. Obviously she had either overlooked something or done something wrong. She thought, *thank God, at least it turned out well.*

Kate had picked up her cup of coffee at the counter, paid for it and was searching for a place to sit when she spied Sister Ellen at a corner table. Ellen, too, had been scheduled for her first delivery today and appeared as composed as she always did.

"There's a lot to be said for faith if you can take a day like this in stride," Kate joked.

Instead of laughing or even smiling, Ellen's face seemed to dissolve slowly. In place of the smile Kate expected, tears started slowly tracing down her cheeks.

"Ellen? What happened?" Kate demanded.

"Dead."

"Ellen!"

"Everything seemed to be going well. Then its little fetal heart started beating erratically. I sent for Dr. Boyd. He came at once. But it was too late. The little one had been strangled by its own umbilical cord. It came out blue and still. Very still."

Kate left her side of the table to embrace Ellen, who leaned against her and wept openly now.

"It wasn't your fault, Ellen, dear. These things just happen." Kate continued to pat Ellen gently on the shoulder.

But Ellen said, "It *was* my fault. I must find the nearest priest and confess."

"Confess? You?" Kate demanded. "After all the work you've put in. Spending more than the required hours in clinic. Going out on your own to follow up on clinic patients? What could you have to confess to?"

"This was God's way of rebuking me. Because I went against my bishop's orders about birth control. Anyone I touch from now on will suffer for it. Maybe, because of the way I feel, I was never meant to be a midwife."

"Ellen, if you feel a need to confess, then do. But I've observed you for almost a year now. I've never seen a better nurse, a more compassionate nurse. You have a devotion that I envy. There's a lifetime of service waiting for you, among thousands of poor patients who need you."

Ellen remained unconsoled and continued to weep. "That helpless little thing, so perfectly formed, and yet so still. Died without having lived."

Within the hour, Kate presented herself at Abbott's office, prepared for an accounting of her shortcomings during the delivery of the Downey baby. Among themselves, Kate, Ellen and Emily McClendon referred to Abbott as Mother Superior, claiming that she would also have made a very strict abbot and had been aptly named.

Abbott leaned back in her desk chair, reached for the open pack of cigarettes on her desk, lit one while observing, "Dismal habit, smoking. Never start.'' It was the one human frailty Abbott ever exhibited, and she confined it to her office.

''Well, then?'' Abbott began the interview. ''Did you learn anything?''

''Yes,'' Kate said. ''All the manuals, medical papers, books, all the nights of studying were worth it. To see that little one emerge healthy, sound and loud was worth it.''

''That's very nice and sentimental,'' Abbott said, ''but what did you learn?''

''That in most cases the mother and nature do the work. And we only assist whenever and wherever indicated.''

''Exactly!'' Abbott said. ''But don't think it will be this easy every time. During the fifteen deliveries you have to complete before you are qualified, a few will be difficult. One may be dangerous. So never take anything for granted. Never relax. Things can go wrong at any time, even up to the last moment. Be alert. Sharp. Quick. Every part of you. Mind. Hands. Instinct. All must work together and swiftly. Life and death can be a matter of minutes. Never forget that. That's all for now.''

Dismissed, Kate made no effort to move.

''Yes, Kincaid?''

''Miss Abbott, about Sister Ellen—''

''Yes. I know. Too bad. But that rarely happens. We haven't lost an infant that way in years.''

''Something has to be done,'' Kate urged.

''The infant was born dead, strangled by its own cord. There is nothing we can do.''

''Sister Ellen thinks it was her fault.''

''Dr. Boyd explained that she had nothing to do with the unfortunate outcome.''

''Still, she feels enormous guilt. She thinks because of her attitude about birth control this was a sign of heavenly disapproval.''

''I see,'' Abbott said.

''She must experience a successful delivery. And soon,'' Kate suggested.

''We can do something about that.''

Several days had passed, days which forced Kate to resent the irony of their situation. Sister Ellen felt it even more strongly, for in a way it concerned the very crux of her conflict with her church.

At Mountain Hospital, no midwife was graduated or certified until she had presided over fifteen deliveries. Yet the hospital's family planning advice had been so successful that the birthrate in the entire area had been sharply curtailed in recent years. There were, therefore, fewer deliveries to afford the three candidates the opportunities they would have liked. There was considerable waiting time between deliveries for these three women who were eager to put to work the knowledge and ability they had acquired.

Emily McClendon expressed their frustration when she said, "I feel like a woman who's been pregnant for the full term, is heavy with child, and now can't deliver. All I want is the chance to do what we've been preparing to do for nine long months."

The very next case was assigned to Sister Ellen. Kate and Emily would have liked to be present if only to encourage Ellen. But they had been assigned to the Prenatal Clinic. As they concentrated on their duties, they eagerly awaited the reports which other nurses brought from the delivery room.

It turned out to be a long labor. The mother, being a primagravida, was having great pain and difficulty. Sister Ellen, her thin face as damp with sweat as that of her patient, cautioned, urged, comforted and encouraged the young woman. The presentation was breech, the tiny feet, not the head, presenting first. The baby's feet were crossed, it faced the mother's right side, and its buttocks were entering the pelvis. The baby had moved down to the birth canal, its arms unfolding. Eventually Ellen saw its right foot appear at the outlet of the vagina.

With her gloved hands she gently supported and guided the tiny legs into the open. She wrapped a surgically clean towel around the legs for a firm grip to assist the infant out. With her other hand she pressed lightly over the mother's uterus to help in delivering the baby's head. She continued the light pressure while lifting the tiny infant upward to help ease its fragile head through the vaginal opening. Once it was out, she aspirated the mucus from its nose, and when it gave its first cry she surrendered it to Abbott who was standing by to assist. The baby's extremities and bottom were edematous, swollen from the trauma of delivery. But its head was beautifully formed.

After Ellen cleansed the baby's red body, she took it in her arms, performed the Apgar test to ascertain its neurological condition. The infant was a perfect specimen, and Ellen was delighted to turn it over to its mother.

Ellen stood back. Wet face beaming, she stared down at the healthy infant cradled in its mother's arms.

Abbott whispered, "Good work, Sister! Go get some coffee."

Kate and Emily excused themselves from clinic to join Ellen in the cafeteria. Without a word the three young women embraced in triumph.

Kate said, "Sit down. Today we'll get your coffee for you."

Once Kate rejoined Ellen and Emily, the young nun said, softly and reverently, "I think He was testing me. A frank breech delivery."

"We know," Kate said. "We kept getting word. But you handled it beautifully. Perfectly."

"Such a nice baby, too. Healthy, strong. Good Apgars. All babies should be born that way."

"All babies should have the help and assistance of women like you," Kate said.

Over the next eleven weeks, Kate presided over thirteen more deliveries. Ellen, too, completed her fourteenth. Emily was lucky, having completed all fifteen. She was ready for certification and passed her state examination with flying colors. She was the first accredited family nurse-midwife of their group to leave. As she had promised from the outset, she left to go south to the fruitlands of Georgia to care for the migrant workers and their families who were due there during the approaching harvest.

At the moment of parting, the three realized how devoted to one another they had become during their year of training. They embraced, they wept, they laughed. They exchanged promises to keep in touch. No matter where in the world their service took them, they would write to each other and Mountain Hospital. A lifelong friendship had been born.

Since Dr. Boyd was driving up to the city to attend a medical seminar, he volunteered to drop Emily at the airport. He waited patiently in the parking lot until the three young women said their last good-byes. Kate and Ellen waved as Boyd's Jeep started down the driveway toward the blacktop road. Emily kept waving back until the car disappeared.

Kate was scheduled for the next delivery. But there had been an urgent message from Sister Ellen's order. A contingent of nuns was being sent to Africa to work among one of the large but poor tribes. If she could qualify in time, the need for a midwife was so desperate that the bishop was willing to overlook her views on birth control. For she would be serving the higher purpose of helping native women give birth to healthy infants.

It was not stated explicitly, but it was indicated that the bishop would appreciate it if during her service there, she kept her views on family planning to herself. However, word was passed along informally by her Mother Superior that the bishop had refrained from exacting any promise from Ellen that he felt she might not be able to honor.

Kate was delighted to yield the next delivery to Sister Ellen. It was a difficult delivery, requiring her to perform an episiotomy. She made the incision before the delivery in order to prevent any lacerations and to preserve the mother's pelvic floor and surrounding areas. Her main purpose was to reduce pressure on the infant's head, since it was an unusually large baby.

Kate was present to observe. She admired the manner in which Ellen executed the surgical procedure. Maintaining absolute aseptic technique, she injected the 1 percent Xylocaine to anesthetize the sensitive area, injecting another dose of Xylocaine when her patient seemed to feel pain during the procedure.

Soon she was able to turn the baby's large head and body and, accompanied by considerable effort from the mother, ease it out into the open. It was a large baby, indeed, but vociferously healthy. Ellen immediately set to work repairing the area of the episiotomy.

Kate could see Ellen's mind working precisely according to the book. Approximate like tissue. Employ minimal amount of suture material necessary to close the incision. Minimize blood flow. Close each layer of tissue so as not to leave any spaces where a hematoma could form.

Kate performed the Apgar test and handed the infant to its mother. Abbott stood off, observing her two students, only her eyes commenting on what she observed. But later that evening she would write on Sister Ellen's record: "The candidate is extremely well qualified. She shows coolness in the face of emergency and great skill in the practical application of her knowledge."

Two days later Kate was saying farewell to Ellen in the parking lot. The two young women embraced, made the same promises, shed the same tears, and felt the same sense of having gained a great deal more than an education in the year they had spent together.

"You *will* write," Kate insisted.

"You, too," Ellen made her promise.

"And when you see the bishop tell him for me he almost lost a terrific lady when he censured you," Kate said.

Ellen laughed. "When you see the bishop, *you* tell him!"

The driver was honking his horn, anxious to start on the long drive up to the city. One last embrace, and the two parted. Ellen climbed into the half-ton truck alongside the driver, waved her last good-bye to Kate and Abbott. The truck started down the road to the outside world.

"She was one of the great ones," Kate said softly as the truck disappeared around a curve in the road.

Abbott agreed. "Devoted. Capable. Strong in body as well as spirit. She'll do fine work wherever she goes. Now, I suppose, you're itching to do your fifteenth and get going."

Kate nodded. "I haven't yet decided where. But it will be good to stop being a student and start doing on my own."

"I know the feeling," Abbott said. "You may have your fifteenth before you know it."

Kate looked at her, most curious.

"I received a call from Danforth at our River Outpost. She has a Mrs. McCready who is due to deliver very soon, but Danforth can't come in to do it herself. She has two emergencies there. The husband is bringing the woman in this evening. Be ready!"

With those words Abbott started away abruptly, as was her nature. Kate took one last look in the direction in which Sister Ellen had disappeared and felt a great sense of loss. She would miss that tiny, determined, inspired young woman who had the true spirit of religion in her. *Wherever she goes,* Kate thought, *a caring God will bless her work.*

CHAPTER 22

In the delivery room Kate Kincaid was scrutinizing the prenatal chart of Mrs. Frank McCready to determine if it revealed any high-risk factors. Carried off successfully, this could be Kate's final and qualifying delivery that would win her accreditation. As usual, Abbott was present to observe.

Fortunately, there were no special risks indicated on the chart. Mrs. McCready was thirty-one years old, a multipara who had been delivered of three children without incident, and she was in good health.

She was now in the first stage of labor, with all indications that it was progressing normally.

Kate pulled on fresh sterile rubber gloves and proceeded to do an abdominal and vaginal examination to determine the lie and presentation of the fetus. She determined the cervical dilatation. With each contraction Kate palpated the patient to ascertain the frequency, duration and intensity of the pain.

Everything seemed to be going normally.

Though in some pain, the woman tried to smile at Kate. She sympathized with the tension this new midwife was experiencing, and she was trying to reassure her. Yet she winced with every contraction.

To monitor the fetal heart, Kate placed the round metal disc of her stethoscope against Mrs. McCready's distended belly. She checked the beat as it varied during each contraction to determine if it returned to normal once the contraction was over. Fortunately, it did. The infant, too, was responding normally. All signs were good.

As she had been taught and had done fourteen times before during the birth process, Kate drew blood for hematocrit, hemoglobin and white-cell count, holding back one tube for type and, if required, cross match.

She checked a urine specimen for ketones and protein. None being present, she did not have to start the patient on an I.V. Instead, she fed her ice chips, cautioning her to allow them to melt slowly in her mouth. She reassured and encouraged her, urging her to breathe normally and shallowly. Mrs. McCready was a sturdy, dark-haired woman, handsome despite the momentary contortions that pain inflicted on her face.

Kate decided there was no urgent need for medication. Why risk fetal narcosis?

The descent of the infant had begun and could be monitored. Mrs. McCready was entering the second stage of delivery. Since she was a multipara with a good history, the infant should be born soon. Based on her training, Kate knew that a multipara should proceed from full dilatation to birth in an hour or less.

The minutes went by. Mrs. McCready began sweating more profusely. Kate looked at the wall clock and started counting the minutes. When the hour had almost elapsed, Kate had to admit to herself that something had gone wrong.

She urged her patient to push. And push again. The woman tried to cooperate, exerting as much pressure as she could. But the baby's head had not engaged in the proper position.

In her mind, Kate ran through the procedure to follow in a prolonged second stage. Was it due to malpresentation or malposition? From her examination that did not seem to be the case. The patient was cooperating by pushing. There was no possibility of excessive anesthesia, since Kate had not found it necessary to administer any. That left Kate only one possible conclusion. The patient was suffering a constriction ring, caused by involuntary contractions of some areas of the circular muscle fibers at different levels of the patient's uterus. The danger was that, being imprisoned in that area for too long, the baby would suffer brain or other damage.

Aware of Abbott's presence and her immobile face, though her eyes were clearly judgmental, Kate urged Mrs. McCready to push even harder. The woman tried. Speaking through her pain, she apologized, "It's never been like this before. Not even with the first."

To Kate that was both a challenge and an affront. As if she, not the birth process, were failing. She could feel sweat break out on her forehead and between her breasts. She kept eyeing the clock. Precious minutes were being used up before she had to make the one decision she hated to make. She continued to perform her examinations in swift repetition. Track the fetal heartbeat. Examine and test for presentation of the infant's head. It had not presented.

The wall clock indicated that fifty-seven minutes had gone by. The permissible hour had almost elapsed and the birth process had been interrupted with what could be dangerous and fatal consequences. Both midwife and patient began to sense that the ability to accomplish a normal birth had eluded them.

More aware than ever of the presence of Abbott, whose expression had not changed at all but whose eyes were fixed on her, Kate went to the wall phone and said, "There is an emergency in Delivery. Page Dr. Boyd."

Then, with full awareness of her continuing responsibility, she proceeded to call for Type B blood, two pints. She started the patient on an intravenous drip of 100 ml of Ringer's lactate with an 18-gauge intracatheter. She was setting out the vacuum extractor when Boyd rushed into the delivery room.

He knew how much this delivery meant to Kate, but he made no comment. He washed quickly, scrubbing hard, while Kate brought him up to date on the details of the situation. Multipara, sixty-four minutes had elapsed, second stage prolonged, infant had strong fetal heartbeats which responded well after contractions.

"Sixty-four minutes?" was all Boyd said. He then proceeded to verify each of Kate's findings. He went through the same process of elimination, trying to determine the cause of this prolonged second stage. In all details his findings corroborated Kate's. His diagnosis was the same. His orders were curt.

"Oxytocin, ten units I.M."

Kate prepared the injection and administered it intramuscularly into Mrs. McCready's arm. By now her eyes were revealing her fear. She realized that something was wrong and that both doctor and midwife were only guessing as to the cause.

To reassure her, Kate said, "This helps when contractions are ineffective. Just keep pushing and breathing the way you've practiced."

Boyd demanded, "Forceps!"

Kate produced a sterile stainless-steel forceps which might become necessary depending on how matters progressed from now on. They would have to await the effect of the oxytocin. Failing a favorable development, the danger this prolonged second stage might pose to the infant would demand a cesarean be performed.

Now Kate, Boyd and Abbott watched the clock alternately while monitoring the progress of events, which Mrs. McCready was enduring as well as she could but with little success.

When Boyd determined that she had been subjected to as much risk as he thought justified, he made his decision.

"We'll do a section!"

Boyd left at once for Surgery. Kate swiftly prepared her patient to undergo a cesarean. Boyd had finished scrubbing. Mrs. McCready was ready. Kate wheeled her into the Operating Room, where the scrub nurse helped her lift the patient onto the table. Kate informed the anesthesia nurse of all the relevant details of Mrs. McCready's condition so that she could determine the proper dosage.

By the time Mrs. McCready was under, Boyd was ready to begin. Kate stood by to observe, feeling great guilt. If she had not failed, this entire surgical procedure would not be necessary.

Boyd was efficient, skillful and effective. In less than half an hour he lifted out and handed to Kate a squirming, moist, red-faced boy with eyes clenched shut and with tiny hands, and feet that seemed too large for such a small baby. The child gave a cry of protest. Kate set about performing the first Apgar to determine his neurological condition. His responses were normal. Kate was greatly relieved. He had suffered no damage during that prolonged second stage. But her fifteenth delivery had eluded her.

After she surrendered Mrs. McCready to the recovery nurse, Kate went down to the cafeteria for some coffee. She missed Emily. She desperately missed Sister Ellen. This was a time when she needed someone for consolation, for comradeship. Someone in whose presence she would not be ashamed to weep, and who would understand.

She was feeling alone and abandoned when Abbott appeared in the doorway. Kate's first reaction was anger. How could this woman who had been such a taskmaster during the entire twelve months be so insensitive as to attack her now? Yes, this was her crucial fifteenth delivery. No, things had not proceeded as they should have for a healthy multipara. But as far as Kate could remember she had done everything according to the book. She was determined not to accept Abbott's reprimand without defending herself.

"Well," Abbott began, slipping into the chair opposite Kate, "quite a morning, Kincaid."

"Yes, quite," Kate agreed, tense and ready to justify every step she had taken prior to calling in Ray Boyd.

"Too bad it required a cesarean," Abbott said.

"I did everything I could," Kate replied.

"You did one thing . . ." Abbott started to say.

But Kate interrupted angrily, "Miss Abbott, you have been picking on me ever since I interceded for little Eloise. And I've taken it. But not this time! Oh, no, not this time! You say I did one thing wrong? Name it! Just name it!"

Abbott listened patiently through Kate's outburst. "Finished, Kincaid?"

Kate relented, then said quietly, "Yes. Finished."

"Then may I continue?" Abbott asked. Kate nodded. "I was about to say that you did one thing today that in my mind is more important than a fifteenth successful delivery."

Dubious, Kate looked across the table to study Abbott's eyes. Was the woman playing some sadistic joke on her?

Abbott continued, "From your arrival here, even before that, from your scholastic record, your application and your reason for coming, I detected an overdetermined need to prove that you are always right, always infallible. I observed that same characteristic in you during the Eloise affair. What I have been looking for these past months is some sign of humility. Some recognition that, along with all the rest of us, you are human, fallible.

"Because to me there's always been one final test for a good midwife. Does she know the limits of her professional expertise? Can she recognize when it's time to call in an obstetrician to complete the procedure? That was far more important to me than if you had carried off another routine delivery. I already know you can do that.

Just as I know you'll have your fifteenth successful delivery any day now. It was humility I've been looking for. The moment when you put your patient's welfare above your own pride. Today you did. That's a beginning, a good beginning.

"I congratulate you. Good work, Kincaid."

Without a smile, without another word, Abbott rose and left the table.

Kate sat silent, but an enormous weight had been lifted from her, not the least of which was the hostility she had harbored against this woman who, in her own way, had been concerned with Kate's own future welfare.

Abbott was right about one other thing. Before the week was out, Kate had delivered her fifteenth normal, healthy baby. It was with more than the usual satisfaction that she tenderly placed the blanketed infant in the arms of its mother.

With that gesture, she had not only delivered a baby, she had liberated herself from twelve long months of study, training, testing and proving herself. She could not resist glancing at Abbott, who signified her approval by nodding but not smiling.

But the nod was enough. Kate breathed a sigh of relief. She was free! Free to return to the outside world!

She must call Howard at once.

His secretary said he was in court but that he would be phoning the office during the lunch break to pick up his messages. She would relay Kate's call. Kate determined to tell him the news herself. What time would he be back in the office? He had two more witnesses to prepare for tomorrow's court session, so he would surely be in the office from six until ten this evening. Kate would call back on his private night line.

She hung up and realized that in her haste to tell him her own news she had not listened as carefully as she should have. She placed the call again, listening attentively as she heard the switchboard operator say, "Brooks, Travers, Klein, Aldrich and Brewster."

Kate smiled, said, "Sorry, wrong number," and hung up, still smiling. She repeated the names to herself. Brooks, Travers, Klein, Aldrich and Brewster. The *and Brewster* sounded just fine. Hawk had made it. He was now a partner in the firm. Why hadn't he written her about it? Was he saving it as a surprise because she was so close to finishing? Was the news going to be his welcome-home Easter present to her?

To make waiting for six o'clock bearable, she volunteered to serve in Family Clinic, spelling any nurse in need of a coffee break.

She kept glancing at the clinic wall clock. If the red sweep second hand had not been so obvious, she would have been sure the clock had stopped. Today, of all days, it must be running slow.

Finally, it was six. The nurses she had relieved were back from their supper break. She was free to make her call. To ensure privacy, she had asked permission to use the phone in Abbott's office. She dialed Howard's direct line. After two rings she heard him answer brusquely, obviously annoyed at being interrupted in the midst of his trial preparation.

"Brewster! Yes?" he demanded impatiently.

Kate mimicked his abrupt attitude. "Brewster? Kincaid! And the answer *is* yes! I passed. I qualified. I'm free. I'll be home for Easter!"

With enforced reserve in the presence of a witness important to his trial, Howard said, "That is excellent news. Let me know exactly when and where, and I will be there."

For all his witness could gather, Howard had just arranged another business meeting. Kate hung up. She sat back in Abbott's desk chair, and in the dark room she smiled a big, broad smile, feeling better than she had in many months.

Kate Kincaid, Family Nurse-Midwife, had achieved her goal. Had weathered a long year of tough training and study, twelve months of isolation and separation. She was now free to resume her life and her career, not as a second-class citizen but as a full-fledged capable professional with the right to treat patients on her own.

Still sitting in the dark, she began, as a surgeon does once the purpose of an operation is achieved, to tie off the relationships she had established during her months here. Mrs. Russell, that dear old lady who had virtually adopted her. Eloise, who had not only proved herself brighter than Kate had suspected, but who lit up the Russell house, making it a three-generational home along with Grandma Russell and Kate. Mrs. Russell had taken to sewing dresses for the child, cooking special dishes for her, answering her never-ending questions, reading with her from the books Miss Talmadge had sent for, books far more advanced than the ones available at the school.

And there was Abbott, that unrelenting taskmaster who demanded nothing less than perfection from her students, yet who could be as indulgent and understanding with an unfortunate patient as any nurse Kate had ever seen.

And Ray. Ray Boyd, a misunderstood doctor in these mountains, who had come back, not because he had failed but out of love for his land and his people.

There were also the families Kate had cared for. She resolved to call on each of them and say farewell in person. She would make one last try to convince Mrs. Persons to give up her chewing tobacco with its heavy molasses content. She would urge the Torrences to see that Eloise received a college education. Any college would be delighted to give her a scholarship. And there was cherubic old Professor Spencer. And . . . the ands seemed to run on and on, including all fifteen women whom she had successfully delivered of their babies, twins in one case.

In the midst of her resolutions, the door suddenly opened. Abbott snapped on the overhead light.

"Oh, sorry, Kincaid, didn't know you were still here," Abbott said.

"You said it was all right to make a personal call."

"I know. Hope I'm not intruding," Abbott said. It was obvious that she was in a state of great personal stress.

"Anything I can do?" Kate offered.

"Owens . . ." Abbott interrupted, then began to weep. The sight of the resolute woman in tears startled Kate.

"What about Owens?"

"Four days ago she felt a lump. Dr. Boyd went in for a biopsy. We just received word from the pathologist up in the city."

"I see," Kate said quietly.

"Poor Owens. A fine nurse. Wonderful woman . . . wonderful . . ." Abbott wept softly.

"It doesn't have to be that bad," Kate tried to encourage.

"We tell that to patients, not to each other," Abbott replied.

"When will the surgery be?"

"Tomorrow. So I have to find a replacement. Wildwood is our busiest Outpost. And with Samuels now in charge of Pine Ridge, Wildwood needs a very competent nurse. So I've got a lot of serious thinking to do. I would like to be alone for a while."

"Can I get you something? Have you had supper?" Kate asked.

Abbott was oblivious of Kate's offer as she began to consider the problem less emotionally. "Where to find a capable, trained woman. . . ." She became aware of Kate again. "Go along, you've had a long day yourself. See you tomorrow."

CHAPTER 23

Kate woke early the next morning, uneasy, disturbed by a mixture of feelings. Her elation at being free to return home after so long was overshadowed by the unfortunate news about Owens.

Kate looked out of her bedroom window at the mountains, green with perennial spruce and pine but with white patches of snow still visible. Soon these mountains would be only a memory, a fragrant memory of one of the important years of her life. So close to leaving, she could appreciate now why people who were born and reared here were in some mystical way drawn back to it, to breathe its clean, brisk air, to refresh themselves with its quaint language and rhythmic music. She knew that she would have such memories and such longings herself.

Laughter from the kitchen beckoned her. Slipping on her robe, she went out to discover Mrs. Russell and Eloise laughing hilariously at some private joke. Those two enjoyed each other enormously. Today was Friday, and since Eloise would be going home to spend the weekend with her family, they were making the most of their day together.

"Well, sleepyhead," Mrs. Russell greeted Kate, "you've had a long night's sleep. But then you got in so late. *Too* late, I must say."

Kate's look of surprise made Mrs. Russell urge, "Go on, Eloise, show her!"

Shyly, Eloise drew out of her schoolbag a folded sheet of lined pad paper. Written across the top in mature handwriting was *This must be submitted to the All-State Grade School Poetry Contest. R.D.*

"R.D.?" Kate asked.

"Mr. Danforth, our principal," Eloise said.

Kate sank into a chair and began to read the poem. It was about a pretty blond lady who had come to visit one day and befriended a little girl who loved to read books and write poems. A little girl who felt all alone because she didn't know anyone else in this world who liked the same things.

A poem about me, Kate thought; how many people in this world ever had a poem written about them? And such sensitive writing, showing Eloise's growing command of the language as spoken in the world outside these mountains. The new books were already having their effect. Kate reached out. Eloise embraced her.

"You'll have to write me, very often," Kate said. "I'll want to know if your poem won, and if you're going to high school in the city and then to the university. For the rest of our lives we will write to each other. Promise?"

Kate toyed with a few wisps of the child's delicate golden hair, still as soft as cobwebs. Eloise stared up at her and asked, "Why do I have to write?"

"Because . . ." For the first time Kate realized that she had told no one. "Because I will be leaving here. Soon. Very soon."

Without a word the child pressed desperately against Kate as if she could reverse the decision.

"Yesterday I assisted at my fifteenth delivery. So my training here is finished."

"You're going . . ." was all the child could say.

"Yes, dear."

"You won't go while I'm up home in the holler next two days, will you?" Eloise pleaded.

"No, I'll pick you up on Monday morning as usual."

The child clung to her, pressing her head against Kate's breast, until Mrs. Russell reminded her gently, "Time, child, time to go off to school."

"Will you be here when I get back?" she asked Kate.

"Here or at the hospital," Kate promised.

One last hug and the child took up her schoolbag and was on her way.

"I never realized . . ." Kate said.

"She never stops talking about you," Mrs. Russell said. "Though she's very young, she knows you've changed her whole life."

"Make sure she writes me how her poem made out in the contest," Kate said.

"I'll miss you, too, my dear," Mrs. Russell said. "You have a way of bringing brightness into a place. You cheer the soul."

The phone rang. Mrs. Russell answered. "It's for you. Abbott."

Kate took the phone quickly. "Yes?"

Abbott's voice was once again efficient and professional, revealing none of the emotion of last evening. "Kincaid, can you be in my office in fifteen minutes?"

"Yes, yes, of course."

Kate found Abbott at her desk, completing a phone conversation. "Tell her not to worry. We'll take care of things here. And I'll come up to the city as soon as I can." She looked up at Kate and said only, "Positive. The nodes were positive. They had to do a radical. Poor Owens. So I have to make plans. Long-range plans. I can't close down Wildwood. Hundreds of people depend on it."

Kate's strong impulse was to say, I'd like to help, but I'm finished here. I've put in my year, done my job. Besides, there's Howard. I promised, "I'm free, I'll be home for Easter." I want to go back there and practice my new-found skills. I am no longer a handservant to arrogant physicians. I have achieved a position of respect. I want to go back and show them all, Dr. Morse, the Medical Board, the Disciplinary Board! And you're asking me to postpone all that for another term of voluntary seclusion in this little place? No! I will not do it! You have no right to ask!

Then she knew what she must do.

"How long would it take to find a replacement for Owens?"

"Weeks. Probably months," Abbott said.

"I'll . . . I'll fill in for her," Kate said.

"With Samuels no longer there, you realize you would be taking on the sole responsibility for an entire busy district? More than three hundred families?"

"Yes," Kate said.

"It won't be easy," Abbott warned.

"I don't expect it will be."

"Okay, Kincaid," Abbott said, adding softly, "and thanks. I'd hoped, but I didn't think I had a right to ask."

"When do I start?" Kate asked.

"Eva, Owens's secretary, called. There are patients waiting now."

"I'll gather up my things and go," Kate said.

"Check the pharmacy and see what medications you have to take."

"First . . . first, I have a phone call to make, a personal call," Kate said.

"Of course," Abbott said. "Use my phone." She left the room to afford Kate the privacy she would need.

She dialed. But when it rang, Howard's secretary said he was on another call and then had to rush off to court. Kate insisted on holding on. Soon she heard his voice, more cheerful and enthusiastic than usual. "Darling? Great news! My trial is over. Just got the call. The other side settled. So tell me what time your plane arrives and I'll be there!"

"Howard . . ." she began, "Howard, darling, please try to understand—"

"What's there to understand?" he asked, his enthusiasm turning to impatience.

"There's an emergency here. Something's come up. They need me."

"Don't tell me you're going to be delayed? I've already made plans for a terrific Easter weekend."

"I'm not talking about the weekend. Or even a week."

"Kate?" he asked soberly.

"It will be weeks, maybe even months."

"Months! But just yesterday . . ."

"Howard, darling, I told you, this is an emergency."

"An emergency does not last for months!" he declared angrily.

"But this is an unusual situation. . . ."

He interrupted sharply, "For the last year your whole life has been an unusual situation. I begged you not to go down there. You wouldn't listen!" Suddenly he demanded furiously, "What if I said you have to make a choice. Either come home now or forget it!"

Kate paused before replying, "In that case, I'm afraid I would have to say forget it."

She stopped at the pharmacy in the basement of the hospital. A large carton of medications was waiting for her. Insulin for diabetic patients. Inderal for several cardiac cases. Thyroid. And quantities of the other drugs that some patients had to take regularly to survive in decent health.

She must check all other basic supplies as soon as she arrived at Wildwood to see what was needed in the way of bandages, antiseptics, sutures, snake antivenin, and many other medications for the very next patient who might show up with any one of hundreds of symptoms, diseases or injuries.

She loaded her saddlebags and supplies into the Jeep and pulled away from the hospital.

The farther up into the mountains she drove, the warmer she felt. This struck her as strange. Last year at this time when she first arrived, it had felt cold, almost wintry. Yet now she was aware of dampness oozing around the collar of her flannel shirt. She loosened it to allow the fresh air to cool her. It did not.

Soon she realized she was entirely bathed in perspiration. The sweat of fear. Suddenly she had had thrust on her the very freedom, responsibility and professional challenge she had been demanding all these years, and now she found it terrifying.

She tried to recall who the writer was who had once said, "There is only one thing worse than not getting what you want. And that is getting it."

Kate Kincaid knew now what he meant.

She began to anticipate the number of emergencies that might confront her at any hour of day or night at Wildwood. There was no predicting what the next tinkle of the little bell over the front door of Wildwood might signal. It could be a routine visit by a pregnant woman in her fourth uneventful month or a man fatally hemorrhaging from a chain-saw accident.

The very first time she had been left in charge of the Maternity Ward at University Hospital was not nearly so terrifying. There, she had only to lift a phone and a resident or staff doctor would be on the floor in minutes.

Now, help would be hours away. If the weather was against her, maybe as much as a day away or more. It was like being on a desert island and sending up a makeshift flag, hoping some passing vessel would see it.

When she reached Wildwood there were five other vehicles already in the parking lot. One could belong to Eva, the Outpost secretary. The other four must be patients' cars. No more time for fantasies or fears. She mopped her damp face, gripped her saddlebags, swung them over her shoulder and started for the door of Wildwood.

Kate Kincaid, R.N., F.N.P., N.-M. She was ready for whatever this day, and all following days, would bring.

The bell over the door jingled as she opened it. The patients in the tiny waiting room turned to greet her. She could see their disappointment. They had been waiting for Owens. Until they grew used to her, it would be unwise for Kate to add to their uneasiness by admitting Owens would be a long time returning, if she ever did.

"Good morning. Miss Owens . . . Leona . . . sent me to take over for her for a while. She's up in the city. At the hospital there. Catching up on some new medical procedures, I think."

She hoped the explanation had reassured them. But she had no way of telling, for they only stared at her, making her feel even more a stranger.

"Well, let's get started," Kate announced pleasantly. "Who was first?"

A young mother with a squirming, active two-year-old rose from her chair. She had brought him for his periodic examination. They followed Kate into the tiny examining room. She performed a complete examination on the child, who was more interested in the shiny metal instruments in the glass cabinet than he was in being examined. It was a struggle to hold him and examine him at the same time.

He evidenced no deviation from normal physical development. She tested him with blocks and toys. He was coming along nicely, neurologically and intellectually, and Kate was delighted to reassure his mother of this.

This first case gave her a modicum of the confidence she needed.

The second case, too, was a checkup. A pregnant woman in her second trimester. Kate consulted her chart before beginning the actual examination. The woman was a multipara, aged twenty-six, with two previous children, both born healthy. She was slightly hyperthyroid, but it created no problem. Kate tested her heart, lungs, pulse rate, blood pressure. She performed a complete pelvic examination and found no indications of future difficulty. She monitored the fetal heartbeat. It was as swift and regular as a normal fetal heartbeat should be. One hundred forty a minute. Kate was relieved to pronounce both mother and fetus in excellent condition.

But her third case was different, alarmingly different. A little girl of nine with the moist, weary eyes of a child in high fever, detectable even by Kate's first touch. The mother, a slender woman with the same straight black hair and dark eyes as her daughter, stood by watching anxiously.

"How long has she been this way?" Kate asked as she took the child's temperature.

"Four days."

"You should have brought her in sooner."

"I couldn't," the mother explained. "There's my others to do for and no one to stay till my mother come this morning."

Kate proceeded to examine the child's throat. The trouble was immediately apparent. A bad inflammation. Kate used a wooden spatula to take a specimen of the white material that exuded from the child's inflamed tonsils. For these signs could be warnings of more serious and life-threatening complications. Kate palpated the child's swollen lymph nodes. They were extremely tender.

Kate felt a surge of anger toward the mother. Four days! Didn't she realize that signs of such throat distress, if not treated soon enough, could develop into rheumatic fever, eventually shortening the life of her child? Four days! Kate would have to obtain an analysis of this culture at once. If it proved to be A-beta-hemolytic streptococcus it could be life-threatening. There were other possible causes of such a red, inflamed throat and high temperature. Infectious mononucleosis, scarlet fever, even gonorrhea. But the prime enemy to guard against was strep.

Kate asked the child to open and close her mouth several times. She obeyed. No signs of trismus. She examined the soft, fleshy part of the palate and found no deviation of the uvula. That ruled out any abscess of the tonsils.

Her concern fixed more and more on the possibility of strep throat and on those four elapsed days, which could have proved critical. She would have to treat for the worst indications.

"Has Marcy ever had penicillin?" Kate asked.

"Penicillin? I don' know," the woman said. "Leona'd be

knowin'. She knowed everythin'," the woman said, obviously rebuking Kate for not knowing.

Kate referred to the child's chart. It revealed no previous injections of penicillin. Kate's decision had to be made now. Prescribe erythromycin by mouth or penicillin by intramuscular injection. Penicillin, which would be more effective, posed a serious risk if the little patient proved sensitive to it. She could have a severe anaphylactic reaction; this would lead to acute respiratory distress resulting from the swelling of the larynx, and might possibly even cause circulatory collapse from shock.

On the other hand, with a mother who had allowed four days of high fever to go by before bringing the child in, Kate could not take the chance that any oral medication she prescribed would be conscientiously administered during the ensuing ten days.

The child's extreme condition forced Kate to decide to use penicillin, injected intramuscularly. But she would have to be prepared for any dangerous reactions. She laid out the medication and the hypodermic, the gauze pads and the alcohol. Before she proceeded, she paused to wipe the sweat from her own face. She drew the medication into the syringe, swabbed the child's arm with alcohol, pushed in the needle and administered the injection. Once she had put aside the hypodermic, she said, "Now, lie back and rest awhile. You're going to be fine now. Just fine. So fall asleep if you feel like it."

She signaled the mother to join her outside the door. "Stay here and watch her. If she shows any pain, any breathing difficulty, let me know right away. Right away, you hear?"

"Yes, ma'am," the mother replied.

"Any sign of difficulty at all!" Kate warned her.

Kate took the next patient into the other small examining room. He was an elderly man with low back pain. She asked him to remove his denim pants. He bridled at the suggestion.

"You want me to tell Leona that you wouldn't do as you were ordered?" Kate asked. The man might resist her, a foreigner, but Kate sensed he would do anything if Leona Owens asked. It worked. He slipped off his denims, protesting all the while.

"Young woman, from off, come here asking a man to do things he'd be shamed to do front of his own granddaughter."

The most sensitive part of the procedure must now take place and for him, undoubtedly the worst indignity. Kate suspected, in a man of his age, an involvement of the prostate, possibly even a malig nancy. She slipped on a rubber glove and proceeded with her rectal examination.

"What air ye doin'? It's only the rheumatiz likely."

Though his protests now included some cuss words, she persevered with her examination. Her gloved finger found a small, hard mass, confirming what she had suspected. This would call for a biopsy.

But before she could explain, she had another urgent duty pressing on her, one in which minutes counted. She tore off the surgical glove, scrubbed, and rushed back to her little patient in the other room. The child was still highly febrile. But fortunately, she had no difficulty breathing. Eight minutes had elapsed with no signs of an adverse reaction. She tried to smile up at Kate before she drifted off to sleep. However, Kate did not relax. Another twenty minutes, Kate knew, before one could be sure.

She returned to her old patient, whom she surprised trying to pull his denims up over his worn, cracked workshoes.

"Damn, used to a man could pull on his pants without no wuhman spyin' on him."

"Mr. Rutledge, I'm afraid you'll have to go into the hospital. You need some tests."

"Testes, is it? And fur what?" he demanded.

Preferring not to alarm him if her suspicions turned out to be unfounded, Kate said, "Certain things that can't be confirmed by a routine examination like the one I just gave you."

"Routine? Ye call what ye did to me routine?" he protested. But the gravity of the situation turned his anger into concerned curiosity. "The hospital, ye say? Which 'un?"

By now Kate had had enough experience with mountain people to know he was asking for her assessment of his jeopardy. If she said Mountain Hospital he could be assured that the situation was not too dangerous. But if she said the hospital up in the city, then the situation might be grave.

" 'Long as you're leaving your holler might's well go to the city. They have more facilities, better facilities," she said.

The look in his steel-blue eyes told her her attempt to minimize his danger had not succeeded. He blinked, then looked past her as if to complain to the world at large.

"Nowadays yer go t' see a nurse, a mere nurse, mind ye, and the look on her face is enough to make ye sick. Ye leave feelin' worse than when ye come. And as fer the city hospital, come without no money nor no medical card and they won't take ye."

"I'm sure that money will be no difficulty. You are on Social Security and Medicare, aren't you?"

He grunted and nodded reluctantly.

"I'll arrange for you to go with the next hospital messenger who leaves for the city," Kate said.

He felt thankful for her concern but tried to conceal it by grumbling, "Knew fer certain when ye did all that testin' wasn't goin' to come to no good."

As he started for the door, Kate said, "I'll let you know as soon as I can arrange it."

"I'll be sleepin' with my Bible under my pillow till ye do," he said, a simple confession that he acknowledged the gravity of his situation.

Kate went back to her little patient, who was sleeping, breathing evenly and shallowly. The full thirty minutes had passed. There was no longer any danger of an anaphylactic reaction to the penicillin. Until the lab report excluded A-beta strep, it would be safest to keep the child here, administer the four injections a day of penicillin rather than entrust them to the mother, who might stop as soon as the child showed any improvement.

Kate glanced at the family chart to find the woman's first name.

"Ellie," Kate began, "I can take care of Marcy here. But there's something you must do. You have to go home, look very carefully into the throat of everyone there. . . ."

"Even into Marmaw's?"

Kate was confused until she recalled having heard the term before in the clinic. A boy had been brought in with an infected foot which still had a fishhook in it. Clinging to his grandmother's hand, he kept whispering through his tears, "Marmaw . . . Marmaw." It was the mountain word for Grandma.

"Yes," Kate replied, "even Marmaw's. Everyone. Your kids, your man. And if any of them has a red throat, bring them to me. *Right away!*"

The woman nodded, her face grimmer than before, for Kate's concern reflected the dangerous condition of her little daughter.

"Treat her kindly. She's afeared of strangers."

"I'll treat her kindly," Kate assured.

"And yer name, ye didn't tell me yer name."

"Kate. Kate Kincaid."

The woman nodded. "I'll do like ye sayed, Kate." She took one last look at her sleeping child, kissed her gently so as not to rouse her, and departed.

CHAPTER 24

The rest of the day proceeded in similar fashion. Ailments, some minor, some warning of graver dangers, presented in a steady flow. Infants, pregnant mothers for routine periodic checkups; old folks with the pains and crotchets of age.

So it went, through the day and into early evening. When the flood of patients had ebbed, Kate administered the third inoculation of penicillin to Marcy, her little in-house patient, who was still feverish but thankfully less so.

Finally, Kate had a chance to sit back and enjoy the cup of coffee Eva forced on her. With a moment all to herself Kate realized that the back of her blouse was wet through. There was a moistness between her breasts that had persisted throughout the day. She had been in a constant sweat.

Each patient had presented fresh fears. Had she misdiagnosed a condition? Or having diagnosed it properly, had she treated it wrong? Had she missed some important sign, failed to pay attention to some crucial symptom which might later result in serious illness or even death? Had she hurt some child unnecessarily while administering treatment? And always, every time the little bell over the front door rang, a new wave of fear assailed her.

Whole families, even to three generations, were dependent on her. From birth until the final days of their lives, people were depending now on Kate Kincaid. The responsibility was greater than she had ever anticipated.

She drew a few exhausted breaths, sipped her coffee and consoled herself, at least it's over for this day. But her respite did not endure for long. She recalled what Abbott had once warned them about in an early lecture on family nursing. "The ones who come to you are only part of your problem. Those who don't come when they should may be the graver part."

Kate called out, "Eva! The files of all patients due here who didn't show up!"

Along with an armful of files, Eva also brought her a sandwich and some fresh coffee. Kate nibbled at the sandwich while she skimmed through the files. Most called for routine periodic follow-ups for previously diagnosed nonemergent conditions. The difference of a day or two would not matter too much.

One case turned out to be critical, possibly life-endangering. The file was labeled *LONGLEY, MARCUS.*

Longley, Marcus, a widower his file indicated, lived alone up what was called Five Mile Holler. He had been a coal miner in his early days. Had a history of black lung disease. Recent X rays revealed the condition was chronic but not acute.

Longley had had no major diseases until the onset several years ago of diabetes. He had been put on insulin by injection, had been instructed how to administer it himself, and for the past three years, had been provided with a steady free supply. Longley came regularly to Wildwood every two weeks to pick up the ampules, which he kept refrigerated in the brook that ran just behind his house. Periodic examinations proved this arrangement kept his diabetes under control.

However, this week he had not appeared for his fresh supply of insulin and hypos. With a start, Kate realized Longley must have run out of medication two days ago! His appearance had been so regular in the past that his absence caused her to consider ominous possibilities. If Longley had been prevented from coming down to Wildwood because of an accident or some other sickness, he would be in desperate need of insulin, possibly even be in a diabetic coma by now. There was no time to lose.

Kate dropped the remaining half of her sandwich, washed up quickly, gave her febrile little patient her fourth and last shot of penicillin for the day. At the same time she called out instructions.

"Eva, get a supply of insulin out of the refrigerator! Pack a two-week supply of syringes and needles in my saddlebag."

"Saddlebag? Where do you think you're going this time of evening?"

"Five Mile Holler. How do I get there?" Kate asked, coming out of the child's room.

"You can't make that trip now," Eva protested.

"Eva, you've never seen a patient in diabetic coma. I have. I must go!"

"It'll be dark before you get there!" Eva warned her.

"I have to go! Now, tell me!"

Reluctantly, Eva gave her the instructions. Saddlebags packed, Kate set out in her Jeep as twilight was closing in.

By the time she came to the narrow unpaved road that snaked off the two-lane blacktop into dense woods, it was already dark. She switched on her high beams, pointed the Jeep up the dirt road until it became so steep she had to shift into four-wheel drive. She could feel the tires grind over a rock here, bounce into a hole there. Finally her headlights picked out a large object ahead. It turned out to be an automobile at least thirty years old but well cared for. Beyond that was the cabin. There was no light. Kate sensed that her worst fears had been confirmed.

She came to a stop beside the ancient car, groped in the saddlebag for her flashlight. After she had played it over the ground to make sure there were no rattlers, she ventured out. Before approaching too close to the house she called, "Mr. Longley! Marcus? Marcus! It's Kate Kincaid from Wildwood. I'm the nurse there! Taking Leona's place for a time. Marcus, do you hear me?"

There was no reply. No light appeared in the cabin windows. No matter what she might find inside, she was in no danger of being fired upon. She started for the porch. The high beams of the Jeep lit up the area so she had no difficulty reaching the cabin. The only thing that slowed her was her reluctance to discover what she was sure she would find.

Even her footsteps on the creaking porch evoked no response, no warning. In these mountains that was a sure sign there was no life inside this cabin. She turned on her flash, then cautiously pushed the door. It opened with a creak of hinges that begged for oil. She played her flashlight slowly around the room.

The old stove was black, gray and cold. She hoped her fears were unjustified, that possibly Longley had gone off to visit somewhere and had not been home in days. But if so, why was his old car still parked outside?

She ventured into the room. There were dishes on the table, one filled with some food. She shone her light on it. Grits. Longley's last meal? Mountain people were clean, respectful of their homes and themselves. If Longley had left, he would have cleaned up before he went. Now all signs were indeed ominous.

She played her flashlight around the room until she found an old handcrafted door that led to another room. If he were anywhere, he must be in there. Kate started toward the door very slowly, her every step straining the ancient boards beneath her. There was no latch on the door. She pushed. It swung slowly back, revealing a plain wood bed.

She discovered a figure in the bed. She shone the light down on him. Longley lay still, partly covered by an old homemade patchwork mountain quilt that his wife must have sewn a half century ago. His gaunt face appeared to confirm her original fear. Then she noticed the faintest signs of breathing as his chest rose almost imperceptibly, then slowly fell.

She dropped down beside him, tried to find a pulse, was finally able to detect one. Her first thought was to test neurologically to determine the depth of his coma. But the man's history dictated an immediate dose of insulin. She prepared the hypo. He did not stir when she jabbed the needle into his arm. Once she had forced the contents into him, she commenced her examination.

She tested his soles with needle pricks. He did not respond. She continued until he pulled back in a vague way, the first hopeful sign. She forced open his eyes and flashed her light into them. There was some response. She took his blood pressure. Low, dangerously so. She took his pulse once more. It seemed to have gained slightly in rate and strength.

There was nothing more to do for him except allow the insulin to work. She left his side to find the oil lamps by which this house must be lit. There was one in the room and two in the kitchen. She lit them all. Using kindling and a few logs, she started a fire in the old cast-iron stove. Every few minutes she checked to ascertain Longley's condition. Her needle pricks now evoked stronger reactions. When she pinched the soles of his feet, he withdrew them with more force. When she flashed the light in his eyes, he tried to turn his head away.

By the time the fire was blazing, Longley had begun to mutter and mumble. Kate could not make out specific words, but she was gratified that he was voluntarily making sounds. She put the old kettle on the stove to boil up some water, and searched the old wood cabinet for food. When he woke, he would be hungry as a result of the insulin.

She found some potatoes, which she peeled and set to cook, some stale bread, which she could toast over one of the open stove holes when she removed the lid. She discovered some coffee. And in the icebox out on the porch, kept cold only by the mountain air, she found some butter and some milk. The milk had curdled. But the butter still smelled sweet enough to use.

She set the table with simple crockery and with utensils which once had been fine examples of seventeenth-century silvercraft but were now worn, bent and scratched from years of being scoured with homemade lye-based soap.

She could hear him now, breathing deeply and sighing with each exhalation. She went into the bedroom.

"Mr. Longley . . . Marcus?"

His eyes opened with a start. "Who be ye?"

"Kate Kincaid. I've come to take Leona's place for a while."

"Leona, oh, yes," he said.

"You're probably very hungry by now. Come out, have something to eat," Kate said.

He turned away from her and said, "Ain't hongry."

"You must be."

"Ain't," he persisted.

Kate knew he had not eaten for a day at least, possibly longer, and now with the insulin in his system he was not only hungry but needed food. Why did he persist in denying it? Then she realized. Over the past few years he had become accustomed to the routine of always taking his insulin before eating. Rather than admit he had had no insulin, he stubbornly chose to pretend he was not hungry.

Kate resolved his dilemma. "It's all right, Marcus, I gave you a shot when you were . . . when you were asleep."

"And I didn't feel it?" he asked, dubious.

"I did it so gently there was no pain," Kate said.

"Ye ain't funnin', are ye?"

Kate smiled. "No, I ain't funnin'. You've had your shot."

"Then, in that case, I kin eat, though I ain't real hongry," he continued to protest.

The ravenous way he ate his boiled potatoes, buttered toast and coffee proved beyond doubt the degree of his hunger. Eventually he became self-conscious and asked, "Ain't ye hongry? Dig in. Have some."

There was hardly enough for him, so Kate said, "I ate before I came. But I'd be mighty pleasured to have coffee with ye."

Longley smiled at her. "Ye talk lak folks, real folks. Be ye mountain born?"

"No," Kate admitted.

"Well, ye shore larn quick." He continued eating.

Kate studied his face by lamplight. The color was back in his cheeks, which were thin and lined with deep creases. His prominent nose was patrician. His gray eyes were now bright and sharp. In his early seventies, Longley was still a handsome man, to whom age seemed to have added nobility. Kate suspected he was also a man of great pride. Something she must reckon with now that she was forced to put important questions to him.

"Marcus . . . two days ago you should have come down to Wildwood . . ." She noticed that he drew back, less open and friendly than before.

"Ye-uh," he replied, but it was not agreement, merely his way of permitting her to proceed.

"You didn't appear. You didn't get your insulin. As a result you went into coma. You almost died. Do you know that?"

"Didn't though, did I?" he countered.

"If I hadn't shown up tonight you would have," Kate pointed out.

"But ye did, and after all, was your bounden duty, so there ain't no real bad trouble, is there?"

He was being evasive, which caused Kate to wonder, had he deliberately chosen to deprive himself of insulin in order to die in a less shameful, less violent way than many suicides? But suicide was not the way of mountain people. They were too stubborn, too proud.

She tried once more. "Marcus, you didn't come for your insulin. Why?"

He looked away. She reached for his thin, bony hand, now warm when it had been icy cold before.

He did not turn back to her. But he did begin to speak.

"Used to, a man could git into his car and mosey down to Wildwood. Wuz nice seein' Leona and Evy. They's right pleasant girls. And we'd fun a little, makin' jokes and all."

"Leona's only been gone for a day. You were supposed to come down two days ago," Kate pointed out.

"Will ye stop from buttin' in?" he replied angrily. "I'm a-tryin' to tell ye. Used to, that's the way it wuz. But nowdays . . . well, man cain't jes' get into his car and go. I mean . . . less'n a man is bad took . . . he can't jes' go wastin' money, not with the price of gas so high," he confessed. "I be on the draw as 'tis. To go spendin' money on gas, over dollar a gallon . . ." He shook his head sadly. "Cain't rightly afford to no more."

So now it was out. He could not afford the price of the gasoline it would take to go down to Wildwood and back. Too proud to say so, he would rather have died than admit it. Out of sensitivity for his feelings, Kate improvised. "I guess you didn't hear. We've started a new service at Wildwood. Patients who need medication will have it delivered to them. So from now on I'll be bringing it to you."

He turned to stare at her suspiciously. She nodded convincingly. He finally believed her.

He confessed, "Times, the last few weeks, I wuz so worrit, I took the big eye." Then he explained, "Hardly slep' a wink all night." He smiled. "So ye gonna be brangin' that stuff yereself. Well, that's right nice. Have some more coffee."

While she was drinking her second cup, Longley stared at her in the glow from the oil lamp on the table.

"Ye're pretty. 'Mind me of 'Lizabeth, our eldest. Lives in Californy now. My, she wuz a beauty. Cotched the eye of this here minin' engineer come through when they wuz first talkin' 'bout strip minin'. Stayed right on to spark her. Next I know he's talkin' to her. 'Bout gittin' married, that is. Now she lives in Californy. And I got littl' uns I ain't never seed."

He stirred the remains of the coffee in his cup before looking off and admitting, "If ye hadn't come . . ." He did not finish the thought.

You must never let that much time go by without your injections again, understand, Marcus?" He nodded, but still would not face her. To emphasize the point she said, "Ye could be bad took if'n ye let that happen again."

At her use of mountain phrases he smiled, then paid her the supreme compliment. "Ye're common like the rest of us." He had accepted her as one of his own.

It was past midnight when Kate found her way down from Five Mile Holler and back to Wildwood. Before she would relax she examined her little patient and was relieved to discover that her fever had completely subsided.

Kate made herself a cup of hot coffee and a sandwich, but before eating it she felt she had to sit down at her crowded little desk and write to Howard after being so adamant during their last phone conversation.

In several different ways she tried to apologize, but tore up each attempt. Finally she decided there was only one way to do it. As simply as possible she would relate all the cases she had handled on this first day alone.

So you see, darling, they need me. Young, old, very sick, or only worried, they depend on me.

And, in my way, I need them and depend on them. They have to teach me if I'm good enough for this work I've chosen. Do I have knowledge enough, skill enough, patience enough, confidence enough? Because to tell the truth I haven't stopped sweating since I took over here this morning. Fear, my darling, fear is what does it. And self-doubt. Yes, me, your Kate, is beginning to have self-doubts. That's one thing they've taught me here. But I keep telling myself, tomorrow will be better.

Tomorrow was no better. Nor the tomorrows that followed. Each was a day of constant fear and sweat until after the fourth day, Kate began to tie a bandana around her neck every morning to catch the perspiration that seemed to trickle down in endless rivulets.

During several times of great stress she was tempted to call Abbott and confess, "I am not up to it! Send someone to relieve me."

Each time she was forced to delay the call because another emergency had presented itself. Some were manageable. Some were beyond help. Some were emergencies of a spiritual or psychological nature. Such as the one brought into Wildwood on Saturday morning.

When the Woodsons were first shown into the examining room, Kate assumed that they were mother and son, for the woman was thin, frail, and seemed years older than the man who aided her. But when Eva brought Kate their family chart, she saw at once what the difficulty was. Leona's notes were cryptic but clear.

"Carcinoma of the uterus, postsurgical chemotherapy. Family insists patient not be informed."

Even if that warning had not been clearly noted on the chart, it was obvious in the eyes of the husband, who hovered so protectively over his wife.

"She says now it's quicky all over," he informed Kate.

"Let me have a look," Kate said, indicating he leave them alone. First, his eyes beckoned Kate out of the room. Once the door was closed he said softly, "I ain't never tol' her. I kinda like to gentle her till the end."

"I understand. But it might be better if she did know. She'd understand her pain and accept it."

"Promised the young'uns I'd never tell her."

"She has a right to prepare for the end," Kate pointed out.

"We ain't tellin'," Woodson said, putting an end to all discussion.

"As you say," Kate agreed. "Now, excuse me."

Mrs. Woodson had already stripped and was lying resignedly on the examining table. This simple act depressed Kate, for she realized that in the past few years the unfortunate woman had become so used to the routine that she undressed with the habitual regularity of cows coming in from pasture every night to be milked.

Kate went through the empty charade of the usual palpation of the woman's stomach. She could feel the hard metastases of the cancer which had totally invaded her body. There was nothing anyone could do for her except prescribe a stronger narcotic to battle her growing pain. It would help but little. Her pain would increase until the end.

Kate completed her examination. Mrs. Woodson asked, "Worse, ain't it?"

"Well, it's not improving as fast as it should," Kate said, avoiding the woman's piercing eyes.

"Ye can tell me the truth," the woman said. "My man won't. My kinfolk won't. But ye could. I'm more'n bad took. I'm dyin', ain't I? The cancer is broke free and nobody can stop it."

Kate could no longer avoid it. The woman had used the one word they had been trying to keep from her. But she had obviously suspected for some time now.

"Yes, Mrs. Woodson." She took the woman's frail, cold hand. "There is nothing we can do to stop it."

"Is there time, much time?"

Kate shook her head.

Instead of shedding tears, the woman breathed softly. "Thank God. I cain't stand the pain no more. Nor the lyin' neither. Tom never lie to me before. As painful as the pain was, was worse to see him try to lie so near to the end."

"He'd like to think he succeeded at it," Kate reminded her gently.

"Still, I got to say farewell afore I go. To Tom, to the young 'uns. How kin I, if I ain't supposed to know?" she asked simply. Then she said with resolve, "I'll find a way, I'll find a way to let 'em know I know."

Kate had to admire the strength of this woman whom life had not prepared for such a tragic end, and who showed more courage to meet it than her family did.

Kate had no time to dwell on that, for she heard Eva cry out, "Kate! Kate! Come quick!"

She raced through the reception room to find Eva out on the porch. At one glance, Kate diagnosed the problem. Seated on the passenger side of an old rusting car at the foot of the steps was a man in his early sixties, his arms clutching his chest as he fought for breath. His pale, drawn face revealed intense pain. Kate had seen those signs too many times. The man was suffering a heart attack.

Two things, Kate's mind dictated at once, *two things! Give him an oxygen supply so there will be no brain damage! And get him to the hospital!* She raced to the car, brushing by the terrified wife who stood alongside her husband, helpless.

"Watch me!" Kate ordered. Pressing his head back to make sure he had a clear air passage, she began to give the man mouth-to-mouth cardiopulmonary resuscitation. Between breaths, she ordered Eva to bring her a hypodermic and medication to ease the man's pain. Meanwhile, she kept rhythmic count as she inhaled and then breathed into his mouth.

As soon as she had administered the medication, she ordered the man's wife, "Now you do it!" She watched as the woman tried to perform the resuscitation maneuver, corrected her when she failed until she was finally executing the procedure in desperate continuity. Once the woman had mastered it, Kate ordered Eva to pull up the Jeep alongside the car. Summoning all her strength, Kate lifted the man out of the car and eased him into the back of the Jeep.

"Now, keep at it!" Kate instructed the wife as she herself climbed into the front of the Jeep. She told Eva, "Phone the hospital. Tell them I'm coming in with a cardiac case. Have Dr. Boyd stand by!"

Kate put the Jeep into gear, turned so swiftly that the gravel flew up behind them as she took off.

CHAPTER 25

The unpaved road was dry from two weeks without rain. A thick layer of dust made it as treacherous as a coating of ice. The Jeep skidded and twisted with each bump and pothole. Kate struggled to keep it on the road and had special difficulty when a huge coal truck came bearing down, forcing her over to the side. She tried to warn it off by keeping her hand on the horn, but the truck only seemed to veer even closer to the center of the road.

As Kate struggled to keep the Jeep at top speed, under control and on the road, she also glanced back from time to time to make sure her patient's wife continued to administer the vital CPR properly. The woman was beginning to show exhaustion.

Kate had to wait to relieve her until she had turned onto the two-lane blacktop. Narrow as it was, it was still safer than the dirt road. She glanced back once more.

She called to the woman, "Can you drive? Fast?" The woman paused in her labors long enough to nod. "You take the wheel. I'll take over the CPR."

Kate brought the Jeep to a stop on the shoulder of the road. She slid out from behind the wheel and into the backseat, and tapped the woman on the shoulder. Kate eased herself into her place and took up the rhythmic function of breathing for the patient. The man's wife started up the vehicle and drove on toward Adelphi.

A gurney and a nurse were waiting in the parking area. As Kate set the patient down on the stretcher, Boyd came racing out of the hospital. While Kate wheeled the stretcher toward the door of Emergency, Boyd hurried alongside, commencing his appraisal of the patient's vital signs.

Kate tried to accompany them into Intensive Care. Boyd said, "You've done enough. Get some rest."

Abbott brought her into her own office, dispatched one of the new trainees for some coffee. As soon as Kate started to sip the hot, refreshing brew, Abbott said, "Now you know what it's like."

Kate nodded, exhausted. "I really should go and see how he's doing."

"He's in capable hands and you can't help him by exhausting yourself," Abbott insisted. "Now I've got things to do." And she left.

Almost half an hour later, Boyd came by to report. "He's under oxygen, with an I.V. And being constantly monitored."

"How bad was it?"

"Would have been fatal except for you," Boyd said. "As it is, failing another episode he should be on his feet again in three to four weeks."

"Thank you," Kate said softly.

"Now, what about his nurse?"

"What about her?" Kate asked defensively.

Boyd took her hand, raised her to her feet, stared into her eyes, gently fingered the creases under her eyes, ran his forefinger over the furrows in her brow.

"I detect all the signs of extreme weariness. You are a tired young lady. Very tired," Boyd said.

"I . . . I haven't been able to sleep," she said. "The responsibility, the pressure, the constant uncertainty at what the next moment will bring. I haven't stopped sweating since I've been there."

Kate turned away from him before she admitted, "I've never quit on anything in my life. But I've been on the verge of asking Abbott to let me out. I want to be free of the burden of knowing all the answers, knowing what to do in every situation. I want out."

When she turned back to Boyd, she had tears in her eyes. He took her in his arms, not as a lover but as a father.

"Kate, Kate, every nurse put in charge of an Outpost for the first time is terrified. Just as every young doctor, even the smug, cocky ones, are. That's why they are so obnoxious. They have to give the impression they know everything at the very time in their careers when they know least."

"But what do I do about the sweats, the constant tension?" Kate asked.

"I think you will find after what's just happened, the sweats will gradually diminish. This was what you needed. That first plunge into the icy waters when a human life depended solely on what you did. And you did it."

Abbott returned in her usual brisk fashion. "Kincaid, there have been some frenzied calls from Eva. Patients are piling up at Wildwood. You'd better get going!"

Kate pulled into the gravel-covered parking area in front of Wildwood. She could see several patients sitting on the porch steps, which meant that all the chairs in the tiny waiting room were occupied. This day, hectic as it had already been, was beginning all over again.

Fortunately, it proved to be an afternoon of routine cases.

It was twilight, the edge of dark, before her thirty-third and last patient departed. Kate welcomed the first opportunity she'd had to slip into a chair and not feel the pressure of having to do everything at once. She could just sit there and breathe easy. When Eva brought her some coffee and a sandwich, Kate realized she had had no lunch. But neither had she missed it. Until she started eating she didn't realize how hungry she was.

After her brief supper she began dictating into the tape recorder her reports on the day's patients. If she did not do these now, there would be no time. Tomorrow there would be a fresh batch of notes to dictate for Eva to transcribe.

It was after nine. All the cares and sounds of the day had receded. Outside, the night was still except for the rustling of the trees and a hound baying.

Kate was ready for bed. She started toward her little room, untying the kerchief she had grown used to wearing around her neck. Damp. Still damp. The magical cure Boyd had predicted had not yet taken effect. She hoped that at least she would regain the ability to sleep without sudden waking.

It was a restless night nevertheless. Emergencies kept parading through her dreams and, try as she might, she could never reach the patient in time. She woke suddenly. It was still dark out. She turned on the light. Only twenty after two. She had not been asleep for more than a few hours.

She tried to fall asleep again. She could not. She went out to the small office, took out a group of files and went through them to discover which patients should have come back for follow-up care and had not, especially the pregnant women. Unless they suffered pain or bleeding some women tended to assume checkups were unnecessary. She started making a list of those women.

She fell asleep in the midst of her chore, sitting in the chair, her head resting on the desk. At dawn she woke to the sound of someone at work outside raking gravel. She peered out. A young man, no more than eighteen, was raking the parking area to smooth out the deep grooves that her hasty tire tracks had dug into the gravel yesterday. Kate pulled her robe about her and went out onto the porch. She discovered it had been swept. She looked over at her Jeep. It had been thoroughly cleaned, the windows freshly washed. The young man paid her no attention, but continued to rake and level the gravel.

She called to him, "Young man?"

He turned slowly toward her. "Yes'm?"

"Who are you? What are you doing?" Kate asked.

"Jethro Haislip," the young man answered and resumed raking.

"We've no money for such work. I can't pay you," Kate said.

"I'd be right angry if ye tried," he said. "After how ye saved my granpaw yesterday, seemed only right I do somethin' fer ye," he said and continued working.

"I see," Kate said, realizing that by their code a good deed done deserved a good deed in return. These proud people did not like to be indebted to anyone for anything.

She went back inside and started preparing for the day. A brisk shower. Then her usual garb. No nurse's uniform, only slacks and a shirt, more practical and utilitarian.

She brushed, combed and put up her long blond hair, applied a little makeup and was ready for whatever the day might bring. As a daring act of confidence she decided she would not tie the bandana around her neck. She was determined not to break into a nervous sweat. Today would be the beginning of new courage and self-assurance for Kate Kincaid.

But before the day was half over she was confronted by a mother who carried in her arms an asthmatic eight-year-old girl who was gasping for breath, turning blue and cyanotic.

Kate had no choice. To keep the child alive she would have to do a tracheostomy.

Between breaths that she forced into the child, she called out instructions to Eva. Once Eva had assembled all the equipment, Kate had her take over the mouth-to-mouth procedure while she slipped on a pair of sterile gloves and reached for the syringe to inject a local anesthetic. Though she had seen the procedure done a number of times, she had never done it herself. She had, in fact, never made an incision in a patient before.

She injected the anesthetic just below the trachea, and waited for it to take effect. Then, as she picked up the scalpel, sweat started to flow more profusely than before. She forced herself to rehearse the rules silently.

Position patient supine. Hyperextend the neck. Find the cricoid cartilage. She brought the scalpel to the area of the patient's neck and carefully made a transverse incision between one and one-and-a-half centimeters below the lower border of the cricoid. She opened the trachea and inserted the endotracheal tube.

It gave the struggling girl access to the air that she so desperately needed. Kate felt the child's body grow less tense as the air filled her hungry lungs. Her breathing became almost regular, her pale cheeks regained a more natural color, her blue lips returned to a normal pink once more. Her struggle for life having been won, she closed her eyes and breathed peacefully. Kate tended the area around the small wound, taped the tube in place and kept watch, being careful to suction the tube clean from time to time to keep open a clear air channel.

She carried the child to the bed in the small treatment room, instructed her mother how to use the syringe to clear the tube and allowed her to fall asleep. Kate went back to the examining room ready for her next patient, an elderly woman complaining of foot trouble, which Kate diagnosed as due to faulty circulation.

But she was still perspiring. Would it never stop? This fear of making a mistake? Of not reacting quickly enough? Of costing some unfortunate patient his life because she did not think clearly enough in a moment of emergency?

She tied a fresh bandana around her neck and carried on.

CHAPTER 26

It was another long day in a succession of days filled with many cases, but fortunately no life-threatening emergencies. Kate was going over the list of patients who were delinquent in their return visits.

There was an elderly woman who had no first name but was called only Marmaw Johnston. She had been suffering the usual aches, pains and inconveniences of old age. Her chart also indicated she was beginning to suffer from hardening of the arteries of the brain. Though not emergent, she undoubtedly needed another examination and probably an increase in her medication.

Kate determined to visit her for follow-up care. Since even Eva did not know the directions to that remote hollow, Kate decided to get them from the general-store owner, who also ran the one-pump gas station in the tiny town adjacent to Wildwood.

She pulled up at the pump in front of the store. Three elderly men were sitting on the porch, gossiping. At the sight of her, the three became silent. Kate was conscious of their staring and one of them said, "Hear they got a new nurse down to Wildwood."

"Some says she is plumb purty," the second man said.

"Dunno," the third said. "I heerd she is kinda piedy, strange like."

"If'n so, it's 'cause she needs a man. Ain't God's way a woman should be livin' all alone," the second man said. "How does Preacher Willis say it? 'An abomination unto the Lord.'"

"Right well said," the first man corroborated.

The second man squirted a brown stream of tobacco juice across the porch. "Likely, she cain't get no man 'cause she's so small and scrawny. Man needs a woman he can grab holt of."

She glared at them as she passed, but this only provoked smiles. She found Cleve Brigham behind his counter going over an old worn ledger in which he kept accounts of customers with bills past due. He finished a page, turned it and without looking up, asked, "Yes, ma'am?"

"I'd like to fill up my Jeep."

"Anybody out there stoppin' ye?"

"No, but I thought—" Kate started to say.

"When ye get done, jes' tell me how much," Brigham said, not raising his eyes from his accounts.

Trust was something that had virtually disappeared from city life. During the worst days of the fuel shortage Kate had grown used to paying in cash before she was permitted to pump a drop of gas. Here there was no thought or suspicion that she might be tempted to cheat.

She went out to do the job herself, but found she had been anticipated. Will Spencer, professor of speech, song and rural customs, was filling the tank for her. But the three mountain men had still not given up.

"Randy, why do ye suppose that there old man is messin' over that young girl?"

"Dunno, less'n they's more 'tween them than meets the eye," the second man said, with a smile that was more a leer.

Determined to ignore them and discourage all further comments, Kate came round the Jeep to the side where Spencer was just screwing the cap back onto the tank. But her annoyance was obvious to him.

"Easy, my girl," he said, smiling. "They are joking about you. That means they've heard good things about you. Not many from 'off' get that kind of treatment. They are only paying their respects."

"It's a funny way to do it," Kate said. "Now, I wonder if you can give me some directions. I'm set to visit a woman named Marmaw Johnston. All it says on my card is that she lives up Two Pines Holler."

Before Spencer could respond, the three men, having overheard, came down to join them, all three talking at once.

"Y'see, ma'am . . ."

But the second man was pointing down the road and saying, "Hit's twicet as fur as ye kin see."

And the third said, "Seems further'n 'tis."

"Hit's twicet as fur as ye kin see," the second man insisted. "Then up the holler a ways."

Kate looked at Spencer, who explained, "If that sounds confusing, it is quite logical. 'Twicet as fur as ye kin see' means it's around the next two curves. Then turn right at the dirt road and follow it up to the end. You'll find Marmaw there. I've been to see her. In her lucid moments she is one of the best historians on local lore and color in this whole mountain range." Then he lowered his voice, "Now, thank them kindly and be on your way. It's late. And I don't like the look of the weather."

Kate thanked the three idlers for their directions and was starting up her motor when one of them called out as a parting shot, " 'Cordin' to the law of the mountains, ev'ry man needs two or three wives. She might yet make one." The other two men laughed, one of them spraying the road with tobacco juice.

Instead of resenting them, Kate smiled and called back, " 'Cordin' to the law from off, it'd take all three of ye to make one good man!"

The three howled with delight and one of them said, "By God, she's common like the rest of us!"

Kate drove off, while Spencer watched, thinking, *she's learning, that girl is learning.*

It was almost dark by the time Kate reached the foot of the holler "twicet as fur as she could see." She surveyed the steepness of the climb, the dusty earth of the unpaved road, and decided to leave the Jeep and climb the rest of the way. She was partway up when she called out, "It's Kate Kincaid. From Wildwood. Anyone home?" She could tell there was because the two small windows shone with the light from a kerosene lamp. So she would not proceed without permission lest she be fired upon.

"Come ye," a woman shouted back from inside the cabin.

By the time Kate reached the porch the woman was outside waiting for her. She was wiping her hands on her faded apron, staring at Kate in the dim light of evening.

"Young, ain't ye?"

"Old enough," Kate said. "Mrs. Johnston?"

"Ye-uh. Ye come to see me or Marmaw?" the woman asked. In the faint light Kate could see the woman's face. She must have been a beauty in her younger days, though she was now hardly more than forty. Hard work and sacrifice had aged her before her time.

"Marmaw. If I may?" Kate replied, ever solicitous of the custom of always asking permission, never assuming. Primitive in some ways, the mountain people had an old English sense of propriety and etiquette.

"Come on in, but fust, I got to tell ye, she's drinlin' bad. Her eyeglasses has a-left her eyes. They ain't helpin' her no more. And she just sets starin'. 'Cept times when she sangs to herself. Other times she don' remember nothin'. Times she can think way back to when she was a mite of a girl and times she ain't among us. If'n they's anythin' ye can do. . . ."

"I'll have a look at her."

Though it was not a cold evening, the old woman was huddled close to the log fire, hungry for any bit of warmth she could glean from it. The flickering light played on her face, revealing pink skin against pure white hair. The blue veins in her temples stood out clearly. Her skin was stretched so tightly against good bone structure that across the bridge of her nose it was white in contrast with the pink. Physically she seemed in excellent condition. But her eyes stared aimlessly, even when Kate spoke to her.

"Marmaw? I'm Kate. Kate Kincaid. From Wildwood."

The woman did not respond. Kate studied her a moment. One thing was immediately apparent, the woman was being meticulously cared for. Her dress, though of cheap cotton, had not only been freshly washed but neatly ironed as well. Her white hair, so thin with age that Kate could see the pink scalp beneath, had been carefully brushed and combed. Incapable of taking care of herself, Marmaw had obviously been bathed and dressed for supper.

Her daughter-in-law stood apart, watching Kate, along with the children, two boys, no more than twelve and fourteen, and a girl of ten.

"I would like to examine her in the bedroom, if I may," Kate said.

"Rafe, help yer marmaw into her room."

The older boy gently lifted his grandmother into his arms. "Marmaw, ye come with Rafe. Nice and gentle like." He carried her into the small room, which by its odd juxtaposition to the rest of the cabin indicated to Kate that it had been built recently and without the aid of any architectural advice. Everything in the room had been hand built, plain but new. It must have been constructed for the old woman once she had started "drinlin'" from age.

Marmaw did not resist the examination. She seemed unaware of it. Kate did not find any startling changes. Her blood pressure was high but not excessive for her age. Her pulse was steady in the main, skipping one beat in every seven, a not uncommon phenomenon.

Physically she was in good shape for a woman in her late seventies. But the damage arteriosclerosis had inflicted on her brain was apparent and beyond the help of Medicine. She would continue to deteriorate, becoming less and less part of the conscious world, though she might go on living for a few years. The medical aspects were irreversible. But about the other aspects Kate felt obligated to speak out. It would be better if the man of the house were here, not only because he was the authority in the family but because Marmaw was his mother.

Kate went out to meet with the daughter-in-law.

"Will your husband be home soon?" Kate asked.

"He's workin' the coal trucks down in Suffolk. Ain't likely to be back 'fore Tuesday," she said. "But ye can tell me. She ain't worse took than before, is she?"

At those words the three children drew close to their mother.

"According to her chart," Kate said, "she's just about the same."

"Good," the woman said.

"But what I would like to discuss with you and your husband . . ." She looked at the children to indicate their presence was not necessary or desirable. But the woman reached out and drew the girl closer to her, indicating the children had a right to be part of this.

Kate continued, "It is obvious to me that caring for your mother-in-law is a burden to the entire family. That room, it must have taken quite a lot of money and a great deal of time to build it for her. And I could see at first glance the toll it's taken on you. The hours you must spend tending her, washing her, doing her clothes, combing and brushing her hair. . . ."

"It's only fit," the woman said, "a woman o' her age desarves the respec'."

"But at what cost to the rest of your family?" Kate asked. "You'd have more time for your children, for your husband, for other things."

The mother looked at her three children, drew the little girl even tighter to her and asked, "Whar else could she be a-goin' 'cept hyar?"

"There are nursing homes for such elderly people. Where they get good care, proper food, and there's a doctor close by at all times. And I think, through the hospital, we could arrange to have her put in a nursing home at government expense," Kate explained.

The older boy ventured to ask, "What kind of place did ye say?"

"A nursing home," Kate repeated.

The boy turned to his mother, puzzled. "I never heerd there was any kind of home but a body's own home. Is there, Maw?"

"Ain't never heerd of it myself," his mother said. "Cain't think yer paw'd let his own maw be the care o' strangers. 'Tain't right."

"But think what it would mean to the rest of your family," Kate urged softly. "The time you'd have to spend on them."

"They ain't needin'," the woman said staunchly. "Ask 'em."

There was no reason for Kate to ask. The three stood staunchly alongside their mother, giving her total support and loyalty.

"Marmaw is our family and she stays. Until comes the day she restes for the last time. Then we will call on Preacher Willis and she be buried up on the hill 'yond the house alongside her man. Only decent way to do," Mrs. Johnston declared.

"I only thought I would mention that there are other choices," Kate said.

"Mebbe, but not for us!"

The older boy escorted Kate down the dark trail, holding a kerosene lamp before her. Twice when she almost tripped he caught her arm and supported her. He was young but strong, his body already well developed muscularly. He must have performed a good part of the labor involved in building that extra room for his marmaw.

He waited until Kate had turned the Jeep around and started away along the blacktop road. She could see the light of his lamp in her rearview mirror.

* * *

On the drive back, around the two bends in the road, Kate thought the outside world might call mountain folk primitive and even burlesque them on television. But these decent people could give the rest of the country some lessons in family and personal loyalty.

Heavy rain had finally begun to fall. There was the far-off sound of thunder. Premature for early April. It was wise that she had put off visiting any other patients tonight. Now, all she wanted to do was get back to Wildwood and into bed after another day too crowded to allow time for rest or a leisurely meal. Still, she had sweat a little less profusely than before. Bit by bit she was conquering her fear.

Once back at Wildwood, she fell asleep with the memory of the white-haired, pink-cheeked old woman who, in her dotage, still had the love and devotion of her family, when other families in other places would have shipped her off to some institution.

The last thing she was aware of was the sound of heavy rain beating down on the shingled roof of Wildwood. This was evidently no passing April shower. Tomorrow the dirt roads would be quagmires.

CHAPTER 27

Kate woke early to the steady sound of rain still beating down on the roof. She slipped out of bed, pushed the window blind aside and peeked out. There were deep puddles in the garden back of the clinic. It had rained all night. She wondered if that would slow the stream of patients today. She recalled that last January, heavy rains combined with a winter thaw caused many of the rivers and streams to swell to flood stage and become impassable in some cases.

Kate went into the kitchenette, put on the water for coffee. She showered, dressed, decided to risk going without a kerchief for her neck again. She had her breakfast of grapefruit juice and coffee. If she had been prescribing for a patient she would have insisted on eggs and bacon or a hot cereal. She promised herself if today did prove a light day in clinic, she would catch up on all the files she had yet to study. It would obviously be impossible to make that call on the pregnant young woman in this kind of weather. She would also call Abbott and check on Owens's medical condition.

She had hauled out a batch of files and was starting to peruse them when she heard the front door bell.

"Eva?"

"Me, all right. What a day!"

Eva came into the doorway of the small office, water streaming off her shiny black raincoat.

"Could hardly get across. The water's 'bout so high to the bridge level.'' She indicated the space between the river and the bridge by holding her thumb and forefinger about an inch apart. ''They won't be coming today. Give me a chance to type up all those notes you've been dictating.''

Kate worked over her files, pulling out those of the cases she must visit first. She glanced at her wristwatch. Almost nine o'clock. Good time to call Abbott.

Brisk as usual, the director answered, ''Abbott!'' The woman always spoke as if there were never enough time.

''This is Kincaid.''

''Something wrong?'' Abbott asked immediately. ''This is a bad day for emergencies.''

''I was just calling to inquire about Leona.''

''She's doing as well as can be expected under the circumstances,'' Abbott said.

It was a guarded response and Kate was fully aware of it.

''How are things at Wildwood?'' Abbott asked.

''I guess you could say the same, as well as can be expected under the circumstances. Problems, but all manageable.''

''Good,'' Abbott said. ''I'm still trying to find a replacement. I've called some of our older graduates. But no one's available at the moment.''

The phone suddenly went dead. Kate jiggled the bar several times until Eva said, ''Happens all the time. Local phone always goes dead during storms. And even when there are no storms. Half the time we never get to say good-bye. Phone company does it for us.''

Kate did not reply, for she had been hoping Abbott would have some word about a replacement, so she could write Howard about coming home. Perhaps that might elicit a more encouraging response from him than his last letter.

Eva went to the window to watch the rain cascading off the slanting porch roof. ''Bad,'' she said. ''Looks like Buttermilk Falls. Ever been out to Buttermilk Falls, Kate?''

The phone rang, stutteringly, never completing a solid ring. Eva answered, then announced, ''Yes, yes, Miss Abbott.'' She held out the phone to Kate.

''Yes, Miss Abbott?''

''We got cut off before I had a chance to tell you about your little protégée.''

"Protégée?" The word puzzled Kate until Abbott said, "She won! Eloise won the poetry contest!"

"Wonderful!" Kate exclaimed. "We must have a party to help her celebrate."

"We'll be celebrating more than that. An offer came with the prize. The Fremont Family Foundation, which puts up the prize money, they've offered to give her a scholarship to a private school in the city."

"Wonderful!" Kate replied. "What did her father say?"

"We haven't been able to tell him yet, they don't have a phone."

"Of course," Kate recalled. "Soon as this rain lets up I'd like to go call on them and tell them."

"Then you can tell Eloise, too, she's up there during the school holiday."

"Good. It'll be a thrill for her." Kate started to say, "And for me," but the phone went dead again. "Damn!"

"You'll get used to it," Eva said, and resumed typing Kate's notes.

The morning passed easily. Only two cases. One from the little adjoining town. The other from the Wildwood side of the river. A baby suffering colic was brought in by its mother. Kate determined there was no serious illness before prescribing a change in the baby's diet. She administered some paregoric. Even before the mother took the infant home its colic had begun to subside.

The other case was a young woman, no more than sixteen, Kate judged. She came unaccompanied, dripping wet, strands of hair pasted to the sides of her face. And she was obviously terrified. Even Eva was startled by her appearance. Kate led her into the examining room, made her get out of her wet clothes. Before Kate had an opportunity to examine her, the dried blood on the insides of her thighs revealed the cause of her fear. She had obviously tried to abort herself but panicked in the process and stopped. Kate pulled on a pair of surgical gloves and began to perform a vaginal examination. The girl pulled back and curled up, more from guilt than pain. Kate forced her to straighten out. She put the girl's legs into the stirrups.

"What did you use?" Kate asked.

"Wasn't much else to use but a handle," the girl admitted, beginning to sob. "Will I die?"

"What kind of handle?" Kate asked, gently proceeding with her examination. She realized that although the girl had inflicted some bloody damage on herself, she had probably not completed the abortion. What she required now was treatment to prevent infection, then surgical intervention to repair the lacerations.

But, first, Kate cautioned herself, follow the rules. Determine the extent of the injury to tissue. Also make sure there are no foreign bodies. Irrigate the area with a saline solution to wash away any dirt or contamination left by the instrument. And as a prophylactic measure, start the patient on erythromycin.

Having done all that, Kate elicited the girl's history. The man had been one of the truck drivers on the coal route. They had met in the tiny general store and poolroom in town. They played a few games. They had a few drinks. What happened after that was inevitable. Except that he was a stranger to the mountains. He had gone on to another job, at another strip mine. She never heard from him again.

Then, weeks later, she discovered she was pregnant. She kept it secret until she decided to do what she did. She tried it in the middle of the night when the rest of her family was asleep. She began bleeding. She ran from the house so they wouldn't know. She couldn't go home now. She couldn't.

No matter what myths the outside world had perpetrated about the loose morality of mountain people, they were deeply religious. They might drink some, resort to the use of guns and rifles to settle disputes, but they were very strict about the morals of their women and the reputation of a family in the community.

Kate put the girl to bed in the small patients' room, gave her a tranquilizer to help her get some much needed sleep.

"We'll have to get her to Dr. Boyd as soon as possible," Kate said to Eva. "And after that, what?"

"You won't often see a mountain girl do something like that," Eva said. "Her family will be even more angry about that than about her getting pregnant. But they'll take care of the young one if it's born. It's their kin and they'll treat it like kin. It'll just be one of the children like all the others. And no one will dare say a word against it for its whole life."

Half an hour later Kate looked in on the girl. She was sleeping soundly. Kate decided to call Ray to check on what she had done and what more she might do. If it weren't raining so hard, she would drive the girl down to town this afternoon.

She lifted the phone, hoping to hear the noisy buzz of a live line, but she heard an excited man's voice. "Hallo, hallo, this the Wildwood?"

"Yes," Kate replied.

"Leona? That you?"

"No, this is Kate, Kate Kincaid."

"Dunno no Kate. I need Leona! Real serious. She got the pains already."

"Who is 'she'? Who are you?"

"Nate Teller," the voice responded. "My wuhman's about to git down."

Kate put her hand over the mouthpiece and called to Eva, "Do we have a file on a woman named Teller?"

Without interrupting her typing, Eva responded, "That's the file I put on your desk yesterday for follow-up."

"That was Taylor," Kate corrected.

"Spelled *Taylor,* pronounced *Teller* in the mountains," Eva pointed out.

Kate seized the Taylor file from atop her desk. "Just hold on, Mr. Teller." She riffled through the file to acquaint herself with the details of the wife's case.

Vera Taylor was a multipara, now thirty-eight weeks pregnant again. She had given uneventful birth to two children, one boy, one girl. Past experience, plus the general conclusion of her clinical evaluation at the start of her pregnancy, was that she had a gynecoid pelvis, eminently suitable for a normal, healthy delivery.

According to her chart she had been seen by Owens once each month for the first thirty weeks. Once every two weeks between the thirtieth and thirty-fourth weeks. Every week during . . . But what Kate had expected to find on Vera Taylor's chart was not there. For whatever reason, she had not come down for her weekly visits during the past four weeks.

That was the only distressing fact in the woman's history. For during the last four weeks of pregnancy, any difficulty that could present itself at birth might have been detected. This did not mean there were any, Kate reassured herself; it only meant there might be. She had no diabetes, heart or respiratory complications.

Mrs. Taylor's picture did not present any special problems.

Those two previous normal births were a very encouraging sign.

Kate kept her hand over the phone when she asked Eva, "What would he mean, 'She's ready to git down'?"

"Ready to deliver. The old method of squatting on the floor in position to give birth when it's time."

"Ready to give . . ." Kate began to say, then interrupted to ask Taylor, "Can you bring her in right away? She belongs in a hospital. We can't get her there but at least we can do better here."

"I jes' 'bout got acrost the bridge to get to a phone myself. The river's ragin'. I got to get back acrost now if I want to make sure," Taylor said. "If'n ye wuz Leona ye'd make it here."

The challenge so provoked Kate that she replied, "Okay! I'll get there!" She hung up and only then realized the mission she had promised to undertake.

The danger of her situation became more apparent when Eva stopped typing, looked up at Kate and said, "You don't know the bridge to the Taylor place. It's no more'n two feet above river level in normal times. Might be under water when you get there or swep' away altogether. You oughten to promise," Eva said. Her reversion to her native speech patterns betrayed her fear. "I hadn't ought to let you go."

"Draw me a map, show me how to get to that bridge!" Kate ordered.

While Eva sketched a crude map, Kate assembled all the instruments, drugs and materials she might need for what should be a routine delivery. Bulb syringe, umbilical clamps, bandages, scissors, needles, lidocaine, drapes, lap masks, scalpels. When she had packed her saddlebags, Eva showed her the map, with every twist and turn in the road and at the two forks. She would have to take the right road at the first fork and the left at the second.

The map ran off the side of the page where Eva had drawn two wavy parallel lines and printed: *The bridge, if it's still there.*

CHAPTER 28

Kate went out into the driving rain, slung the saddlebags into the backseat of the Jeep, started up the motor, activated the windshield wipers to high, turned the Jeep about, slowly crossed the puddled gravel parking area and pulled up onto the blacktop. She turned left and started along the slick, treacherous road. The rain pelted down so hard the wipers could not clear the windshield sufficiently to permit a safe view of the road.

The high beams of her Jeep barely cut the mist. Finally she was forced to slow down. She followed Eva's map, looking for landmarks. At the second fork she made the indicated turn from the slick blacktop onto a muddy side road that should take her to the bridge. She crawled along at less than five miles an hour, peering into the darkness in an effort to spot the bridge. She could not. Then suddenly the road seemed to drop away. She jammed her foot down on the brake and brought the Jeep to a skidding halt. She climbed out, made her way slowly through the mud, keeping her flashlight pointed at the ground. The Jeep's headlights pointing straight ahead made it possible to see the outlines of the rusting iron stanchions of the old bridge. But the bridge itself seemed not to be there. She drew close and aimed her light down. The river had risen so high that the wooden roadway was submerged below almost a foot of water.

It was too dangerous to try to drive a heavy vehicle over so precarious a span. She went back to the Jeep, removed her shoes, peeled off her stockings, rolled up her pants legs. With her saddlebags over her right shoulder, which left that hand free to grasp the rail of the bridge and her left hand to point the flashlight, she started across the submerged bridge in the driving rain. The water was not as cold as she expected but far stronger. Tales she had heard about how suddenly swift these mountain streams could become in a heavy rain were proving true. Three different times she was shoved violently against the downstream side of the bridge and forced to hold on. Each time she had to raise her shoulder high to keep the saddlebags from slipping into the raging water.

The first sign that offered any hope was a light approaching from the opposite shore. The light of a kerosene lamp. As it drew closer, she made out the figure of a man. He called to her through the darkness, "That you, Nurse?"

"It's me," Kate called back.

"I'll come git ye," Taylor called.

"No! Wait there! I'll make it!"

With Taylor's light as her guide she finally reached the other side.

"I'll be takin' that," he said, freeing her shoulder from the heavy burden of the water-soaked leather bags. The light from the cabin windows led Kate the rest of the way. Relieved and exhausted she climbed up onto the porch and out of the rain. She let the water drip from her soaking raincoat before entering the house.

Once inside, Kate stripped herself of the coat and squeezed the water out of her pants legs. When she had carefully washed with surgical soap and hot water from the kettle on the back of the wood stove, she was ready.

Taylor, a lean, leathery man who could be no more than thirty, led the way to the bedroom. As Kate went by the door of another room, it opened slightly and two small faces peered out, curious and frightened at this unaccustomed activity in their house.

"Nurse come to see yere maw," Taylor said. "Now git back inter yere bed!"

Aware of strict family discipline in mountain families, Kate was surprised to see the little boy stand firm, though his sister had retreated behind the door at once. The boy stared up at his father, fearful yet defiant. He came toward Kate, took her free hand and pressed his face against it.

"Don't let my maw die, please?" he implored. "Don't!"

Kate dropped to her knees to look into his eyes. "I am going to do my very best for your maw. Now you do like your paw said."

Tears shining in his eyes, he said, "Ye-uh. But you look after my maw."

He glanced at his father, to beg forgiveness for having disobeyed, then slipped back into the room. Just before the door closed, Kate caught a glimpse of the wide, staring eyes of his sister peering at her in silent entreaty.

Kate was reminded of the many times Abbott and her other instructors had impressed on them: "In our work we treat whole families. All the generations depend on what you do."

She turned to Nate Taylor. "Let me see her."

Taylor opened the door to the other bedroom. It was a small room, barely able to accommodate the big, old carved bed. A family heirloom, Kate surmised.

She found Vera Taylor sweating profusely but not exhibiting any obvious signs of pain. Kate looked at Taylor, who explained, "When I went to call she was havin' a spell of pain. When I come back 'twas 'bout gone."

Obviously the woman was not ready to deliver immediately.

"Has your water broken yet?" Kate asked. The woman shook her head. Good sign. Once the patient's water had broken, the longer delivery was delayed, the greater the chance of infection.

First things first, Kate cautioned herself. Determine the lie and the condition of the fetus, since its position could have changed at any time since her last clinic visit.

"You should have come in for your examination weeks ago," Kate said.

"Couldn't," Vera Taylor said. "First Nate come down with the flu. Then the little 'uns. Was more'n I could do to see to them."

Tracing her stethoscope over Mrs. Taylor's belly, Kate located the fetal heartbeat. It was 140 to the minute. Normal. But then, a less-than-reassuring sign: She had located the fetal heart in the mother's upper left quadrant. Putting aside her scope and using her fingers gently, Kate palpated Mrs. Taylor's abdomen until she located what she sensed to be the baby's head. It proved to be where she had feared. The infant was presenting not in the normal and usual vertex position with head down, but head up and with the buttocks down. It was a breech presentation, she realized grimly.

The problem now was to determine if it was a frank breech, with one leg or both extended, or a complete breech, with only the buttocks presenting bluntly because the legs were drawn up close to the body. A frank breech, dangerous as it was, might still be delivered safely if done quickly. But if it were a complete breech . . .

Instead of speculating on the most dire of possibilities, Kate continued gently to probe the mother's stomach. Fortunately, her abdominal walls were thin enough to permit accurate palpation. Kate could feel the head at the upper pole, the buttocks at the lower. She kept feeling to find the limbs. She found one arm. But she could not find the legs. She was finally forced to accept the fact that this was indeed a complete breech—legs drawn in, buttocks presenting in the bluntest form possible.

In any hospital, and surely back in University Hospital, the doctor would have decided to do a cesarean section at once. For during a breech delivery, especially a complete breech, if delivery was too slow the head might be damaged. And since the cord was drawn into the pelvis, it became compressed, which would cut off oxygen, possibly creating hypoxia, which could cause potential brain damage if it continued long enough, and even death.

To attempt to hasten delivery in order to avoid that danger could lead to other dangers. Any outside effort to speed the birth process might well damage the infant's brain, spinal cord, skeleton and abdominal viscera.

Mrs. Taylor sensed Kate's fears and indecisions, for she looked up at her and asked, "What . . . what are you going to do?"

With a cesarean out of the question, no communication with a physician, no chance of moving the mother to the hospital, Kate knew as never before the awesome responsibility of having not one but two lives in her hands.

She was overcome by a surge of self-doubt and fear. Naked fear. Fear in a way she had never experienced before. Something within her cried out, it isn't fair to thrust this responsibility on me! I want to be any place in this world but here in this primitive cabin, with no help, no facilities, no doctor to turn to, with only a bag of basic drugs and equipment and not enough experience to do what's demanded of me. I can't, I won't take this woman's life in my hands!

In panic, she turned from the bed and would have fled if Nate Taylor had not been standing in the doorway, his eyes pleading with her for help while she fought hard to hold back her own tears.

"Ma'am?" was all Taylor said, but the way he said it meant, you can't desert us now, you can't let her die, we're depending on you.

Slowly, Kate turned back to the bed and her patient.

Now Vera Taylor was beginning to evidence pain. Her contractions had commenced in earnest. The infant was waiting to be born, or to die.

"It's hurtin' now," the woman said. "What are we goin' to do? Nurse?"

"Do?" Kate echoed, then, silently, as she fought to allay her own panic, she decided, we are not going to do anything precipitous. I know what we *don't* have. Let's try to make do with what we *do* have.

She began to marshal in her mind everything she had studied and learned about breech presentations. What she had heard in class. What she had read on those long nights when she sat up in Mrs. Russell's kitchen, drinking coffee to stay awake while poring over medical books and tracts.

Think. Think and remember.

The first word that came back was *Dystocia. Dystocia: difficulties in delivery. Dystocia Caused by Abnormalities of the Fetus.* That was the title of the medical tract she remembered, giving a detailed description of how under the proper circumstances one could correct the dangerous lie of a fetus which prevented a normal birth. *Version* was the word, *cephalic version.* They had touched on it once in class. That was what had stimulated her to read up on the topic. Cephalic version was the procedure for reversing the position of an unborn fetus by pressure from outside the mother's body.

Now she had to recall precisely what she had read. Four conditions were necessary to make it possible to perform the maneuver.

First? The uterus must contain a sufficient amount of amniotic fluid to permit easy movement of the fetus. Mrs. Taylor's water had not broken. Condition one prevailed.

Second? The mother's abdominal and uterine walls must not be irritated. Under palpation Kate had determined they were not.

Third? The abdominal walls of the mother must be sufficiently thin to allow for accurate palpation. Kate had already established that by locating the infant's position.

Fourth? The presenting part of the infant must not be so deeply engaged in the mother's pelvis as to be unmovable.

Kate would now have to determine that. For if the fetus were deeply engaged, none of the other three factors mattered. Just as Kate was about to feel gently for the baby's buttocks, Mrs. Taylor suffered another and sharper contraction.

Kate had to abandon feeling for the baby to monitor its heartbeat. For it was crucial to learn if the baby was suffering late decelerations. Normally its pulse rate should drop with the contraction and resume thereafter. But if the drop in pulse rate came after the mother's contraction, this would be a warning of danger and could thwart all her efforts to effect a successful delivery.

She found the fetal heartbeat, kept her stethoscope on it, awaiting the next contraction. When it came she listened closely. Contraction followed by recovery of the fetal heart rate. Another contraction, but this time the recovery was not as immediate as before. Bradycardia—a falling, unrestored fetal heartbeat—could be fatal.

Kate would have to decide what to do and do it with dispatch.

She began once more to locate the infant's butt. When she felt it in the pelvic area, she tried to move it gently from where it was resting. It responded to her pressure. This was encouraging. Knowing now that she had satisfied all four requirements necessary to perform cephalic version, she had to accomplish the procedure before the mother's water broke and made it impossible. She had to risk doing it now or lose the child, and possibly the mother as well.

She turned to Taylor, who hovered over her like a troubled conscience.

"Ye-uh?" he asked, challenging her.

"I want you to go out there and wash your hands."

"Warsh?" he asked, puzzled.

"Warsh! In water as hot as you can stand. And with strong soap."

"What fer?" he asked, without moving.

"I might need your help. So warsh!" she ordered, this time in a voice so authoritative that he obeyed at once.

Meantime, she searched through her saddlebags for a drug to relax the mother's muscles and make what she was about to attempt feasible and safer.

Terbutaline or ritodrine was what they would have used back at University Hospital when a general anesthetic was not advisable. Kate had neither of those drugs. She cautioned herself that now especially she had to get out of the habit of recalling what they would have done back at University. At the hospital you would not even be in charge. You would only be a messenger or at best an assistant, being told what to do and how to do it.

This was what you wanted, the responsibility, the right to be in command. Well, you have it now. And you are here, in the mountains, with no doctor at your beck and call, no delivery room, no help of any kind. Only your knowledge, your skill, and whatever your agile brain can improvise can help you now.

With those things in mind and fully aware of the dangers, Kate began what could end in disaster, but for which she had no alternative. She would attempt, from memory, to perform a cephalic version.

It must be done delicately, slowly, applying only enough pressure to turn the infant around gradually in its mother's uterus, while not applying so much pressure that it might break the delicate, soft bones in the baby's hip or shoulder. Not so much pressure that she might cause the uterus to rupture, thus dooming both mother and child. Not so much pressure that she would cause the placenta to separate from the uterine wall and thus cut off the infant's oxygen supply.

And she must hope all the while that, without her being aware of it, the movement was not causing the umbilical cord to wrap around the infant's neck, thereby suffocating it.

It was one of those times in a medical case when there are no safe alternatives. And worse, because of the infant's late decelerations, time had now become a factor. She must proceed with skillful yet deliberate haste.

To relax Vera Taylor so that her body would be more amenable to the procedure, Kate injected a dose of Demerol. While it took effect, she located the infant's head at the upper end of the uterus. She rested her left hand over it. Then, palpating with her right hand, she found the lower part of the fetus in the pelvic area.

Now Kate slowly started to turn the tiny body floating in the mother's amniotic fluid so that its head gradually moved counterclockwise to its mother's right side, while its bottom turned to the left side.

It was a slow, careful process. Kate could feel the sweat pouring from her own face and neck. Drops of it fell onto Vera Taylor's belly. But gradually, in slow, careful stages, Kate succeeded in moving the fetus to the point where its head and feet were lying horizontally across the mother's belly.

Kate paused, took a few deep breaths, then resumed slowly, carefully. It seemed a bit easier now, as if the fetus had resigned itself to cooperating, had accepted that it would be born in a normal position. Eventually Kate had moved it to the point where its head was lower than its buttocks. Carefully she tried to guide the head into the pelvis and engage it there.

She had done it! She leaned back from the bed, drew a deep breath, wiped the sweat from her face with the back of her wrists, not wanting to contaminate her surgical gloves.

She glanced at her wristwatch. It had seemed like an hour, but only five minutes had elapsed.

With the head slightly engaged in the pelvic area, she could begin now to facilitate the delivery. She turned to her saddlebag to lay out the required instruments and medical supplies. But when she turned back, she was horrified to see that without any outside influence the fetus was slowly and perversely turning clockwise back to the breech position. Kate was powerless to stop it lest she inflict some harm. In fewer minutes than it had taken her to perform the maneuver, the fetus had returned to its original dangerous position.

The first thing she must do was check its condition to determine if version and the reversal had damaged it in any way. Raising her stethoscope to her ears, she pressed the metal disc against the mother's belly, located the fetal heartbeat once more and listened. She studied her wristwatch, matching its second hand against the thudding in her ears. The rate was now distinctly slower than the normal 140 to the minute.

She dared not make another attempt at cephalic version while the heartbeat indicated trouble. She was fighting time desperately now. She waited a few moments, then took another fetal pulse. Still under 140. If it did not return to normal or near normal, she would have no choice but to try to effect a breech delivery of the most dangerous kind. Very soon she might have to decide on the alternative, to let the infant die in order to save the mother.

The fourth time she took the pulse, it had risen to almost 140. Given a choice, she would not have risked version again. But out of sheer necessity, she had to. This time, she must be sure the head was deeply engaged in the pelvis before she let go.

The process was much slower now. Either because she was more cautious or because the fetus seemed in some willful way to be resisting more. But Kate kept her left hand firmly on the head and her right on the buttocks, and she moved the tiny body slowly, inch by inch, holding it in position before starting each new move. She had finally brought it to the transverse position, across the plane of the mother's body. She held it there, breathing hard, sweating more profusely.

Then she continued, gradually forcing the fetus's head down toward the pelvic area. She had succeeded in turning it completely around again. She guided the head gently into place in the pelvic area. Kate held it there, hoping it would become so engaged that it would not move back on its own again. She lifted her hands slightly, watched it closely. When it seemed about to move again, she placed both her hands in the proper position, left hand on the head, right on the buttocks, and held them there. It appeared that the fetus was content now to rest where she had placed it, engaged in the pelvic area. But she dared not let go.

She called to Taylor who was standing in the doorway, staring in bewilderment and fear.

"Have you touched anything since you washed?" she asked.

"No."

"Then come here," Kate ordered.

The gangly man came to the side of the bed.

"Put your hands where I have mine."

Awkwardly, hardly daring to touch his wife's belly, he did as he was told, replacing Kate's right hand with his own and her left hand with his.

"Hold them like that! Don't press!" Kate instructed.

With this momentary freedom from tension, Kate had to gather her thoughts and plan her strategy. Since the fetus was now in the most favorable position, she must try as soon as possible to effect a normal delivery. That had two advantages. Once the mother went into labor, the head of the fetus would remain engaged in the pelvis. And for the sake of the infant, whose condition could not be absolutely determined, a swifter delivery would be safer.

Having decided on that course of action, Kate poured alcohol over her surgical gloves and then proceeded to rupture Mrs. Taylor's membranes, causing the water to leak out. Now labor commenced in earnest. Pushing Nate Taylor back from the bed, Kate raised up his wife's knees, placed a pillow under the back and urged softly, "Push, push, push!"

After a while, Kate saw the head crowning. Now it began to emerge, wet, covered with the gelatinous substance that lubricates the birth process. Kate reached under it to lift it and ease its entry into this world. Gradually it emerged, finally resting in her gloved hands, a small, red, writhing, clenched-eyed creature. At once, Kate took up her bulb syringe to aspirate its nose of anything that would impede breathing. No longer supplied with oxygen by the mother, now it had to draw breath on its own, as it would for the rest of its life.

Kate rested the infant on the bed. She picked up two umbilical clamps, fixed them in place inches apart, and with her bandage scissors, cut the cord, severing the infant from its mother. Then she wrapped some umbilical tape around the cord at the infant's navel and snipped it. She extracted some of the cord blood for laboratory purposes, administered the preventive drops to the infant's eyes and wiped its body clean.

To determine if the procedure had inflicted any harm, Kate began to perform the first Apgar test. The trauma of birth, and of those events which had preceded it, did not appear to have done the infant any neurological damage.

It was in all respects a normal, healthy little boy.

She handed the new son to his mother, who took him and cradled him in her arms. When his lips made a sucking motion, she eased her nipple into his mouth. So soon after giving birth she had no milk to give him. But the infant seemed content to suck.

Since Mrs. Taylor had delivered the placenta and the cord without difficulty, Kate's work was over for the moment. There was only the usual postdelivery observation to do, periodically checking on mother and child for any aftereffects.

Kate stood at the bedside and stared down at them. All the terror she had experienced was worth it. She had a sense of accomplishment such as she had never experienced before in her nursing career. *This,* she thought, *will always be one of the great moments of my life.*

She went out to the kitchen where Nate Taylor had brewed some coffee for her. She needed it. But before she permitted herself to enjoy it, Kate went to the door of the other room, pushed it open and was greeted by two pairs of eyes shining up at her from the darkness.

"Maw?" the boy asked. "Is my maw all right?"

"She's fine. And you have a new baby brother. Go and see."

The two small children attired in plain homemade nightgowns skittered across the floor on bare feet into their mother's room. From their sounds of surprise and delight, Kate knew how they had received the miracle of birth, adding to her pride and satisfaction.

Through the night Kate monitored the vital signs of mother and infant. There were no indications of trouble, no sign of abnormality, no effects of her need to perform the version.

Dawn. The rain still continued, heavier than before. Nate Taylor went down to check if the bridge was intact. The river had risen but the bridge was still crossable.

Taylor saw Kate down to the bridge. As he handed her her saddlebags, she cautioned, "Make sure to get them both in for a checkup within the week."

She had to put the Jeep into four-wheel drive before she could extricate it from its muddy bed. Turning the vehicle about, she started down from the holler toward the road to Wildwood.

When she turned onto the blacktop, she experienced the full force of the storm. The dirt road, even with its deep gullies and rivulets, had been shielded from the brunt of it by overhanging trees. Out on the open blacktop, the fat drops beat down with vengeful force. Her wipers could not keep up with the deluge. She realized how fortunate she had been to be able to cross the Taylor bridge.

She drove on toward Wildwood, which now seemed a sanctuary instead of the crucible in which she was tested every day, every hour, almost every moment. She had met her toughest case and handled it successfully. She had left behind a healthy baby boy, a mother in good condition, and two of the happiest, most reassured children she had ever seen. With this driving rain, today promised to allow her to catch up on her lost sleep.

She drove slowly, carefully, but more relaxed. Until she heard in the distance behind her a low, rolling rumble of thunder which seemed to persevere far longer than most. This noise was accompanied by a sound she had never before associated with thunder.

Even from this distance she could hear a sharp, very loud, cracking sound, like gunfire. It had no rhythm, but came first in single explosive sounds of rifle fire, and then with the rapid fire of a machine gun. The noise was so strange that she stopped the car to listen more intently. The rumble continued, the cracking sounds continued. Finally they stopped.

Unable to decipher what this meant, she waited until all was quiet except for the pelting rain. Still puzzled, she started the Jeep up again and headed for Wildwood. She tried to explain it by assuring herself that early spring storms could bring almost any phenomenon, out-of-season snow, thunderstorms, anything. But not that cracking sound, she had to admit.

Kate was still much more than a mile from Wildwood when she saw what she assumed to be a mirage, to her a particularly ominous mirage. Red and white revolving lights, which since childhood had always frightened her, were approaching out of the blackness of the storm. She came to a halt. The lights continued to approach. Now she could hear the sound of a siren blaring.

Finally, through the mist and the heavy rain, she could make out a familiar vehicle. The patrol car of state troopers headquartered in Adelphi. That car had brought in many a case when she was on duty in Emergency. Despite the weather, it seemed to be approaching at a fast clip. But it slowed down as it reached her. It pulled alongside. Trooper Helms lowered his window, signaling Kate to do the same.

He leaned a bit out of his window to get a closer look at Kate through the rain and the darkness.

"Kincaid? From the hospital?" he asked.

"Yes."

"You'd better turn around and follow us. They's going to be help needed," Helms said.

"Help? Why?"

"Didn't you hear it?"

"Hear what?" Kate asked, completely baffled.

"The slide. You wuz coming from that direction."

"Heard something, like a long rumble of thunder, yet different. Cracking sounds. Like machine-gun fire. What was it?"

"Moved. The whole damn rain-soaked mountain moved. Slid right down into the valley. Snapping off giant trees like matchsticks. Reached a few hollers, far as we know. Buried them, we're afeared," Helms said.

"Which mountain?" Kate asked.

"Hell's Mountain."

"Big Betsy's mountain," Kate realized.

"Right," Helms said. "Harlan kep' warnin' them. Plant whilst we dig. They wouldn't listen. Now it's come down. The whole mountain and that damn machine with it," Helms said. Meanwhile, his shortwave radio crackled frantic orders from the barracks. "So you turn around and follow us. They's going to be help needed, lots of it. We're trying to get Dr. Boyd and a rescue team up here soon's we can."

Weary though she was, Kate turned her Jeep around quickly. Helms's car started, Kate fell in behind him.

In a little while she noticed in her rearview mirror another set of revolving lights. Probably an auxiliary police car. They must be mobilizing reinforcements from all over the area, from all over the county. Helms's flashers began blinking suddenly. He was coming to a halt. Instead of slamming on her brakes and risk skidding, Kate pumped to a slow stop. Helms and his partner, Henson, piled out of their car into the rain. Kate joined them and found she was standing in deep, thick mud. All three stared into the darkness.

Before them loomed a mountain of black, moist, steaming earth, high as the trees used to stand, and visible in the earth were jagged pieces of white which reminded Kate of human bones as they presented in a compound fracture. But these were the broken, twisted parts of trees that had been shattered by the avalanche of mud. There were masses of underbrush mixed in as well as large chunks of the blacktop road, which had been torn up and swallowed by the mud as it moved along with inexorable force.

As the mass of mud started to lurch forward again, Helms seized Kate by the hand and pulled her back.

"Let's get out of here!"

They ran to their cars to back down the road before they could be engulfed by the slide, which had resumed moving, more slowly now but still taking with it some giant trees, which cracked with sickening sounds that echoed in the early dawn.

When they were a safe distance down the road, Kate leaped out of her Jeep and joined Helms and Henson. They stared at the devastation.

"Cain't hardly believe it," Henson said.

"If'n that thang widened out like it 'pears, musta filled more'n one river and one holler and taken some houses with it," Helms said.

"And people," Kate said. "We've got to do something!"

"Got to find 'em first," Helms said.

"I've got patients up this way. The Clintons. Mrs. Persons. Mr. Spencer. And the Torrences . . . God, Eloise and her family!"

Following her impulse, Kate started forward toward the wall of rough, wet earth and shattered trees, but Helms seized her by the arm.

"You cain't do anything up there 'cept get yourself killed. A rescue crew's on the way. You just better wait and do what you can for the survivors."

"But the Torrences—" Kate started to protest.

"You wait here! In your car!" Helms ordered. He pointed her toward the Jeep.

As she turned, she caught sight of a piece of wreckage she identified as the pitched angle of what had been a roof. It jutted slightly above the mass of timber, blacktop and rock. Only an hour ago that had been a house, someone's simple, neat, clean home until the avalanche of mud had swept it away like refuse. Possibly it was the Torrences' house. Kate's impulse to scramble up over the mud to find those people was forcibly overruled by Helms's strong hand.

She heard the cracking sound again, this time in rapid-fire, machine-gun style.

"She's movin' again," Helms said. "Just took another stand of trees with her. And you want to go up there? Back in your car!"

As Kate turned toward the Jeep, she saw a caravan of vehicles drawing up behind it. Through the darkness she heard an excited voice, tense but familiar, calling orders, demanding digging equipment. She recognized Harlan Jessup. He was commandeering a volunteer work crew to follow him toward the devastation.

As he approached, he saw her.

"I told them, begged them," he said. "Plant while we dig. But no. Now, look! I ought to be hung. Hung!" He went past her, followed by men with shovels, pickaxes, powerful portable lights, stretchers.

She heard a helicopter's blades whipping overhead, looked up to see its searchlight come on, a piercing beam of white light. Despite the dangerous weather they had ordered out the troopers' rescue copter. It headed toward the slide, its powerful beam probing the rain, mist and darkness to assess the conditions.

They won't find anything, Kate thought fearfully. *They won't find anyone.*

Her very next thought was *But if they do . . .* She knew what was required of her. She was the only medically trained person in the immediate area. She must set up a place and equip it, as best she could, to be ready for survivors, if any.

She sought out Helms and instructed him, "Give me one man to help! I'm going back to Wildwood for supplies. Then I'll set up in the nearest safe building. . . ."

"Nearest safe building." Helms evaluated from his intimate knowledge of the area. "That'd be Redeemer's."

"Redeemer's?" Kate asked.

"Pentecostalist Church. Ever hear of it?"

Yes, indeed, I've heard of it, Kate thought, recalling the snake-handlers' service.

But she said, "Okay, I'll set up there. Send in any survivors!"

CHAPTER 29

With the help of Trooper Henson, Kate had piled in as many emergency medical supplies as the Jeep could carry—bandages, gauze pads, sutures, basic instruments, antibiotics, I.V.'s, bottles of saline solution, anesthetics. She raced back to the Redeemer's Pentecostal Church swiftly, at times dangerously. When she arrived, she found one survivor had already been brought in. She ordered Henson to start unloading. Looking around the tiny church with its seven rows of pews, she decided that the altar would be her best treatment area, the pews would serve as beds.

She had Henson move the patient to the altar, the same altar, Kate reminded herself, where she had once seen a man drop that gunnysack of rattlesnakes. She began to examine the victim only to discover that the single naked light bulb was not sufficient for the purpose.

"Get me a portable light! A strong one. And radio back for more lights!" she ordered Henson.

"Just hope the line can power 'em without blowin'," Henson said.

"Get 'em," Kate ordered. "Meantime, get me the most powerful flash you can. I can't work in this light!" She proceeded to make as careful an examination of the man's condition as the poor light would allow.

He was unconscious, and his face showed a nasty bleeding

wound where something had cut through his skin and flesh down to the cheekbone. She could not determine if the bone was broken, but she debrided the wound, clearing away any signs of dirt or foreign matter. Under the sting of the antiseptic, the man regained consciousness and reacted in pain.

"What happen . . . ?" he asked, dazed and in shock.

"Just be quiet. And hold still," Kate said as she began to suture the cleansed wound.

While she worked, she could hear a large truck pull up outside the little church. Henson came in to report.

"Supplies from the hospital. All they had. But more'll be comin' from the city. They're coptering 'em in fast as they kin."

"Lights!" Kate insisted. "I need more light!"

"On the way," Henson informed her. "They'll be on the copter."

Kate was just knotting the last suture and reaching for a protective bandage to cover the wound when four more survivors were brought in. A woman, two children, a man. Kate scanned them quickly to determine who needed help the most urgently. But also to discover if any of them were Eloise, or Benjy, or any Torrence. They were not.

She carried the little boy to the altar and ordered Henson to make the others comfortable on the pews. Then she began to assess the boy's injuries.

From then on, for what would prove to be hours, Kate worked without ceasing. She no sooner treated one patient than Henson replaced him with another. While her work went on under the beam of the strong flashlight, new lights were brought in, portable, powerful, used to supply auxiliary light when the permanent lights in Mountain Hospital went out.

She heard some man call out, "All hooked up! Try 'em! And hope they don't blow!"

There was a moment when Kate paused in her work to see what would happen. The lights came on, flickered, but then became steady. As if the sun had suddenly come out from behind a cloud, her work area was lit up so she could see without difficulty.

"Thanks," she breathed softly. "Thanks, guys," and went on working, examining the little girl who lay before her on the altar. She palpated for possible internal injuries but could detect none.

Which meant only that they might not have become apparent in such a short time. But when she began to examine the child's arms and legs, she found what she feared, then affirmed, was a broken femur.

With great care, and exerting only sufficient pressure to accomplish it, she set the bone, then wrapped it tightly and applied surgical tape to hold it in place temporarily. She made a mental note, handle with care, X ray and reset at the hospital the first moment possible. She administered an antibiotic as a precaution, and a sedative to allow the child to rest without pain. She carried the little girl to one of the pews herself and set her down gently.

By the time she turned back to the altar, Henson had another patient ready for her. After that, Kate never left her station, for survivors began to stream in, some brought by all manner of vehicles, some on their own, on foot, while others limped in with the aid of relatives or friends.

She went on working, debriding wounds, bandaging, suturing, probing for internal injuries, administering medications, sedatives, affixing I.V.'s, doing all those things she reminded herself she would never have been permitted to do at University Hospital.

Every time she appeared ready to falter, having gone without sleep since the day before when she had been summoned to deliver the Taylor baby, a fresh victim demanded another burst of enforced energy from her, and she responded.

When there was no longer any room in the pews for those who were awaiting help and those who had received it, she ordered Henson to commandeer a truck, convert it into a makeshift ambulance by spreading some blankets in it, and remove as many as possible of the treated patients to Mountain Hospital.

But more victims had been found and dug out, or had wandered into the little church on their own. Kate continued emergency treatment, wondering, where is Ray, where is his rescue team? But there was little time to wonder, for now Henson brought her an elderly white-haired woman, across whose forehead some sharp object, a splintered branch, rock or other piece of debris, had torn a ragged, ugly gash.

The woman was barely conscious but sensitive enough to feel the pain as Kate cleansed her wound with alcohol. She tried to conceal her distress, but trembled under Kate's hand.

"It's all right, my dear, cry if you want to, let go," Kate urged softly. Tears began to stream down the woman's wrinkled cheeks, but she made no sound as Kate continued to clean the wound, then carefully suture it, finally wiping away blood that had begun to crust. She signaled to Henson to move the woman to one of the pews. Immediately, another man set down a new victim, and Kate continued her work.

She examined a deep cut on the scalp of a young woman. To make sure the injury was no more serious than it appeared, she performed the basic neurological tests. She found no evidence of brain damage. As she cleaned and sutured the wound, she hoped that the woman's condition would not deteriorate, since head traumas had an unfortunate tendency to do so.

She was thinking that, and was completing the tying of the last suture, when without being aware of it, she slid forward and eased into a sleep of exhaustion. She came to with a start when she felt herself being lifted. She looked up. She was staring into Abbott's face.

"I'm sending you back," Abbott said. "I'll have someone else take over here."

"All I need is some coffee and I'll be fine," Kate protested. "I've never felt better."

"Kincaid, that's an order! You've had it for today."

Another attempt to protest, another of Abbott's forbidding stares, and reluctantly Kate started away from the altar, then stopped and turned back to ask, "Dr. Boyd? What happened to Dr. Boyd?"

"Once we heard what good work you were doing here, he set up another station at the Baptist Church. We've got two other emergency stations working, one at Wildwood. But you've done your share. Get into one of the cars and back to the hospital. Get some sleep! Lots of it!"

Kate made her way up the short, narrow aisle between two banks of pews filled with the injured and refugees.

Outside, she discovered that while she had been totally immersed in caring for her patients, an enormous rescue operation had been mobilized. A commissary truck had moved in with coffee and food for survivors and rescue workers. Heavy land-moving equipment was preparing to attack the mudslide and search for more victims. Two helicopters, their blades whirling, were ready to take off. Harlan Jessup, in command of one, was taking to the air to get another overview of the extent of the devastation.

To add to the powerful beams of light supplied by a huge generator truck, three crews from the networks had moved in to cover the disaster for national television, adding their own lights, trucks, cameras, cables and sound equipment. The whole area had taken on the look of wartime mobilization for an impending battle.

In dire need of coffee, Kate headed for the commissary truck where a volunteer was filling cups of coffee from a steaming urn. As the woman turned to hand a cup to one of the rescue workers, Kate realized she was Mrs. Persons.

"Hildy! Thank God, you made it," Kate said.

"Ye-uh," Hildy Persons said, adding, "so you's the one."

"Which one?" Kate asked, puzzled.

"They comin' out of Redeemer's talkin' 'bout this piedy little girl who wuz doin' such fine work in there," Mrs. Persons said. "Wuz you all along, wuz it? Have some coffee."

As the woman handed her a cup, Kate noticed, "You're not chewing tobacco anymore. Good!"

"Good, mah foot!" Hildy exclaimed angrily. "Had to clear out so fast hatn't nary a chance to take some. Somewhere up in that house o' mine is three plugs of the finest chewin' terbaccy in this county. And ah'll probably never get to see 'em again."

"Was it that bad, Hildy?"

"Wuz lak Preacher Willis allus says Judgment Day'll be. Whole world shakin' and tremblin'. A powerful roarin' sound. And trees snappin' off like they's matchsticks. Ditn't take mah house, leastway not yit."

Someone must have identified Kate and spread the word, for in a moment she was surrounded by network cameras. Interviewers were shoving microphones into her face, asking questions.

"Are you the Angel of Mercy they're all talking about?"

"What was the worst case you treated?"

"Did you get any fatalities?"

She tried to escape but they surrounded her. The questions continued. Finally, she felt she had to answer.

"It was bad, very bad. And I did what I had to do. Any nurse would have done the same."

Though she refused to answer, the questions continued; the interviewers gave up only when another rescue copter appeared overhead and started to descend. They rushed to surround it.

Alone again, she turned away and for the first time noticed that to one side of the church steps was a large area covered by a huge army tarpaulin. Under it she could make out a neat row of mounds which she realized were human bodies, some large enough to be adults but some much smaller. She approached with great trepidation and realized that the body closest to the edge was not quite fully covered. A tuft of white hair protruded, causing her to kneel down and peel back the tarp.

She saw the face of old Will Spencer, his cheeks no longer florid but ashen gray in death. Eyes closed, face at peace, he seemed to be sleeping.

Alone, Kate thought sadly. *He died alone. At least he's with his beloved Claire now.*

She kissed him on the cheek and covered him once more, brushing back his white hair under the tarp. She rose to her feet, staring down at the forms that lay so still, especially at the smaller ones. She tried to banish the thought but was unable. Eloise. One of those smaller forms could be Eloise. She resisted trying to find out but could not. She folded back the stiff wet covering. She recognized one child whom she had treated, the little girl on whom she had performed a tracheostomy. Now she was still, lifeless, her head turned away so that the tiny white scar on her throat was visible.

Kate had only one consolation, little Eloise was not here. Nor were any of the Torrences. Then where were they? Buried under the slide? This time she was determined to find them, no matter what restrictions the rescue workers might try to impose on her.

She rose to her feet, started away from the church, fought her way through the clutter of assembled vehicles, power cables, patrol cars and trucks, and broke free to begin climbing the mountain of mud, rock and shattered timber. With no sure footing under her, she slipped and fell, sliding back at some moments, crawling forward at others, but she managed to clamber up the oozing mass.

She climbed for a long time. Her hands were covered now not only with mud but with her own blood from the bruises and cuts suffered on the sharp edges of torn trees and sharp rock. She finally reached that place where she had once climbed Torrence's hill. There was no longer any hill there, no brook. The mountain had moved down to fill in the brook and the land so that the top of the hill was almost level with the mud and debris around it.

She rose up and dared to look in the direction in which the Torrence house should be. It was still there. Spared by only a few feet from the devastation that Hell's Mountain had inflicted on those who had dared to rape it. Quickly as she could, Kate started across the mud, rock and broken trees, calling as she went, "Eloise! Eloise! Can you hear me! Can anyone up there hear me?"

There was no sign of life from the modest little cabin.

"Eloise!" she shouted one more frantic time.

From higher up the hill came a voice, finally, "Kate?" It was Eloise's voice.

"Yes, it's me! Kate!"

Down the hill the child came running. Kate started forward until they met and embraced each other in tears.

"When there was no one in the house, I was frightened," Kate confessed. "So frightened for all of you."

"Paw said it was coming too close, we was safer up there," Eloise explained.

"As long as you're all safe, my dear, dear Eloise," Kate said, kissing the child once more.

In the law offices of Brooks, Travers, Klein, Aldrich and Brewster, new partner Howard Brewster was shouting at his secretary.

"Damn it, Miss Sands, there has to be some way to get to that place! There must be an airport close to Adelphi!"

Trembling, since she had never seen him in such an agitated state, Miss Sands tried to explain. "There is an airport, sir. But it is restricted to rescue aircraft. Army planes. Marine copters. Red Cross personnel. All passenger planes have been banned."

"Then, damn it, get on the phone! Get through to that hospital! God knows what's happened to her!" Howard shouted. "No, never mind! I'll drive down. A thousand miles. Can't take more than fifteen hours. Cancel all my appointments for the rest of the week and . . ."

From down the corridor the voice of senior partner Elton Travers interrupted, "Howard! Quick! My office!"

Howard ran down the corridor, still shouting instructions back to his trembling secretary. "Call my garage! I want my car in front of the building in fifteen minutes. Full of gas!"

He burst into Travers's office to find Klein and Aldrich, their eyes glued to the television screen. One glimpse and Howard Brewster moved to the set, dropped down to kneel on one knee.

He was staring at live television coverage of the devastation. A trench-coated reporter standing in the rain, microphone in hand, was reporting the destruction around him. Behind him the mountain of mud, with torn trees and other debris, added proof to the tone of his voice which reflected his personal shock.

At his first glimpse of the devastation, Howard Brewster murmured an awed "Good God . . ."

". . . the mountain moved," the TV reporter was saying, "and an entire valley was wiped out. There is no estimate of the number of homes lost or the number of casualties . . ."

Something he heard on his earphone made him look into the camera and say, "Ladies and gentlemen, we are cutting away to an interview that was taped only a few moments ago."

On the screen they cut to another camera which revealed a woman reporter, standing amid a number of rescue vehicles, with a small church in the background.

"We are outside Redeemer's Church, the first rescue station set up in this devastated valley outside Adelphi, West Virginia. Here at my side is the young nurse from Mountain Hospital who, because of the wounded she treated and the lives she saved, is being called the Angel of Adelphi. Miss Kincaid . . ."

The camera widened its angle to include in the shot a weary, stunned Kate Kincaid, oblivious of the attention being focused on her, as she tried to answer the questions being hurled at her by a number of reporters.

Howard stared and dared to say, half-aloud, "She's okay." He turned to his partners. "Did you see? She's okay. She's alive. Alive!"

He started toward the phone on Travers's desk, saying, "Angel of Adelphi . . . she saved lives . . . you heard her . . . 'because of the wounded she treated and the lives she saved' . . ."

He had dialed the operator and was saying, "I want to get through to Adelphi, West Virginia . . . Mountain Hospital. I want to talk to Miss Kate Kincaid. Kincaid, right!" He realized he was weeping.

CHAPTER 30

Once she had led the Torrences down to Redeemer's Church, Kate was given a ride back to Adelphi with one of the troopers. She dozed off before the car even got under way. He had to wake her when they arrived at Mountain Hospital. She apologized for falling asleep, got out of the car, and with a show of bravado and false energy, headed for the front door.

As she opened it, she discovered that the waiting room, which had been her first introduction to Mountain Hospital, had been converted into one enormous emergency ward. Cots were crowded together, and where they had run out of cots, the terrazzo floor was covered with blankets, all of them occupied by women, men, children, nursing mothers. Some were simply homeless refugees. The bandages on others showed the medical treatment they had required.

Kate recognized a familiar figure kneeling to tend a small boy. She went to relieve her. "Mrs. Russell, I'll do that," she said. "Let me."

Mrs. Russell rose to her feet and said, half in jest, "What do ye mean, let ye? Ye're talking to one of the bestest and most experienced nurses in this here county. 'Tween us, feels good to be useful again."

The women embraced. "Thank God ye're safe, child. We hear ye did great work up there."

"I did what I could."

"From the ones came down here, they said ye did more than ye could. Ye was like an angel. And knowin' ye like I do, I believe it. Now, I got my own patients to look after." And she was off to the next cot.

Kate discovered that Abbott had returned. She went to report for further duty. She found the administrator on the second floor, where the Maternity Ward had been converted into another emergency area. Every nurse had been drafted for twenty-four-hour duty. Kate also saw many unfamiliar faces, obviously nurses from other towns and from the city hospital. When Abbott had finished giving orders, Kate approached her.

"I'm back. What can I do?"

Abbott reached out, ran her forefinger around Kate's weary eyes. She shook her head reprovingly. "Not satisfied, just nursing. I hear you had to become a one-woman rescue team, too. You could have become a casualty yourself. Find the Torrences all right?"

"Thank God."

"Good. Now, then, Kincaid, first thing, go to my office."

"Yes, and—?" Kate asked, puzzled.

"You'll find a cot set up there. Get some sleep!"

When Kate began to protest, Abbott said, "That's an order. Not for your sake. But because I don't want any patient here getting less than our best treatment simply because you happen to be exhausted. I'll wake you when I think it's time."

"There's just one thing . . ." Kate started to say.

"I said, no!" Abbott interrupted, on the verge of anger.

"A family named Taylor . . . Teller . . . anything heard of them? She just gave birth only twenty-four hours ago."

"I know. Cephalic version. Good work. They were brought in hours ago. All safe and in good shape."

"That's a relief," Kate said, and started for Abbott's office.

She was not conscious of lying down on the cot before falling into a sleep of total exhaustion.

Kate had no sense of time when she was jolted awake by the incessant ringing of the telephone. Half-asleep, she was tempted to shout, "Abbott's not here! Stop that damn ringing!" It continued until she could no longer ignore it. She staggered to the desk, lifted the phone. A man's voice, heard over the usual interference of the local phone system, kept insisting, "She *has* to be there! Somewhere! Find her. The name is Kincaid. Kate Kincaid! I know she's safe! I saw her on television!"

Even over the loud hum and the static, she recognized the voice. "Hawk? Is that you?"

"Kate? Katie? Honey, are you all right!"

"Exhausted. But otherwise all right."

"I was scared to death when that news first started coming in. Landslide. Adelphi. Hell's Mountain. I remembered what you'd told me about that place. When I began to see that devastating footage on the TV news, I thought, she was right in the path of that thing. Maybe even buried by it. But then I saw you. You didn't say much, but when I saw you I . . . I just broke down and cried. Yeah. Me. Cried. Just to see you alive and safe. And I regretted every harsh thing I ever said to you about nursing. Can you forgive me?"

"Yes, Hawk darling, I forgive you," she said and found she was crying now, too.

"Look, I don't know how to say this, but you stay on there as long as they need you, and then hurry home. I mean, I'll wait, as long as it takes. Days. Weeks. Months, even. You don't have to explain or apologize. Not anymore. I understand now. And I'll wait."

"I'll be back as soon as I can," she promised.

"I love you, Katie."

"I love you, Hawk. Now I have to go back on duty. They need me."

"Of course. But you're sure you're okay?" he asked one last time.

"Yes, sure, okay," she said, then hung up, smiling. She did not need any sleep now. She went down to report to Abbott and be reassigned.

CHAPTER 31

Since the Torrences had been moved into Adelphi until the road could be cleared, instead of driving Eloise to school, this morning Kate walked with her. The child clutched her new books to her breast as she asked, "This is the last time? For real the last time?"

"Yes," Kate said. "This afternoon I drive up to the city, take the plane and go back home."

"I won't ever git—get—to see you again?" the child asked.

"I'll probably come back here to visit. Or else you can come up and visit me. I'd love that. But we'll be writing to each other all the time. I want to know everything you do. Especially when you go to the school in the city. I hear it's a wonderful school. I'll want to know all about it. Promise you'll write."

"Oh, I will for sartain—I mean I surely will," Eloise said.

They walked on, silent for a time, until Eloise asked, "Are ye—are you ever going to be birthin' one of your own?"

"I'd like to have a child of my own, especially one like you."

"If'n you do, kin I—can I still write to you?"

"Of course. We'll write to each other forever," Kate said.

"I thought oncet you had your own, you wouldn't be carin' for anyone else," the little girl said.

"I'll always care about you, Eloise. About everything you do, everything you think, everything you learn, everything you write. I'll want to know it all."

At the school door, Kate knelt down and kissed Eloise. The child clung to her for a moment, then ran swiftly into the school building.

Mrs. Russell hovered over her while she packed her two bags, saying, "It'll be lonely, terrible lonely."

"There'll be a new student here next week," Kate reminded.

"Won't be the same. There's been many a young woman come to stay, but none like you, Kate. I ain't felt so grieved since Louise went off to the war."

"You have Eloise, and will till she goes to the city."

"True. She's a heap o' pleasure. Did I show you the sweater I've started for her to take along? Blue, with little white crocheted flowers around the collar and the pocket."

Kate had made one last tour of the clinics, saying her farewells to the nurses with whom she had worked for the past year. When she was done, she went up to the second floor.

Abbott was on the phone, lighting up a cigarette, while saying at the same time, "Yes, my dear, I know what you saw on television about our work during the disaster. And it is very fine of you to want to train and serve here. Believe me, I appreciate that. But first we have to see your record. So let me mail you an application. But I must warn you, the competition is very stiff. We take only the best here." She looked up at Kate and smiled. "Only the very best."

Abbott hung up, exhaled some smoke, and said, "Like you, Kincaid. I must say I'm a little vain about you. First time I looked over your application I said to myself, there's a woman with fight. Give her the right training, the right incentive, and she can become one of the great ones. And you have. You did us proud during the disaster. Setting up your own first-aid unit. I've seen many a young doctor who wouldn't have done as well."

"Thank you, Miss Abbott."

"If ever you get the urge to come back down, to work or teach, or just to visit, I'd appreciate that," Abbott said. "I'd like to keep in touch anyhow. And Kate, when you write, my name is Christine."

Abbott rose. When Kate held out her hand to shake, the older woman embraced her tenderly.

Ray Boyd had taken the afternoon off to drive her up to the airport. On the way he said little. She said little.

Finally he asked, "You're sure there's no way we can make you stay?"

"No. I'm glad I came here. And very sad about leaving. But I'm going back stronger and sure now that my sacrifice was worth it. I know what I'm going to do. What Doctor Abrams said."

"Bring Medicine to the people?" Ray asked.

"I'm going to do family nursing and midwifery among the poor in the inner city. Where they need trained, experienced nurses. Especially where the children need someone like me. There are lots of Eloises in the inner city. Lots of little Kate Kincaids, too."

Ray took his eyes off the road only long enough to react with great curiosity to her last statement.

"When I was young, a very kind nurse gave me warmth, reassurance and a sense of security though I was terrified watching my home burn. I want to comfort, reassure and treat children who feel deprived, afraid and abandoned in this difficult, hostile world."

Then Kate smiled. "You have to grant one thing. In the end, your people did accept me."

"Accept you? They love you so much that I pity the next new nurse who goes calling on them. I can hear them now, 'Ye sure ain't much. Used to, we had a nurse, Kate Kincaid. Now there was a nurse. Pretty. But darn good! Ye'll sure never measure up to the likes of her.'"

They both laughed, until Ray asked, "And what about Howard?"

"We're going to get married, of course."

"Of course," he said.

"And buy a house. Have a baby or two, I hope," Kate said. "Then he'll have his work. I'll have mine. And we'll just live, I guess."

"Does he know how lucky he is?" Ray asked.

"I think we're both lucky," Kate said.

After a pause, and just before he brought the car to a stop at the airport terminal, Ray said, "I'll never forget you, Kate."

"Nor I you, Ray. Nor Adelphi. Nor Wildwood. Nor the people there. Never."

The plane was on the runway, waiting the signal to take off. She felt the engines gain power as the plane surged forward, increasing in thrust until she was forced against the back of her seat. In moments they were off the ground, airborne, and the landing gear was retracting.

Soon she would be seeing the tall green mountains stretching off to her right. Hidden somewhere among those mountains were Adelphi and Mountain Hospital and a part of her life that she would always remember with warmth and love.

She had come here as Kate Kincaid, Registered Nurse. Somewhat vain about her ability. Aloof from these people. Determined, even overdetermined, to soak up all the knowledge she could and leave the moment her year was over.

Now, a year and a half later, she was Kate Kincaid, Family Nurse-Midwife, a trained, thoroughly experienced, accredited professional, equipped not only to render health care to whole families, but to help women bring new healthy children into this world.

Now she was no longer vain about her abilities. No longer overdetermined. And she found herself reluctant to leave.

Mountain Hospital had taught her much about nursing and midwifery. But mountain people had taught her much about life. About honesty. Devotion. Friendship. Pride. Trust. And family loyalty. Such values might seem old-fashioned to many. But in this world of planes, satellites, television, computers, H-bombs and dispersed families, they were more necessary than ever.

Hawk, she promised silently, I will not only be a great nurse, I will make you the best wife, the best mother for our children, that any man has ever had.

Then, amused at her own resolve, she asked herself, am I being overdetermined again?